The Left-Handed Marriage

A. O'CONNOR

POOLBEG

Published 2015
by Poolbeg Press Ltd
123 Grange Hill, Baldoyle
Dublin 13, Ireland
E-mail: poolbeg@poolbeg.com
www.poolbeg.com

1

A catalogue record for this book is available from the British Library.

ISBN 978-1-78199-940-0

Typeset by Poolbeg Press Ltd
Printed by CPI Group (UK) Ltd, CR0 4YY
www.poolbeg.com

About the author

A. O'Connor is the bestselling author of eight previous novels including *The House* and *The Secrets of Armstrong House*, and is a graduate of NUI Maynooth and Trinity College Dublin.

Also by A. O'Connor

Acknowledgements

A big thank-you to the team at Poolbeg – Paula, Kieran, Ailbhe and David. Thanks to Gaye Shortland for the ever-diligent edit.

On this centenary of the First World War, I'd also like to acknowledge that generation whose lives were affected and whose experiences helped inspire this book.

For Pat

PROLOGUE

Present Day

The Mercedes was parked outside the manor house in Munich. The front door of the house opened and a man in his late fifties came out and walked down the steps in the sunshine to the waiting car. The chauffeur quickly got out of the car and opened the back door.

"Good morning, Your Excellency," said the chauffeur.

"Good morning, Peter," said Eric Von Hoffsten as he sat in.

Peter drove through the grounds of the manor house. Approaching the electric gates, he pressed a button and they smoothly opened. The Mercedes slid out into the street outside.

Eric opened his briefcase and began to work on papers as Peter drove the regular morning route to Eric's office through the quiet affluent streets of the district.

Peter noticed a motorbike carrying two people coming out from a side street and travelling close behind the Mercedes. He slowed down to let it pass and, as it overtook them, a white van emerged from another side street and drove behind them.

As the motorbike pulled ahead it suddenly swerved in front of the Mercedes, forcing Peter to jam on the brakes.

"What the – ?" shouted Eric in the back as he was flung forward and his papers went flying to the floor.

The pillion passenger leapt off the motorbike and came running towards the Mercedes, holding a gun.

"Get out of the car! Get out of the fucking car!" the man screamed, wielding the gun in front of the windscreen.

Peter went to reverse but saw the white van had jammed him in

1

and the driver was at the back door of the Mercedes, pointing a gun through the window, shouting at Eric to open the door. Just as Eric reached hesitatingly toward the door handle, Peter suddenly slammed on the accelerator and the car leapt forward, swerving around the parked motorbike. The man in front fired his gun as he jumped out of the way, shattering the side window of the car. Peter continued to accelerate down the road and didn't reduce speed until he reached the nearest police station.

The car screeched to a halt in front of the station. Peter was shaking as he jumped out of the car and opened the back door to let Eric out. Then he froze in horror as he saw Count Eric Von Hoffsten slumped there, shot, on the back seat.

Sam Cantwell stood at the top of the lecture hall in Trinity College Dublin, looking out at a sea of youthful faces.

"It is therefore believed that the First World War was the watershed between the old order and the new. Everything changed in four short years as society was turned upside down. In 1918, the people who had survived the war could hardly recognise the new world. Monarchies gone, empires crumbled, but new opportunities for people who didn't have them before, women of property having the vote . . ." Sam trailed off as he saw one of his young students staring out the window, preoccupied by something he found more interesting than the aftermath of the Great War.

Sam sauntered over to a window and saw it was a football match that had robbed the student's attention.

"Mr Kelly!" called Sam, causing the young man to jolt.

"Yes, Professor Cantwell?"

"I understand that the intricacies of the Great War find it hard to compete against the joys of the beautiful game," said Sam, "but I think what's going on here inside the classroom will be more beneficial to you in the long run than what's going on outside. Do you agree, Mr Cantwell?"

The other students were sniggering.

"Yes, Professor Cantwell," said the student, embarrassed.

"Anyway," said Sam as he returned to his desk and gathered up his papers, "I think we're finished here today, so if you hurry you might be able to catch the end of that match from a better ringside location than your present one."

"Thank you, Professor Cantwell," smiled the student as the lecture hall erupted in the usual chatter and noise that signalled the end of a lecture.

Sam Cantwell was a man of thirty-nine, tall with brown hair. He had been a history lecturer in Trinity for five years and he enjoyed the job. As he always said, he was lucky enough to be paid for doing what he liked most.

As he drove home through the sunlit streets, he turned the radio on and caught the end of the news.

"*In Munich today, Count Eric Von Hoffsten, of the famous brewery family, was shot in an attempted kidnap. The count is in a critical condition in hospital. Hoffsten beer is famous throughout the world as –*"

Sam changed channels and easy-listening music began to play.

Sam drove his car into the driveway of his home, an Edwardian semi-detached on a leafy street and, getting out, walked across the gravel and let himself into the house. He could hear the children playing at the back of the house and, walking through to the back garden, he saw his wife Julia relaxing in the sun as their son and daughter, Brian and Eva, played. There were only two years between the children, eight-year-old Brian being the oldest.

"Hello," he said, bending down and kissing his wife.

"Good day?" she asked as she tied back her blonde hair.

"The usual," he answered. "At least it's Friday."

"Yes, at least it's Friday," she agreed, smiling guiltily.

Julia was a chemist who had presently taken time off work to complete a PhD. The PhD had so far been neglected as Julia found that, after a fifteen-year career, she was enjoying being a stay-at-home-mum more than she cared to admit.

She stood up. "Right, I'm going to get a move on in the kitchen, if you mind the kids. Thomas and Colette are arriving at half eight."

Sam pulled a face. "I could have done with a quiet night in front of the television."

"You can do that tomorrow night. Anyway, who are you kidding? I'll be trying to get them to go home at two in the morning and it'll be you who'll insist on keeping the party going!"

That night Sam and Julia were sitting with their two guests in the dining room, lingering over coffee and liqueurs after finishing dinner.

Sam was smiling as he told a story. "So I said to the student, if you're not interested in studying then why are you a student? And she turned to me and said: 'For the same reason that *you* probably became a lecturer – because my parents forced me to be one!'"

The others started to laugh.

"She sounds a bit cynical for one so young," said Julia.

"So speaks the enthusiastic PhD student!" Colette said, laughingly raising an eyebrow. "I've been afraid to ask! How's it going?"

"So far so slow!" said Julia.

The telephone started to ring out in the hallway.

Sam looked at his watch: it was half past eleven. "Who's that, I wonder, at this time?"

"It might be my mother," said Julia, looking worried.

Sam got up, went out into the hallway and picked up the receiver.

"Hello?"

"Could I speak to Sam Cantwell?"

"Yes, that's me."

"Mr Cantwell, my name is Sophie Essen. I'm a lawyer in Munich and I represent the Von Hoffsten family."

"Sorry?"

"Sophie Essen – I'm the lawyer for Count Eric Von Hoffsten."

Sam was confused. "I think you've got the wrong number."

"No, I haven't – if you are the Sam Cantwell who works at Trinity College?"

"Well, yes, that's me, but – why do you want to speak to me?"

4

"Mr Cantwell, Count Von Hoffsten has been involved in an incident and is in hospital."

"Yes?"

"His condition is quite critical, Mr Cantwell, and we require your help."

The sound of laughter and chat came from the dining room as the door opened and Julia popped her head out. "Is it Mum?"

Sam shook his head and gestured for her to go back inside and close the door.

"This is the Count Von Hoffsten who was shot?" he asked.

"Yes."

"But what on earth has that to do with me?" Sam was flabbergasted.

"Mr Cantwell, we are contacting relatives of the count in the hope that they match his very rare blood type."

"I don't understand . . ."

"You are a distant cousin of the count's, Mr Cantwell. None of his immediate family match his blood type and so we are hoping a more distant relative might provide a match."

"Right, I'm going to put down the phone now," said Sam, annoyed. "You're obviously one of my students playing a practical joke, and it's not in very good taste."

"Mr Cantwell! This is not a joke! This is a case of life and death!" said the woman angrily.

"But what are you suggesting I do?" Sam was baffled.

"Do you know what your blood type is, Mr Cantwell?"

"I actually don't. I've never been ill."

"We would be very grateful if you went to Doctor Gordon Ryan's surgery in St Vincent's Hospital in the morning in order for them to run the tests to see if you are a match. An appointment has been made for you for eleven in the morning."

"This is ridiculous! How did you get my details, my telephone number? I know the name Hoffsten is in my ancestry but I've never even heard of these Von Hoffstens before, apart from drinking their beer!"

"You are related to them, Mr Cantwell. The Von Hoffstens have always had your details and those of all their relatives."

"And how exactly am I related to them?" demanded Sam.

"Mr Cantwell! That is irrelevant. The count is going to die if we don't get a match. If you are not a match then none of this matters. If you are, then you're crucial to the count's survival." She sounded frantic. "Will you attend Dr Ryan's surgery in the morning?"

"Well, I don't know! I'll have to discuss it with my wife."

"Please, Mr Cantwell. I can't emphasise how important this is."

Sam walked back into the dining room.

"Who was that?" asked Julia.

Sam sat down, looking mystified. "It was a lawyer from Germany saying . . . saying I'm related to that count who was shot in Munich and wanting me to do a blood test tomorrow to help him survive."

There was silence around the table and then everyone started laughing.

"I know!" said Sam, starting to laugh too.

Julia was intrigued. "The brewery guy?"

"Yes. I don't know anything else. She was very much to the point and very insistent. She said he would die if they don't get a correct match. Apparently he has some peculiar blood type – something rare. I don't know what mine is – so she wants me to get it tested."

"You didn't know you were related to him?" asked their friend Thomas.

"I hadn't a clue. I know there is German ancestry in my background but that was a hundred years ago. My grandfather's family changed their name from Hoffsten to Cantwell as there was so much anti-German feeling at the time. But I never knew it was *Von* Hoffsten, an aristocratic name."

"Sam's grandfather died young, so he never really knew much about that side of the family," explained Julia. "Pity your parents aren't still here – they would love the intrigue of all this, Sam."

"True," said Sam with a smile.

"And you've no brothers or sisters?" Colette, Thomas's wife, asked.

"No, my family weren't big breeders," laughed Sam.

"A count? I always thought you had a regal air about you!" joked Thomas.

"And are you going?" asked Julia.

"Well, I don't know. I wouldn't want to be responsible for anyone dying because I didn't help, I suppose."

"But it's nothing to do with you, really," said Colette. "Strangers ringing up when they want something! I'd tell them to take a running jump."

"Besides, how much blood can they take from you? A pint?" wondered Thomas. "Would that be enough to save this man's life?"

"I imagine they need plasma donations from you, Sam," explained Julia. "Plasma replenishes itself after twenty-four hours, allowing them to take much more."

"Ah! I knew the chemist I married was still there somewhere, hiding behind the Stepford Wife of the past few weeks," said Sam, laughing.

Julia ignored the jibe. "It's kind of exciting though, isn't it? I wonder how you're connected to them? There's nothing more interesting in my family background than ten generations of farmers."

"Like most Irish people's families," said Thomas. "Go do the blood test, Sam – it's the only way you'll find out anything more."

"What do you think?" Sam asked Julia.

"Well, you've nothing to lose but a couple of hours and then your conscience will be clear when they tell you you're not a match," suggested Julia.

Sam shrugged. "I've nothing to lose as you said."

"I thought it was a joke when I got the phone call last night," said Sam as Doctor Ryan took the blood sample the next day.

"No joke, I'm afraid. The man is desperate for a transfusion according to his consultant in Munich."

"Did they tell you anything else?"

"No, other than he was badly wounded."

"He's a count, you know."

"So I gathered," said the doctor as he finished up. "Thank you, Mr Cantwell – we'll run the test and be in contact shortly."

Sam was in a strange mood for the rest of the day. It all felt surreal.

A phone call came through at eight that evening.

"Mr Cantwell, it's Sophie Essen."

"Hello again."

"The blood matched. Your flight to Munich is leaving at eight o'clock tomorrow morning. I will personally be at the airport to meet you."

"*What?*"

"Your ticket will be waiting for you at the Aer Lingus customer service desk."

"Now hold on a second! I can't just fly out to Munich in the morning."

"Why not?"

"Because I have responsibilities. I have children!"

"Can't your wife take care of them?"

"But I can't just disappear off like that! How long would I be there? I have to work on Monday, you know!"

"Mr Cantwell! As I said before, this is a matter of life and death. If you do not come to Munich, Count Von Hoffsten will die!"

"Well, I – this is an awful lot to be putting on my shoulders for a man I've never even heard of, let alone met!"

"In that case, it depends on what kind of a person you are, Mr Cantwell. If you can live with the fact you have refused to save a man's life, that is your prerogative. But he will die, Mr Cantwell, if you are not on the flight tomorrow morning. Do you have a pen? I'll give you my number and you can ring me back once you've discussed it with your wife."

"I think you should go," urged Julia that evening as they discussed it in the sitting room.

"But what about work?"

"I'll ring them and say there was a family emergency. Which is the truth actually!"

"But this woman Sophie couldn't give me any details of how long I'd be," warned Sam.

"I don't think you have a choice, Sam. Imagine the guilt if he does die. I'm sure it will be only a couple of days. And to think you'll get to meet the Von Hoffstens and discover all about this part of your family you never realised you even had!"

"Well, they are very distant relatives. And they knew I was here all this time and never offered the hand of friendship before."

"They live in a different world from ours. They probably thought we had nothing in common."

"Except blood types as it turns out."

PART 1

1913

CHAPTER 1

The flag waved. The horses stampeded down the racecourse at a furious pace towards the finishing line of the Irish Derby. The crowds on either side of the racecourse fencing erupted in an orchestra of excitement and screams of encouragement.

The young thoroughbred Halcyon struggled to maintain his position among the main body of horses.

Standing between her father and mother, Diana Cantwell gripped the fencing at the racecourse edge.

"Come on, Halcyon! *Come on*!" she shouted as she watched her horse gain ground.

Halcyon suddenly galloped ahead of the other horses, joining the frontrunners. Diana gripped her father's hand as Halcyon and the favourite Civility began a neck-to-neck battle.

"I can't bear to watch!" declared Diana as she turned away.

Simon Cantwell excitedly grabbed his daughter. "You *have* to look! Your horse is about to win the Irish Derby!"

Diana forced herself to look back at the racecourse.

As the two horses continued the fight to the finishing line, Halcyon drew into the lead.

"*Halcyon!*" shouted Diana in delight.

But as they drew near the finishing line Halcyon suddenly lost ground, as the greater experience of the other horse became evident, and he galloped over the line in second place to his rival.

"*The winner is Civility!*" came the announcement.

"Well done!" shouted Simon as he embraced his daughter.

"For a moment I thought Halcyon was actually going to win," said Diana who was in shock that her horse had come second in his first major race.

"But he came second! Second!" said Simon.

"Nobody ever remembers the name of which horse came second," said his wife Maud.

People excitedly came rushing over to the Cantwells to offer congratulations which they gratefully accepted as they made their way through the crowd towards the winner's enclosure.

"Thank you . . . thank you, most kind," smiled Maud to the passers-by as the family reached the horse. Then she muttered under her breath to her daughter and husband: "Well, at least the prize money will help with the bank overdraft."

"Oh, you beauty!" said Diana as she put her arms around Halcyon's neck and kissed him.

"Now, Maud, Halcyon does belong to Diana. The prize money is hers," cautioned Simon.

"And she is welcome to keep it," said Maud, continuing to smile at the well-wishers. "Of course, if she does, she'd better enrol in cookery lessons, as we won't be able to pay the kitchen staff this month's wages."

"Oh, I don't want the prize money," said Diana, smiling happily as she continued to hug Halcyon. "I just want the glory for Halcyon."

"You can keep the glory then in that case, and the bank can have the prize money," said Maud. "Diana, come – they want us for photographs."

A short distance away a Mercedes automobile was parked with a tall dark-haired man in his mid-twenties leaning against it, smoking a cigarette. The man and the glamorous vehicle were attracting almost as much attention as the winning horse. The man's eyes were trained on Diana Cantwell as she posed for a photograph with Halcyon.

"Who is she?" he asked, his eyes not leaving Diana.

"That's the girl who owns Halcyon," said Tommy Robinson, the man's guide.

"Well, I've guessed that! But who *is* she?"

"Diana Cantwell. She's Simon Cantwell's girl."

Max Von Hoffsten studied Diana. He judged her to be about twenty. She was dressed in a cream summer dress with a matching summer hat. He thought she was very beautiful with her porcelain skin and shining brown hair that came to just below her shoulders. She had an unusual prettiness that made her stand out from the crowd. Her father Simon stood proudly beside her, a pleasant distinguished-looking man in his late forties. A tall elegant woman Max assumed was Diana's mother was busy talking to people as Diana posed for the photographs.

"The Cantwells are a well-known Anglo-Irish family," said Tommy. "They have a farm in Meath. Very popular with the hunt crowd. Like most of their kind, I think they are all airs and graces these days, with not much money left. The mother, Maud, is a lord's granddaughter and was quite a looker in her day, I believe."

"I'm sure she was, if Diana is anything to go by," said Max.

Some children began to crawl over the bonnet of the car.

"Here, get off the car!" shouted Tommy at them. "Clear off!"

Max suddenly threw his cigarette on the ground and stood up straight.

"Do you know them?" he asked.

"I know Simon, yes," said Tommy.

"Good, then you can introduce me." Max smiled at him and tapped him on the shoulder.

Max cut a path through the crowd, followed by Tommy. He stopped abruptly in front of Diana and stood smiling at her. She had spotted him earlier driving through the crowd in his motor car.

Tommy came and stood beside Max.

"Good show, Cantwell," said Tommy in a jolly voice.

"Thank you, Tommy, but it's my daughter who deserves all the credit. She's nurtured Halcyon since he was a foal," said Simon.

Max continued smiling at Diana. "Aren't you going introduce us, Tommy?" he asked.

"Eh, yes, of course. Simon, this is Max Von Hoffsten over for the races from Germany."

"Pleased to meet you," said Max who didn't even look at Simon but continued to smile at Diana.

His smile unnerved her and she held the reins of Halcyon even tighter.

"Oh, and this is his daughter, Diana," said Tommy.

"So very pleased to meet you." Max nodded to her. "I understand this is the horse's first race?" he added as he began to stroke Halcyon.

"That's right," said Diana. "His first professional race anyway."

"Quite a performance. With the right training and guidance he could go far," said Max.

"Oh, he will go far, Mr Von Hoffsten – you can be assured of that," said Diana confidently.

"Do you think you have the resources to train him to reach his full potential?" asked Max, looking sceptically at her.

Diana felt he was insulting her ability. "Quite sure, Mr Von Hoffsten – you have no need to worry yourself." She nodded, indicating something behind him. "I'm afraid that flash motor car of yours is about to be stolen."

Max glanced over and saw there were now half a dozen children excitedly sitting in his car. Max didn't move but Tommy went storming over.

"Clear off, you rotten little bastards!" he shouted.

"It's only a motor car," said Max, smiling.

"Good day, Mr Von Hoffsten," said Diana as she led Halcyon away to another photographer.

She had found her encounter with the stranger a little unnerving. The way he stared at her. The way he spoke to her as if he knew her. Yet she couldn't help turning around and looking at him again. To her surprise she found Max Von Hoffsten was in deep conversation with her father and mother.

CHAPTER 2

Diana drove the Cantwells' motor car through the country roads of Meath, her father beside her and her mother in the back.

"A little slower, Diana, there's a dear," cautioned Maud.

"Slower didn't make Halcyon nearly win the Derby!" said Diana.

"No, but slower may save me from meeting my Maker before I'm ready," said Maud.

Diana slowed down as a gateway came into view. She turned in through it and drove past a small gate lodge and up a long driveway. Garonglen quickly came into view. It was a small manor house set in rolling countryside which was dotted with ash and beech trees. The driveway led directly into the forecourt and the black open-topped car screeched to a halt there.

As Diana got out, four black and brown Labradors came bounding across the gravel to her and she enveloped them in hugs.

"Welcome home!" came a voice.

Diana looked up and saw her brother Warren come out the front door and down the steps towards them.

"Warren! Did you hear? Did you hear that Halcyon nearly won the Derby?" Diana said excitedly as she rushed into his arms and hugged him.

"I heard. Congratulations, I knew you and he had it in you," said Warren, smiling broadly at her. "Where is Halcyon?"

"Billy is bringing him back in the trailer," said Simon as he and Maud walked up the steps and into their home, followed by Diana and Warren.

Warren, aged nineteen, was a year younger than Diana and the youngest child. Diana had one older brother Dashiel who was studying law at Trinity in Dublin.

"To be fair to poor Billy, he put in as much work as I did with Halcyon over the years and he was almost forgotten about today," said Diana.

"Stable boys are always forgotten about," said Maud as she took off her gloves and threw them on the sideboard.

"I could never forget Billy," said Diana as the four made their way into the drawing room on the right.

Diana walked over to the drinks cabinet and poured herself a glass of wine.

"Anyone for a drink?" she asked.

"Gin and tonic for me," said Simon, sitting down, and he gave her a secret wink. "More gin than tonic."

She laughed, winked back and fixed him his drink.

Maud went and yanked the bell pull before going over and fixing her hair in the mirror over the fireplace.

"I suppose this sudden fame you've found at the Derby today can only enhance your reputation for when we eventually get you to do the Season in London, hopefully next year," said Maud as she admired herself in the mirror.

Diana handed the gin and tonic to Simon and sat down beside him.

"I thought we couldn't afford to send me to London to do the Season?" said Diana.

"Well, we can't, but you're still going." Maud turned and looked at her daughter. "I've been waiting until after the race to tell you. How we'll get the money to send you I don't know but I have it all arranged now with my cousins, Lord Ashenbry's family, who you'll be staying with." She spoke the name with pride.

"Lord Ashenbry's family, Diana – lucky you!" jeered Warren, his voice heavy with mockery.

Their second cousins, the Ashenbrys, were a long-standing joke with Diana and her brothers. These distant cousins in London, who they never saw and rarely heard from, were held in high regard by their mother who relentlessly kept the connection alive with pride.

"Although I've never really met them they sound perfectly civil," said Maud. "Lord Ashenbry's wife is an American called Thelma, and she has offered to be your chaperone."

"Well, if we can't afford to send me, I'm just as happy not to go," said Diana. "I'm quite happy attending the races, hunt balls and parties here in Ireland where I'm sure some poor fellow will eventually take pity on me and ask me to marry him as a great act of kindness on his part."

At this, Diana and Warren erupted in laughter.

"Well, I'm glad you two find it all so funny," Maud said angrily.

"We do!" Diana and Warren sang in harmony.

In through the door came their cook Caitríona. She was a woman in her fifties, stout, with a no-nonsense approach.

"Ah, Caitríona, Miss Diana's horse did rather well today at the Derby so we're planning a small celebration tomorrow night here, if you can manage it," said Maud with a smile.

"How small is small?" asked Caitríona.

"About thirty people. Not a sit-down affair in the dining room, but plenty of splendid food laid on," said Maud.

"Thirty people! That's not small! That's a small army to feed!" Caitríona looked indignant.

"Yes, well, I'm sure you and your staff will manage just fine," encouraged Maud.

"My staff! There's only me and Fiona down there and that half-witted girl Molly you thrust on us, who I often think took a wrong turning on her way to a lunatic asylum and instead arrived here at Garonglen!"

"Nonsense, Caitríona, the girl is perfectly adequate for assisting you in the kitchen," Maud said.

"That's your opinion, Mrs Cantwell. I've told you before that you're trying to run Garonglen on too tight a budget. All the staff are double-jobbing!" Caitríona looked irritably around the room.

Maud glanced at Caitríona in a bored fashion. "A tight budget is better than no budget, Caitríona. We're all having to cut our coats to suit our cloth."

"But —" Caitríona began to object.

"I'll meet you in the morning," Maud headed her off, "and we can go through the menu. And we need something Germanic, so put your thinking hat on."

"Germanic!" Caitríona repeated, horrified.

"Yes, we're having a German visitor, so let's make him feel at home."

Caitríona huffed and walked out of the room.

"Really," sighed Maud. "I don't know what to do with her. She resents it when you ask anything of her."

"Let's tread carefully, Maud," advised Simon. "We don't want to upset the locals, with independence coming."

"If it ever comes," said Maud. "But it's true that inside every Irish peasant is a Republican — that's what my father used to say. I don't know what this country is coming to when you can't ask your paid staff to show a little respect. Times have changed and families like ours are trying to get by as best we can. There simply is not the money there to run a full household staff any more."

"Never mind all that," said Diana. "Who is the German visitor?"

"Max Von Hoffsten," Maud informed her. "We met him at the races today."

"And why have you invited him to my party tomorrow?" asked Diana.

"Oh, it's your party, is it?" asked Maud cuttingly. "He's invited because he's a very charming and interesting man. He also happens to be Count Von Hoffsten's son, and heir to that family."

"So what interest does he have in coming here then?" asked Diana.

"He was impressed by Halcyon's performance and expressed an interest in seeing the facilities we have here," explained Simon.

"Well, I wish you'd checked with me first," said Diana.

"I didn't realise I needed your approval of whom I may invite to my house, Diana," said Maud.

"I just don't like the look of him," said Diana.

"Well, I like the look of him," said Maud. "Very handsome, I thought."

Warren got up, went over to a table and riffled through some magazines, brought one over to Diana and opened a page.

"Is this him?" asked Warren, showing a photo of Max in an automobile at the Monaco Grand Prix.

"Yes, that's him," said Diana, still sounding unimpressed.

"He races cars, horses – anything that takes his fancy," said Warren, excited at the thought of meeting him.

"And with his money, anything that takes his fancy is in his reach," said Simon as he knocked back his gin and tonic.

CHAPTER 3

Max's car swung through the gateway and up the driveway to the house. He stepped out and surveyed the elegant small manor house set in beautiful grounds.

Suddenly he saw Diana in the distance riding Halcyon through the green fields. He stood staring.

"You managed to find us all right?" came a voice from behind and he turned to find Simon Cantwell coming down the steps to greet him.

"Good afternoon, Mr Cantwell, nice to meet you again." He crossed over the forecourt and shook the older man's hand.

"We're delighted to have you as a guest."

"She rides the horse beautifully," said Max, nodding at Diana in the distance.

"Yes, she adores Halcyon and is getting a reputation for being one of the finest horsewomen in the country," said Simon proudly.

"I can see why," nodded Max.

Warren came walking into the forecourt, leading a horse.

"This is my son Warren," said Simon.

Warren shook Max's hand enthusiastically. "A real pleasure. I'm an avid follower of your car-racing career."

Max laughed. "More a hobby than a career."

Simon glanced at the car and asked, "Is your valet not with you?"

Max laughed. "No, I make a point of never having one. I like to travel light and fast and I don't want a valet in my shadow. Besides,

22

I found my last valet was reporting everything I did back to my family!"

"I see!" laughed Simon as he put his arm around Max's shoulder and led him up the steps to the house. "Warren, get Max's bag from the car, there's a good man."

Inside, Max took in the interior. There was a wide tiled hallway that ran through the centre of the house. At the end of it was a mahogany staircase that ran up to a landing over which was a large arched window. The landing then divided into two stairs leading up to the first floor. Beyond the staircase were French windows that led out to beautifully cultivated gardens.

There were six mahogany doors leading off the hallway and Simon led Max through the first door into the drawing room, which managed to be cosy and ornate at the same time. Two large cream antique couches faced each other, resting on a red Persian rug that stretched over a dark wooden floor. Beyond the couches was a cream marble fireplace with a flamboyant gold-embossed mirror over it.

Dotted on various sideboards were photos showing the family enjoying what seemed like a multitude of idyllic Edwardian summers and Christmases. Max couldn't help but stare at a very large photo portrait of Diana smiling enigmatically into the distance. He immediately got a sense of a warm and happy environment – one that he was almost envious of, despite Garonglen being an insignificant house compared to what he was used to.

Maud entered the room and came to greet him warmly.

"You are most welcome, Max," she said, offering her hand.

"The pleasure is all mine, Mrs Cantwell," Max said as he bent over to kiss her hand.

Diana made her way from the stables through the back gardens of Garonglen. The lawn was long and wide and surrounded by ash and oak trees, an abundance of paths leading off to more gardens beyond.

Diana quickly walked up the steps to the French window at the back of the house and let herself into the hall. As she walked through the hall to the front drawing room she spotted a maid carrying a suitcase up the stairs.

"Molly, whose luggage is that?" asked Diana.

"The German gentleman's, miss," said Molly.

"The German gentleman?" Diana was confused. "Max Von Hoffsten? But why is he staying here tonight?"

"Don't know, miss!" Molly, as ever, when asked a question she was unable to answer, looked as if she were about to burst into tears.

Diana nodded and continued into the drawing room. There she saw Max sitting on one of the cream embroidered couches, her family clustered around him in admiration as if he were some rare jewel.

". . . and I turned around and said – 'Dear lady, I most certainly will carry your handbag, but in return you must carry my suitcase!'" Max finished his tale and Maud, Simon and Warren erupted in laughter.

Maud noticed Diana standing there.

"Ah, Diana dear, there you are. Our guest has arrived – Max – you remember him from the races?"

Smiling, Max stood up and bowed. "Lovely to see you again, Miss Cantwell."

"Yes, I remember . . . hello again." Diana nodded at him then walked across the room and poured herself a brandy. She sprayed some soda into her drink.

"I didn't realise you were staying the night?" she said, turning and walking over to the other couch.

"Your parents kindly invited me," Max said.

"Really? They never said."

"Well, we can't have poor Max driving back to stay in a hotel in Dublin after he's had a few drinks," said Maud. "We couldn't be responsible for him ending up in a ditch." She smiled happily at him.

"I'm sure a racing driver as experienced as Max would never end up in a ditch, no matter how many tipples he's had," said Warren, smiling.

Diana looked at her brother curiously. She wondered why her whole family were fawning over this stranger.

"What an attractive painting!" commented Max as he looked at one of the portraits on the wall.

"Do you like it?" Maud asked excitedly. "It's one of mine."

"You painted it?" checked Max.

"Yes, I'm an artist."

"Of a sort," suggested Diana who, glancing up at the ugly portrait, knew Max had to be flattering Maud in admiring it.

Max stood up and examined the portrait. "A most individual style."

"Well, that is true, at least!" smirked Diana as she took a drink.

"Diana!" Maud cautioned with a warning look at her daughter. "Are you an enthusiast of art, Max?" She stood up and joined him.

"Yes, indeed. In fact, I collect art," said Max.

"Really? Perhaps you would like to see some of my other work. I use the gate lodge as my studio as a rule. I call it my sanctuary. I disappear in there and let my mind run wild on canvas."

"She really does," agreed Diana. "Quite wild, judging by her paintings."

"I have some paintings in the conservatory here at the house. Would you care to take a look?" asked Maud.

"I'd be delighted to," said Max, offering his arm, and he and Maud walked out of the room.

Diana leaned forward to her brother and father. "Why is he staying here tonight?"

"Your mother insisted," said Simon, absolving himself of the responsibility.

"But he won't fit in with our set. He's not one of us," said Diana.

"Because he's German? I never had you down as prejudiced," said Warren.

"I'm not! I'm just saying!" Diana defended herself.

"I think he's smashing," said Warren. "You know, he's been to everywhere, met everyone."

"Nobody's been to everywhere, met everyone," dismissed Diana.

"He went to school in America," said Simon.

"And university in England," added Warren.

"His home is a magnificent hunting estate near the Alps in Germany," said Simon.

"But he spends half his time travelling – London, Monte Carlo, Paris, Madrid."

"One day he'll be Count Von Hoffsten –"

"When his father dies and he inherits the title –"

"Enough!" said Diana, putting her drink down quickly. "I'm already tired of hearing everything about this man under whose spell you all seem to have fallen."

A little while later Maud came back in, holding Max's arm possessively and with a grin on her face.

"Max has bought one of my paintings!" she declared with delight.

"Really? Which one?" smiled Simon.

"The one of the dandelions," Maud informed him.

Diana raised her eyes to heaven. "You must have more money than sense, Mr Von Hoffsten."

"I pride myself on being able to spot talent in its early stages," said Max.

"Early stages! She's been painting for forty years!" said Diana with a laugh.

"Diana, don't you need to go and get yourself ready for tonight?" said Maud sharply.

Diana finished her drink and stood up. "Good idea."

As she walked past Max she smirked at him. "I'll leave you to your fans."

Max turned and watched her walk confidently out of the room.

As Diana got ready that evening she felt unnerved by Max Von Hoffsten's presence. It wasn't just that he was so different from the usual men in their set, with his glamour, looks and sophistication. She knew her parents and they were keeping something from her. Maud and Simon usually spoke freely and easily about everything. But they had been clandestine about the fact Max would be staying with them.

She could hear motor cars arrive outside and laughter and cheer as the summer's evening turned into night. She stepped back and looked at herself in the mirror. Satisfied, she left her room.

Walking down the stairs she saw that the tiled hallway below was already filling up with guests.

"Diana, darling, congrats on Halcyon's performance!" said a young woman, grabbing her and kissing her. Hannah Roundtree was from one of the Anglo-Irish families in the county.

"Thanks, Hannah, though you've seen nothing yet. I fully expect to return to the Derby next year where Halcyon will come first."

"Good for you," smiled Hannah, putting her arm around Diana as they walked into the drawing room which was full of people. "I didn't know you knew Max Von Hoffsten."

"I don't. Not in the least. He seemed to have just appeared here from nowhere, or at least as a result of my parents' manoeuvres. Do you know him?"

"I met him briefly when I did the Season in London last year. All the gals were throwing themselves at him. Including me, for that matter!" Hannah pulled a face.

Diana started to laugh. "You are atrocious, Hannah! He had no interest?"

"In me? He didn't seem to, unfortunately. He wasn't there to find a wife anyway, by all accounts. He was there to have fun."

"Nobody caught his attention?" Diana found herself annoyed by her own curiosity.

"Plenty of flirtation and interaction. But he'll marry some German or Austrian aristocrat. They always do. You know what the German nobility is like. They are so strict on these matters."

"I'm afraid I don't know anything about the German nobility, and I don't think I'm that interested in learning."

"Oh, you'll learn all right. When you get to do the Season in London, you'll learn all the bloody politics of it all." Hannah spoke with the bitterness of somebody whose one and only opportunity to do the Season had not been an overriding success, due to her own family's financial constraints.

Diana watched Max by the fireplace happily chatting with a group. He looked up and caught her looking at him. He held her gaze and smiled at her. She quickly turned away.

CHAPTER 4

Max circulated freely among the other guests at the party. All the time he kept one eye on Diana, whose friendly manner and light laughter seemed to mix with a quick wit. He waited for an opportunity to approach her but the right moment didn't seem to arise as she moved effortlessly between the guests. She was the centre of attention that night as she accepted everyone's praise and admiration for Halcyon's unexpected success.

Max saw a tall dark-haired man enter the room and when he saw Diana's face light up on seeing him he suspected the man was a romantic interest of hers. But, when Maud crossed over the room, declaring loudly, "My son! My beautiful son!" and embraced him warmly, Max realised the young man was Diana's older brother Dashiel.

Maud was leading Dashiel over to Max.

"Max, this is our other son, Dashiel. He came down from Dublin for the party tonight. He's studying law at Trinity."

"Yes, you already informed me," said Max. Several times, he added mentally.

Dashiel smiled warmly and shook his hand. "Pleased to meet you. Are they looking after you with drinks?"

Max raised his full glass. "They certainly are."

"As long as they're keeping you well fed and watered," said Dashiel.

"Indeed they are," smiled Max.

"Now, you are enjoying yourself, Max, I hope?" said Maud.

"How could I not with such charming hosts?" said Max. He found the whole family pleasant and jolly in that way he generally found the British upper classes to be. And yet the Cantwells and their set weren't the British upper class. He knew that. These Anglo-Irish might have all the manners and etiquette of the British upper class, but they were in fact Irish though living an almost colonial existence.

As Diana approached them she was amazed to see Dashiel appeared to have fallen under the same spell that Max had cast on the rest of her family.

She tapped Dashiel on the shoulder and he turned and embraced her tightly.

"Diana the Victorious!" he declared.

"*Almost* victorious! She only came second, remember," corrected Maud.

"We were expecting you hours ago! What delayed you?" asked Diana.

"I had to sit a bloody exam," said Dashiel.

"Which you will come first in, I have no doubt," said Maud.

Dashiel made a face at Max. "*I* doubt it very much!"

"I think I should warn you, Dashiel," said Diana. "Hannah Roundtree has been looking for you all night. Keeps asking where you are."

"I bet she does!" Maud pulled a displeased face. "Looking to snare herself a successful husband since she was an utter failure during the Season in London. Didn't get herself one enquiry for a meeting, let alone a marriage, that's what I heard."

Dashiel smiled widely. "In that case I'm quite safe! Since I'm not successful in any shape or form."

Maud reached up and kissed him tenderly. "But you will be one day, when you're a successful barrister."

"Anyway, I'm starving. Where's the food?" asked Dashiel, looking around.

"Come along and we'll feed you." Maud put her arm around him to lead him away. "I'm not leaving you alone for one second, in case that Hannah Roundtree comes hunting for you."

Dashiel waved at Max and Diana. "See you later!"

"Now, you will enjoy yourself, Max, promise me you will?" Maud called back as she departed.

"I promise," said Max as he smiled down at Diana.

Diana felt awkward left alone with him and her eyes strayed around the crowded drawing room where people were talking and dancing to music from a gramophone.

"You bought a pig in a poke incidentally," she said then.

"I'm sorry?"

"My mother's painting – she sold you a dud. She really is quite talentless."

"Rather unkind of you to say."

"That's not just my opinion. She has bullied some art critics to view her work and they all came to the same conclusion."

At the far end of the room was a table laden with lavish food and, as Diana saw Maud instruct Caitríona on what to put on a plate for Dashiel, she smiled fleetingly at Max.

"He's her favourite, you see," she said.

"I'm sorry?"

"My brother Dashiel is my mother's favourite. Always has been, always will be. She says they're so alike they're like two peas in a pod. Funny thing is, they're nothing alike!"

"I don't like it when parents have favourites, do you?"

Diana smiled nonchalantly. "It doesn't bother me in the least. It's just a fact of life. All parents have favourites, even if they try to hide it. My mother doesn't even bother to try and hide it."

"And what of your other brother, Warren?"

"Warren is wonderful, but Dashiel got all the brains. Warren is quite happy to raise horses here and take over when the time comes."

Max moved closer. "Which just leaves you?"

"What about me?" She looked at him warily.

"What is your life plan?"

"My life plan? I don't have any. I'm far too busy enjoying the here and now."

"But I understand you're planning to go and do the Season in London and meet everybody there is to meet."

"That's my mother's plan, not mine. I think it's a waste of money we can ill afford, to be honest. All I'll do is go over to London, attend lots of balls and rush back to Ireland with my tail between my legs just like Hannah Roundtree, after being fittingly humbled by all those London sophisticated beauties."

He stared at her, mesmerized by the open cheeky carefree way she spoke, uncaring of how she came across.

"I can assure you that when London gets to meet you, it will not let you go," he said, staring into her eyes.

She felt herself blush at his flattery and turned away to glance around at the party which was now in full swing.

"Do you dance, Max?" she asked suddenly.

"Eh, yes, though I usually do the asking," he said.

"Oh, I wasn't asking you to dance with me, I was just asking *could* you dance." She smiled then winked at him and walked across the floor to a couch where Warren was deep in conversation with Hannah Roundtree. Diana pulled him up and, dragging him over to join the other couples, started dancing in a vigorous fashion with him. As Max looked on, she turned and smiled at him and then winked at him again.

By two all the guests had gone home. Maud and Simon had retired upstairs to bed leaving Max, Diana, Dashiel and Warren in the lounge while the music still played on the gramophone.

"And you've really been in an aeroplane?" asked Warren again, overexcited at the thought.

"Sure. I flew over Paris," said Max nonchalantly.

Diana sat back, crossed her legs and smiled at Max wryly. "Weren't you frightened of crashing into the Eiffel Tower?"

Max looked over at her and smiled. "I was with a very good pilot."

"If the Good Lord had wanted us to fly he would have given us wings," said Diana.

"In that case, if the Good Lord didn't want us to cross water why did he give us boats?" he replied.

Diana smiled to herself and swirled her wine in her glass.

31

"Well, I'm off to bed. I'm exhausted," said Dashiel, standing up.

"Must you?" asked Diana.

"'Fraid so." He bent down and kissed her cheek, then turned to Max and shook his hand energetically. "It's been such a real pleasure to meet you, Max."

"And you," Max smiled back.

"See you in the morning," said Dashiel. He ruffled Warren's hair, bounded out of the room and up the stairs.

"And then there were three," said Diana.

"You're not going to bed just yet, are you?" asked Max.

"No, I'm a night owl."

"Good, so am I."

She stood up. "Another drink?" she asked as she walked over to the drinks table. She ran a finger over the bottles. "Wine, whiskey, gin or . . ." she turned around and got a start to see him standing close behind her, ". . . something else?"

She looked behind him and saw that Warren had fallen fast asleep on his armchair.

"And then there were two," said Max, smiling crookedly at her.

She turned around again and went to unscrew the whiskey bottle.

"I'm going to have a whiskey –" she began.

Suddenly his hand was on hers, pushing the bottle back down on the table.

She turned and looked at him, confused.

"Why don't I make you a cocktail?" he said.

"A what?"

"A cocktail."

"What's that?"

"It's all the rage in New York," he said, gently pushing her aside.

He studied the bottles of alcohol before them. Then he took a glass water jug and emptied the water in it into a potted plant. He poured a large amount of gin into the jug, then picked up a bottle of vermouth and, judging carefully, poured some into the jug. Taking a long spoon he stirred the contents vigorously and tasted the results with the spoon. He nodded to himself. She looked on, transfixed. He suddenly looked at her, then turned and walked away quickly. She looked after him as he left the room, confused. She waited, wondering where he had gone to. She sauntered back to the couch and sat down.

Looking at Warren's sleeping form, she said aloud, "And then there was one."

The minutes ticked by and when there was no sign of Max she decided he must have gone to bed. She was just about to reach forward to shake Warren awake when Max arrived back at the doorway, holding a lemon aloft.

"I couldn't find any olives in your kitchens, but a slice of lemon should suffice," he explained and walked past her to the drinks table where he cut up the lemon. She watched as he poured the contents of the jug into two glasses and garnished them with the lemon. He then walked towards her, handed her one of the glasses and sat down opposite her.

He reached forward and chinked his glass against hers. "It's called a Martini."

She sipped at the drink and decided it was the best thing she had ever tasted.

They drank their Martinis in silence, she looking warily at him.

She smiled at him. "These – cocktails – are basically concoctions of different drinks put together?"

He nodded.

"All right . . . let's see . . ." She put down her drink and walked over to the drinks table.

He followed her and stood beside her.

She put her hands together as she thought, then reached out, picked up the whiskey and poured an amount into another glass jug. Her face was creased in thought. Then she reached out, picked up the vermouth and poured an amount into the whiskey. She glanced at Max who shrugged at her. Her fingers reached out, picked up the vodka bottle and poured a dash into the drink. She glanced at Max who looked surprised but intrigued. She then reached out for the gin and went to unscrew the cap. Max's hand came out, took the bottle out of her hand and placed it back down.

She looked at him and he was shaking his head disapprovingly.

"Too much?" she enquired.

"Definitely!"

She nodded and smiled, then reached out for the soda and looked at him for his opinion. He nodded and she sprayed some soda into the jug. She stood thinking then turned and walked out of the room. She walked down the hallway, past the stairs, down a corridor and into the kitchens.

The kitchens were large with big windows looking out on to the back gardens. She knew what she was looking for – she just didn't know where to find it. She started opening the larders and searching through the stock kept there. She frantically looked through the tins and boxes, not wanting to leave Max alone too long. She smiled happily as she spotted a box of cherries and took it out.

She put the box of cherries on the kitchen counter and opened it. At a sound from the door she looked up and got a start to see Max standing there, holding two balloon glasses filled with the alcoholic concoction she had made. He walked slowly to her and smiled as he saw the box of cherries.

She arched an eyebrow quizzically to enquire if the cherries were a good idea. He nodded and put the two glasses down on the counter and, reaching for two cherries, put one in each glass. She picked up her glass and drank from it, making a face at the strength of it. He raised his glass and sipped it. He savoured the taste and then nodded approvingly.

Reaching into his pocket he took out a silver cigarette box, took out a cigarette and lit it. He took another sip of his drink and then offered her the cigarette.

She felt he was standing too close to her. "No," she said, almost alarmed. "I don't smoke, of course not!"

He smiled almost mockingly at her and put the cigarette between her lips, brushing his fingers against them as he did so.

She inhaled the cigarette and the mixture of the cocktails, smoke and his scent began to overwhelm her.

"Diana!" came Warren's voice from somewhere down the corridor.

Her brother's voice jolted her back into reality from this strange spell she was under. She quickly took the cigarette out of her mouth and threw it on the ground, stamping it out. Max's eyes were boring into hers. She took her glass and poured the contents down the sink and then quickly walked out of the kitchen.

"Where were you?" asked a bleary-eyed Warren in the hallway.

"Oh, nowhere – come on, let's to bed." She linked her arm through his as they climbed up the stairs.

Max came sauntering out of the kitchen, still drinking the cocktail she had created for him.

CHAPTER 5

Max walked down the stairs, looking at his watch and seeing it was well after noon. He paused in the hallway, not sure which direction to go. He could see the French windows were open at the bottom of the hallway and then he heard talking and laughter from that direction.

He walked out the French windows into the sunshine. Maud was sitting at a garden table on the terrace reading a newspaper, a silver coffee pot beside her. Down the gardens on the tennis court Diana and Warren were playing each other.

"Ah, there you are!" said Maud, smiling at him. "When you missed breakfast, I sent yours up to your room."

"Thank you, it was very considerate of you," he said, sitting down at the table opposite her.

"I imagined you weren't allowed to go to bed at a civilised hour. My children are notorious across the county for being the last ones to leave a party," she said with an almost proud air as she poured him coffee.

"They were very hospitable," said Max as he sat back and watched Diana playing tennis in the sunshine.

Maud sighed as she pushed the newspaper to the other side of the table.

"All this political turmoil in Ireland. I can't bear to read any more. Are we to become independent – are we not? I wish they would just make up their bloody minds and decide and put the rest of us out of our misery!"

"You would not like the country to be independent?" Max asked.

"I worry where it might leave families like ourselves – the gentry. There have always been undercurrents of hostility from the people towards us."

"All populations are envious of the aristocracy. My family in Germany are resented too."

"That's different – you are all German. The people here perceive us as British overlords, even though we've been here hundreds of years . . . The Irish have long memories. That's why it's so important for me that Diana goes to London and does the Season. I want her to be given every opportunity to meet and marry well there. I'd prefer to see her married in London than here. It would be a safer future for her there, I believe."

Max nodded, taking in everything she said. "I imagine she'll be a big hit in London," he said.

"Of course she will! With her beauty and charm! I've seen those circus ponies they trot around London masquerading as debutantes. Diana will outshine them all."

Max nodded. He studied Diana as she glided across the court.

"Game, set and match!" she declared triumphantly.

Maud smiled at Max. "And now. with your help, we'll be able to send her to London."

As Diana walked across the lawns to the terrace, Warren waved over to Max.

"Good morning! How are you today?" he called.

"Very good!" Max waved back.

"I'll see you down at the stables in a while," called Warren as he headed off.

Diana sat down at the table and poured herself coffee.

"I understand you kept poor Max up till all hours," Maud accused her.

"I didn't see Max objecting," said Diana, glancing over at him.

"Poor Max is too much of a gentleman to object."

Diana sat back with her coffee and looked at Max. "I wouldn't be too sure about that."

Caitríona came out onto the terrace.

"Ah, Caitríona, more coffee please," instructed Maud.

Caitríona took the pot and looked accusingly at Diana. "Somebody has been messing with my lemons – and my cherries!"

"What on earth are you going on about now, Caitríona?" said Maud irritably.

"I'm sure we can't have anybody messing with your cherries," said Max as he smirked at Diana.

She started giggling.

Maud looked at the two of them, confused, as Caitríona walked off with the coffee pot. "What is she going on about?"

"I was teaching your daughter how to mix cocktails last night," said Max, smiling at Diana.

As Maud looked at him, nonplussed, Simon emerged from the house.

"Are you ready to see the stables, Max?" he asked.

"Yes, ready when you are, sir," said Max, putting down his coffee cup and standing up. He nodded to the women. "See you later."

Diana watched as her father and Max walked across the gardens to the stables which could just be glimpsed through the trees from the terrace.

"It's a pity Max can't stay longer, but he has to get back to Dublin – pressing business, he said," Maud remarked. "Such a charming man! I'm glad you've had the opportunity to converse with him. It's good experience for you before you go to London."

"I really don't know why you keep going on about London," said Diana irritably, "when it's plain to see we can never afford to send me."

"I wouldn't be too sure," said Maud as she watched Simon lead Halcyon out of the stables and Max inspect the animal.

Diana looked on concerned as Max mounted Halcyon.

"What's he doing getting on my horse?" she said.

Max turned Halcyon around and trotted him out to the open fields. Diana looked on in horror as he began to race Halcyon.

"What's he doing?" she demanded, jumping to her feet.

"Riding the damned horse of course," said Maud. "What does it look like?"

"But he has no right! I didn't give him permission! Only Billy and I are allowed to ride Halcyon. Everyone knows that!"

"Oh, don't be so ridiculous, darling, and sit down," commanded Maud.

"That man knows no boundaries – he should have checked with me first – as should Papa have!"

"Oh, I'm not going to sit here while you make a fuss about nothing," said Maud, standing up. "I'm off to my studio to paint. You know, I have renewed confidence since Max bought my painting. I might get an art critic to take another look."

"Don't waste his time!" spat Diana as Maud went into the house.

In the distance Max rode Halcyon out of view.

Late that afternoon Diana was in her bedroom, sitting at her dressing table brushing her hair. She and Warren were due to go to a hunt ball later and she was preparing herself for the night ahead. She wondered what time Max would be leaving for Dublin. She stopped brushing her hair and thought about the enigmatic stranger who had so beguiled her family. And, if she had to be honest, had also beguiled her – she thought about their encounter making cocktails the previous night. She wondered where he would be off to next on this fabulous life adventure he seemed to be on. This man who could go anywhere, do anything, meet anyone he chose. She could imagine what a life like his would be.

She heard a commotion in the front courtyard. Getting up, she went to the window. She was surprised to see Halcyon there with her father and Billy. She hurried out of her room and downstairs. By the time she got to the forecourt Warren had driven up in the automobile with a trailer attached to the back of it.

"What's going on?" demanded Diana as she saw them lead Halcyon to the trailer.

"Diana, go back into the house," ordered Simon.

Diana rushed over to the horse. "I most certainly will not! What are you doing with my horse?"

Nobody said anything as Billy opened the back of the trailer and Simon and Billy began to lead the horse into it.

"*Papa!*" Diana suddenly shouted, giving everyone a start including Halycon who started to resist going into the horsebox.

"Diana! Stop disrupting things! You're making the damned horse nervous."

"He's not a damned horse – he's *my* horse!" Diana lunged forward and grabbed Halcyon's reins. "*Now where are you taking him?*"

Simon sighed loudly. "He's not your horse any more, Diana. Max has bought him."

"*Max!*" Diana screeched, horrified. "He can't have bought him because my horse is not for sale!"

Simon tried to remove Diana's hands from Halcyon's reins. "It's done, darling, let him go!"

"No! You're not taking my horse! You can't, Papa! It's the only thing I have!" she pleaded.

"It's for the best. It's for your own good," insisted Simon.

"We'll see about that!" Diana's eyes blazed with fury as she glanced over at Max's motor car. She turned and rushed across the courtyard and into the house.

"Where is he?" she demanded of Molly who shivered at the sight of her storming through the hallway.

"Who, miss?" quivered Molly.

"The bloody German!" shrieked Diana.

"In his room, miss – packing!" managed Molly.

Diana stormed up the stairs and down a corridor.

Max was just closing his suitcase when his bedroom door swung open and banged into a cabinet. Startled, he saw Diana march towards him.

"Who do you think you are that you can just walk in here and take my horse?" she demanded.

"I didn't take Halcyon. I've paid quite a lot of money for him."

"But he wasn't for sale!"

"That's not what your parents said."

"Halcyon wasn't theirs to sell! He's mine!"

"*Was* yours! He's mine now!" said Max who couldn't help

smirking at the sight before him. He'd never seen a girl in such a temper before.

"How much did you pay? You can have the money back."

"I don't want the money back. I want Halcyon. It's my belief Halcyon is going to be a great champion and I want to own him. I want to be the person to turn him into the champion."

"It was *I* who moulded him. *I* who sat up nights with him in the stables when he was sick, and raced him and nursed him and loved him – Billy and I!"

"And you've done an excellent job – thank you!"

The tears that had been threatening to spring to her eyes now ran down her face.

"He's the only thing I've ever loved and you're just taking him from me. You can have any horse, anything you want, and you're taking what I love away – just because you can!"

"Because I want to have the best – and Halcyon will be the best," he said. His face softened. "I'll take the best care of him."

He reached out and tried to wipe away a tear. Her hand hit his away and then slapped him hard across the face.

"Get out! Get out of my home and I hope I never see you again!" she hissed.

He nodded and walked past her and out of the room. She quickly wiped away her tears and raced out and down the stairs and out to the forecourt. To her horror she realised that the motor car and trailer containing Halcyon had already left. She looked over at Billy who looked as upset as she did.

Max was at his car, putting his suitcase in the back. Then he opened the front door and sat in. He smiled over at her.

"Till next time?" he said.

Diana felt herself consumed with fury at his smug face and quickly reached down and picked up a stone from the forecourt. As Max started the car and began to drive off Diana fired the stone at the car, smashing one of the headlights. Max just laughed and waved in the air as the automobile drove down the drive and disappeared from view.

"Where's my father?" Diana demanded of Billy.

"He drove away with Halcyon," said Billy.

"Delivering my horse somewhere for his new owner," she said angrily.

She looked at the gatehouse in the distance at the bottom of the drive and set off walking furiously towards it.

The inside of the gatehouse was small and Maud had converted it into a comfortable studio for her painting. Various creations of hers lay hanging on the walls or lying against the antique furniture she had stored there. That afternoon she was standing at a canvas as she dabbled a paintbrush on it.

Her peace and quiet was shattered by the front door of the gatehouse opening and slamming and Diana shouting, "*Mother!*"

Maud raised her eyes heavenward in anticipation of Diana's fury.

Diana came marching into the small parlour.

"How could you? *How could you?*" she demanded, her face a mask of stress and anger.

"Diana, dear, could you lower your voice? I come here for peace and quiet. It's my sanctuary as well as my studio."

"Answer me!"

"If you're talking about Halcyon – very easily, darling, with the amount of money Max offered us for him." Maud didn't look at her daughter but continued to paint.

"But you had no right. I *love* Halcyon!"

"Oh, there'll be other horses, Diana."

"I knew you and Papa were up to something. I sensed it from the start when we met that terrible man."

"You didn't think him so terrible when you were mixing – what did you call them – cocktails? – until the sun came up this morning."

"I should have trusted my instinct on him – and you!"

"As I said, my darling, there will be other horses, but there may not be other chances for you to attend a Season in London." Maud stopped painting and looked at her daughter "We had to raise the money to send you to London somehow, and this is how we did it. We sold the horse to enable you to go next year – as you know it costs so much, all the dresses, and the parties, and the –"

"You sold my beautiful horse for *that?*" Diana was incredulous.

"Of course. As I said, there will be other horses but there may not be other years that you can go to London. A year here, a year there, and suddenly a gal is past her prime." Maud resumed painting.

Diana sat down on the green velvet couch, distraught. "But I told you all along that I wasn't fussed about going. I was just as happy here going to parties with Warren and Dashiel."

"Well, you won't know that till you try London. Anyway it would have been ridiculous to turn down what Max was offering –"

"He only offered it because he knows Halcyon will be a great champion," said Diana.

"He doesn't know that, nobody knows anything for sure . . . Halcyon might have stumbled and fallen and broken a leg by next year . . . and then where would you be, without your horse and without the Season in London?"

Maud painted away in silence for a while as Diana wiped away her tears over her lost love.

"I never loved your father, you know," Maud suddenly said as she continued to paint. "Not really."

"Why did you marry him then?" Diana looked up at her, confused and bewildered.

"He didn't give me any choice. He turned up at every hunt ball and shoot I was at. He was so insistent we married I had no choice but to agree . . . but then when Dashiel arrived I did love him . . . and then you and Warren of course . . . But I often think about what might have been, if I'd gone to London to my cousins, the Ashenbrys. What would have happened to me? I've made sure you never ask yourself that question, even if we had to sell your precious Halcyon to get you there."

Diana refused to come down from her room for dinner that evening. She sat in her room, despondent. Nobody seemed to understand how much she loved that horse. How much she had cared for him. How little doing the Season in London really mattered to her, and certainly did not matter to her if it meant sacrificing Halcyon. And as she thought of Max Von Hoffsten, she was consumed with anger and hatred. His attitude inflamed her – the attitude that he could go through life and just take what he wanted, just because he had the money and power to do so, without any thought or consideration for the pain he would cause. She thought of how he had seductively mixed drinks with her the previous night, all the while planning to rob her horse. She would never trust a man again, she thought as she finally fell into an exhausted sleep.

CHAPTER 6

She woke up the next morning and got out of bed. A night's sleep hadn't made her feel any better as she couldn't even bear the thought of going down and joining her disloyal family for breakfast. Sighing, she opened the curtains. She squinted in the sunlight, rubbed her eyes and stared again disbelieving.

Halcyon was there in the forecourt, strolling around. Not understanding, she quickly put on a long dressing gown and went racing from her room down the stairs and out to the forecourt to Halcyon who she embraced and kissed.

"You've come back to me," she whispered to him.

"What's all this?" demanded Maud as she came down the steps with Simon, both of them looking concerned, followed by Warren.

Billy, who had been standing by the wall, stepped forward.

"The German gentleman turned up this morning with him," he explained.

"Max? Is he here?" questioned Maud, worried Diana's exhibition yesterday had disrupted the sale and Max was looking for his money back.

"No. He delivered Halcyon and then drove off in that fancy motor car of his," said Billy.

"I don't understand. What did he say?" demanded Diana.

"He said the horse was to be left here under Miss Diana's window, and he left this for you, miss." Billy handed over an envelope with *'Diana'* written across the front.

Diana tore open the envelope and read the note inside: *'As if I could deny you anything – M'*

Her family gathered around and read the note with her.

"I don't understand," said Maud. "Is he giving the horse back?"

"Looks like it!" Simon was amazed.

"And what of the money he paid for him?" Maud didn't like this unorthodox commercial transaction in the least.

"He said he was returning to Germany today," said Billy.

"In that case he has gifted the horse back to you, Diana," said Simon.

"*Woa! What a gesture!*" roared Warren excitedly.

"But why would he do such a thing?" Maud was confused. "It's as you said, Diana – the man obviously has more money than sense. Do you know he left without taking the painting he bought and paid for from me?"

"A man of good taste after all!" said Diana.

Maud gave Diana a filthy look. "I'm going to return to my breakfast – my poached eggs will have gone cold."

Taking Simon's hand, Maud turned and walked back to the house, Warren following them. Then she turned around.

"All I can say, Diana, is you embarrassed the poor man into handing you Halcyon back! I've rarely heard of a young woman behaving less like a lady. That temper of yours will have to go before you go to London, or else nobody will want to receive you!"

As Billy took Halcyon back to the stables, Diana stood there staring at Max's note to her.

CHAPTER 7

There was a strange restlessness in Diana over the following days. One she had never had before and couldn't understand. A feeling of loss. But she had managed to keep Halcyon and not lose him, so she really could not understand this emotion.

She spent the summer days riding Halcyon through the country or going for walks on her own. And one image refused to leave her: Max Von Hoffsten. She couldn't stop thinking about this strange, charismatic, inexplicable man. She couldn't understand his generosity in handing Halcyon back to her when it was obvious he wanted the horse from the moment he set eyes on him at the Derby. She thought back to the night they mixed the cocktails together and the strange intimacy between them. And she thought of how he had smirked at her mockingly the next day, almost as if he had enjoyed her distress, probably delighting in knowing he could restore her happiness at a whim by giving back Halcyon – which he had done. But it hadn't restored any happiness, which is what confused her. And then there was his note: '*As if I could deny you anything – M*' What did he mean by that?

She was strolling along a river that wound its way through their farm when she saw Warren galloping towards her on his horse.

"Come on, Diana," he said as he reached her. "Why aren't you getting yourself ready for tonight?"

That night they had been invited to Hannah Roundtree's party. Dashiel was making the trip from Dublin to attend with them.

She shook her head. "I'm not going, Warren."

"You? Miss a party? Are you ill?"

"No – I just don't feel like it."

"But Dashiel is coming down for it and anybody who's anybody in the county will be there!"

Max Von Hoffsten won't be there, she thought.

"You'll just have to manage without me tonight." She smiled sadly and walked off down by the river.

Warren watched her wander off and wondered what was wrong with her lately. She had her horse back, she was getting to go to London. What more could she want?

That evening, Diana came down the stairs and crossed over to the drawing room. The family was gathered there and Dashiel had arrived from Dublin. He was sitting on a couch telling some hilarious story from university. Maud, as ever, sat beside him, hanging on his every word and looking adoringly at him.

"Here she is!" exclaimed Dashiel. "Come on, get ready! We'll be late for the party."

"I've told everyone I'm not going, Dashiel." She reached down and greeted him with a kiss on the cheek.

"Not going? Of course you are. Now get up them stairs and put on your glad rags!" ordered Dashiel.

"She's been like this for days now. She's a complete bore. I'm trying to get her up to Dublin for fittings for dresses for London, but she won't go," said Maud.

"I still haven't forgiven you for that trick you pulled trying to sell my horse." Diana looked at Maud and Simon accusingly.

Simon looked suitably ashamed, Maud looked as if she couldn't care less.

"Oh, get over it, Diana!" snapped Maud.

"Yes, I heard you came into a bit of a windfall from Max and you will go to the ball in London, Cinderella!" Dashiel said laughingly.

"We've taken that money under false pretences. He didn't get the horse so we shouldn't have got the money," Diana retorted.

"Let it go, Diana!" snapped Maud, raising her eyes to heaven.

Dashiel stood up, grabbed Diana's arm and marched her out of the room.

"That's right! Force her to go, Dashiel!" Maud laughed to herself as she sipped her sherry. "Save me and her father from having to look at that gloomy face for the night!"

"You are going to the party and that's the end of it!" Dashiel insisted as he hauled her up the stairs. "Who else is going to save me from Hannah Roundtree tonight?"

CHAPTER 8

The Roundtrees lived in a crumbling castle and, as Dashiel drove up, their forecourt was already filled with motor cars. Diana got out of the car and her two brothers linked her arms and walked her swiftly over the gravel and up into the castle. Warren and Dashiel's good humour was infectious and Diana decided to force herself to enjoy the night as they walked through the Roundtrees' huge ancient hallway which was filled with smartly dressed party guests.

"There you are!" said Hannah. "What kept you so long?"

"All Diana's fault, I'm afraid," said Dashiel.

"Well, not to worry, you're here now!" said Hannah who was looking at Dashiel in an almost gluttonous fashion. "I've been saving my first dance for you!"

She grabbed Dashiel's arm and led him to the dancing in the drawing room.

Diana laughed as Dashiel looked back and mimed "*Help!*" at her.

An hour went by and Diana danced and chatted with the others as best she could but it was very forced.

"What is wrong with you?" demanded Dashiel.

"Oh, I don't know, Dashiel – ignore me! I told you I shouldn't have come!"

"But you look so unhappy. I know what happened to your horse was a bit of a shock, but you managed to keep him," said Dashiel.

"It's not that – it's Max, I think."

"Max? Is there something you want to tell me? Do you like him?"

"I don't know. I can't stop thinking about him. I wouldn't mind, but I treated him so badly! I was rude and unwelcoming and unpleasant . . ."

"Have *you* – Diana – fallen in love?" Dashiel's face was full of amusement.

"I hope I haven't! Or at least I hope this is not what love feels like . . . Anyway it doesn't matter any more. I behaved so appallingly the day he left. I slapped him and even broke the headlight on his motor car!"

"Oh Diana!" Dashiel's face became a mixture of amusement and sympathy.

"So he'll never want to see me again," she said, "not even as a friend."

Diana left the party and wandered into the large darkened conservatory that ran along the Roundtrees' castle. As the music swirled out from the French windows that led into the castle she stared at her reflection in the glass wall.

Suddenly, in the glass, she saw a figure behind her and felt very confused as it looked like Max. She stared at the reflection and Max's features became more recognisable as the figure behind slowly approached her.

She turned around and Max was standing there.

"*Ahhh! You!*" she all but screamed in shock.

He laughed lightly. "Did I startle you?"

"But what are you *doing* here?"

"I organised to come here."

"You said you were leaving Ireland. Why aren't you in Paris or Rome or –"

"Did you enjoy getting Halcyon back?"

"This doesn't make sense. You don't even know Hannah Roundtree, do you?"

"No. I contacted Dashiel at Trinity and explained the situation to him and we organised for me to be here tonight to surprise you."

"Dashiel arranged for you to be here tonight?"

"I wanted to surprise you. And I couldn't just call up to see you because I wasn't sure how you'd react. You gave me quite a send-off last time I saw you." He rubbed the cheek which she had slapped.

"I'm – I'm sorry about that . . . and breaking your headlight."

"You were certainly spirited that morning."

"Of course I was! You were buying my horse without my permission!"

"Or at least I thought I was!" he laughed.

"But I still don't understand – why are you here?"

"I thought that was obvious. To see – you." He smiled at her.

She felt thrilled and that emptiness she had been feeling since last seeing him vanished. "Well, I wish you would just contact me directly rather than planning things behind my back with my family all the time!"

"I had to be sure you wanted to see me." He looked at her knowingly. "Dashiel indicated to me that you liked me. And tonight he just confirmed it."

"Dashiel! My brother betrayed me! I told him that in confidence! He had no right!" Her voice raged as her face became inflamed with embarrassment and anger.

He reached and took her hands. His touch had a strange calming effect on her and the embarrassment and anger she felt evaporated. She felt it didn't matter what this man knew about her.

He pulled her closer and they began to kiss.

"Diana? Diana!" called Hannah Roundtree in the distance.

Diana quickly pulled away from him.

"Diana?" called Hannah again as she entered the conservatory.

"Hannah, we're here."

Diana quickly stepped out of the darkened shadow, followed by Max.

"Do you see who's here?" Diana asked, smiling brightly while she patted her hair.

"Yes, I'd heard you had come tonight – hello again, Max." Hannah smiled at him in a suspicious way. "You're missing all the food."

"Oh." Diana turned and smiled at Max. "Are you hungry?"

"Famished!"

"We'd better go and get some food then." Diana smiled at him and led him past Hannah into the party.

For the rest of the night Diana and Max didn't leave each other's side. They danced together, talked together, ate together, laughed together.

"What on earth is going on there?" demanded Hannah of Dashiel as they both watched Diana and Max dance closely together.

"I don't know. All I know is he asked me to arrange for him to meet her again, without her knowing."

"I see!" said Hannah, looking even more suspicious.

CHAPTER 9

Over the following weeks Max Von Hoffsten became a regular fixture on the Anglo-Irish circuit. He was at all the shoots, balls and soirées. And always not far from the beautiful young Diana Cantwell. The Cantwell family seemed to be his permanent hosts, he stayed so often with them.

All the time Diana felt happier than she ever had before in her life. She knew this time would end. That Max would leave Ireland, return to his exciting life in glamorous places and that she would soon be sent to London to stay with her cousins the Ashenbrys where the foundations of her future life would be set down. But for now all she cared about was being with Max.

As she sat on the terrace at the back of Garonglen having tea with her mother, Dashiel and Max were on the tennis court engaged in a bitter battle to the end.

"You're letting the side down!" Maud called to her son as Max took the lead.

"Come on, Dashiel! You can catch him up!" Diana called.

"I now know whose side you're on!" Max called to her.

"Of course you do! The underdog! I'm always on the side of the underdog!" she answered.

"Ah, in that case – I will let him win!" said Max.

Smiling to herself, Diana sat back in her chair.

Maud studied her daughter. "He's so charming, isn't he? Max?"

"Yes, I guess he is," said Diana.

"We'll all miss him, when he goes."

Diana's face soured.

"And he will go, Diana, you do realise that?" Maud looked earnestly at her but Diana said nothing. "By the way, since you won't come to Dublin to do the dresses for London, I've arranged for some dressmakers to come here and measure you up."

Diana sat up, looking angry. "Will you stop pushing me all the time! I'll do the bloody dresses in my own time! I'm too busy at the moment."

"Too busy escorting Max around!"

"I thought you liked him?"

"I do, very much so. But he's a friend, not a fiancé, darling. And you need to start thinking of fiancés."

"Game, set and match!" shouted Max.

"I thought you said you were going to let me win!" objected Dashiel as he reached over and shook Max's hand.

"I was! I gave you every opportunity to win, but I was still far too good for you," laughed Max.

The two men headed over to the terrace.

"Everything all right?" asked Max, looking at Diana's unhappy face.

"Fine!" Diana forced herself to smile. "We're looking forward to the theatre tonight!"

One day the following week Max and Diana were walking along the river in the afternoon sunshine at Garonglen.

"Thank you for taking me and Warren to The Shelbourne for lunch yesterday. He very much enjoyed it, we both did. But it was a real treat for him. He rarely gets to Dublin."

"I think Warren shouldn't be forgotten about. Dashiel will go on to have a glittering career in law and you will go on to have a glittering marriage. But his future will be at Garonglen forever. He'll never see anything beyond this county, so it's good he gets an opportunity now and again."

Max speaking about her having a glittering marriage angered her. That he could so easily see her with another man.

"Yes, I'm going to Dublin this week to be fitted for dresses for London." She said it out of spite.

He looked at her knowingly. "Oh, your mother has finally got you to commit, has she?"

"Of course. That is my destiny, is it not?"

"It's probably just as well. I'm leaving tomorrow for the Continent."

"*What?* But why didn't you say something before?"

"Well, I only made my mind up recently. I need to get back to Germany, check on business there, with my father, my family. Before heading to – oh, I don't know, Madrid maybe."

"Madrid?" Her voice was furious. "Well, I hope you manage to find hosts there as hospitable as you did here. And a girl to show you around and keep you company as well as I did." She turned and started walking quickly back to the house.

He followed her. "What's wrong with you now?"

"Well, if I have to tell you, then there's no point in doing so!" she said, her pace not slowing.

"I'm sorry – I don't understand what has you so upset."

She stopped and faced him. "You come here, disrupt all our lives, blind us with us with your money and glamour and then just say you're off with hardly as much as a ta-ta!"

He looked at her, bemused, smirking at her.

"My gosh, if you don't remove that smirk, I'll remove it for you!" she threatened.

He put his hands up defensively. "Oh, please, don't hit me again!"

"You deserve a beating! I don't know why you've been messing around here for the past few weeks. All you do is go from pillar to post around the world."

"Do you think I've been toying with your affections?"

"As if I ever took you seriously!" Her own voice became mocking. "I am off to be fitted for dresses for my spectacular appearance in London. I wish you well in Madrid – good day!" She walked off quickly.

Max caught up with her and turned her to him.

"You're a fool, do you know that?" he said, smiling at her.

"A fool to ever spend any time with you!"

"I'm going to Germany to inform my father and family about my forthcoming marriage," he informed her.

"*Your marriage!*" she shrieked. "To whom?"

"To you, my Diana."

"I can't take any more of your jokes, Max." She turned to pull away.

"I'm not joking. I'm going to marry you, if you'll have me."

"Don't joke with me like this," she begged, shaking her head.

"I'm not. I've asked your parents and they have given their permission and their blessing."

"But they never said!"

"I asked them not to. I wanted to tell you myself."

"More deceit! I really can't believe you. I know women haven't got the vote yet, but I will not have you going around organising my life behind my back, which you seem to insist upon doing."

"I only want what's best for you. I'm in love with you – will you marry me?"

"Yes, of course I will!" She reached forward and held him tightly.

They walked into the house through the French windows hand in hand.

In the drawing room Maud, Simon, Dashiel and Warren were waiting expectantly.

"She said yes!" declared Max excitedly.

They all cheered.

"Thank goodness for that!" said Simon as he opened a bottle of champagne.

"As if she would have said no!" Maud replied, coming over to congratulate them.

"You could never tell with Diana!" said Dashiel as he kissed his sister and shook Max's hand.

"You all knew?" Diana didn't want to spoil the moment by feeling angry, but she really didn't like how Max had orchestrated the proposal, involving her whole family without even giving her a hint. But she was more angry with them as they seemed to care more about pleasing Max than her! But as she looked at Max she pushed the thoughts out of her head. She couldn't believe he was marrying her. It was what she wanted more than anything else, but had been afraid to let herself even think of the possibility as it seemed out of the question. But, as a glass of champagne was put in her hand and her father toasted their future happiness, she looked at Max's loving face and realised that he had made her the happiest girl in the world.

Later, as another bottle of champagne was opened and the men laughed and joked, Maud sidled up beside her daughter.

"It's absolutely wonderful news. You know, he was in love with you from the first moment he met you. All that nonsense with Halcyon was just a ruse to get to know you."

"Did he say that?" asked Diana.

"No, but it's obvious, isn't it? Well, I'd better write to the Ashenbrys and tell them you won't be going over to do the London Season after all." She smiled smugly. "Just think, Diana, you will one day be a countess! The Countess Von Hoffsten. You couldn't have made a better match. Do you know how wealthy the Von Hoffstens are? All of society will be stricken with jealousy!"

"I guess. I haven't given all that any thought. I'm just happy, that's all."

"Where will you live, I wonder? Did he say?" enquired Maud.

"No. We haven't talked about anything. It's all so new."

"Everything is new until it becomes old, Diana. We must attend to the practicalities." She then called out to Max. "Max, have you given any thought to where you and Diana will live?"

"We will base ourselves at the family hunting estate in Germany, and from there we'll travel to wherever we wish – South of France, London, or here – home to Ireland." He smiled at Maud.

"Sounds divine! And what about your family? When will you tell them so we can announce the engagement officially?"

"Mama! I'm still recovering from my engagement myself – please give us some time!" pleaded Diana.

"I shall tell my father without delay. I'm sure he will want to meet Diana as soon as is convenient."

"As I would have thought. Your mother is no longer with us, of course."

"No," said Max sadly.

"Is it long since she passed away?" asked Maud sympathetically.

"A few years," said Max quietly.

"Was it sudden?"

"Yes . . . she had a fall," answered Max.

"Tragic," Maud shook her head.

"I must inform my brother and sister as well, of course," Max said.

"Well, I can't wait to meet them all," said Maud as she held up her glass. "To Diana and Max!"

"To Diana and Max!"

CHAPTER 10

As Diana walked down Grafton Street, shopping with Maud in Dublin, she suddenly felt very different. It wasn't just that she was engaged to the man she was besotted with. Or that he seemed to be besotted with her. It was that her life would change so much so very soon. She would be whisked away to a life of extreme wealth and glamour. She would one day be Countess Von Hoffsten. Although she knew she had been brought up with privilege, despite their lack of cash, marriage to Max would bring her into the nobility. It was very hard for her to get her head around it.

"What about the wedding itself?" pushed Maud. "Has Max said anything of the plans? Would he prefer a marriage in Germany or here in Ireland? It would be normal for the marriage to be in the bride's place, but considering who his family is I imagine they would want a kind of state wedding in Germany?"

"He hasn't said anything," said Diana.

"Hmmm, I wonder about finance for the occasion?" Maud looked worried.

"Oh Mama, will you be quiet!" Diana snapped.

"I'm just saying! You've never had to worry about money as your father and I took on all the worry. And now, with marriage to Max, it looks like you never will."

"I'm sure Max will insist on taking care of the financing of the wedding," Diana reassured her.

"Isn't he just fabulous!" sighed Maud as she and Diana reached The Shelbourne.

They walked up the steps into the hotel.

In the restaurant Max was waiting for them for afternoon tea. He waved over to them and stood up as they reached the table. He pulled out the chairs for them and they all sat down.

"How are you today?" Max smiled adoringly at Diana as he held her hand.

"Very good," she smiled back at him.

"We were just talking about the marriage arrangements," said Maud.

"Mama!" objected Diana.

"No, your mother is quite right, Diana, to discuss the wedding plans. I personally don't want to wait that long to marry you. As soon as possible is my choice. Why wait around?"

"My thought exactly," nodded Maud.

"That is why I'm delighted to give you my news. My father is travelling to Ireland next week to meet you."

"Your father is coming here?" Diana felt panicked.

"I know. I was surprised when he sent a telegram. He rarely leaves Germany. He's quite old now, you know," said Max.

"But that's wonderful!" Maud clapped her hands together. "I can't wait to meet the count. He must stay with us at Garonglen."

Max made an awkward face. "That's very kind of you, but he said he was staying here at The Shelbourne. He has already booked a suite of rooms."

"But you must tell him there is no need. We would love him to stay with us," said Maud.

"I shall certainly say it to him, but he is very set in his ways. He likes to have his own space and I don't think he'll accept the offer, as grateful as I'm sure he will be."

"Whatever he is more comfortable with," said Diana.

"In that case he will come to dinner at Garonglen and we can meet him at our home and get to know him there," said Maud.

"I think that would be delightful." Max squeezed Diana's hand again and smiled at her.

CHAPTER 11

Garonglen was in a flurry of activity. Max's father Count Conrad Von Hoffsten had arrived safely in Ireland and was ensconced in The Shelbourne in Dublin. He was due for dinner at Garonglen that evening. Maud was clucking around the dinner table like a mother hen as Caitríona and Molly put the finishing touches to the feast being prepared.

"And remember the count is to be addressed as *Your Excellency*, is that clear?" ordered Maud.

"Perhaps if Mrs Cantwell invested in some extra servants for the night, she might be more at ease with the service being provided to *His Excellency*. We're going to be run off our feet!" snapped Caitríona.

"Budgets, Caitríona, budgets!" dismissed Maud.

Caitríona raised her eyes to heaven as she slammed down a fork.

Molly had been issued so many orders she was now too petrified to look left or right.

Maud walked out of the room and across the hall into the drawing room where Diana was dressed in a new chiffon gown. She was pouring herself a sherry.

"And you can do without that!" said Maud, taking away the full glass and putting it down. "We don't want you in an inebriated state by the time your future father-in-law arrives."

"I'm just so nervous of meeting him. What if he doesn't like me?"

"Of course he'll like you. What is there not to like about you? If you had gone to London, you would have been debutante of the year!"

Max and his father were being driven along country roads towards Garonglen.

"It's not that much farther," said Max. "They are only an hour from Dublin."

"It seems much longer," said Conrad.

Max looked at his father. Conrad was a man in his seventies. He had a stern unsmiling expression that Max had rarely known to leave his face.

"They would have come to meet you in Germany, you know. There was no need for you to come to Ireland."

"I thought it wiser I should come here," said Conrad.

"They are very excited about meeting you . . . Diana especially."

"I'm sure."

"Garonglen is very beautiful . . . it's not palatial, but it's a beautiful old Georgian house."

"I'm sure I'll see it for myself shortly," said Conrad.

"The Cantwells have been there for centuries. And Diana's grandmother was a daughter of Lord Ashenbry. You know, the Ashenbrys in London?"

Conrad sighed loudly. "So you keep telling me, boy. So Diana is second cousin of the Ashenbrys. You don't need to tell me again."

Max nodded and bit his lower lip as he looked straight ahead.

"Diana was about to go to London to do the Season."

"I know!" Conrad snapped loudly, causing the driver to glance at them in the rear mirror.

Max sat back in silence.

"They're here!" shouted Warren, who was standing at the window of the drawing room.

Maud knocked back her sherry and stood up. She was feeling quite nervous herself by now. She quickly inspected the family. Warren, Dashiel and Conrad looked distinguished in their tuxedos. Diana looked resplendent.

"Everyone to the hall!" shouted Maud.

"We're here!" snarled Caitríona and then she whispered to Molly, "The sooner we get independence and send this lot packing the better!"

In the hall all the servants from the house and farm were standing in a row as Maud had trained them to. Garonglen hadn't had a butler for ten years and Maud had spent an afternoon training Billy the stable boy in a quick course to act as butler for the night. As she looked at Billy nervously waiting by the door, she hoped the count wouldn't notice the boy's lack of training.

The family gathered around Diana as Billy, on Maud's nod, opened the front door. Outside in the forecourt they could see Max assisting his father from the back of the motor car. Then the two of them walked towards the house and up the steps to the front door.

Simon stepped forward to greet them.

"Welcome to Garonglen, Your Excellency – and Max," he said.

"Simon, if I could introduce my father, Count Conrad Von Hoffsten," said Max proudly.

Simon offered his hand and Conrad took it and shook it quickly, then walked into the hallway, silently observing the house and the decor.

"And, Father, this is Mrs Maud Cantwell," said Max.

Maud smiled delightedly. It was already all over the county that the count was coming to dinner. Maud could only imagine the shockwaves once the engagement was announced.

"You are so very welcome to Garonglen, Your Excellency." Maud waved a hand at her sons. "This is my eldest son Dashiel and my youngest Warren."

Conrad nodded to them as Maud turned towards Diana.

"And may I present to you my daughter – Diana Cantwell," she said proudly.

Conrad stopped abruptly in front of Diana and stared at her.

Diana stepped forward and smiled. "I'm so pleased to meet you. Max has told me so much about you."

Conrad said nothing but continued to stare at her, his eyes inspecting every part of her. She felt embarrassed and exposed by his scrutiny and felt herself blush. As Conrad's silent glaring became unbearable she quickly glanced from her mother to Max, who were standing on either side of the count.

"Shall we go to the drawing room for an aperitif?" suggested Maud.

Conrad's glare did not waver with this suggestion.

"Father?" urged Max.

Conrad turned and began to follow Maud into the dining room. As he walked he passed a cursory glance over the servants assembled on the other side of the hall. As he passed Molly, she made an exaggerated curtsy, and Caitríona gave her a swift surreptitious kick to stand up.

Conrad entered the drawing room and silently studied his surroundings. Maud invited him to sit in an armchair by the fire.

By now, as Max and the Cantwells took their positions around the room, Conrad's silence was unnerving everybody. Maud glanced nervously at her husband.

Billy, loosely trained in the etiquette of footman for the night, stood waiting for his orders by the drinks cabinet.

"Billy, you may serve the drinks," Maud nodded.

As Diana sat on the couch where Maud had earlier instructed her to sit in the rehearsals that had been going on all day, she really didn't know what to make of Max's father. His staring eyes, his silence – she was completely intimidated. Perhaps he didn't speak good English, she suddenly thought, although Max had never said he didn't.

Billy walked around and offered sherry to the guests.

Maud froze as she saw the glasses wobble on the tray.

"Our butler is down with a cold, Your Excellency," she lied. "Our footman is filling the post for the night."

The count gave Billy an uninterested glance.

Simon, who was standing at the fireplace, leaned forward to Conrad. "Did you have a good trip?"

"It was certainly a long one," Conrad declared, and there was a tangible relief around the room that the man had at last spoken.

Diana felt Max was different in his father's company. He wasn't the relaxed carefree confident man he usually was. He was quieter, on edge. Of course he was introducing his future bride so he had every reason to be nervous, she reasoned. She herself wasn't being her normal self either and was more reserved. As the party moved across the hall to the dining room and began dinner, it was lucky for all that Maud and Simon were seasoned conversationalists.

"It's very sad that Max's mother is no longer with us," said Maud. "I'm sure she will be much missed at the wedding."

Conrad paused in eating his pheasant and glanced at Max.

Max quickly looked away.

"Is it long since the countess passed away?" asked Simon.

Max and Conrad looked at each other momentarily.

"The Cantwell shoot is one of the best in the country, Father," Max quickly informed him.

"Although from what we hear of the Von Hoffsten hunting estate in Germany, our shoot bears no comparison," said Simon.

"Yes – I understand from Max that the hunting estate will be their main residence when he marries Diana," said Maud.

"Max had shown me photographs of it – it looks marvellous," said Diana, smiling at Conrad.

"Do you visit the hunting estate much, Your Excellency?" asked Simon. "I understand from Max that you yourself reside in the family *schloss* in Munich?"

Conrad glanced at Max and then took a sip of his wine.

"Of course Diana has never been to Germany, but she's incredibly adaptable. And her German is word perfect, along with her French," said Maud.

Diana looked lovingly at Max across the table from her. "I'm very much looking forward to my new life in my new home country with my husband."

Still no response from Conrad.

"Max has a brother and sister, I believe?" said Maud to him.

There was a moment's silence and when it was obvious Conrad was not going to answer Max quickly said, "That's right – Brigitte and Hugo."

"I can't wait to meet them," said Diana.

"It's a pity they couldn't have come with you to visit us," said Maud.

As Conrad continued to say nothing the conversation fell into another lull.

"Have you met my cousins, Lord Ashenbry and the Ashenbry family, Your Excellency?" Maud smiled over at him.

After a dessert of bon-bons and ice cream was tidied away by Caitríona and the staff, coffee and chocolates were served.

The servants then left the room, leaving just the family with Max and his father.

"I really need to be leaving – to get back to my hotel in Dublin," said Conrad.

It was the longest sentence he had said all night, causing everyone to look at him, startled.

"We would have been delighted if you had stayed with us instead of at a hotel," said Maud. "After all, we'll soon be family."

"Hmph!" said Conrad. "I would like to thank you for your hospitality tonight, and indeed the hospitality you have shown my son over the summer."

Maud smiled happily at Max. "It's been our pleasure. He's like one of the family already."

Max smiled appreciatively back at her.

Conrad looked at Diana. "I hope my son hasn't given any false . . . hopes or . . . indications . . . to you during his time here?"

Diana looked at Conrad, perplexed. "I'm sorry?"

"Of course –" Conrad paused before he continued, "– a marriage between you and my son is quite out of the question."

Diana felt as if someone had stolen her ability to inhale as everyone at the table gazed at each other with open mouths.

"I beg your pardon?" said Maud.

"No, I'm afraid I'm the one who must beg your pardon on behalf of my son. You see it is quite impossible that Max marries your daughter as he is already engaged to be married to somebody else."

"*Father!*" shouted Max.

"What is the meaning of this?" demanded Simon.

"Max is engaged to be married to the Princess Alexandra of Howstein."

"Max, what is he talking about?" demanded Diana as tears sprang to her eyes.

"Who on earth is Princess Alexandra of Howstein?" Maud shrilled.

"Princess Alexandra is a second cousin once removed of Max's. We Von Hoffstens always marry from within our own family circle."

"Hence there is a strong streak of insanity running through the family!" snarled Max.

"I think somebody had better explain to me what is going on very quickly before I lose my temper!" Simon's face was red with anger.

"I am not engaged to anybody else but Diana!" Max insisted, looking earnestly at her across the table.

"But who is this other woman then?" demanded Diana.

"His fiancée, I told you!" said Conrad.

Max slammed both his hands down on the table. "*Not* my fiancée!"

"The arrangement was made when you were sixteen," said Conrad.

"I have never given my consent or agreement to that arrangement. You made it with her family, but I never did!" Max shouted.

"I don't care much what you agree to – the contract is unbreakable," said Conrad.

"I've never heard anything like it!" said Maud, horrified. "Trying to force the poor lad into a marriage that he doesn't want!"

"Sir!" said Simon, looking at Conrad. "I believe a person has a right to marry whoever they choose – it is a free country last time I checked!"

"You, sir, may live in a free country, but I and Max do not live in a country that has quite the same democratic freedoms, not the last time I checked with the Kaiser in any case."

"Max, why did you never mention this arrangement before?" demanded Diana.

"Because it has nothing to do with me!"

"Well, it obviously has!" shouted Diana.

Conrad observed Diana's anger. "Yes, they said you were spirited . . . Max will return to Germany with me and arrangements will be made for his marriage to the Princess Alexandra without further delay."

"*Damn you!*" Max shouted at him.

"And what of the promise Max made to my daughter?" demanded Maud.

"He was not in a position to make it. Your daughter seems like a perfectly adequate young woman –"

"*Adequate!*" Maud nearly screamed.

"Yes, adequate! And that is as far a compliment as I can pay her . . . I'm afraid your pride is misplaced in many areas." Conrad looked Diana up and down and then started to laugh unpleasantly. "But it is ridiculous to suggest that she could ever marry Max and become the Countess Von Hoffsten . . . She absolutely does not come up to scratch. She has neither the pedigree, the background, the wealth, the connections or the breeding."

Maud's face was horrified. "We are cousins of Lord Ashenbry's!"

"Distant cousins but you are not aristocracy in any way, as much as the Anglo-Irish like to masquerade as such. Families like you are on the fringes of high society. Put bluntly, your daughter is simply not good enough!"

Dashiel and Simon jumped to their feet in fury.

"Sir, I think you had better leave my house before I do something I regret!" advised Simon loudly, his face a mask of fury.

"And I!" added Maud.

Conrad rose to his feet. "It will be my pleasure to leave."

"You are the most ghastly man I have ever met!" Diana accused him, wiping away tears as she jumped to her feet.

"I understood before you met my son you were en route to do the Season in London. I daresay you will now head off there to try and snare another wealthy young man. By the time you finish the Season you'll have met far more ghastly men than me . . . Max, come along, we must return to Dublin."

"Do you think I will go anywhere with you?" snapped Max as he went around the table and put his arms around Diana.

"Max, you will leave with me now and not ever return to this house," commanded Conrad.

"Diana?" Max said gently as he held her tenderly.

"Just go, Max, go with him now!" said Diana. "Get him out of my home and out of my sight!"

"You heard the . . . *lady*," said Conrad.

Max stayed stationary beside Diana.

"Max, it's best you go," Simon said.

Max tore himself away from Diana. "All right. But I will be back!"

Conrad walked out of the room with his head in the air.

Max looked at the Cantwells.

"I'm so sorry," he whispered before walking out and following his father.

As the motor car started up outside, Maud and the family gathered around a sobbing Diana to comfort her.

CHAPTER 12

As Conrad entered his suite of rooms at The Shelbourne Hotel, Max stormed in after him.

"*How could you?*" Max screamed at him across the suite's drawing room.

"And how could *you?*" retorted Conrad calmly. "How could you drag me to this infernal country to that dreadful chalet to endure the most tiresome company and mediocre food I have ever had the misfortune to be presented with?"

"They are wonderful people, a wonderful warm and cultured family."

"I think I have already expressed my opinion on those people. Need I repeat myself?"

"You make me so angry!" Max in his frustration grabbed a crystal ashtray and sent it flying across the room.

"Dear boy, please stop! Remember what we had to do to you as a child to stop these irrational tantrums you suffer from."

"You were invited by that family, my future wife's family, and given their utmost hospitality and you degraded them and insulted them!"

"They degraded and insulted themselves by assuming they could ever be married into the Von Hoffstens."

"Why did you come here then?" demanded Max. "Why make the journey here to meet them when you were so set against me marrying Diana?"

"Quite simply because I *was* so against it! When I learned that you had gone so far as to propose to the girl without my permission, I knew I had to come straight here and let her, her family and you know in no uncertain terms that this engagement is not proceeding."

"You didn't even give Diana a chance. If she went to London she would have been catapulted to the top of society with her beauty and charm."

"And there lies the heart of the matter. She is like everything else you want in life – a possession you want to acquire and nurture so that you get the credit for turning her into a success."

"That's not true!"

"Yes, it is. You're like this with a racehorse, a yacht, a new racing car or anything new – you want to get there before everyone else. You see potential in this girl and want to marry her before anyone else gets the chance. Marriages should not be based on such thoughts but on the sound basis of wealth and common ground, which is what you and Princess Alexandra have."

"Alexandra! I cannot even stand being in the same room as her!" snapped Max in disgust.

"In that case, dear boy, you will only be enduring the same kind of marriage that the rest of us did."

"I want a marriage with somebody I love and worship and not a contract."

"And you think you love this girl?" Conrad sneered.

"I love her. I can't live without her." Max spoke with pure determination.

"Nobody is suggesting that you live without her. You can set her up in a flat somewhere, visit her twice a week if you care to. She looks like the type of girl who would readily agree to such an arrangement."

Max raced across the room in a rage, stopping short in front of his father who didn't falter. "Don't you ever speak about her like that again. I don't want a marriage like you and Mother had, with your women in Munich and Berlin and Paris. I want Diana and I will marry her, and there's nothing you can do to stop me!" Max turned and stormed out of the room.

"Yes, there is – you need my permission or the marriage will not be recognised!" Conrad called after him.

Diana and the rest of the Cantwells were in the drawing room, still in a kind of shock. Diana sat in a trance, ignoring the large gin and tonic her father had poured for her and which rested on a table beside her.

"Just who does he think he is?" demanded Maud. "Speaking to us in such a manner!"

"He's a bastard, that's what he is!" said Warren.

"Warren, language, please!" corrected Maud. "I realise we may not be titled aristocracy . . . but we *are* landed gentry!"

"All your airs and graces in the world didn't matter a damn to him, Mama," said Diana. "He made it crystal clear what he thought of me."

"He's a stupid old fool, Diana – old-fashioned and bitter," said Simon.

"That's as it may be, but I fear Max will not go against his father's wishes," said Diana.

"The whole thing is so archaic!" said Maud. "Marrying a woman he doesn't want or love!"

Diana stared at her mother accusingly. "I believe many successful marriages begin with such circumstances."

Guiltily, Maud raised her wine and took a large gulp.

"I wonder what Max meant by saying there was insanity in the family?" mused Dashiel.

"I should have known the whole thing was too good to be true," said Diana. "I was warned that those German aristocratic families only intermarry with each other. I remember Hannah Roundtree told me that before, when she mentioned Max couldn't marry any of the debutantes who were pursuing him when he visited London. Who was I to ever think Max would break the rule for me?"

"You thought it because Max is mad about you – it's plain for everyone to see," said Simon.

"What good is that, when he is forbidden to marry me?" sighed Diana.

"He'll be back tomorrow, and he'll have the whole thing straightened out, you'll see," Simon assured her.

Diana stood up. "I'm going to bed – I'll see you in the morning." She walked around and kissed everyone before walking slowly upstairs.

She hardly slept that night. She was wounded by the vicious words from Conrad that had cut to her core and undermined her so much that she felt inferior. She could only imagine the row that had continued on into the night between Conrad and Max. If the count spoke so insultingly and freely before her, she could only imagine what terrible things he would say about her when alone with Max.

The next morning she waited anxiously for Max to arrive. She couldn't wait to see him yet was terrified of seeing him as well. Would he look at her differently after his perception was so coloured by his father? Would he love her less? How could he ever apologise on behalf of his father to make it right between them again? All the scenarios played in her mind as she waited . . . and waited . . . and as morning drifted into afternoon which fell into evening . . . waited.

CHAPTER 13

It was four days since Conrad had visited and Diana sat staring out the drawing-room window, visualising Max's car racing up any second.

Three days and Max had made no contact with her. He hadn't arrived, he hadn't telephoned, he hadn't written or at least, if he had, it hadn't reached her yet.

Maud came in, her face stressed, and walked over to her daughter who didn't take her eyes from the long winding driveway.

"I could telephone The Shelbourne and ask to speak to him," Maud suggested. "That is where he probably is."

Diana swung around and raised her voice. "No! Don't you dare! I will not chase him! Am I not humiliated enough?"

"In that case, I think it's time you face facts, my darling . . . Max isn't going to come back for you. If he hasn't by now, then he won't. His father has obviously forbidden any further contact with you."

"Max would never leave me like this. He's too strong a character to just obey his father."

"You would be surprised what people do when they are put under pressure. Max is the heir to a vast fortune and, as his father said, they do not live in a free country. They have rules and regulations."

Diana wiped away a tear.

"I'm sure he did love you, Diana, but he will not go against his father's orders obviously."

"Max would never abandon me like this, without a goodbye.

You don't understand what we share together."

"Perhaps it's all for the best. Having met the father, do you want to be married into a family like that? And as the engagement was never announced your reputation is intact. I'll write to the Ashenbrys and say you are going to London to do the Season after all." Maud smiled sadly at Diana and turned and left the room.

Diana began to cry as she continued to stare down the driveway.

It was six days since the confrontation and Diana was left in a state of confusion and despair. And she was feeling angry that Max's love for her was so obviously broken. One command from his father and he unceremoniously dumped her, without even an apology or explanation.

But most of all she missed him.

On the sixth day she went out for her first ride on Halcyon since the count's visit and even that didn't distract her from the pain she was feeling. Her family seemed to be as shocked as she was but no words from them could comfort her. Not even her mother continuously saying: "Your miss is your mercy. It's just as well you found out now what he is like."

She took Halcyon back to the stables and walked back through the gardens and into the house.

"Mama?" she called and hearing no answer she realised Maud and Simon hadn't returned yet from a trip to Dublin that day. She riffled through the post on the sideboard in the hall and was despondent to see there was no letter again from Max.

She took off her riding gloves and walked into the drawing room.

With a terrible start she saw a figure standing there, silhouetted against the sun shining through the window behind.

"Max?" she asked as she blinked, trying to see for sure if it was him.

Max stepped out of the light and they stared at each other. He moved first and they rushed to each other and embraced and kissed.

"Diana, you have no idea how I missed you," he whispered.

She kissed him passionately. Then she angrily pulled away from him.

"Why are you here?" she demanded unpleasantly.

"For you, of course," he said, moving towards her, but she slapped his hand away.

"Where have you been all week?"

"I had to make arrangements," he tried to explain.

"*Arrangements!*" she screamed. "Your awful father comes here and insults me beyond what I could ever imagine and then you just abandon me for the week!"

"It was you who told me to go that night!"

"Yes, because I knew he wouldn't go without you and I had to get him away from me as quickly as possible. But I expected you to come the next day, or the next day after that or write or telephone or . . ." Her anger and upset took over and she could no longer talk.

"I'm sorry, Diana, but I had to have everything in place before I met you again."

"I can understand why we can't be married – your father made all the reasons perfectly clear, but you could have come sooner to tell me yourself. Rather than leaving me here and –"

"Can't be married?" Max cut in and then started to laugh in that mocking tone that so enraged her.

"And you *laugh* at me!" Diana was incredulous.

"Diana!" Max moved towards her and grabbed her. "My darling Diana, I have absolutely every intention of marrying you."

"Don't be ridiculous! It's impossible now!"

Max walked over to a table and picked up a pile of newspapers he had placed there. He began to riffle through the first paper.

"*The London Times*," he said, holding out a page of the paper to her.

She took the paper and studied it. On the page was a large photo of her and Max, taken at a racecourse, under the headline: '*Max Von Hoffsten to Marry Miss Diana Cantwell*'.

Her eyes widened as she read on.

'*In an official announcement, Max Von Hoffsten, son and heir to Count Conrad Von Hoffsten, is to be married to Miss Diana Cantwell, daughter of Simon and Maud Cantwell, County Meath, Ireland . . .*'

Diana read the article to the end.

"And this is *The Irish Times*." Max handed her another paper. "And the French one and of course the German one."

"I don't understand," said Diana as she looked at the same photo in all the newspapers, announcing their engagement.

"It's quite simple, my darling," he said, putting his arms around her. "Yes, my father forbade me to marry you, so I had to outsmart him. I was busy these past few days arranging this announcement and photos in all the newspapers. Now there is nothing he can do to stop our marriage. It's gone too far."

Diana was stunned. "But he will be enraged! He will hit the roof!"

"Let him hit the roof! He's hit it many times before I can assure you. I'm so sorry about how he spoke to you and your family, who have been nothing but generous and kind to me."

"But Max, why didn't you tell me about this? Why didn't you tell me what you were arranging?"

"I wanted it to be a surprise."

"But Max," Diana shook her head in disbelief, "this was no time for surprises, it was time for reassurance. I've been going through hell these past few days. Your not contacting me, not coming here. I thought your father had whisked you back to Germany and I would never see you again!"

"As if that could ever happen! I love you too much."

"But Max!" Dina felt herself becoming angry, but her anger was quickly overcome by relief and delight. And as she looked into his adoring eyes and looked down at the photos of them in the newspapers announcing their marriage to the world, she pulled him close.

"Well, Max certainly knows how to do things!" said Maud who was flabbergasted by the announcements in the newspapers and the following outpourings of congratulations.

"He's certainly nobody's puppet, especially his father's!" said Simon.

Diana was in the drawing room with her parents, going through all the letters of congratulations.

"Here's a letter from Lady Devonshire in London," said Maud. "I never even heard of the woman, let alone met her. She says she knew my grandfather, Lord Ashenbry, and was delighted to hear about Diana's engagement to Max! She's invited us all to stay at her house in London!"

Maud crumpled the letter in excitement.

Diana smiled over at her mother. She was happy for her. After spending a lifetime as the poor relation on the fringes of society, as Conrad had said, the engagement to Max had given her the recognition she always craved so desperately.

"Well, I suppose now we must concentrate on the wedding and the arrangements for it," said Maud.

"Max says we are to be married in Germany, near his ancestral home," said Diana.

"Germany!" said Simon. "Well, I can't see many of our friends being able to make it there for the marriage. It's too far and too expensive to travel there. Most of the people we know can barely afford to pay their staff. Roundtree was telling me this winter he's going to close up most of their castle and only live in a part of it. That's all they can afford to heat."

"Oh, Simon, be quiet!" interrupted Maud. "If they can't afford to go to the future Countess Von Hoffsten's wedding then that's that!" She gestured to all the invitations and letters before her. "There's plenty more who can afford and wouldn't miss it for the world!"

"Max wants a December wedding."

"Oh, how gorgeous!" sighed Maud. "A winter wedding."

CHAPTER 14

The arrangements for the December wedding were in place. In the weeks and months leading up to it Diana felt she hardly had a free moment. She found she had gone to the very top of society and was being invited everywhere.

Max regularly stayed at Garonglen and when he had to leave to travel back to Germany she could barely contain her anguish.

"Don't worry, darling, I'll be back in a couple of weeks. Besides, I'm going back to continue with organising our wedding!" he would point out to her.

She stood in the forecourt in front of Garonglen under the evening sky as summer turned into autumn, holding him closely.

"Cheer up, cherub, I'll always come back to you," he promised her and then went to his automobile and got in.

He smiled and waved to her as he drove off.

She didn't turn and go back towards the house until the car was out of sight.

"Come along, Diana, we've got a wedding dress to design!" said Maud, coming down the steps and walking across to her.

Seeing her daughter's sad face she put an arm around her as they walked.

"For goodness' sakes, Diana! You'll be with him every minute of the day and night soon. I daresay you'll be sick of the sight of him in no time!"

"I'll never be sick of Max," said Diana as she put her arm

around her mother.

Suddenly it was December before Diana even realised it and she was packing for her wedding and the move to Germany.

After taking Halcyon out for a ride she came into the drawing room where her mother sat surrounded by letters and paperwork.

"You know, I really think we should have insisted on the wedding being here in Ireland. It's too difficult to co-ordinate the whole thing from here!" Maud was beset with last-minute nerves.

"It's a tradition for the Von Hoffstens always to be married in the same church in Bavaria."

"That family have more traditions than Christmas! I just hope this church can contain all the people who have accepted."

"Mama, will you stop fretting! You've been told from the beginning that the Von Hoffstens and Max will arrange everything."

"That's what I'm afraid of, having met Max's father! It's a terrible pity his mother isn't around to help organise things that end."

"Well, she's not! Mama, families like the Von Hoffstens have huge resources and staff to organise any occasion and event! Besides, his sister Brigitte has been very much involved in the organisation according to Max."

Maud sighed loudly. "I fear we will merely be window-dressing at this wedding."

"I thought this is what you wanted, me marrying aristocracy?"

"It is."

"Well, then, of course a family like that were going to take over the occasion and all arrangements."

Maud got up and came over to Diana. "Of course they were. Don't mind me, just last-minute nerves, I daresay. We're delighted about the wedding, and we adore Max."

"Good, and so do I."

It was three days before the wedding and Diana, Maud and Simon were in the dining car on The Orient Express en route for Munich.

They had made the crossing to the continent by boat where Max had arranged the train transportation from Paris. Dashiel and Warren were due to follow on with more luggage just before the wedding.

"I have to say when Max said he was arranging the train tickets to take us to Germany I didn't expect him to arrange the Orient Express," said Simon as he took in the elegant grandeur of the train.

"Did he not tell you, Diana?" asked Maud.

"No," smiled Diana. "But that's Max, he likes to surprise me."

"Well, as long as they are nice surprises, then who cares?" said Maud. "Besides, this is a fitting way for the future Countess Von Hoffsten to arrive in her new home."

"I won't be countess until after Max's father has died," said Diana.

"Which hopefully won't be long!" said Maud.

"Mama!" said Diana horrified.

"I'm sorry, that was in bad taste," apologised Maud.

The three sat in silence for a few seconds. All were dreading meeting Conrad again.

"Well, hopefully it won't be too long," said Diana, looking guilty, and the three suddenly began to laugh.

That night before Diana went to her sleeper car on the train she left instructions with the staff to awaken her. She wanted plenty of time to dress before she met Max who was coming to the station to collect them. And she didn't want to sleep it out and miss her departure and continue on the Orient's journey to Vienna.

Before she went to bed she sat in the small luxurious sleeper car looking out at the moonlit countryside whizz by. As the train left France and entered Germany, she forced herself to go to bed so she wouldn't be tired for Max.

Munich was covered in snow as the Orient Express made its way into the Hauptbahnhof, the main train station. Diana had a window open and she was leaning out to see if she could spot Max.

Her eyes searched the crowds standing on the platform.

"Diana!" Max called and she saw him on the platform waving frantically. As the train continued to move to its halting position, he ran alongside her window smiling at her.

"Careful, you'll fall!" she warned as he raced along the snowy platform.

Finally the train came to a stop and she went to the door, opened it and stepped out onto the platform into his arms. He pulled back and stared at her in her pale gold dress covered in a white fur coat.

"Is it you, are you really here?" he asked, smiling at her.

"It's her all right! And us!" said Simon as he helped Maud onto the platform.

"Welcome, welcome to my country," said Max as he embraced both of them.

"The luggage, we have quite a lot," said Maud, gesturing behind her.

Max clicked his fingers and two red-tunicked attendants arrived.

Max issued them some orders and they rushed into the train.

"They'll bring your luggage up to the hunting estate, no need to worry. We must hurry, our train is departing shortly." Max took Diana's arm and quickly guided her through the train station, followed by Maud and Simon.

As their luggage no longer seemed to be their responsibility, Maud whispered to Simon, "I could get used to this!"

They got on another train. This train, Max informed them, would take them on the final leg of their journey to the Von Hoffsten estate which was an hour south of Munich in the Alps.

Diana could feel the train gradually rise higher and higher as it made its journey through the lower Alps. As they went higher the snow became thicker. It seemed incredible to her that this would be her new home. It seemed so different from Ireland, different but exciting. A beautiful lake that stretched for miles came into view and the train ran alongside it and entered the town of Tegernfrei which was beside the lake.

The train pulled into the station.

"We are nearly home!" smiled Max as he led her and her parents off the train.

To Diana's delight, a sleigh with horses was waiting for them.

"Easiest way to get around here this time of year," said Max as they all got in and the awaiting driver took off through the town.

Diana remembered once getting a chocolate box as a gift from Germany. On the lid was a painting of a beautiful German town. As the sleigh whisked them through the town's streets and she marvelled at the beautiful traditional wooden buildings, it reminded her of that chocolate box.

Max told them the Von Hoffsten estate was only a couple of miles outside the town. The sleigh brought them swiftly up further into the gently sloping hills around the lake. Diana realised how high up they were when she could see some clouds touch the snow-covered peaks above them.

Suddenly the house came into view. It was a sprawling three-storey building perched up on the hills, facing down on the lake.

Diana felt an excitement but also dread at the thought of meeting Max's father Conrad again and she pulled her fur coat closer to her not just for warmth. None of them had so much as mentioned his name up to now.

"Max, how is your father?" she asked, unable to keep the stress out of her voice.

Max reached and took her gloved hand in his. "He's not here today – he's been kept in Munich on business."

He could see her visibly relax as the sleigh drove up the long avenue to the house.

The sleigh went under an arch in the building and into a large central courtyard.

As Max helped her out of the sleigh, through another arch Diana could see the lake glistening in the distance.

The house was a very faint yellow, with a red-tiled roof, and was typical of the German architecture of country manor houses. As Diana looked at the four wings stretched around the courtyard she suddenly felt overwhelmed and wished for the comfort and familiarity of Garonglen. How could she ever be the lady of such a house and estate? How could she be expected to be a countess and run and live in this place that seemed so foreign to her? All Conrad's cruel words came rushing back and she realised he was probably right, in spite of her mother's lofty ambitions for her.

She felt a strong and firm arm around her and she looked up to see Max's reassuring face.

"Are you all right?" he asked, almost as if he could read her mind.

She shook her head and smiled. "I didn't think it would be like this."

"What did you think it would be like?"

"Smaller, I guess," she said, shrugging.

"But I am here with you, so there's no need to fear anything."

She looked up into his loving eyes.

"I'll always be with you, remember that, Diana, I'll always be with you."

She suddenly felt relaxed and smiled.

"Shall we go in?" suggested Maud. "I'm absolutely freezing!"

Diana held Max's hand firmly as they walked up the steps to the main front door where a butler waited.

They walked into the house. They were in a large hall with dark wooden floors, wooden panelled walls and a sweeping staircase that led to the upper floors. To Maud's delight the hall was heated with a blazing fire.

"Brigitte! We're here!" Max shouted as he took off his gloves and coat and threw them on a circular table that was in the middle of the hall.

Through large double doors Diana could see a luxurious drawing room.

A woman suddenly emerged from this room, walking briskly. She was of medium height with a confident smiling face, her blonde hair styled into a bob. Although she wasn't pretty or beautiful, Diana felt she had a face you would remember with its warm smile and twinkling curious blue eyes.

"What joy!" the woman said as she quickly embraced Diana warmly, then pulled back from her, still holding her shoulders tightly as she studied her. "I'm Brigitte. I've just been so excited about meeting you! I could hardly sleep last night with excitement!"

Diana smiled back warmly. Although Brigitte's welcome was not what Diana was used to in the polite, reserved Irish Edwardian world, she was relieved that Max's sister was in no way like his father.

Brigitte continued to scrutinise her as Max came up behind his sister and said quietly, "Well, will she do?"

"She's perfect! Absolutely perfect, Max. She's exactly as you described her!" Brigitte suddenly took off Diana's hat and started to toss the shining strands of hair back from Diana's face.

As both Brigitte and Max seemed to be in a trance staring at Diana, Maud glanced at Simon uneasily and coughed loudly.

"Oh, and Brigitte, these are her parents, Maud and Simon Cantwell," said Max.

Brigitte forced herself to look away from Diana and it was as if she hadn't seen them before, even though they were standing close by. She reluctantly left Diana, came over to them and proffered her hand.

"I'm so delighted to meet you. Max has told me all about you. You're so good to come," said Brigitte, shaking their hands warmly.

"Well, we're delighted to be here," said Maud.

Two servants had heard the commotion and arrived to take the Cantwells' coats and gloves.

"You must be freezing and starving." Brigitte turned to the servants and instructed, "Bring coffee, tea and sandwiches immediately to the drawing room."

Then she turned her attention back to Diana and linked her arm as she led her through the open double doors and into the drawing room.

Maud whispered to Simon as they followed Brigitte and Diana in. "She said *we're so good to come*? We're the parents of the bride! We're hardly going to miss our own daughter's wedding!"

Diana loved the drawing room. It was airy and bright and luxuriously furnished. But it was the view that took her breath away. There were six French windows along the main wall which opened up onto a terrace balcony. This was the ground floor, but the balcony had been built out of the hill that swept down to the lake.

Diana stood at a French window and declared, "What a wonderful view!"

"Isn't it?" said Max, delighted she was happy, and he opened the French window.

She stepped out onto the balcony. Down at the side of the lake was the local town they had just come from and across the lake the hills led into the highest mountains of the Alps.

"That's Austria," said Max, pointing to the lofty peaks.

"Diana, please close the door," insisted Maud from inside.

Max put his arm around Diana and led her back in. They sat down on the couches around the blazing fire as the servants brought in beef sandwiches, coffee and tea.

"Do you like it here?" asked Brigitte expectantly.

"It's breathtaking."

"I'm so glad you like it," said Brigitte. "I told you she would, Max."

"So much snow!"

"Yes, we have the snow usually between November and March," explained Brigitte. "Max prefers it here in the winter because all his glamorous friends come and stay for the skiing."

"The house here is a necessary stop-off for anyone who is anyone during the winter," agreed Max.

"It's become nearly as famous as the Cowes Regatta in certain circles," said Brigitte. "I prefer it in the summer, when the snow is gone and meadows blooming."

"Yes, I'm looking forward to my horse Halcyon arriving and riding him here when the weather improves," said Diana.

"Ah, yes, Halcyon, or Cupid as we call him," Brigitte said, giggling in a conspiratorial manner at Max.

"Cupid?" asked Diana.

"Yes, he brought you two together, didn't he?"

Diana looked at Max. "Yes – yes, I guess he did."

Brigitte reached forward for the large silver teapot. "Shall I be mother?"

"Please do, as long as *somebody* pours me a cup of tea soon!" said Maud.

"My father is so sorry he can't be here to greet you," said Brigitte.

"Yes, Max explained he was detained in Munich," said Simon.

"I'm afraid so – it was completely unavoidable," Brigitte said. "He really wished he could have been here when you arrived."

Suddenly from out in the hallway came the unmistakable voice of Conrad. As Diana and her parents looked out through the double doors, to their astonishment they saw Conrad Von Hoffsten marching down the staircase with a man who looked like a servant.

"Is my transport ready?" demanded Conrad.

"Yes, Your Excellency, waiting for you in the courtyard."

"Good, I want to be gone before those confounded people from Ireland arrive and I'm forced to see them!"

As the servant put on his coat, Conrad looked up and through the double doors, and saw Diana and her parents sitting there looking at him in amazement. Conrad looked away, put on his gloves and walked out of the house at a steady pace.

Diana looked at Brigitte for an explanation.

"One lump or two?" asked Brigitte good-naturedly as she picked up a sugar lump with a miniature silver tongs.

"What on earth?" said Simon, his face red with anger.

"Two!" said Maud, giving her husband a swift discreet kick to be silent.

Diana looked at Max for some kind of explanation, but he seemed as unconcerned as his sister.

"Of course he's seldom here, Father," continued Brigitte as she handed cups of tea around. "He's based in Munich in his *schloss* – his castle."

"Yes, Max did tell us that," said Maud.

"Yes, it's near the brewery and he likes to be on hand for business," continued Max.

Diana and Maud glanced at each other, concerned that they were being blatantly lied to about Conrad. Maud shrugged.

"And what of you, Brigitte? Do you spend much time here?" Maud asked, smiling and deciding to play along.

"It is where we grew up mostly, so I do see it as home. But I'm not here that much as I'm studying in Vienna."

"Really, Max never mentioned. What are you studying?" asked Diana, intrigued.

"Psychoanalysis," said Brigitte with a satisfied smile.

"That's all that mumbo jumbo invented by that man Freud, isn't it?" checked Simon, looking unimpressed.

"Oh, it's not mumbo jumbo, it's truly the most fascinating thing I've ever encountered," Brigitte said emphatically. "The mind is like an unexplored continent. So many chapters in the mind not read, so many corridors not travelled."

Maud took a sip of her tea. "I think there are no hidden chapters or corridors in my mind. I think I know myself far too well!"

"Does anyone really know their own mind?" asked Brigitte, smiling.

Diana turned to Max, perplexed. "Why did you never mention Brigitte was studying psychoanalysis, Max?"

Max looked up from his cup of tea. "It must have slipped my – mind!"

Brigitte and Max looked at each other and then they burst out in convulsions of laughter.

A couple of hours later, after the luggage had arrived, as Maud and Simon were being shown to their bedroom through the hall a cuckoo clock began to sound.

"That's not the only thing that's cuckoo around here!" said Maud as they climbed the stairs.

Brigitte had gone to deal with a query from the staff, leaving Max alone with Diana in the drawing room.

"I can't believe you're here. I'm so happy," said Max, pulling her close and kissing her.

Diana pulled away. "Max! Your father wasn't in Munich at all as you said, but still here in the house!"

"Are you sure?" asked Max, looking perplexed.

"Don't be ridiculous – of course I'm sure! I saw him with my own eyes in the hallway! As did you and Brigitte but you chose to ignore both the fact that he was here and that you had just been caught red-handed lying!"

"Well, I'm sorry – I thought he had left for Munich already."

"But Brigitte hadn't left the house – she must have known he was here!"

"There are several exits from the house – she probably assumed he had left as well."

Max looked concerned and tried to come near her but she walked away from him.

"I was so embarrassed, as were my parents. Then you and Brigitte just continued as if nothing were the matter!"

"As did you and your parents!" Max retaliated. "Of course everyone was going to try and ignore an embarrassing situation and continue with the social niceties."

"Well, I've never experienced anything like it. And of course worst of all was the fact that your father obviously did not want to meet us – to meet *me,* his daughter-in-law in a couple of days!"

"That's not true –"

"No more lies, Max! I heard him call us 'those confounded people from Ireland'!" Diana's voice had risen several octaves and her face blazed with anger. She quickly turned around and stared out the window at the snow-covered Alps in the distance across the lake.

Max walked behind her and put his arms around her, nuzzling his head into her neck. "I'm sorry, darling."

"You said he was fine about the wedding now. But he hasn't changed at all, has he?"

"Well, he hasn't said any more about it."

"He hasn't discussed it once?" Diana was incredulous.

"I'm afraid not. But silence is good in his case. He knows there's nothing he can do. It's us that matters, Diana, nobody else." He held her tightly.

Diana sighed and turned to face him. "You're right, of course. I'm not going to let him ruin our wedding." She reached forward and kissed him.

In the next couple of days, in the lead-up to the wedding, there was much activity at the estate house, but still no sign of Conrad making an appearance. Diana didn't have much time to think about it as she was whisked around by Max and Brigitte, with rehearsals and arrangements. There was a banquet hall in the house and the reception was to be there.

"It's been so hectic this past while, getting everything arranged. I haven't had a moment to myself," said Brigitte to Diana as she led her around the banqueting hall, indicating where everyone was sitting.

"You've been very kind. I can never repay you for all the consideration and kindness you've shown me," said Diana. In actual fact she knew she really could never repay Brigitte's kindness, but she did find it overpowering and she wished she had more of a hand in her own wedding arrangements.

Brigitte stopped walking around the tables and embraced Diana. "But you've already repaid me by marrying Max and becoming my family."

Diana smiled and continued to follow Brigitte around the banqueting room.

"The guests are starting to arrive tomorrow," said Brigitte. "From all over Germany and the aristocracy from around Europe. We'll have a party here tomorrow night for selected guests."

"Well, I hope it won't be a late one. I'll need to be in bed early for an early rise to get ready for the wedding the next morning," laughed Diana.

Brigitte looked at her, concerned. "But all of Max's parties are late ones so I imagine this one will be no different. You simply can't sneak off to bed early. Your new role as Max's wife will be filled with late-night entertaining – it's what will be expected of you. You might as well start as you mean to go on."

Diana smiled and nodded.

"And your brothers will arrive tomorrow – dashing Dashiel and wonderful Warren – I can't wait to meet them! Max speaks so highly of them –"

Suddenly Brigitte's hand shot to her forehead where she held it firmly as her eyes closed and her expression creased in pain.

"Brigitte, what's wrong?" asked Diana, concerned.

"It's nothing – no need to worry." Brigitte's face winced with pain and she gripped a chair for support.

"Brigitte!"

"It's just these pains – I get – sharp, piercing pains through my head – my mind –" She stopped abruptly as the pain seemed to overcome her.

"Sit down!" pleaded Diana as she pulled up a chair.

Brigitte sat down, the palms of both her hands now to her temples.

"I'll fetch somebody, get a doctor –"

"No!" Brigitte grabbed her wrist and stopped her. "A doctor can do nothing. I get them regularly. It will pass . . ."

"But what causes them?" asked Diana, kneeling beside her in concern.

"They . . . don't . . . know . . . they . . . can't . . . tell . . . me," Brigitte said, struggling to speak. "It's going now. It's subsiding . . ." There was relief on her face as she spoke.

Finally she opened her eyes and smiled at Diana.

"Looks like my little sister has landed on her feet!" said Dashiel as the two stood out on the balcony of the drawing room, enjoying the view while drinking cognac.

"I'm worried about tonight, Dashiel – meeting all his friends and relatives," confessed Diana.

"Yes, we are going to be outnumbered all right – not many of our set managed to come, as predicted. Hannah Roundtree is devastated she can't be here, begged her mother to sell the family silver to buy the ticket for her to come."

"Poor Hannah!" sighed Diana.

"You're leaving our county set behind now, Diana, moving on to bigger things," he said, hugging her.

"Diana!" called Max from the other side of the room. He beckoned her over.

He was standing beside a tall handsome man with a slightly nervous air about him.

"Diana, I'm pleased to introduce you to my brother, Hugo!"

said Max happily, clapping a hand on his brother's shoulder.

"Oh, hello!" smiled Diana warmly. "I've been so looking forward to meeting you."

Hugo began to stammer. "Y-y-yes. Nice to m-m-m-eet you."

"Aren't we all just one big happy family!" smiled Max.

"I b-b-better see if everything is a-a-a-ll right for Ff-f-father's arrival," said Hugo and then he quickly left the room.

Diana looked after him, concerned. "Is he all right?"

"Oh, yes, that's him being talkative!"

CHAPTER 15

On the eve of her wedding Diana was dressed in a sequinned black dress as the guests began to arrive. Max and Brigitte proudly and eagerly introduced her to everyone. The drawing room and the rooms around it soon filled up.

As Diana strenuously tried to understand the accents of a Swedish baron and his wife, Maud made her way through the crowd with a tall handsome man and an elegant woman who was very slim with a striking angular face and short black hair. Both of them looked to be in their early thirties.

"Diana! These are our cousins! Lord and Lady Ashenbry!" said Maud in an over-excited voice.

Diana had grown up with the Ashenbry name constantly in her ears, so she hardly knew how to greet them now that they stood here before her.

"Please!" said the woman in a strong American accent. "Call me Thelma, and this is Elliott." She reached out and kissed Diana's cheek and Elliott did the same.

"We were delighted to be invited to the wedding. Your mother informs us we were top of the invitation list," said Elliott.

"Don't doubt it for a second," smiled Diana.

"Of course we're great friends of Max as well," said Thelma.

"Really? He never mentioned," said Diana, curious as to why he hadn't as he had heard the Ashenbry name mentioned enough around Garonglen.

"I remember playing with your father when we were children –

we were first cousins," said Maud.

"Yes, of course," said Elliott and was immediately cornered by Maud in a private conversation.

"I think we were destined to meet, Diana," smiled Thelma. "You were due to visit us in London after your mother wrote to us asking to have you for the Season."

"Yes, thank you so much for the invitation. I do apologise for my mother attempting to foist me on you like that."

"Oh, we were looking forward to having you. Elliott vaguely knew of his Irish cousins. The main Ashenbry family got out of Ireland when the politics became too hot to handle thirty years ago. But Elliott remembered his father speaking well of your mother, so we were happy to give a relative a leg up the social ladder in London. I found all this social manoeuvring weird when I moved from New York ten years ago, but it all makes perfect sense to me now." Thelma winked and smiled at Diana. "Of course, no need for all that now with your engagement to Max."

"How long have you known Max?" Diana was curious.

"Oh, years! We tend to come skiing here during the winter."

"You've been here before?" Diana was very surprised.

"Often. And of course we meet up in London or at the Regatta at Cowes. You know Max usually has one of the biggest yachts at Cowes, nearly as big as the Kaiser's. You know the Germans – they always have to be the biggest and the best!"

"Sounds like you're great friends of Max then?"

"Oh, we are. And I can tell you there are a lot of girls fairly pissed off that you've managed to snare him. A few broken hearts in London."

"I can imagine!" Diana glanced over at Max appreciatively.

Thelma moved closer to Diana and adopted a conspiratorial tone. "Of course, *she* was the real competition." She nodded over at a very glamorous woman in a silk burgundy dress, with blonde hair neatly pinned up in waves.

"Who is she?" asked Diana.

"That's Princess Alexandra. Have you heard about her?"

Diana got a start. She was unnerved to see her there on her

wedding eve, obviously a guest for tomorrow. And shocked that nobody had told or warned her that she would be there.

"Everyone thought she and Max were set in stone," confided Thelma. "That's why all the young women weren't too disappointed to be passed over by him – because they thought the position of Countess Von Hoffsten was reserved for her."

Diana couldn't take her eyes off Alexandra. She had an alluring dramatic attractiveness. She was deep in conversation with two men. Then, almost as if she was sensing Diana's stare, she looked over and stared back. Diana quickly looked away.

Thelma smiled and hugged Diana. "I'm delighted Max chose you! Alexandra isn't known for being good fun! I know we're going to be the best of friends."

Diana made her way through the crowd in the drawing room till she found Max.

"Max, I need to speak to you," she said.

"Ah, there you are," said Max. "I was looking for you. Where are your parents?" He looked around anxiously.

"Max, I've just learned that this Princess Alexandra is here. Why didn't you tell me?"

"Of course she is here. It would be impossible not to invite her, our two families are so close."

"But Max, I don't want your ex-fiancée, if that is what she is, at my wedding!"

Max looked irritated. "Never mind all that now, Diana – we have more important things to think about. Father has arrived back from Munich."

"At last! I was beginning to think he wasn't going to come to the wedding! Where is he?" She looked around the room.

"He's upstairs in his study. He has requested that we and your parents report there without delay."

"Report there!" Diana looked amused and annoyed. "What does he think this is – a military parade?"

"Please, Diana! We don't want to keep him waiting."

"You mean *you* don't want to keep him waiting! After his

96

appalling manners in Ireland and his avoidance of us here, I don't care if he's kept waiting till next year!"

"Diana, *please*! For me?" Max's eyes were pleading.

Diana sighed loudly. "All right! I've been dreading meeting him, so we might as well get it out of the way and enjoy the wedding. I'll go get Mama, if I can drag her away from the Ashenbrys."

Diana and Max walked down a corridor upstairs followed by Maud and Simon. The music and laughter could be heard in the distance downstairs.

"He's not exactly a social man, your father, is he?" said Maud.

"At least he's here!" said Max.

"Do you mean he might not have been? That he would miss his own son's wedding?" Simon was incredulous.

Max stopped at a door and turned and smiled at Diana. She smiled back. He took her hand and then knocked on the door and opened it.

This was Conrad's study, a dark wood-panelled room, with a chaise longue in front of the fire. Conrad sat at a large desk, in front of a window that looked down on the courtyard.

"Good evening, Father," said Max as he led Diana into the room.

"Good evening – please be seated," said Conrad as he sat back on his chair and studied the small party.

"Hello again," said Simon good-naturedly as he sat down.

Maud nodded coolly to Conrad as she took her seat.

Max smiled reassuringly at Diana as they both sat down and he continued to hold her hand.

Diana smiled at Conrad. She could see that outside it had started to snow and the snowflakes bounced off the window behind him.

"We meet again," said Conrad. "I trust you had a good journey here?"

"Very good, thank you, and Max has been the most excellent host to us," said Maud. "We've had a wonderful few days." Then she added acidly, "It's a pity you were detained in Munich."

"Yes, I brought my son up well," said Conrad.

"Someone certainly did," said Maud under her breath.

"I'm not a man to beat around the bush," began Conrad.

"We noticed that before," said Maud.

"I'm very surprised that, after I made my opinion clear to you, these wedding arrangements have gone this far," said Conrad.

"What do you mean?" asked Diana, becoming disturbed.

Maud had prepared herself for Conrad. He might have got her off guard last time, but this time she would not let him take control.

"Yes, the church is booked, the priest is booked, everything is on course for a beautiful wedding tomorrow," she confirmed with a thin smile.

Conrad fixed a steely look on Max. "Despite everything I have said, you are still determined to go ahead with this marriage?"

Max gripped Diana's hand tightly. "Yes, sir."

"Even against my wishes?"

Max glanced at Diana. "If that's what it means – then yes."

Conrad sat forward and put his hands together. "In that case, you have left me with no option but to insist on a morganatic marriage."

Max visibly paled.

"A what marriage?" Simon asked, looking utterly confused.

Diana turned to Max. "What is he talking about?"

"A morganatic marriage," repeated Max quietly. "A left-handed marriage."

"Could somebody please explain to me what you're talking about?" demanded Diana.

Conrad looked at Diana. "A morganatic – or left-handed marriage – is a legitimate marriage that is legal in the eyes of the state and the church. The wife of such a union enjoys full status as the legal spouse. The only difference being that the wife does not get her husband's title or inherit his wealth and any children of this marriage, although completely legitimate, inherit neither their father's title nor his property rights."

"I've never heard of such a thing!" Maud was disgusted. "Such a marriage has no legal standing!"

"Of course not in your country where primogeniture is

sacrosanct. But here among the aristocracy of Germany and Austria, Russia as well, such marriages are legal. They are enforced when the son and heir of the family insists on marrying a woman who is not of the same background as her husband and who his family do not approve of."

"*Ohhhh!*" Diana let out a cry of horror and disgust.

"I don't believe you, sir!" Simon turned to Max. "This barbaric arrangement can't be legal?"

"I'm afraid it is," said Max quietly as he looked down at the floor.

Conrad sat back. "It is in place to ensure that the line of the family is passed through to correct heirs and not diluted to mongrels."

Simon stood up in a rage. "How dare you!"

Maud put her hand out to Simon and gently pulled him back down to his chair.

"Max, is all this correct?" she demanded.

Max nodded grimly. "Yes."

"And the custom of primogeniture, the automatic inheritance of the first-born son, is overruled if the marriage is a left-handed one?"

"Yes," said Max.

"But surely you can ignore what he says, Max!" said Diana. "We just marry and when you become Count Von Hoffsten I become countess and our children will have all their rights."

"No, Diana! I can't marry without his permission," insisted Max. "This isn't your country – there are so many laws and by-laws here stretching back centuries and this is one of them. I need his permission to marry, and he will only give permission for a left-handed marriage."

Conrad sneered at Diana. "A left-handed marriage is a true love match. The couple marry despite the fact that she won't get the title and the children are disinherited before they are even conceived."

Maud glared at Conrad. "And you left it to the last minute to tell us of this?"

"Dear lady, I did try to tell you when I visited your cottage in Ireland," said Conrad.

"Cottage!"

"Dear lady –" began Conrad.

"Stop calling me that!"

"Indeed, you are correct – dear *woman*, no one was listening to me. My son told me he could not live without this young woman. Now he does not have to. But the future of the Von Hoffsten family will not be infiltrated by her. Max as the rightful heir will have all the rights and privileges of being Count Von Hoffsten during his lifetime, and his wife can enjoy that life beside him, though not as a countess. She will be plain Mrs Von Hoffsten and the title and wealth will then pass through to my second son Hugo's children and not to Max's."

"On condition Hugo will make a correct marriage!" Maud pointed out.

"He will, I assure you."

"Diana, we must leave this place immediately and return to Ireland," insisted Simon.

"No!" begged Max.

"You are forcing us into the most humiliating situation, Count Von Hoffsten. It will be the talk of the place when we leave on the eve of Diana's wedding," said Maud.

"But far more humiliating to stay here and accept these draconian rules," said Simon.

Max's face was red with anger as he spat at his father, "You bastard! You plotted all this."

Conrad smirked. "You thought you had outwitted me by announcing the engagement in all the newspapers like you did. Nobody outsmarts me. You forced my hand and this is the consequence!"

Diana stared at Conrad, her eyes brimming with angry tears. "Why are you behaving like this?"

"I've made my thoughts on you perfectly clear – I have no reason to elaborate." He stood up. "I will leave you, you have much to discuss. There is transport ready to take you to the train station any time you need to leave."

Conrad walked out of the room.

Maud turned to Diana. "Diana, as embarrassing as walking away is, you can't accept these measures. You will not be a countess and your children will have no rights!"

"It is a common practice," said Max as he looked imploringly at Diana. "Even the Emperor of Austria's son, Archduke Franz Ferdinand, has a left-handed marriage. The family didn't approve so his wife will never be empress."

"Are you suggesting I accept this?" Diana was shocked.

"Diana, my father holds all the cards, as I have explained to you."

Simon stood up. "Come along, Diana. We need to pack and leave this place immediately."

"Oh, for God's sake!" Diana shouted as she ran her hands through her hair.

"Please stay! Please don't leave me!" Max begged as he fell to his knees.

"I need to be on my own!" Diana jumped up and ran out of the room.

"Diana!" Maud shouted after her.

Diana wrapped her fur coat around her as she walked down the steps from the terrace balcony. It had stopped snowing and she scrunched along the snow below. The party was still going on inside even though it was now midnight. Little did they know there would be no wedding now tomorrow, she thought.

She looked out at the lake shining under the full moon, the snow-covered hills and mountains around it glistening in the moonlight. To the left down the hills she could see the town all lit up. There was the sound of much merriment drifting up from it. By the volume of the noise Diana thought the whole town must be out celebrating, for her to be able to hear them up in the hills. She wondered what the occasion was. Then fireworks began to soar into the night sky and their multicolours were mirrored in the lake below.

"So this is where you're hiding," said a voice behind her and she turned to see Max standing there in a long grey coat.

"I'm not hiding, I'm thinking," she said, turning away from him and looking out at the view again.

He came and stood beside her.

He nodded to the merriment in the town and said, "They are celebrating for us."

"Us?" She glanced at him, confused.

"For our wedding tomorrow. We've been here for centuries, so it is a time of joy for them when the next count marries his bride."

"Well, they're going to have hangovers tomorrow for no reason when they find out there is no marriage."

He turned to her. "Diana!"

"There can't be a marriage, not under these circumstances laid down by your father."

"I can't believe what he has done. I'm so ashamed of his treatment of you and your family."

"He's appalling. But it's his treatment of you that's much worse!" She turned to him. "To ignore your wishes and your happiness, to coldly cut your future children out of their destiny without any consideration for you!"

"I don't care about me – it's only how he treats you that angers me."

"We'll return to Ireland first thing tomorrow."

"Diana, no!" He grabbed her shoulders.

"It's no use, Max. I can't be responsible for the disenfranchisement of your children. You are the natural heir through a long line of ancestors. For me to be the cause of that line being broken – I can't let that happen."

"We can't make decisions on the basis of children that are not even born yet," objected Max.

"Of course we can. My mother said she only found real happiness when Dashiel was born. You don't know how this arrangement will affect you until your own children are born and you realise they will not have your title or the privilege and status that is yours."

"If your mother said this, then she must not have loved your father," insisted Max.

Diana looked away as she remembered Maud also having said that.

102

"Don't you realise that it is so much more important for our children to grow up in a loving family where the parents love each other? That would give them so much more happiness than a title or lands or a brewery in Munich!"

"I doubt they will see it the same way."

"Well, they will never exist if you don't marry me tomorrow so it will be of no concern to them!" He smirked and gave a small laugh.

"You can laugh at a time like this?" she asked incredulously.

He moved towards her. "Marry me tomorrow."

"You would sacrifice this just to marry me?"

"It's you who are sacrificing not being the rightful countess."

"I suppose it's a mutual sacrifice, which is why your father said a left-handed marriage is a true love match. Did you really tell him you couldn't live without me?"

Max nodded.

"Oh Max!" She reached out for him.

He held her close. "I will make you happy every day of your life. You will not be a countess only in name. We will have the best times and the best marriage."

She reached up and kissed him.

A fresh burst of fireworks went off from the village, filling the sky and the lake below with colour.

"Looks like the locals won't be disappointed after all," he said, smiling at her.

CHAPTER 16

The next day, the morning of the wedding, Diana stood in her room in her wedding dress, her family around her, as the maids fussed over her and groomed her.

"Diana, I can't believe you're going through with this." Maud stood beside her daughter, looking visibly upset.

"Don't let the old bastard do this to you, Diana," advised Dashiel. "Walk!"

Simon put his hand on his daughter's shoulder. "Come home with us, darling. I can't abide this situation you're getting yourself into."

"You can still do the Season in London. We can do a damage limitation and say you walked out on Max – that might even enhance your marriage prospects to others," said Maud.

"You're all wasting your breath. I am marrying Max today."

"But the sacrifice –" began Maud.

"It's Max who is making the sacrifice – his children will not inherit all this. He must really love me more than anything."

"And you must either love him more than anything or you're quite out of your mind!" said Maud.

The maids started to put on the veil.

There was a knock on the door and Brigitte entered.

"I've only just heard the awful news!" said Brigitte, walking quickly to Diana. "A left-handed marriage! You poor darling!"

"I can't say I'm pleased with the way I've been treated by your father," said Diana.

"Yes, he's being such a brute!" said Brigitte who didn't look overly upset.

"Isn't there something you can do or say to make him change his mind?" Maud challenged Brigitte.

"I?" Brigitte said, surprised, and then laughed lightly. "As if my father would ever listen to anything I ever said. I remember when I wanted to go to school in Munich and he overruled me and off to Switzerland I went!"

"This is hardly the same thing," said Maud.

"There's no use talking about it any more," snapped Diana. "The decision is made and that's the end of it!"

"I, for one, think it's terribly romantic," sighed Brigitte as she began to fiddle with the veil. "You and Max are going to be together despite all the odds and opposition."

"As far as I can see there is only one source of opposition – your father, the count!" snapped Maud.

"And you and Max will still have the most wonderful life together. He will still be the count and heir and you will be his wife."

"A kind of second-hand, second-rate wife!" said Maud.

"Now, has anyone explained the change in procedure to you?" asked Brigitte, becoming very serious and putting her hands together. "The marriage ceremony is exactly the same *except* the groom offers his left hand to the bride instead of the traditional right hand, hence it is called a left-handed marriage. And when you accept this it signifies to everyone that you accept this is a morganatic marriage and you and your children will have no rights over your husband's title or estate."

"Yes, the whole thing has already been explained to me," confirmed Diana.

"Such a thing has no basis in law," snapped Dashiel.

"Perhaps in the British law you are studying but it does in German law."

Dashiel shook his head in disgust.

As the veil's fitting was completed Brigitte stood back and admired the bride.

"*Wunderbar!*" she exclaimed, clapping her hands together.

As the caravan of bridal cars pulled into the churchyard Simon turned to Diana, took her hand and said, "Not too late to change your mind, you know."

Diana shook her head and smiled. "Not for all the titles and money in the world."

He nodded and squeezed her hand.

The rest of the party made their way into the church while Simon, Diana and her bridesmaids prepared themselves to make their entrance.

The church was perched high in the hills, looking down across the valley and lake.

Brigitte, who had appointed herself chief bridesmaid, gave the signal and they proceeded into the church as the music began to play loudly.

Safe on her father's arm, Diana walked slowly up the aisle, seeing Max standing at the top beside Hugo. He beamed a smile down to her and she smiled back. As she reached the top of the church, she passed Conrad who was staring coldly ahead.

As they reached the altar, Simon kissed Diana and left her, going to take his seat beside Maud.

Diana and Max looked at each other for a moment. Then Max went and took a position in front of the altar that was not the traditional place for the groom. He turned to her and held out his left hand to her.

She stared at the hand, waiting to signify to everyone that this was a morganatic marriage. She could already hear the murmurs behind her from the congregation as they realised what was happening. Diana stepped forward and took his left hand with her right.

The congregation behind her erupted in loud whispers and gasps, but Diana didn't care. As she held Max's left hand tightly she felt completely safe.

Despite the loud chatter in the church, the bishop began to officiate in the traditional way, the only difference being the irreversible symbolic positions of the bride and groom.

The music in the church blared loudly as Max and Diana walked down the aisle, smiling happily. They reached the end of the aisle, the doors were flung open and they stepped out into the crisp snow-laden landscape.

Max walked down the steps outside the church first and then he turned and smiled at Diana at the top of the steps. He held out his right hand to her. She looked at his right hand and smiled appreciatively at him, then accepted it and he assisted her down the steps.

The congregation came swarming out of the church and began to congratulate the couple. Though they were smiling, Diana could see in their expressions the shock that it was a left-handed marriage, as there had been no hint of it.

Thelma and Elliott Ashenbry came hurrying over to her and embraced her.

"Congratulations, Diana," shrilled Thelma.

"Thank you, Thelma."

Thelma drew near to her and lowered her voice. "You created quite a stir in there. Nobody realised it was to be a morganatic marriage."

Diana sighed. "Nor did I until yesterday."

Thelma looked concerned and anxious. "Diana, you do understand it, don't you? It was properly explained to you what you've entered into?"

At the end of the churchyard Diana saw Conrad walking briskly to his chauffeured car, away from the crowd.

"Oh, yes, it was all meticulously explained to me," said Diana as she saw Conrad drive off without so much as a backward glance.

Even though nobody spoke about the reason for a left-handed marriage, and no explanation was offered, there was no doubt in anyone's mind what the cause was. As the guests celebrated the wedding in the banqueting hall and champagne, wine and food flowed, there was no sign of Count Conrad Von Hoffsten.

"Couldn't even sit at the head table and pretend for the day!" spat Maud bitterly.

Diana wasn't too worried that he didn't make an appearance for the meal. She hadn't expected him to and she would rather not have his sour face clouding the occasion. What did unnerve her was the presence of Princess Alexandra. Because of the shock of the enforced left-handed marriage, she had almost forgotten that Max's unofficial ex-fiancée had been invited to the wedding. But here she sat now at the wedding banquet, next to the head table, not touching her food but sitting back in a confident manner smoking continuously. What's more she seemed to know everybody intimately and her strong voice and continual laughter was making Diana feel like a stranger at her own wedding.

"Max, I tried to bring up the subject earlier and you changed the topic. Why didn't you tell me that Alexandra had been invited to our wedding?" she questioned her husband as dessert was served.

"Did I not?" he asked.

"No. I think under the circumstances I would have preferred if she wasn't here," said Diana.

"Wasn't here? But I told you – we would not have got away with not inviting her. She's my second cousin once removed."

"She's also your dumped fiancée!" Diana pointed out.

"According to my father, not to me."

Diana took the opportunity to study Alexandra who was preoccupied with what appeared to be a most enjoyable conversation with several guests.

"She's not at all as I imagined."

"And what did you imagine?" asked Max.

"Someone quieter, timid almost, and rather plain. The way you presented it, you were about to be forced into a marriage to the dullest woman ever!"

Max reached forward and took her hand. "But she is, compared to you."

"I doubt that very much. Anyway, I hope that's the last either of us have to see of Princess Alexandra of Huton Tuton, or wherever she's from, second cousin once removed or not!" Diana arched her eyebrow.

Max started laughing and bent forward to kiss her.

CHAPTER 17

After the dinner there was music through the house as the wedding guests enjoyed the rest of the day. Max proudly introduced Diana to his friends and relatives. As she chatted away with guests in the drawing room, she could see Conrad through one of the French windows on the terrace. He was talking to somebody and she moved slightly to get a better view. He was deep in conversation with Alexandra.

"Diana? Diana?" asked Max, jolting her back to the people she was with.

"I'm sorry?" she said, smiling at the circle around her.

"Lady Furlong is asking do you prefer Biarritz or Monaco at Easter time?" said Max.

"Oh, I haven't been to either, but I hope to be an expert on both very shortly," said Diana and everyone gave a light laugh.

Conrad stayed out on the terrace with Alexandra for ages, making Diana more uneasy. Then she was distracted by more guests and when she looked again, he was gone.

"Diana, darling, a word to the wise," said Brigitte, cornering her and linking her arm. "If someone asks you a question like Lady Furlong did about Biarritz or Monaco, it's far cleverer to just pick one rather than admit ignorance, don't you think?"

"I don't want to lie, Brigitte."

"Oh everyone lies, Diana, and it would save Max from looking foolish."

Diana looked at Brigitte, confused. "And how does my answer

make Max look foolish?"

"Well, this marriage has been controversial enough without people thinking he's married someone who doesn't know Biarritz from Monaco."

"But I don't!" Diana's eyes became steely.

"Well, of course you don't, but no need for anybody to know that. Just because you won't be Countess Von Hoffsten it doesn't mean the pressure is off, you know. You will still be the count's wife and he can't be embarrassed by you."

"Embarrassed!" Diana said, becoming angry.

Suddenly Alexandra came walking by and Brigitte stopped her.

"Ah, there you are, Alexandra! Have you met Diana yet?" she asked, smiling broadly.

"I haven't had the pleasure," said Alexandra who inhaled on her cigarette and looked coolly at Diana.

"I've heard so much about you, Alexandra – it's so nice to meet you," said Diana.

Brigitte leaned forward and whispered in Diana's ear. "I thought you said you didn't lie!" She then erupted in giggles.

Diana, alarmed at Brigitte's rude behaviour in front of Alexandra, stepped away from her.

"I hope you're enjoying the day?" she said, smiling at Alexandra.

"Yes – everything is as I expected it," said Alexandra. She never smiled and maintained a cool distance. Then she looked at her watch and looked concerned. "But it's getting late and you're still in your wedding dress?"

Diana was confused. "Yes, I hadn't planned on changing – why?"

"But you will miss your train!" said Alexandra.

"Train?" Diana became more confused.

"For your honeymoon," Alexandra said.

"But we're not going on honeymoon – we're staying here," said Diana.

"No, you're going to Venice on the night train," Alexandra informed her.

"Alexandra!" Brigitte appeared horrified. "It was a secret. Max didn't want her to know and was going to surprise her!"

"Ooops!" Alexandra put her hand to her mouth but didn't look in any way upset.

"Excuse me, please," said Diana, not bothering to hide her anger and walking away.

As she walked away she heard Alexandra say, "I must have misheard you. I thought you said Max met her over a horse, not that she *was* a horse!"

Diana paused for a second and then quickly walked on.

"Max, may I speak to you for a minute?" said Diana, interrupting him as he chatted with a group of friends.

"Certainly," he smiled, breaking away from the others and joining her in a corner.

"Max, what's all this about us going to Venice?"

Max's smile dropped. "How did you find out?"

"Alexandra informed me." She looked at him accusingly.

Max looked across the crowded room, searching for Alexandra. He spotted her on her own, looking directly at them and smiling.

"She had no right to tell you, it was supposed to be a surprise," he said.

"Max! She had no right to know of our honeymoon plans when I didn't know myself! Did you tell her?"

"Of course I didn't," said Max, becoming annoyed. "It must have been either Brigitte or Hugo who let it slip."

"It was very unnerving to be told by her. Her very presence here is completely unacceptable to me, Max, knowing that in hers and everyone else's mind it should be her marrying you. *And* the fact that she was approved by your father while I must make do with this left-handed marriage."

"Darling, you will never have to make do with anything, not as long as I'm by your side."

"I've just found the whole thing so upsetting – everyone's whispers and sympathy today – your father's brutal treatment."

Max reached forward and took her in his arms. "That's why I

111

arranged for us to go to Venice. I thought we'd get away from everybody and just have time to ourselves."

Diana nodded. "And it was a good idea, just not a good idea the way I was told."

"I'm sorry, I had no idea that Alexandra knew and would say it."

"Well, as I said, I won't be sorry to leave her company and let's hope we won't have to see her again after this," said Diana.

Max said nothing but stared over at Alexandra who was staring back in equal measure.

When Diana entered her room to change, she found Max already had all her clothes packed for the honeymoon. She knew there was no point in protesting that he wouldn't have known what she wanted to bring. Max would just look at her with his large dark eyes in that confused way he always did when she confronted him about doing things behind her back. She quickly changed from her bridal dress into a smart travelling suit. Max had warned her not to delay as they had to get into Munich and not miss the connecting train to Venice.

It was a lovely idea of his to arrange the Venice trip, she thought as she came down the stairs.

Just as she reached the hall she saw Conrad walk out the main door, dressed in a big coat and hat. She thought for a moment and then followed him out. In the courtyard Conrad was marching towards his chauffeur-driven car. She quickly walked towards him.

"Are you not going to wait to wave us off on our honeymoon?" she said loudly as he reached the car and the chauffeur held the door open for him.

Conrad glanced at her before turning to get into the car.

She marched over to him, grasped his arm and blazed, "I'm talking to you!"

He looked at her, momentarily alarmed, and then shook her hand off. "What do you want?"

"How does it feel to have treated your son so badly?"

"It is he who has treated me badly. Marrying against my wishes."

"It's his life!"

"His life comes with certain requirements, ones he has just ignored. Because of you four hundred years of our family is being interrupted. Four hundred years of primogeniture, of direct succession through the eldest son has been brought to a halt."

"Because you chose to make it so!"

"I hope my son knows what he's doing, but I doubt it. Now if you'll excuse me, young lady, I have to get back to Munich."

"If Max's mother was alive, she would have never allowed this to happen," said Diana.

Conrad turned and looked at her and then for the first time she saw an expression other than the serious look he always had. He started to smirk in a mocking way as he sat into the car, then he started laughing.

The chauffeur closed the door and got in himself, and as he drove the car out of the courtyard, she could still hear Conrad bellowing a hollow laugh.

After an emotional farewell to her family, Diana and Max left the wedding party and travelled through the night to Venice.

Late the next morning Diana found herself installed in a luxurious suite at their hotel, having breakfast at a table in their room at the open French windows, looking down onto the canal beneath.

"Are you happy?" Max asked, reaching for her hand across the table.

"Perfectly!" she said as she took a sip of her strong coffee.

He suddenly got up and marched to a drawer and returning handed her a velvet-covered box.

"What's this?" she asked.

"Open and find out!"

She unclasped the catch and saw inside an emerald necklace lying on a satin bed.

"It's my wedding gift to you," Max said, taking the necklace and placing it around her neck.

"But there was no need for a wedding gift," she objected as she fingered the jewels.

"Every need," he said, bending down and kissing her neck.

CHAPTER 18

Present Day

The plane landed in Munich Airport and Sam made his way out though security and into the arrivals hall. Amongst the people waiting there was a rather stern-looking man holding up a sign with the word '*Cantwell*' written on it. Sam made his way over to him.

"I am he!" he said, pointing to the sign.

"Follow me, please," said the man, taking Sam's suitcase and heading towards the exit.

Sam just about managed to keep up with him.

Outside they went to an awaiting car and the man put Sam's suitcase into the boot before opening the back door for him.

Sam sat in to find a well-groomed woman in her thirties, dressed in a sharp suit, sitting there.

"I'm Sophie Essen, Mr Cantwell," she said, stretching out her hand.

"Call me Sam," he said, shaking her hand.

The man who had collected him got into the front seat and drove the car at high speed away from the airport and to the autobahn en route to the city.

"We are going straight to the hospital to start the transfusions," said Sophie. "You are booked into the Hilton Hotel. Please do not venture out without informing us. We can't have anything happen to you until the transfusions are complete."

"Your concern is very touching." He didn't hide the sarcasm in his voice.

"Under no circumstances must you speak to the press. Please

114

sign this document." She handed him a sheet of paper. "I had it printed in English."

Surprised, Sam took the document. It was a short statement that he would not talk to the media concerning Count Von Hoffsten's health, condition or Sam's involvement.

"Is this really necessary?" Sam was perplexed.

"We have to take precautions to ensure the Von Hoffstens' privacy and security," said Sophie.

Annoyed, Sam took the pen being offered and scribbled his signature at the bottom of the page.

"Perhaps if you had taken more precautions to protect the count's security in the first place, he might not have got shot!" he said, handing back the paper. "Have you any more details about how I'm actually related to the count?"

"No."

"I believe my great-grandmother, Diana Cantwell, is the connection. She married a German."

"Really?" Sophie sounded disinterested.

"A Hoffsten – well, now obviously a Von Hoffsten. I'd like a look at that peerage family tree if you get a chance to get me a copy."

"Mr Cantwell! You are not here on a family jamboree. You are here to save a man's life!"

"Really? I always wanted to be a hero," said Sam sarcastically.

Sam found himself swept past a large police presence outside the hospital and up an elevator to a private wing that had been reserved for Eric Von Hoffsten.

Sophie never left his side until he was delivered into the hands of the doctors who whisked him into a room where they started tests.

"How is the count now?" he asked the doctor, who didn't respond.

The day seemed to speed by.

When he wasn't needed he was left in a hospital bedroom until he was required again.

He rang Julia.

"There's a lot of press outside," he said, looking out the window to the street downstairs. "And police."

"It's probably one of the biggest news stories in Munich this year," said Julia.

"And they have cordoned off this ward and nobody can get in or out except the medical team."

"And you!" said Julia, loving the drama of it all.

The driver of the car from earlier walked into the room.

"There's somebody here, Julia, I'd better go."

"You're finished here for the day. I'll drive you to your hotel now," said the man, taking Sam's bag.

"Okay," said Sam as he followed him out.

On the way to the elevator they passed a waiting area behind a glass partition. Inside was a very elegant beautiful woman of around fifty, her hair tied back in a bun. She looked very stressed and was being comforted by a young man and woman.

"Who's she?" asked Sam.

"That's the Countess Von Hoffsten," said the driver. "And their children."

Sam stopped and stared at the woman. She looked up and at him through the glass and then quickly looked away again.

"Mr Cantwell!" snapped the driver who was at the elevator. "If you could follow me, please?"

That night in his hotel room, Sam sat at the desk eating a sandwich while he looked up anything he could about the Von Hoffstens. He could find very little about the present count and his wife. They were obviously very private people and weren't the types to be featured in *Hello* magazine. The count, Sam discovered, was fifty-nine years old and had inherited his title and the brewery from his father when he was thirty. His wife Nova was Swedish, and the daughter of a baron. They had two children, a daughter who worked for a charity foundation run by the Von Hoffstens, and a son who was studying at Harvard. They had a *schloss* in Munich and an estate in the Alps. They were one of Germany's wealthiest families, and the brewery had grown into a global brand over the past half-century. Sam found himself becoming dazzled by them.

Their lives seemed so removed from his. And yet he was related to them, connected to them. He shared the same blood as the count, that rare blood type that had brought him into their lives. And the connection was his great-grandmother, Diana Cantwell.

As the week progressed in Munich Sam was summoned into the hospital as required. The ever-watchful Sophie Essen was never far away.

The countess and her children seemed to be there all the time. They were usually in the waiting room as he passed by there to go to the surgery or the elevator. He kept expecting them to call to his room and introduce themselves. He had been looking forward to meeting them. But he realised they had more on their minds at that time. He found himself looking forward to getting a glimpse of the countess each day. She wasn't like any woman he had seen before. Her refined beauty seemed so distant, so unobtainable.

He was on his way down to the surgery one afternoon when he saw the countess come out of the waiting room and walk down the corridor. He decided it was a good opportunity to say hello and, to the nurse's surprise, he walked away from her and up to the countess.

The countess looked startled.

"Hello, I'm Sam Cantwell," he said. "I'm so sorry about your husband. I hope he's doing well?"

The countess said nothing. Her eyes quickly glanced around the corridor, looking for assistance. Help was at hand as Sophie Essen spotted what had happened and came rushing over.

"I'm sorry, Countess," she said. "Mr Cantwell is just on his way to the surgery. If you could follow me, Mr Cantwell?"

The countess walked on down the corridor without saying anything.

Sam looked after her, shocked but mesmerised.

"Mr Cantwell, if you could follow me!" said Sophie crossly.

Sam walked alongside Sophie down the corridor.

"Whatever did you think you were doing, going up to the countess like that?" demanded Sophie angrily.

117

"I wanted to introduce myself," said Sam.

"But you don't just go up to the Countess Von Hoffsten."

"Why not?"

"Because she's the Countess Von Hoffsten!"

"I think I get that bit! I am over here for her and her husband, you know! Away from my family and job for their benefit!"

"Yes, Mr Cantwell, and your efforts are most appreciated. But please do not approach the countess or any of her family again without permission," insisted Sophie.

Sam felt angry. "Excuse me! Are you saying I'm not good enough to meet them?"

"It's just not the right protocol."

"In other words you *are* saying I'm not good enough. How dare you! My blood is good enough to save the count's life though, isn't it?"

"Mr Cantwell, can we just get on with it?" said Sophie as they reached the surgery.

Sam found himself angry for the rest of the day. He couldn't get over the treatment he had received. He knew the Von Hoffstens had much more important things on their minds than him at present, and he didn't need them to express gratitude, but he didn't expect outright ignorance and rudeness either.

There was a knock on his bedroom door. He opened it to find Sophie Essen standing there.

"Good evening, Mr Cantwell," she said, marching past him into the room.

He closed the door after her.

"I have good news for you. Your presence is no longer required. The transfusions are completed."

"Oh!" He was surprised.

"I've arranged a flight for you at seven in the morning, leaving Munich Airport."

"That's very early," he said.

"There's no point in you hanging around."

"Where I'm no longer wanted?" he said knowingly.

"I'm sure you're anxious to get back to your wife and children." She opened her folder. "If I could just get you to sign this."

"What's this now?" he asked, taking the sheet of paper warily.

"Just basically a disclaimer saying that you won't claim any further finance from the Von Hoffsten estate for the assistance you provided this week other than what you are being paid now."

"What are you talking about?"

She held up a cheque. "This is a cheque for 10,000 euros for your time here this week in Munich. Once you sign the disclaimer, relinquishing any further claims, you can have the cheque."

He stared at her in disgust. "You are unbelievable!"

"I think it's quite a generous amount."

"I didn't come here for money! I came to help a dying relative."

"Indeed! Now could you just sign the disclaimer?" She thrust a pen towards him but he ignored it.

"Do you not realise how insulting this is?" he asked.

"I never before heard that being handed a cheque was an insult," she said.

He took the disclaimer and tore it in half.

"Mr Cantwell!" She was horrified. "I can warn you now that if you think you can extract more money from the Von Hoffstens you are sadly mistaken. That was your one and only offer."

He reached forward, snatched the cheque from her and tore that in two as well.

"That is what I think of your offer and your money – now get out!"

"You are acting very unreasonably."

"All I wanted was to help that man and his family. I didn't want payment. A simple thank-you from them personally would have sufficed. I would have liked to have met them and not be ignored when I said hello. And then you're getting me to sign papers about stuff that never even crossed my mind!"

"You are being silly. Did you honestly think you would be sitting down and having tea with the countess and her family? You're deluded."

"I asked you to leave. Now please go!"

"Suit yourself, Mr Cantwell. Safe journey home. I can take it you can find your own way to the airport in the morning?"

With that, Sophie marched past him out of the room.

He stared after her, consumed with anger.

Back in Dublin, Sam was describing everything that had happened during the week to Julia.

"They were just appalling," he concluded.

"They sound it. Although I kind of wish you'd taken the cheque. We do need a new kitchen."

"I wouldn't have given them the satisfaction. Who did they think I was? They treated me like a nobody."

"You are a nobody to them, darling – but you're everything to me." She leaned forward and kissed his forehead.

"Well, I wasn't a nobody a week ago when they were demanding I go to Munich to save his life!"

Julia sighed. "It's nothing personal. It's just the way they probably have to be. People are probably always trying to get money from them – extort it, blackmail it, any way they can. Only a week ago a bunch of kidnappers tried to take the count and now he's fighting for his life. They obviously can't trust or relax with anybody. It's an awful way to live your life."

"I did get a glimpse into that life. Chauffeurs, private wings in hospitals."

"But, yes, it's disappointing that you didn't speak to any of the family. After going all that way. What did she look like, the countess?"

"Beautiful. I've never seen anyone like her before," said Sam.

Julia looked at Sam, concerned. She hid her reaction and smiled, getting up from the couch.

"I'll go put on the kettle," she said, quickly leaving the room.

Sam was very unsettled over the following week. His experience in Munich had affected him and he wasn't sure why. The way he had been treated perhaps. The way he was dismissed. The fact that he discovered he was related to this family whose lives were almost unimaginable to him. And he had been part of their world for a few days. Escorted around by security, chauffeurs, in private wings of hospitals. He imagined the countess sitting there in the waiting room.

He sat in his office at the university looking at the piles of essays sitting on his desk that needed correcting. Instead he pushed them aside and started going through newspaper archives on the internet. He was determined to find out something about his ancestor Diana Cantwell and her connection to the Von Hoffstens. He knew the Cantwells were originally from County Meath. They had been part of the landed gentry a hundred years ago, but the estate and everything else had been lost after Irish Independence.

Since the revelation that he was related to Count Von Hoffsten his world had been in a spin – coming to terms with what was demanded of him, travelling to Germany, letting it all sink in, then catching up with the work he had missed while away. He hadn't time to look up about Diana before.

He typed in Diana's name and added 'Von Hoffsten'. Suddenly an article came up from *The Irish Times* in 1912. It was a large photograph of a man and woman smiling happily together and underneath was written: *'In an official announcement, Max Von Hoffsten, eldest son and heir to Count Conrad Von Hoffsten, is to be married to Miss Diana Cantwell, daughter of Simon and Maud Cantwell, County Meath, Ireland.'*

Sam was taken aback. There was the connection in black and white of how he was related to the Von Hoffstens. Diana had married Max Von Hoffsten. But he was perplexed. The article said that Max was the eldest son and heir to the count. He had imagined Diana had married a distant cousin of the main branch of the family, not the son and heir. He studied the photograph of the handsome couple. They looked very happy and in love. But if Max was the son and heir then he too one day would have been Count Von Hoffsten, and Diana would have been the countess.

That evening they were driving over for a dinner party at Thomas and Colette's.

"Oh, incidentally, I've made an appointment for you with the Dublin Blood Clinic on Monday," said Julia.

"Why?" asked Sam.

"I've spoken to them about your rare blood group, and they're going to keep a permanent bank there of your blood that you can draw on in emergencies. We don't want to find ourselves in the same situation as the count did if anything happened to you, frantically searching for a match at the last moment. The children have the same blood type as me, thankfully. Type O." She smirked at him. "Common!"

"Thank God for that!" He smiled appreciatively at her. "Thanks, Julia, I'll give my first donation on Monday. Let's face it, if anything ever did happen to me, having met the Von Hoffstens I don't think the count would come running to my rescue as I did to him."

"Well, I hope they've done the same thing and registered with a clinic. I hope they never come knocking at our door again!"

"I'm sure they have, now they realise the situation."

He drove along in silence for a while.

"Don't you think it strange?" said Sam. "I never knew my great-grandmother married a count!"

"But she didn't marry a count, Sam – she married the heir to a count."

"But he would one day be count, wouldn't he? Same thing. She was right in the heart of the family, not some distant relative."

He pulled into the driveway.

"Maybe he never became count, maybe he died?" said Julia.

"But their eldest son would still be the heir in that case," said Sam.

"Well, perhaps they didn't have children?"

"Of course they had children!" Sam became annoyed. "Otherwise I wouldn't have the same blood as the Von Hoffstens to give the man the transfusion! I wouldn't be here!"

"All right, all right!" she said, calming him down.

They got out of the car and walked up to the front door.

A few seconds later Thomas answered the door.

"Ah, here he is – His Royal Highness!" said Thomas, laughing loudly as he greeted them.

Colette put beers out beside the dinner plates as everyone sat down at the table.

"Because of the recent revelation of Sam's family connections, we decided instead of serving wine with tonight's dinner, we'd serve Hoffsten beer!" she said, laughing.

"Very funny!" said Sam, smiling.

"To think of all those Hoffsten beers we had at university and we never thought we were putting money into your relatives' pockets!" said Thomas.

"Hmmm, they don't look as if they need much money put into their pockets," said Sam.

"Was it fabulous?" asked Colette excitedly, sitting down at the head of the table.

"Well, I was mostly in the hospital or in the hotel," he said.

"But you met them? The family?" asked Thomas eagerly.

"I met the countess, his wife, briefly," said Sam.

"Very briefly," said Julia, taking a sip of her beer.

"What's she like?"

"Well, she's what you'd expect. Elegant, sophisticated," said Sam.

"You'll have to excuse my husband, everybody," said Julia. "He's developed a crush on this German countess."

"Don't be so daft, Julia," snapped Sam irritably. "And she's not even German, she's Swedish."

Julia raised her eyes to heaven. "A Swedish countess at that! How could I ever hope to compete with that?"

"And one with an endless supply of beer to boot," laughed Thomas. "You're fucked, Julia!"

Everyone but Sam started to roar with laughter.

"You may well all laugh!" said Sam, smiling through his irritation.

"You know, Sam, you shouldn't have saved her husband. She's not free now!" said Julia through her laughter.

Despite his wife and his friends' mockery, Sam was back in the library at the university on the Monday. He began to trail through newspaper archives on the internet in the months after the article about the engagement, to see if there was any further information about the actual wedding. Finally he found a small announcement in *The Irish Times*.

'The wedding took place last Saturday of County Meath resident Miss Diana Cantwell to Max Von Hoffsten. The wedding took place in the Church of St Benedict near the Von Hoffsten estate in Tegernfrei, Bavaria. Father of the bride, Mr Simon Cantwell, gave his daughter away and there followed a reception at the Von Hoffsten estate which was attended by dignitaries and nobility from around Europe. The new Mrs Von Hoffsten is a keen horsewoman, and her horse Halcyon came second in the Irish Derby this year. Mr Von Hoffsten is a keen yachtsman, and a regular competitor at Cowes Regatta.'

Sam reread the article, intrigued. These were his great-grandmother and great-grandfather. Two such accomplished people. He realised they were obviously what today's media would call a 'power couple'. He needed to find out more. He should google the church where the couple were married. Hopefully it would be still there and have records.

Julia was stacking the dishwasher as Sam came downstairs after putting the children to bed.

"I was thinking, when you are away with the kids at your mother's next weekend, I might take a little break myself," he said.

"Good idea. Anywhere interesting in mind?"

"I was thinking Munich."

"*Munich!*" Julia slammed the dishwasher shut and turned to face him.

"Yes, I didn't get a chance to see it properly when I was there. It's such a beautiful place I'd like to go back and see it."

"This hasn't anything to do with those Von Hoffstens, has it?" she demanded.

"Of course not!"

"They haven't been on again looking for you to donate some

other part of you, have they?"

"No. Sure they were delighted to get rid of me," he said.

Julia folded a tea towel, hung it up and sighed. "Whatever you want, Sam."

PART 2

1914-1918

CHAPTER 19

The engagement and marriage had been so fraught with politics that those first few weeks of their marriage were like a dream for Diana. She had expected a short trip to Venice and then back to the estate in Germany. Max had other plans. After Venice they travelled down to Rome and all along the coast to Southern Italy. When he was bored with that they moved on to the South of France. She had known what Max's life was like before she'd married him. He did what he wanted when he wanted where he wanted. She had supposed that when they were married this might change. But it seemed Max had no intention of changing and, to be fair, he had never given her any indication that he would.

Diana was on the telephone to her mother from their hotel suite in Cannes before they were due to go out to dinner with friends of Max's that night.

"Sounds divine!" said Maud as she heard the details of their married life.

"Well, so it does, but all this travel is a little tiresome, Mama."

"How on earth could it be tiresome? You have the life of Reilly! And let's face it, the more you travel, the less you have to see that ghastly family of his back in Germany!"

"Well, that's true."

"Any word from the Ashenbrys?" asked Maud.

"Yes, they've invited us to stay with them in London."

"How marvellous!" Maud was thrilled at how Diana's marriage

had made them in demand with her English cousins.

Diana was in their suite in the Grand Hotel in Monte Carlo, writing a letter to Dashiel. They were due to return home to Germany the following week and she was looking forward to spending some time there and getting to know her new home.

Max walked into the room, came over and kissed her.

"Who are you writing to?" he asked.

"Just a letter home."

"Send them my love. Look – this is a telegram from Brigitte. All is organised for the ski party next week. She has received acceptances back from everyone we invited, including the Ashenbrys."

"Ski party?" Diana looked up, concerned.

"Yes, I've been organising one."

Diana put down her fountain pen. "How many have you invited?"

"Oh, forty, fifty. I'm not sure – I left the finer details to Brigitte."

"And they'll all be staying with us?" Diana was incredulous.

"Of course. Where else would they be staying? They are our guests."

"But, Max, I wish you had discussed this with me before. When we left the estate it was full of wedding guests, and now when we arrive back it will be full of skiing guests."

"So?"

"So, I wanted to have some time to ourselves in our new home. I wanted to get to know it and the staff. How long do you plan for this ski party to go on?"

"Who can say? A couple of weeks."

"Oh, Max, I *really* wish you had discussed this first!" Diana was annoyed. "And why is Brigitte organising it for you? Why isn't she in Vienna studying under Mr Freud?"

"Because Brigitte organises everything for me. I always leave everything for her to arrange."

"That was before you had a wife, Max."

Seeing she was annoyed, he came over to her and put his arms around her. "Don't be angry. You'll enjoy the skiing as much as anyone as soon as you get used to it." He kissed her cheek quickly and then walked out, whistling a happy tune to himself.

CHAPTER 20

The sleigh approached the *schloss* and Diana, wrapped in furs, linked Max's arm tightly.

"When are the first of the guests arriving?" she asked.

"I think tomorrow, according to Brigitte," said Max.

"Well, at least we'll have tonight alone," she said as the sleigh drove through the gateway into the courtyard and pulled to a halt.

The driver assisted Diana out of the sleigh while Max jumped off on the other side.

Suddenly the main door opened and Brigitte came rushing out.

"Max!" she squealed and threw herself into his arms. "I missed you so much!"

Diana stood by awkwardly, watching them as they clung to each other, making no attempt to separate.

"Hello, Brigitte," Diana said eventually, forcing Brigitte to look at her.

"Ah, and Diana, welcome back," said Brigitte as she left Max's embrace and came and kissed Diana's cheek. "You look radiant. Marriage suits you."

She linked Diana's arm and the two of them walked into the house, followed by Max.

Diana took off her fur and hat and gave them to the butler. "Yes, I have to say we've had a ball. I've seen more of the Mediterranean than I ever thought possible!"

"I wish I could have gone with you," sighed Brigitte.

"Eh, yes." Diana nodded awkwardly. "But it's nice to be back.

131

Max tells me you have been terribly busy organising this ski party."

"Oh, yes, I think you'll be happy with the results, Max," said Brigitte.

Linking both their arms she walked them through the double doors into the drawing room.

"I hope it hasn't distracted you too much from your studies . . ." said Diana, her voice trailing off when she saw who was in the drawing room.

Alexandra was sitting smoking beside a roaring fire.

"Welcome home, Max," said Alexandra and then she nodded at Diana. "Diana."

Diana removed herself from Brigitte's vice-like grip and walked carefully on into the room. "Hello again, Alexandra."

Max looked awkward for a second and then bounded over to Alexandra and kissed her cheek. "Are you all set for the skiing?"

"I'm always set for skiing," she answered.

Max laughed. "Shall we have a drink?"

"Hugo went down to the cellars with the butler to choose some schnapps. We've run out of it up here," said Alexandra, indicating the empty schnapps bottle on the table.

"Yes, he's been gone so long we might have to send a search party!" Brigitte said, laughing lightly.

Diana smiled and sat down on the armchair across from Alexandra.

Alexandra reached for Max's hand and squeezed it. "So tell me, darling, where did you go? Who did you see?"

Max went and stood beside the fireplace and lit a cigarette. "Oh, all the usual haunts."

"That's good." Alexandra smiled acidly at Diana. "Now hopefully you'll be able to answer if you prefer Monaco or Biarritz."

Diana glared back coldly at Alexandra.

"Ah, here he is!" said Brigitte, quickly standing up and clasping her hands together as Hugo came into the room holding a bottle of schnapps. "Schnapps all round, I say!"

"*What's she doing here*?" demanded Diana as she stormed into their bedroom upstairs, followed by Max.

"Shhh! They'll hear downstairs!"

"I don't care if they do! Nobody is ever worried about insulting me here, so why should I worry about insulting them?"

"What are you talking about? Apart from Father everyone has been most welcoming to you here."

"Hugo has hardly said two words to me!"

"Hugo hardly says two words to anybody! He's quiet, not much confidence."

"I'm not surprised – with you and Brigitte dominating everything, he doesn't get a look in! The point is – who invited Alexandra?"

"I don't know! She's always invited to the ski parties here."

"So Brigitte did! Didn't you warn her not to invite her?"

"But it would have been awkward not to invite her."

"It's far more awkward for me that she's here!"

"For goodness' sake, Diana, you are being childish. Myself and Alexandra were never involved romantically with each other, and our supposed arrangement is in the past. She's an old friend who –"

"Is no longer welcome here! You might have no feelings for her, Max, but it is obvious to me that she has feelings, and strong ones, for you. She's also rude to me."

"How is she rude?"

"She makes snide remarks . . . and she called me a horse!"

"*What?*"

"I heard her make a comment to Brigitte about me – that she knew we had met over a horse but she hadn't realised I *was* a horse!"

Max fell on the bed, laughing. "Oh, Diana! You are priceless!"

"Well, I'm glad you find it so funny!"

He came over to her and put his arms around her. "Diana –"

"No, Max!" Diana snapped and pushed him away. "You are not going to sweet-talk me this time. That woman is no longer welcome in this house or in this family."

Max's face went deadly serious as he stared at her. "But, Diana, what you ask for is impossible."

"Why?"

"Because –"

Suddenly the bedroom door opened and Brigitte came walking happily in.

Diana stared at her, amazed that she would just enter without knocking and in the midst of a loud argument between husband and wife.

"Can we help you, Brigitte?" she asked, perplexed.

"Great news! Great news!" Brigitte declared.

Diana looked at her sister-in-law's gleeful face but no information was forthcoming.

"Well?" asked Diana eventually.

"Halcyon has arrived from Ireland!" Brigitte declared.

"Halcyon!" said Diana, her face lit with excitement. She turned to Max. "You never told me he was here!"

Max smiled indulgently at her. "I wanted to surprise you."

"Oh, Max!" Diana's eyes filled with tears and she leaned forward and hugged him tightly. "Where is he? Can I see him now?"

"Of course!" said Max. Taking her hand, he led her quickly out of the room.

Outside, they raced across the courtyard and through the arch to the extensive stables behind the house. Max asked directions from one of the stable boys and then led Diana into a warm stable filled with hay where Halcyon waited for her.

"Halcyon!" she whispered as she hugged him tightly and she found herself crying slightly. She turned and kissed Max. "Thank you, Max."

He smiled at her. "As I've said before – as if I could deny you anything!"

CHAPTER 21

Diana and Max's bedroom was at the back of the house. On either side of a large double bed were French windows that led out to a balcony which looked out over the lake and the Alps.

Diana sat at her dressing table brushing her hair that evening as she and Max were getting ready for dinner. Max was fiddling with his cufflinks and she had noticed he was fidgety and not relaxed.

"Are you nearly ready yet?" he asked irritably.

She looked at him in the mirror as she fixed her earrings. "Nearly."

"We don't want to be late for Father."

Diana turned around, startled. "Father?"

"Yes, he's back from Munich and joining us for dinner."

"And why are you only telling me now?" she demanded.

"I only knew myself a short while ago."

Diana stood up and walked towards him. "And what's he doing here?"

"I may be his heir, but this still is his house, Diana. He is entitled to come whenever he wishes."

"My point is," her voice hardened, "since he did everything to avoid me before the wedding and didn't even sit in at our wedding banquet, why does he want to dine with us tonight?"

"I have no idea. I haven't seen him yet."

Diana turned and took off her earrings. "Well, I'm not going down, Max. You'll have to dine without me. I'm sure your father will only be too delighted at that."

135

Max looked at her in horror and then hurried over to her. "Of course you must be there!"

"Of course I must do nothing! I'm in no mood to spend an evening being insulted by that man again. In fact, I wouldn't have come back here from the Riviera if I had known all this was going to be waiting for me – your father, your ex-fiancée –"

"Diana! You are being unreasonable. You are my wife and I am his heir – you have a responsibility to meet him and be at my side."

"Well, as far I can see this left-handed marriage leaves me with all the chores and none of the benefits!"

Max's eyes filled with tears and his face became pleading. "Please, Diana. You have to come to dinner tonight. If you don't it will set a precedent and he will never receive you again."

"Sounds good to me!"

"You are my wife, Diana, and you have to meet him or you won't be included in family events."

Diana saw the pain and anguish this was causing Max and she sighed loudly.

"All right, Max, but I'm only doing this for you."

He smiled and embraced her.

Diana braced herself as she and Max entered the long dining room. Conrad was sitting at the head of the table. To his right sat Alexandra and to his left sat Hugo. Brigitte was seated opposite him at the other end of the table.

"There you are," said Conrad. "We were about to send a search party to find you."

"I only found out twenty minutes ago you were even here," said Diana.

She hesitated as she reached the table as she realised a seat had been left vacant beside Hugo and another beside Alexandra. She chose to sit beside Hugo, leaving Max to sit beside Alexandra.

The servants quickly began to serve dinner.

"I trust you enjoyed your honeymoon?" asked Conrad.

"It was very enjoyable, thank you, Father," said Max.

Alexandra sat back in her chair, ignoring the food that had been served to her, and lit up a cigarette.

"Did you meet Matilda Von Hausen there?" she asked of Max as she inhaled. "I believe she was in Cannes the same time as you."

"Yes, we met her. We had dinner with her one evening," said Max.

"I adore Matilda," said Brigitte, leaning forward conspiringly. "You realise she was a patient of Freud's last summer?"

Alexandra shrugged. "It doesn't surprise me. The woman has always had a nervous disposition in my opinion."

As Diana observed them she felt a complete outsider. They seemed to know each other so intimately and nobody, including Max, was making an effort to include her.

"Tell me, did you go to the Emperor's Vienna ball?" asked Max.

"Of course," said Alexandra. "Hugo accompanied me."

"Did you enjoy it, Hugo?" smiled Diana.

Hugo looked up from the food on his plate which he had been studying. "Y–y-yes. It was good to go."

Conrad glanced at Hugo. "Hugo is to attend far more balls in the future. I've insisted he is to get out more and be sociable."

Diana leaned towards Hugo and smiled. "Yes, Hugo, you are to enjoy yourself whether you want to or not!"

Conrad looked at Diana acidly while Alexandra blew smoke at her across the table.

Conrad sat forward. "I'm very pleased that we are here together before all Max's guests arrive tomorrow as I have something important to announce." He glanced at Hugo. "It is my absolute delight and pleasure to announce the engagement of Hugo to Princess Alexandra."

There was silence around the table for a few moments.

"Congratulations!" said Brigitte happily as she began clapping excitedly. She got up, walked over to Alexandra and kissed her cheek before doing the same to Hugo.

"Yes – yes, congratulations to both of you," said Max awkwardly and then he leaned forward and kissed Alexandra's cheek before reaching across the table and shaking his brother's hand.

Diana sat stunned by the news. There had been no indication that this was on the cards, no hint of a romance between Alexandra and Hugo.

As her mind tried to fathom the consequences of the announcement, Max smiled over at her and said, "Isn't that good news, Diana?"

Diana was jolted out of her trance and managed to smile. "Yes, congratulations to both of you."

"We are delighted that you are becoming a proper member of our family," said Conrad as he raised his glass to Alexandra.

She picked up her own wineglass and chinked it against his. "And I am delighted to become part of the family too."

"Well, that was a turn-up for the books," said Diana as she and Max entered their room that night.

"Hmmm . . ." Max sauntered over to a French window and gazed out at the night view.

"I never heard Hugo had feelings for Alexandra before, did you?"

"Hmmm, no." He took out his cigarette case and lit one.

"I suppose we'll never be rid of her now," she sighed as she sat down on a couch in front of the roaring fire. "But they don't appear as a couple in love."

Max turned and looked at her. "Of course they're not in love! Wherever did you get that idea from?"

"It tends to be a condition before people announce their engagement," she said sarcastically.

"Hugo and Alexandra were always going to get married when I refused to," he announced.

"What are you talking about?" she asked.

"My father was determined that Alexandra be married into the family. He arranged for us to have a left-handed marriage and then organised for Hugo to marry Alexandra so their children will inherit the title and everything else in the future after me."

"So you were aware of this arrangement with Alexandra?"

"Yes."

"Well, why didn't you tell me? Warn me?"

"What good would it have done?"

"Quite a lot actually, rather than having this sprung on me downstairs! And Hugo is just going ahead with his father's plan?"

"Yes, like a good son should!"

"I've never heard anything so ridiculous. Your father is a monster, arranging everyone's lives, bullying them, manipulating us all!"

"Oh, I'm sure Hugo doesn't mind being manipulated at all. It will be his children who will be the ultimate heirs, not mine."

She stared at him. "Oh, Max, why did you marry me? I've brought nothing but disruption and turmoil to your life. Was the sacrifice ever worth this?"

He stormed over to her, his face twisted in anger. "Don't ever say that again! I have never regretted marrying you and I never will. I don't care about anything except that I have you, is that clear?"

Diana observed the intensity in his face and she felt almost scared for a second. What was this love he had for her that led him to give up so much for her? She stood up and held him.

"It's fine, Max, calm down. All I want is you too – nothing else matters."

A scream echoed through the house, frightening Diana out of her sleep. She sat bolt upright. There was a silence and then another scream.

"What on earth is that?" asked Diana as she quickly turned on the lights. She turned around in the bed and saw that Max wasn't there.

"Max!" she called, getting out of bed and going into the bathroom off their bedroom. It was empty.

She quickly slipped on her satin dressing gown and, tying it at the waist, left the room. The corridor outside was dimly lit as she made her way down it. As she reached the top of the stairs she paused, looking down at the lobby below in darkness, and listened. There wasn't a sound through the house and she was amazed the screams hadn't woken everyone up.

Suddenly the scream came echoing through the house again.

She turned and followed where the noise had come from, down a different corridor. As she walked along the corridor she could see the courtyard through the windows that ran along it, glistening in the midnight snow.

The scream came again and then again until she reached the door it seemed to be originating from. She paused at the door and listened intently. She could hear a woman whimpering inside and then another scream.

Panicked, she reached for the door handle, twisted it quickly and opened the door.

Inside was a big sprawling bedroom.

Brigitte was seated on a couch in front of the fire, her head in her hands.

"Brigitte!" Diana gasped as she hurried into the room towards her. "What on earth is the matter with you?" She sat beside Brigitte and put her arms around her.

"It's just the – headaches – I get – the ones I was telling you about," Brigitte managed to say.

"But why didn't you call for a doctor?"

"It's no use, he can't do anything – it will pass eventually," said Brigitte.

Diana stood up. "I must fetch a doctor and get your father and Max."

"No!" Brigitte demanded, grabbing Diana's wrist and gripping it so tightly it hurt.

Diana reluctantly sat down again and began to cradle Brigitte. She tried to fathom how the whole house hadn't been woken by Brigitte's screams. Where was everybody? Why hadn't they come rushing to her aid? Every so often, as Diana soothed her, Brigitte would suddenly let out a further scream, frightening and upsetting Diana.

It seemed like an eternity passed before the pain in Brigitte's head finally subsided. Exhausted, she allowed herself to be led to the bed. Diana tucked her in, took a final check on her and left the room, closing the door firmly behind her.

Diana ran her hands through her hair, unnerved and perplexed by the whole situation. She walked down the corridor back in the direction of her bedroom, wondering where on earth Max had got to.

As she reached the top of the stairs she saw a light was coming from the drawing room downstairs. Curious, she walked down the stairs and across the hall.

In the drawing room was Max, fully dressed, smoking a cigarette as he stared out the French windows.

"Max? What are you doing?" she asked, coming into the room.

He turned in surprise and she saw he was deathly pale and seemed agitated and nervous.

"Just having a cigarette."

"I woke up and you were gone," she said. "Did you not hear the screams? Brigitte's screams?"

"Of course I heard her, that's what woke me up. I had to get out of the house and go for a walk to get away from her screaming."

Diana was shocked. "But why didn't you go and check on her?"

He shrugged. "What's the point? I can't do anything to stop it."

"But why didn't you call a doctor?"

"As I'm sure she has told you, a doctor is of no use."

"I'm sorry, but I don't understand you at all. Your sister is in pain – and – and you just go out for a walk in the snow?" Diana was incredulous.

"What do you suggest I do?"

"Go to her! Help her! If it was Dashiel or Warren, I'd have gone through fire to get to them if I heard them in such pain!"

"Diana, leave it!" he insisted.

"And where's your father and Hugo, not to mention Alexandra and the servants? How could any of them sleep through that howling?"

"I said – *leave it, Diana*!"

His voice was so stern she almost didn't recognise it. He then walked quickly past her and up the stairs to their bedroom.

CHAPTER 22

Max was gone when Diana awoke the next morning. As she got ready she thought about the night's events and mostly Max's reaction to Brigitte's cries. She couldn't understand it. Max and Brigitte seemed so close and yet he was not interested in her pain.

Walking into the dining room she found Max, Alexandra and Hugo eating breakfast while a smiling happy Brigitte was standing, refilling her coffee cup.

"Oh, there you are!" said Brigitte, smiling broadly at her. "We were wondering if we should wake you in case you missed breakfast."

"Good morning, everyone," said Diana as she took her seat.

"Coffee?" smiled Brigitte, holding the coffee pot over Diana's cup.

"Please," nodded Diana.

"Did you sleep well, my darling?" asked Max, smiling over at her.

Diana glanced at Brigitte, who looked refreshed and full of vitality, and answered, "Not very, I'm afraid."

"Really?" said Brigitte, sitting down concerned. "Most people here find they have excellent nights' sleep – it's the fresh mountain air."

Diana stared at Brigitte and Max in amazement.

"P-p-p-perhaps you are overly tired from all the travel recently," ventured Hugo.

"Conrad had to leave early to go back to Munich," said

142

Alexandra as she lit a cigarette. "He sends his apologies for missing you."

"I'm sure!" said Diana under her breath.

"What time are the first guests arriving?" asked Brigitte excitedly.

"Just after lunch," said Max.

Diana watched as they all carried on a mundane good-natured conversation, as if nothing had happened during the night.

Diana tried to put the previous night's events to the back of her mind as the guests for the ski party began to arrive. Looking at Max greet people he seemed a different man from the deathly pale nervous man she had seen in the drawing room in the middle of the night.

Dressed in one of the new gowns Max had bought her in Rome, Diana set about playing hostess, although with the engagement announcement she found that attention gravitated towards Alexandra.

"Diana!" called a friendly American voice and Diana was delighted to see Thelma and Elliott Ashenbry had arrived.

She hurried across the crowded drawing room

"You look swell, Diana, just swell, doesn't she, Elliott?" said Thelma as they embraced.

"You certainly do – marriage to Max is obviously suiting you." Elliott embraced his cousin.

"I'm so happy you're here," said Diana genuinely. "I know we are only distantly related but I've met so many new people since marrying Max that I do think of you as family."

"That's because we are family!" said Thelma earnestly.

The French windows were open onto the terrace balcony. The drawing room had emptied out as most people had gone out skiing. The butler carried a bottle of champagne out to the terrace where Diana, Thelma and Elliott were sitting wrapped in full-length fur coats, watching the skiers swoop down the hills to the lake. The skiers swept by quite close to the house. Diana thought it unusual that, unlike the big houses in Ireland, the hunting lodge wasn't surrounded by gardens but the sloping meadows came nearly right up to it.

The butler opened the champagne and refilled their glasses.

"This is the life," said Thelma as she sipped. "You're a lucky woman, Diana."

"Yes, I suppose I am."

"No supposing about it, sweetheart," said Thelma, reaching forward to break off some chocolate from a bar on the table in front of them.

"Look!" said Diana, pointing at Max who went zooming down on his skis. "This is what he wants," she said then, studying his figure as it grew smaller in the distance. "This is when Max is at his happiest. A party going on around him, lots of glamorous people, him being the centre of attention."

"Sounds good to me!" laughed Elliott.

"Of course," said Diana. "But I'm beginning to realise that Max isn't very good at dealing with real life, or real problems. He just brushes everything under the carpet and pretends it's not happening."

"Well, I suppose he's got the money to allow himself to live in a bubble, Diana."

"He's a playboy, Diana – you knew that when you married him," Elliott pointed out.

"And I love him for being fun and jovial . . . but . . ." Diana's voice trailed off.

Thelma reached over and took her hand. "What's the problem, sweetheart?"

"It's just he seems to keep things from me. He never tells me anything until I've found out myself – like Alexandra's engagement to Hugo. He knew about it, or at least suspected, and never told me."

"He's probably just trying to protect you, doesn't want to worry you," said Thelma.

"I think he doesn't want to worry himself so he just puts anything unpleasant out of his mind."

"The engagement has upset you a lot, hasn't it?" said Thelma.

"Of course it has. Conrad made sure Alexandra's children would be the ultimate heirs to this family and not mine, and he didn't care which of his sons she had to marry to ensure that in the end."

"Diana, that might be the case. But Alexandra or Hugo will have no rights – only their children will when the time comes. It is Max as the count and you as his wife who will control the wealth and the power in this lifetime."

Diana reached forward, took her champagne glass and sipped. "I'll take comfort from that then."

The days passed and the skiing party enjoyed the full extent of Max's hospitality. Diana continued to hope each morning that there would be an announcement that Alexandra would be returning to her own home, but she seemed intent on going nowhere. After a while Diana was secretly wishing the party was over and people would leave her and Max alone.

Diana took out the emerald necklace Max had given her the morning after their wedding and put it on one night before she went down to dinner. As she went down the corridor she met Alexandra coming from her room, dressed immaculately in a long figure-hugging satin dress, her hair immaculately groomed.

Alexandra smiled at her as they descended the stairs together. "I haven't seen you out on the ski slopes yet," she commented.

"No, I don't think skiing is for me. I think I'll stay safely perched on the terrace cheering the rest of you on," said Diana.

Alexandra nodded and smiled. Then, as they reached the hall, she stopped and, reaching out, fingered the emerald necklace. "What a beautiful piece of jewellery," she said.

"Thank you. It was a gift from Max."

"He always had exquisite taste, most of the time," said Alexandra as she continued to study the emeralds. "When did he give it to you?"

"On our honeymoon."

Alexandra drew back with a knowing smile on the face. "The morning after your wedding?"

"Well, yes, actually."

Alexandra gave a low unpleasant laugh. "Ah, in that case it's your morning gift!"

"What do you mean?"

"The word *morganatic* comes from the German word for morning – *morgen*. In a morganatic marriage, on the morning after the wedding it is the custom for the groom to give his left-handed bride a gift. This gift is symbolic as it is the only part of her husband's estate she or their children will ever be entitled to."

Diana stared at Alexandra in speechless amazement.

"This is all you will ever really own of the Von Hoffsten fortune." Alexandra suddenly smiled at her. "It's a very pretty trinket though."

Alexandra turned and walked into the drawing room to join the other guests.

Diana was upset for the rest of the night. Even as they all enjoyed a sumptuous dinner of roast pork in the banquet room she found it hard to pretend to be a happy hostess.

As Max fussed around her, she managed to keep the upset from her face.

"Is everything all right, Diana?" he asked, reaching forward and taking her hand.

She nodded and smiled.

Diana waited until after dinner and then, unable to bear any more of Alexandra's smug looks at her, she slipped away from the party and up to their bedroom. She put on her fur coat and, opening the French window, went out onto the snow-covered balcony. She looked out at the star-filled night over the lake and nearby mountains. In the distance from downstairs, she could hear the music and guests and she imagined the party would continue into the early hours.

"Diana?" called Max as he came into their bedroom looking for her.

"Out here," she called.

Max came bounding out, smiling. "What are you doing up here? Everyone is looking for you downstairs."

"Are they?"

"Yes, come on, I have a surprise for you!"

He reached forward and, taking her arm, led her into the bedroom. There she halted and resisted him.

"Diana?" he asked curiously.

She fingered the emerald necklace around her throat and then she unclasped it and held it out to him.

"I don't want this, Max, take it back," she said.

"What are you talking about?"

"Your 'morning gift', isn't that what it's called?"

Realisation dawned on Max's face. "Diana, it's yours. Keep it."

She spoke softly to him. "But this is your custom not mine." She pushed the necklace into his hand. "If I didn't marry you for your title and estate, then I certainly didn't marry you for this necklace."

"I've insulted you by giving it to you?" he asked.

"This left-handed marriage is your custom, your law, nothing to do with me."

"Or me! My father forced it on us."

"But, by giving that necklace, you showed that you were going along with the decision, following its rules," she said, trying to reason with him.

"All I was doing was following tradition," he said

"When I agreed to marry you in these circumstances," she said, "I was telling the world that I loved you regardless of the cost to me, and I believed you were doing the same."

"I was!"

Diana's eyes filled with tears. "Then keep that necklace . . . I thought it was a token of your love to me, not you telling me that it was all I was worth as a bride, all that I would get."

She went and stood at the open window, looking out as the snow began to fall again.

He came and put his arms around her. "I'm sorry, you were never meant to see it that way."

She turned and faced him. "Don't you see? You never explain to things to me. If you had explained the meaning behind this gift I would have rejected it outright."

147

"I just don't want to burden you with things that are unimportant."

"But they are important, Max." She sighed loudly.

He hesitated, then placed the necklace on the dressing table.

"Take it with you, Max. I never want to set eyes on it again."

He nodded and placed it in his pocket. "I'll have it put back in the family safe," he said.

CHAPTER 23

When Diana awoke the next morning she found the bed beside her empty and realised Max hadn't come back the previous night. Maybe she had hurt him too much . . .

She dressed and made her way downstairs for breakfast.

She was nervous about seeing Max as she walked into the dining room.

He was at the top of the table. He looked up at her and smiled. She smiled back.

"Well, aren't you going to greet your brother?" asked Max.

Diana looked, confused, at the man sitting beside him.

"Dashiel!" she exclaimed, hardly believing her eyes as she rushed to him and embraced him.

"I was waiting for you all night to come down, but Max said you were tired," said Dashiel, hugging her closely.

"But what are you doing here?" asked Diana.

"Max organised for me to come over as a surprise for you," said Dashiel.

Diana smiled at Max then bent over and kissed him. "Thank you, Max."

She was so delighted to have Dashiel visiting her that she couldn't continue to be angry with Max.

"Well, they were really all my friends here for the ski party, so I thought I'd bring Dashiel over," said Max.

"You think of everything." Diana sat down beside her brother. "What news of home, Dashiel?"

"Warren and Hannah Roundtree seem to be getting serious," said Dashiel.

"Really?" Diana was surprised. "I never suspected that was on the cards."

"Well, it is. Mama and Papa are the same but Mama is quite nervous over the political situation at home."

"Political situation?" enquired Brigitte.

"It looks like independence may be coming to Ireland, which might cause a civil war with those who don't want it," said Dashiel.

"Oh no! It won't happen, Dashiel," Diana said. "There will never be a war in Ireland – it's been threatened for decades and nothing comes of it."

"I think it's different this time. The northerners are arming themselves," said Dashiel.

Alexandra lit up cigarette. "But if Ireland breaks away from the United Kingdom, Britain will just be a small island."

"With a very large overseas empire," stated Elliott, affronted.

"Pew!" Alexandra dismissed him with a wave of her hand. "Britain with this empire reminds me of an old lady who lives in a mansion she can no longer afford. Let's face it, Germany has raced ahead as a bigger, richer country. Far superior in every way."

"Actually –" began Elliott.

"More coffee?" said Brigitte loudly as she stood up with the coffee pot. "I always think you can't have enough coffee to set you up for the day ahead."

For once Diana was glad of Brigitte's intrusive courtesy as it staved off the argument.

"I think I'll set myself up with my skis for the day," said Elliott as he got up and hastily left the table.

Diana and Dashiel looked at each other, a silent fear passing between them of how a civil war would impact on their family in Ireland.

The next two weeks flowed by and, the night before most of the guests were due to leave, Diana and Dashiel were out on the balcony.

"Is everything all right, Diana?" he asked.

"Yes, of course, why wouldn't it be?"

"You've just seemed a little on edge while I've been here."

"I'm fine, just adapting to my new life with Max and his family, that's all."

"But you are enjoying life with Max?"

"Yes, I adore him . . . it's just . . ."

"Yes?"

"Sometimes I'm not sure if I can read his mind."

"And why do you want to read his mind?" asked Dashiel.

"There just always seem to be surprises with him."

"Like the one he planned bringing me here for the ski trip?"

"Well, yes."

"Do you know the amount of planning he put into bringing me over here, all of course as a surprise for you?"

"But we don't seem to plan anything together."

"But are not all the plans wonderful and to your benefit?"

"I suppose so."

Dashiel put his hands on Diana's shoulders and smiled. "All Max wants is to be with you and to make you happy. He loves to see you happy. If he is dedicating himself to thrilling you – is that so bad?"

"Of course not. You're absolutely right. I'm a very lucky woman," she said, reaching forward and hugging Dashiel.

Diana decided that Dashiel was absolutely right. And as the guests departed and she was left alone with Max she vowed to enjoy these first few months of marriage with him. She was particularly glad to see the back of Alexandra who returned to her family palace in preparation for her marriage to Hugo. Hugo returned to Munich where he lived with his father and where Diana imagined he was at his constant beck and call. Brigitte returned to university in Vienna but was a regular visitor to the hunting lodge.

And so Diana began to feel at home in the hunting estate which they used as a base for the constant travel Max organised for them. Max seemed to get a thrill out of introducing Diana to the elite in London and Paris and Berlin and soon Max's beautiful young wife became as well known as Max himself.

CHAPTER 24

They were in Paris and Max said he had business that day to attend to, so Diana busied herself shopping. Max had arranged to meet her for dinner in The Ritz that evening and Diana got a cab there, delighted to be dining for the first time in the world-famous Ritz restaurant.

As she walked through the lobby she realised that despite marriage to Max and all the distinguished people who she now counted as friends, she felt insecure and unworldly without Max by her side. She kept feeling somebody would tell her she didn't belong there and to leave.

"May I help you, madame?" asked the maître d' as he approached her.

As Diana looked around the restaurant she realised there was something wrong. Despite it being after nine in the evening the place was completely empty.

"I'm sorry. My husband told me he had made a reservation – he mustn't have realised you weren't open tonight," she said, turning around to leave.

"No mistake, madame. You are Madame Von Hoffsten?"

"Eh, yes."

"Please follow me, madame," he said.

Hesitantly Diana followed him through the empty tables and chairs until they reached a centre table. He pulled out a chair for her and she nodded to him as she sat down. He then walked away and left the huge dining hall. She looked around nervously, wondering what was going on and where was Max, not to mention all the other dinners. Ten minutes went by and then fifteen and then, as there was no sign of a waiter or Max, she decided to leave.

As she stood up she suddenly heard a man singing in the distance. She strained to hear. The singing became louder and she recognised the song as 'If You Were the Only Girl in the World'.

Then she saw Max walking into the restaurant, singing the song loudly.

She watched, confused, as he walked through the empty tables to get to her, all the time singing. He reached the table as he finished the song.

"Max, what's going on? Where is everybody?"

Max sat down opposite her, smiling, and suddenly an army of caterers came filing through the restaurant towards them.

"Max?" she asked as a waiter popped champagne and filled their glasses and another began to serve the hors d'oeuvres.

"This is your first time eating in The Ritz," he said.

"So?"

"Well, I didn't want anyone distracting you from your enjoyment and so I booked the whole restaurant."

Diana stared at him in amazement. "You booked the whole restaurant?"

"Yes." He raised his champagne glass to her and said, "Cheers!"

Diana, in a state of shock, raised her own glass, chinked it against his and managed to say, "Cheers".

Next stop London. They stayed with Elliott and Thelma.

"What has you so happy?" Diana asked Max as they made their way to a party.

"I'm delighted to be the man introducing you to London society," he said, reaching forward and kissing her.

Their stay in London was a constant whirl of invitations and Diana found herself growing close to Elliott and Thelma who she found as warm and welcoming as ever.

One night Diana and Max were at the Palladium and he had organised the royal box. Diana sat entranced by the show.

Suddenly Max stood up.

"Where are you going?" Diana hissed at him. "You'll miss the finale."

"I forgot something," he said and slipped out of the box.

Diana continued to be engrossed by the show and, as it came to an end, she clapped rapturously along with the rest of the audience.

Suddenly to her amazement she saw Max walk out onto the stage below.

A voice off stage addressed the audience. "Ladies and gentlemen, may I present to you – Mr Max Von Hoffsten."

Max approached the front of the stage and turned and smiled up at the box where Diana sat. Suddenly the spotlight shone on her and everyone was looking up at her.

"Ladies and gentlemen, I want to introduce you all to the most beautiful woman in London – my wife, Diana!"

The amused audience looked up at the embarrassed Diana.

"And if I may, I'll serenade you with a song, my wonderful Diana!" he said, and he started to sing 'If You Were the Only Girl in the World'.

Aware everyone was looking at her she managed to smile as he sang, though she was wishing the whole episode was over.

Later, as she waited for him in the foyer, he came bounding over to her.

"Max! Whatever possessed you? How did you organise it?" She was still astounded.

"I wanted to tell the world how much I love you," he said, picking her up and swinging her around.

"Max! Put me down!" she insisted and he let her go.

"Come on!" he said, taking her hand and marching her out. "We have to get to a party at the Café Royal."

"I think it's terribly romantic," said Thelma the next morning as the two women had breakfast.

"Well, I was terribly embarrassed. And I heard one woman say how crass the Germans were and how they think they can use their money to buy anything, even the London Palladium."

"Well, I for one would love if Elliott did something as romantic for me. The most romantic thing he has done for me since we were married was order me a tweed coat from Liberty department store! All of London is jealous of you, Diana."

"I just think he might be overcompensating because of the morganatic marriage we were forced into."

"Who cares? Just enjoy it. Anyway I think you're wrong, He loves you and it's in his nature to be like this."

"You and Elliott are coming down to the regatta as guests on Max's new yacht next month, aren't you?"

"Of course, wouldn't miss it for the world."

Diana was walking along the port at the regatta with Elliott and Thelma. Max had told them he would meet them there on his yacht.

"I had no idea there would be so many yachts here," sighed Diana.

"Which one is Max's?" asked Thelma.

"He didn't give me the name of it but just said it was the biggest here," said Diana.

"Well, that would be that one there. It's the biggest by far," said Elliott, nodding to a gigantic moored yacht.

"Let's go aboard then," said Diana.

Reaching the yacht, they walked up the gangplank and on to the boat.

"Max!" Diana called loudly.

A man came walking down the deck. "Can I help you, miss?"

"Yes – is this Max Von Hoffsten's yacht?" asked Diana.

Suddenly she heard her name being shouted and she saw an enormous yacht moored further out in the sea, much bigger than the one they were on. There on the deck was Max, waving at them.

"You're on the wrong boat!" he shouted at them.

"How were we to know which was the right one?" Diana shouted back, excited at the sheer size of the new yacht.

"I thought the name would be a giveaway!" he shouted.

And Diana saw her name – 'Diana' – engraved on the yacht's side.

Later that evening Diana and Max had an intimate dinner together on a table set up on the deck of the yacht as they sailed down the coast.

"Do you like your yacht?" asked Max.

"My yacht?" smiled Diana.

"Yes, it's got your name on it," said Max.

"That doesn't make it my yacht," said Diana with a smile.

"What's mine is yours, my darling."

After Diana's success in Paris and London, Max was most proud to display his new wife in Berlin, the capital of his own country.

Diana met with so many of Max's friends she could hardly remember their names, and she was even presented to the Kaiser.

But of all the delights Max showered on her in Berlin, the one that thrilled her most was when they returned to their hotel room one night after the theatre. To her astonishment, the entire room was filled with bouquets of flowers.

As ever Max watched her expression, savouring her look of surprise and delight.

In Ireland Maud, Simon and Warren were having breakfast in the dining room at Garonglen. Maud was scouring through the newspaper.

"Ah, here it is," said Maud and turned the paper round so that Simon and Warren could see the large photograph of Max and Diana in it.

"Don't they look smashing?" said Warren.

"What's does it say?" asked Simon.

Maud began to read the caption under the photograph: "*Max Von Hoffsten and his beautiful wife Diana pictured at Ascot yesterday. Diana Von Hoffsten, daughter of Maud and Simon Cantwell of County Meath, was voted the best-dressed woman on Ladies Day. Diana, dressed in an apricot ensemble, wooed the judges with her glamour and style.*" Maud looked up, baffled, and repeated, "Apricot?"

"Maud, isn't that wonderful? Who'd ever have thought we'd

have got to here?" said Simon.

"I knew we would," said Maud with a smile, then fixed Warren with a steely look. "You could do a lot better than that Hannah Roundtree, Warren. Take a leaf out of your sister's book. Or Dashiel's example – he's seeing a millionaire's daughter now. Don't hold this family back, Warren – we're heading to the top!"

Warren grabbed some toast and hastily left the room. "I'm going to check on the horses."

CHAPTER 25

The snow had melted away by the time they returned to the hunting estate in Germany. Diana marvelled at how different it looked, the rolling foothills of the Alps now swaying in meadows and wild flowers. As they drove up along the lakeshore to the house, she saw cows grazing in the fields.

As the car pulled through the arch into the courtyard off the house, Diana reached forward and kissed Max.

"What's that for?" he asked.

"No reason. I'm just so happy to be home," she smiled.

They left the car and walked arm in arm up the steps to the door and into the hall.

"Welcome home, Frau Von Hoffsten," said the butler, taking their coats.

"Oh, thank you, Marc. Our luggage is in the motor car," said Diana.

"Very well," nodded Marc.

"And if you could have tea brought to us immediately, please?" requested Diana as she and Max walked hand in hand into the drawing room.

Diana was startled to see Brigitte there.

"Here you are!" said Brigitte, rushing towards Max and embracing him.

They held each other tightly for what Diana thought was ages.

Brigitte drew back from him and seemed lost in an admiring trance as she stared at him.

"You look wonderful," she breathed. Then, as if suddenly remembering Diana was there, she turned and went to her. "As do you, Diana." She kissed her cheek.

"Brigitte, how lovely to see you. We didn't expect you to be here," said Diana, managing to smile.

"Well, I came back especially from Vienna to be here for when you arrived."

"Very thoughtful of you," said Diana.

Brigitte grabbed Max's hand and led him over to the couch to sit down. "I've been so busy organising Alexandra and Hugo's wedding. They are getting married in Munich."

As Brigitte droned on about the wedding arrangements to her attentive audience, Diana raised her eyes to heaven and left the room to go upstairs to change.

Max had gone to Munich early to meet his father about brewery business. Diana, being a deep sleeper, hadn't been woken by him leaving and as she awoke the light was streaming in through the French windows. Diana turned and saw a rose left on Max's pillow beside her. Smiling, she reached for the rose then got out of bed and went to the French window. She opened it and walked out onto the balcony. She smiled happily and inhaled the fresh early-summer air as she looked out across the sparkling lake in the morning sunshine.

Her peace was disrupted by the bedroom door opening and Brigitte walking in, calling loudly, "Diana?"

It unnerved Diana that Brigitte tended to walk into their bedroom without ever even knocking.

"Good morning, Brigitte," said Diana, coming back into the room and putting on her dressing gown.

"Hello, Diana. I just wanted to check if you were up yet."

"Well, if I wasn't I would be by now." Diana sat down at the dressing table and began to brush her hair. "Can I help you with something, Brigitte?"

"I just thought since Max is away we could spend the day together."

"Well, I'd planned to go riding on Halcyon."

"Oh that's fine, I can go with you."

Diana felt irritated even though she knew Brigitte was only trying to be friendly.

Brigitte approached Diana and, taking the brush from her, began to brush her hair.

"You know, Diana, Max was so proud of you in Paris and London and Berlin."

"Was he?"

"Oh, yes. The way you handled yourself in society. That's what he wanted. He's getting full credit for finding you and discovering you. You were a find, an unpolished diamond that he has brought to full potential."

Diana reached for the brush and snapped it from Brigitte's hand. "Brigitte, Max loves me for who I am, not what he could turn me into."

"Of course he does, that goes without saying."

"Then what exactly are you saying?"

"I'm saying you're wonderful, that's all! As I keep telling Max, I approve of you."

Diana placed the brush down on the dressing table. "I'm a little tired of being approved of or disapproved of around here. When is everyone just going to accept me for who I am?"

Brigitte looked at Diana in amused confusion.

Diana stood and quickly walked to the door and held it open.

"Thank you, Brigitte. Would you mind if we didn't go riding today together? It's just that I need to concentrate on Halcyon. I've been neglecting him with all the travel."

Brigitte shrugged. "Of course. You don't want to neglect Halcyon. I know how much he means to you. Max told me how you lost your mind when he tried to buy him at the beginning of your courtship." She smiled at Diana as she left the room.

Diana felt invigorated as she rode Halcyon through the meadows around the lake. As she trotted along, the workers in the fields waved and smiled at her.

"Hello, Frau Von Hoffsten? How are you today?" a worker called to her.

"Very well, thank you!" she called back.

It was the same in the town when she went down there. The people on the streets and in the shops welcomed her kindly.

That evening she got back to the stables and handed Halcyon over the Paul who was the head groom. He was a man of around fifty who had been always respectful to her.

"Is my husband back from Munich yet?" asked Diana.

"Yes, he's back an hour," said Paul. "Frau Von Hoffsten, I was thinking that Halcyon has been out of his routine since arriving from Ireland. If you like we could start training him again so he can race soon."

"That would be wonderful, Paul. I've certainly been neglecting Halcyon's training with all the travelling and entertaining."

"A new foal was born last night. Would you like to see him?"

"Oh, I'd love to, Paul."

"I'd welcome any input from you with his nurturing. I believe you are one of the best horsewomen in Ireland."

That night Diana came into the drawing room and found Brigitte there reading.

"Did you have a good day with Halcyon?" asked Brigitte.

"Very much so . . . I'm sorry if I was a bit off earlier . . . I'd love to spend tomorrow with you."

Brigitte closed over her book and smiled. "Of course. Let's go into Munich to shop."

That night in bed Max had his arms around Diana.

"It's such a wonderful country," she said. "Everyone looked so happy today. I think I'm really going to love my life here."

"Well, they are delighted to have a beautiful and wonderful lady of the manor," he said.

Diana giggled. "I don't feel like the lady of the manor."

"Well, you are. I am the heir here and you are my wife. The Von Hoffstens used to own and run this whole county. Even when we were absolute rulers here, we and the people always got on well. And you are following that tradition."

"That's a nice relationship to have. My father says in every Irishman lies the heart of a republican. So at home in Ireland there's always some resentment against our class. Life at Garonglen is wonderful, but there's always a feeling that we're on borrowed time there. But here, there's a feeling nothing could ever go wrong." She leaned forward and kissed him.

"Well, in that case, why don't you help organise this year's festival?"

"What festival?"

"It's tradition every year during the summer that the local gentry family hosts a party for the estate workers and the locality. We're having it in June this year. You can help organise it."

"But isn't that the kind of thing Brigitte usually does?"

"You are the lady of the manor, so it should be your role. Besides, I think Brigitte is too preoccupied with Hugo and Alexandra's wedding."

CHAPTER 26

The cream of German and Austrian society turned out for Hugo and Alexandra's wedding in Alexandra's home state Howstein. As Diana watched Alexandra glide up the aisle in a fittingly regal dress towards Hugo and his best man Max, she couldn't help thinking they were robbing her and Max of their proper destiny.

After a rather hesitant-looking Hugo stammered his vows, the marriage was sealed, and Diana observed Conrad with a happy expression on his face for once.

Max and Diana followed the caravan of vehicles after the marriage ceremony to the wedding reception that was being held at Alexandra's family seat.

As Diana got out of the car and looked up at the yellow-painted palace she said to Max, "It's no wonder your father turned his nose up at Garonglen."

"Well, he might have turned his nose up at Garonglen but I turned my nose up at Alexandra." He leaned forward and kissed her.

As they mingled with the rest of the aristocracy for the champagne reception Diana noticed that Conrad steadfastly avoided her and didn't even attempt to greet her. For that matter, apart from a quick acknowledgement of her congratulations at the cathedral, Alexandra and Hugo ignored her as well.

The bell sounded and the guests all made their way into a gigantic reception room, the walls of which were painted a powder blue, where the light from the large arched windows flooded onto the long exquisitely dressed tables.

Max and Diana were among the last to enter. They followed a footman to their table.

"This table is at the bottom of the room," Max said, frowning at their un-prestigious placing.

The footman pulled out a chair. "Frau Von Hoffsten, this is your place."

As Diana sat down Max looked at the full tables and saw there was no other spare seat.

"And where is my seat?" questioned Max in bemusement.

"If you could follow me to your table, sir," said the footman.

"What do you mean – my table? I'm naturally sitting at the same table as my wife," said Max.

"Actually you are being seated at the head table with the groom's party, sir," said the footman.

"There must be some mistake. Of course I and my wife are sitting together," said Max.

"No mistake, sir. The seating arrangements are as planned."

"Under whose orders?" demanded Max, becoming angry.

The footman blinked a few times but remained silent.

"*Well?*" shouted Max, causing the footman to jump and others to look over concerned.

Diana got up quickly and went to Max and whispered, "Max, please don't make a scene. Just let it go."

"No! I will not have you treated in this way!" Max said loudly.

"Max, it really doesn't matter," she pleaded, conscious that the scene was attracting much attention.

"Of course it matters!"

At that moment Conrad, at the head table, rose to his feet and walked down to Max and Diana.

"What's going on here?" he demanded.

"There has been a mix-up with the seating and Diana has been placed down here instead of at the top table," said Max.

Conrad glanced at Diana. "So what? What does it matter? Max, come up to the head table – you're delaying the meal being served."

Seeing what was going on, Alexandra made her way through the tables to them.

"There will be no meal served until we are given the respect deserved by me, your heir, and my wife."

"Your *morganatic* wife," Conrad sneered under his breath.

"My wife in the eyes of the law and the church, and no matter what you do it will not change that, dear father." Max's voice was low but stern.

Alexandra looked at the two men staring at each other defiantly and then at the guests murmuring and whispering to each other. She waved her hand in the air. "So go! Take her to the head table." She turned to the footman. "Quickly, bring another chair to the table and squeeze her in."

"For goodness sake, boy, do you always have to make a fuss about everything?" snapped Conrad as he and Alexandra walked off together.

Max turned to Diana.

"Thank you," she whispered to him as she slipped her hand into his. The two of them walked hand in hand across the hall to take their seats side by side at the head table.

For much of the wedding banquet Diana and Max held hands under the table. As Diana observed Hugo, who looked unhappy and quiet throughout the day, she felt sorry for him as she wondered what pressure and blackmail he had been put under to marry Alexandra to achieve his father's dynastic ambitions.

Diana leaned over to Max and whispered, "I may have been a left-handed bride, but better that than a reluctant groom!"

CHAPTER 27

Diana ploughed into organising the annual festival and found it a wonderful opportunity to get to know the estate workers and locals even more.

It was a beautiful June morning, the day of the festival, and Diana and Max were having breakfast in the dining room.

Gerti, the head housekeeper, cleared away Diana's plate.

"Thank you, Gerti. How is your husband now?"

"Oh, he's much better, Frau Von Hoffsten. The flu is nearly gone. Your cure worked, thank you so much," said Gerti.

"What cure is this?" asked Max, looking up curiously.

"Oh, it's a cure my old nanny had in Ireland. You take whiskey and add honey, sugar and lemon and then boil it and drink it down in one go," said Diana.

Max pulled a face. "Sounds revolting!"

"Nanny used to say it will either kill you or cure you, to be fair," laughed Diana.

"Well, it cured my husband," smiled Gerti as she left the room.

Max finished his coffee. "You've put so much work into today. All the workers appreciate it so much, Diana."

"It's been a great opportunity to get to know them better. Besides, at least with me organising it I will ensure I'm not seated out in the middle of the lake! When are the clan arriving?"

"Brigitte arrives from Vienna at eleven. Father and the newlyweds arrive from Munich at eleven thirty."

"I wonder how Alexandra and Hugo are doing living with your

father in Munich. It's not exactly the most romantic situation for newlyweds."

"I believe they are getting on famously. Besides, the schloss is so large they're not living exactly on top of each other."

"I wouldn't know, having never been invited to your father's home. He invites one daughter-in-law to live with him, and his other not even for a cup of tea."

"Well, when I'm count, it will be our home to do what we want with it."

"Indeed – caretaking it for Alexandra and Hugo's children," said Diana, unable to keep the resentment out of her voice.

The town hall was a large traditional building with a wide forecourt that ran along the lakeshore and that was where the festival was being held.

As Diana and Max circulated amongst the people there, Diana looked around, feeling content. There were long rows of tables set out in the forecourt overlooking the lake and seated at the tables were the estate workers and their families as well as many of the townspeople who owed their livelihood to the Von Hoffsten estate. There were German and Bavarian flags hanging all around the area. Traditionally dressed waitresses were rushing back and forth from the beerhaus with jugs of beer for the tables. A band was playing traditional music. A long stand had been erected in front of the lake, on which there was a table for the Von Hoffstens. Diana glanced over at the table where Alexandra and Hugo sat, Alexandra smoking and looking unimpressed as she surveyed the crowd.

Conrad was talking to Paul, the head groom, at the foot of the steps leading up to the stand.

"Another wonderful year for the estate, Paul," he said. "And wonderful work done at the stables."

"I'm glad you are pleased, Your Excellency," said Paul. "I think it is going to be a bumper year with the harvests."

Conrad viewed Diana suspiciously as she went around chatting to the workers.

"The Irishwoman has not being getting in the way, one hopes," he said.

Paul looked surprised. "On the contrary, Your Excellency. She has fitted in extremely well. She has a genuine interest in the estate."

"I'm sure she has," said Conrad cynically.

"She has been a great help in the stables," said Paul.

"She helps in the stables?"

"All the time. She loves horses, and has been a great help to us, advising us on nurturing foals," Paul informed him.

"Really?" said Conrad, surprised.

Alexandra sat at the table, the lake dotted with small boats sailing behind her. She inhaled from her cigarette as she observed Diana go around the tables, chatting to the workers as they ate the feast laid on for them.

Brigitte sat beside her, eating.

"For the life of me, I don't understand what Max sees in her," said Alexandra.

"They say love is blind," said Brigitte.

"She doesn't even know how to deal with the workers, the farm peasants. She is going around talking to them as if they are friends, instead of keeping an appropriate distance from them," said Alexandra.

"They love her though, the locals," said Brigitte.

"Who needs their love? It's their respect that is needed," said Alexandra. "No sign of a baby yet?"

"No, none," said Brigitte.

"I suppose there is no pressure on them to produce an heir, as it will be my baby who will be the ultimate heir here," said Alexandra.

Brigitte paused from eating her pork and stared at Alexandra as she tossed her cigarette into the lake behind her.

Max and Diana walked up the steps to the stand and were followed by Conrad. They all took their seats at the table.

Paul the groom walked up to the stand and signalled for the band to stop playing.

"Friends, it a great pleasure for us to be here again today enjoying Count Von Hoffsten's hospitality. We have enjoyed another year of prosperity and good health and happiness and we look forward to another year of the same."

The crowd clapped.

"We all owe the count and his family gratitude not just for today but for their patronage and continued support."

The crowd got to their feet and clapped loudly while Conrad waved to them.

"And a big welcome and thank you to the new lady of the manor, Frau Diana Von Hoffsten!"

The crowd clapped and cheered. Paul walked down from the stand and took a little girl from the crowd by the hand. The girl was holding a large bunch of wild daisies and he led her up to the stand towards Diana.

"My daughter, Celine, would like to present you with this little bouquet."

Tears sprang to Diana's eyes as she got up and walked over to the little girl. She bent down, kissed her cheek and thanked her for the flowers.

Max then gestured for Diana to say something.

Holding Celine's hand and the daisies in her other hand, she said, "Thank you all, I –"

Suddenly a man came running from the street in amongst the tables. Diana recognised him as the town mayor and he looked panic-stricken.

Suddenly the man started shouting. "They've shot Franz Ferdinand and his wife! The Austrian emperor's heir and his wife have been assassinated!"

"Well, that kind of ruined the day!" said Brigitte.

The family had returned to the house and were in the drawing room.

Alexandra shook her head. "I can't believe it! I can't believe they would do such a brutal thing!"

"What exactly happened?" asked Diana.

"The Archduke and his wife were visiting Serbia, a corner of the Austrian empire, when an assassin jumped out and fired shots at them, killing both of them stone dead," said Alexandra.

"It was probably the Serbians separatists, looking for independence," said Conrad.

"Savages!" said Alexandra. "Well, they've crossed a line this time, to kill our heir! We must do everything possible to find the culprits and make them pay!"

"And the German empire will be behind you every step of the way," said Conrad.

Although Diana doubted that Alexandra and Conrad were responsible for German and Austrian foreign policy, she understood they reflected their government and people's positions.

CHAPTER 28

Over the next month, while the consequences of the assassination pushed the Continent towards war as frantic diplomacy failed, Max arranged for him and Diana to make a trip back to Ireland to see her family at Garonglen.

Diana was so thrilled to be going home that she was almost oblivious to the growing danger. She marvelled at how much her own life had changed since she had left and all the new things she had experienced. She imagined the magic of home was that nothing would ever change there. It would always remain the same.

And so it seemed when she saw Garonglen again.

The family had a lavish dinner to welcome Diana and Max home.

"I just can't imagine what the shooting of this archduke has to do with us, tragic as it is to shoot a man and his wife in cold blood," observed Maud as she sipped her wine.

"On the surface nothing, but in reality it is going to affect everybody," said Max.

"I'd never even heard of this archduke before," said Simon.

"I suppose it's as serious an issue as if an Irish republican had assassinated the Prince and Princess of Wales," said Diana.

Maud shuddered at the thought. "I suppose, if you put it like that."

"My sister-in-law, the Princess Alexandra –" began Max.

"I recall her," said Maud acidly.

"Well, she's so outraged she's ready to take a gun and go to war herself," said Max.

Diana looked at Max wryly. "And I'm sure she'd make an excellent warrior."

"If there is a war and we are involved, I think it would be quite exciting," said Warren.

"Warren, don't!" snapped Maud.

"I'm just saying I never thought I'd ever get to see any life beyond Garonglen and the county hunt balls. It would be the most exciting thing that ever happened to me."

Max sighed and took Diana's hand. "It's excitement we could do without." His face creased as he realised that nobody seemed to understand the consequences for them as a couple, least of all Diana.

"Anyway, enough of this war talk," said Maud. "After your stay here, you're on to London to stay with the Ashenbrys?"

"Yes," smiled Diana.

"I always knew they would be great friends of yours. You just needed to meet the right husband on their level!"

Diana managed to catch up with all her old friends during her stay, but she noticed Max had become more solemn and by early August realised the worsening situation in Europe was the cause. The tangled web of political alliances around Europe was drawing everyone into the conflict. Germany and Austria declared war on Serbia, which was followed by a declaration of war with Russia. France's alliance with Russia ensured that France was involved. As Britain tried to stay on the sidelines it looked as if it would soon be obliged to honour its alliance with France and Russia.

After their trip to Ireland Max and Diana were due to visit London, but, as Max and Diana talked with her parents and Dashiel in the drawing room at Garonglen, that trip looked out of the question.

"We'll naturally have to cancel our trip to London," said Max.

Diana was slightly dazed. She had never expected it would come to this, thinking that a solution would be found at the last minute.

"Yes, of course," said Diana. "We'll have to pack and return to Germany immediately."

Max looked at Diana. "I'll be returning to Germany, Diana, but you'll be staying here at Garonglen."

Diana was confused. "I don't understand. Why would I be staying here? Of course I'm going home with you."

"Diana, you don't understand anything. I'm to report for duty as soon as I return to Germany. I've been given a commission as an officer in the German army. I'm going to war."

His words filled her with fear and terror. "Regardless, Max, I'm still going back to Germany. Of course I am, what else could I do?"

Max was becoming angry. "You stay here in safety in Ireland, well away from the war and with your parents' security around you."

"And abandon my husband as he goes to war?" Diana was horrified.

"It's the only option." Max went and sat down beside her and took her hand.

"Max is absolutely right of course, Diana. You have to stay here," agreed Maud.

"I will not stay here!" said Diana. "I will be there, waiting and supporting him until he comes home."

"Supporting me? Supporting me against your home country?" he said.

"Max is right, Diana," said Simon. "You're in a very precarious situation. You're British. I don't think you can be seen to support Germany."

Diana laughed dismissively. "I don't care for politics. And frankly I don't care who's right or wrong. As far as I can see from the whole absurd situation, they're having a war about nothing. What I care about is my marriage and my husband and I will be at his side or waiting for him."

"Diana! You're being ludicrous!" Maud became angry.

"I'm being a wife, and a loyal and dedicated one," said Diana.

"But this means we'll be fighting on different sides," said Warren. "We'll be fighting on one side and Max and you will be on the other. We'll be enemies."

"*You* won't be fighting on any side, Warren," said Maud crossly.

"Why won't I?" Warren demanded.

"Because – because you'll be staying here at Garonglen. You have work to do here so you'll be excused from military service because you are an essential worker," said Maud.

Warren laughed dismissively. "Essential worker? What – breeding racehorses?"

Diana looked at Max accusingly. "This is why we're back here, isn't it? This is why you arranged our holiday back to Garonglen – so you could dump me here with the war situation getting worse."

"I only want to do what's best for you."

"Easily known you wouldn't discuss it with me beforehand! Trying to arrange things to your own liking again."

"None of this is to my liking, Diana. The last thing I want is to go to war against my wife's country where I have so many friends."

"That's enough of that," said Simon, seeing Maud was getting very upset.

He went over to Diana and sat down beside her.

"Diana, you've always been headstrong. But I really urge you to take Max's and our advice and not return to Germany. There could be grave consequences for you if you go back."

"I have made my mind up. I'll be going home with my husband."

Max and Diana arranged to leave early the next day. As she hugged the family in the forecourt outside Garonglen Diana had a dreadful feeling in her stomach. She felt nothing would ever be the same again.

Maud seldom cried but she was in a full flight of tears that morning.

As Diana got into the motor car and saw Max shake hands with Dashiel, she looked up at Garonglen and all the memories of it over the years came flooding back to her.

CHAPTER 29

Max and Diana just managed to get back to Munich in time as war was declared.

The streets of Munich were thronged with excited people singing patriotic songs and celebrating. She wasn't sure what on earth they were celebrating. The newspapers reported similar scenes across Europe from Ireland to Russia. It was like a cloud of madness had descended across the continent and people didn't understand what they were marching towards. She saw it with her own brothers Dashiel and Warren, excited at the prospect of going to France and seeing the world, and the perceived excitement of war. She was glad that Max seemed to abhor the thought of war as much as she did. But then, as a couple married from two different sides, they had more to fear, she realised.

When they got home to the hunting lodge, Max's call-up papers were waiting for him.

"So I'm to be Captain Max Von Hoffsten," he said in the drawing room that night.

"I've always loved a man in uniform," Diana said wryly.

They walked through the French windows and out to the balcony. There was much merriment and celebrating down in the town as all the men had signed up for the army straight away.

"Will you be all right here on your own?" asked Max, his face creased with concern.

"Of course I will. It's you we need to be worried about. Getting you home safe and sound."

"The last time Germany went to war with France, it was over in a few weeks," said Max.

"Yes, but Britain, Russia and everybody else wasn't involved that time," said Diana. "And what will happen, Max, after the war? Regardless of who wins, we are caught between the two sides. What will happen if Germany loses – how will it affect our lives? And if Britain loses, what will happen to my family?"

"Everything will return to normal, you'll see," he said, smiling at her reassuringly.

"Will you promise me something, Max?"

"Anything."

"From now on just tell me everything. No more secrets, only the truth. I can handle it, you know. I'm not a child. I'm a strong person. You can tell me anything."

Max nodded and held her close.

Those last few days together with Max, before he was to be transported to training and then the front, were precious. Diana kept expecting a heartbroken and wailing Brigitte to arrive at the house to disrupt their time together. But the chaos on the trains caused by the outbreak of the war meant she couldn't easily get a train from Vienna.

To Diana's surprise Hugo was excused from military duty due to the fact that he suffered from asthma.

"He was always quite weak with it," Max explained.

"It seems unfair that Alexandra, with all her warmongering, should be spared from her husband going to the front, while I, who hate war, am losing you! What's he going to do while the rest of you are at war?"

He smiled at her. "I imagine continue to work at the brewery and deal with Father, not to mention Alexandra. He doesn't have an easy life, Diana."

"I have always felt slightly sorry for him, despite everything. A father like that, a wife like that, a stammer – and asthma on top of everything!"

"Of all people, going to war might have released him from the

176

life he has. But he won't even get that opportunity."

"Well, he could have stood up to your father and made his own life like you did."

"It's different for him. I'm my father's heir, he's not. As my father's heir I'm entitled to my income, but Hugo could be cut off at any moment. Will you write to me?"

"Of course I will – but you'd better write back!" she said, suddenly feeling tearful.

"I'll send my letters scented with my cologne. It will be a signal to you that all is okay, and I'll come back to you."

Diana was reading a letter from her mother.

It's hard to believe what is happening here. Everyone is going to war. Both Dashiel and Warren have enlisted as officers, despite my pleas that they are essential workers. They insist it is their patriotic duty, but I sense they are excited to be going, especially Warren. Yours brothers are positively jingoistic these days. Dashiel has just graduated top of his class with his law degree. But instead of going to practise at the bar, he's going to France to fight a war! Myself and your father will be left alone here. I wish you had stayed with us.

CHAPTER 30

The day that Max was to depart for the front, there was a lunch at Conrad's *schloss* in Munich. As Diana and Max were driven through the gates and the gardens to the *schloss*, Diana marvelled that this was the first time she had been invited to Conrad's home.

Max was wearing his officer's uniform.

"It took a war to get me through these gates," said Diana as they walked up the steps and were shown inside by a butler.

"Max!" screamed Brigitte as she came rushing down the circular staircase and threw herself into his arms. She gripped him tightly. "I was so frightened I wouldn't get back in time before you left! Vienna was hectic – the whole city is mobilising. I couldn't get on a train out of there!"

Max stroked her hair as he soothed her. "It's all right, darling – you're here now." He kissed her hair.

Even now, on the brink of Max going to war, Diana was overtaken by discomfort as she watched her husband and his sister. In moments like this it was like the rest of the world didn't exist for them.

"Hello, Diana," said Brigitte eventually, wiping away her tears. Diana nodded at her.

"I kept hoping you'd fail your medical like Hugo did," said Brigitte as she led Max down a corridor towards the dining room.

Diana followed them.

"No, I'm in my full health," smiled Max.

"I don't know how I'm going to cope without you," said Brigitte as she opened the dining-room doors and they entered a large circular room with French windows which opened up onto beautiful lawns.

There at a circular table were Conrad, Hugo and Alexandra.

"Ah, you're here," said Conrad. "Hurry up and sit down, boy – the food is ready to be served this past thirty minutes."

"You look well in your uniform, Max," complimented Alexandra as she lit her cigarette.

"Good afternoon, everybody," smiled Diana as she sat down.

"G-g-g-good a-a-afternoon, Diana," stammered Hugo.

"How was your journey to Ireland?" asked Alexandra.

"Wonderful. It was good to see everybody before the war started," said Diana.

"What side of the fence does your family sit on with the war?" questioned Alexandra.

"What do you mean by that?" asked Diana, confused.

"Well, one never knows with the Irish, does one?"

"My family are pro-British naturally and they and all our friends and relatives are on the British side."

"Are they actually involved in the war?" asked Conrad.

"Both my brothers have taken their posts as officers in the British army," said Diana.

Nobody said anything as silent looks were exchanged.

"So what are you doing here then?" asked Alexandra eventually.

"I'm here because my husband is here," said Diana. "I think I should explain I don't support this war in the least. I don't know what it's about. I don't think anyone does really."

"It's about power, you fool – everything in life is," snapped Alexandra.

"Alexandra!" objected Max angrily.

"My point is there is nothing that couldn't be resolved without this stupid war and I'm not going to take sides in it," said Diana defiantly.

"Your neutral position sounds all very commendable, but unworkable," said Conrad. "Of course you'll have to take up a position as the war progresses. You're in an impossible situation with your husband and your family. But you'll have to take sides. Even cousins the King of England and the Kaiser of Germany have to take sides, so I don't think your claiming immunity will get you very far."

"I shouldn't worry, Diana," said Max. "The Germans will smash through France in a few weeks and will be in Paris by Christmas."

That evening Diana walked Max down the platform in the Hauptbahnhof, Munich's main railway station. The platform was packed with excited troops being waved off by their cheering loved ones.

"I've instructed the driver to take you straight back to the estate," said Max.

"Yes, well, your father and family didn't extend an invitation to me to stay with them the night in Munich," she pointed out.

He sighed. "I wished you'd stayed in Ireland."

"Well, I'm glad I'm here, waiting for you when you return," she smiled.

The conductor blew his whistle and the troops quickly got on the train.

Max kissed Diana.

"You'll miss the train if you don't get on now, sir," said the conductor.

Max tore himself away from Diana and quickly got on the train as it began to take off.

She stood there as the train gathered speed and she waved him off along with all the others on the platform.

CHAPTER 31

Life at the hunting estate changed overnight with the war and Max gone. Diana found herself alone in the rambling historic house. Even the staff were whittled down to nothing. All the male staff of a certain age had enlisted and the female staff had migrated to Munich to start work in the factories and jobs vacated by the men. Paul, because he was fifty, was excused from going to war and Diana was grateful he was still there to run the stables and help run the estate.

"I'm not going yet, but who knows when I might have to go," he said to her one day out in the stables.

"I'm sure the war will be over long before they start enlisting men of your age," said Diana, thinking of his young family and hoping he wouldn't have to go.

"I'm not sure what is going to happen to the estate," he said as they left the stables and he walked her towards the house.

"How do you mean, Paul?" asked Diana.

"There are no workers left to attend to the harvests or the farming. We're trying to manage with the older men and women and children. But there's not nearly enough of them."

"Well, what instructions and plans did my husband leave?" asked Diana.

"None. The war came so quickly the running of the estate was the last thing on his mind."

"And what of my father-in-law, the count?"

"He's forwarded no instructions or contingency plans."

"Well, I shouldn't worry about it," said Diana. "I'm certain His Excellency will put something in place soon to run the estate efficiently."

"In Britain, farm workers have been named as essential workers and are not expected to enlist in the war – to make sure agriculture isn't disrupted," said Paul.

Diana nodded and headed back to the house.

Diana was sitting alone in the dining room having breakfast when Gerti came in holding an envelope.

"The post has arrived," said Gerti, smiling as she handed over the letter.

Seeing the handwriting was Max's, Diana held it to her heart in delight. Max had kept his word and managed to write to her often.

As Gerti cleared away the breakfast plates, Diana asked, "Any word from your own husband?"

Gerti smiled sadly and shook her head. "Not since the letter three weeks ago."

Diana reached out and took her hand. "I'm sure he's fine."

Gerti nodded. "To think a few months ago all I was concerned about was him getting over his flu!"

Diana left the dining room and crossed the hall into the drawing room. She closed over the doors and nestled into the couch, holding the letter close to her. She then slowly opened it and allowed herself to be immersed in the emerging smell of Max's cologne that he, as he had promised, always doused the writing paper with. And as she let the scent overpower her and closed her eyes it was as if Max was there with her for a few seconds.

She began to read the letter.

My darling Diana,

Well, we're not in Paris yet! We appear to have got bogged down in Northern France as I'm sure you've heard. Two great armies came face to face here and instead of a giant battle to the finish as has happened in all previous wars, we all sort of dug in. Giant trenches on both sides. Facing each other across this area we call

182

no-man's land. I can see the Tommies across from us in the distance and they can see us. The men's morale is very high but we didn't expect the casualties to hit us quite so fast. We are just biding our time for now. We expect that we'll make an advance very shortly and overpower the British and French. The trouble is, darling, that every time we go to make a move, their machine guns start spraying, putting an immediate stop to our advance. I think of you all the time. Morning, noon and night. I picture you there in our home and all the happy times we had together. And all the happy times we'll have again. I like to get your letters. The post is coming through fine to us, so please write to me as often as you can. Just seeing your handwriting makes me happy.

I love you, M x.

Diana clutched the letter close to her as she wiped away a tear.

As Diana had envisaged there was little contact from Max's family except for Brigitte. Conrad, Hugo and Alexandra remained in the *schloss* in Munich while Brigitte travelled out to her to stay regularly. Sometimes Brigitte became so morose and distraught over Max that Diana wished she didn't come as she only managed to upset her further.

"I've been wondering whether your father has made any mention about the running of the estate here, Brigitte?"

"No, not from what I've heard." Brigitte looked unperturbed.

"It's just some of the workers have expressed concern that there's no one to run the estate," said Diana.

"Who cares? When Max isn't here! The newspapers are saying we've made huge advances and suffered very few casualties. But that's not what I'm hearing on the streets. I've heard about a lot of families in Munich who have had someone gunned down."

"There is strict censorship, as I understand it," said Diana.

"I received a letter from Max last week. He sounded in good spirits."

"Yes, he does."

"When did you get a letter from him last?"

"Yesterday."

Brigitte looked excited and suddenly sat forward. "Diana, may I read it?"

Diana was astonished. "No, Brigitte, I'd rather you didn't."

"In fact, if I could read his last few letters, it would give me a bigger connection with him, make me feel not so alone."

"No, Brigitte, I'm afraid that is not going to happen."

"But Max wouldn't mind in the least!"

"But I would!"

"But I don't understand – why would you mind?"

"Because they are personal letters between a husband and a wife." Diana was incredulous.

"Love letters! You simply have to let me read them, Diana," Brigitte insisted.

Diana became angry. "No, Brigitte! I will not let you read our personal letters. And I think you have some audacity to ask!"

"But I've known Max so much longer than you!"

"As his sister! There is a difference!"

"Are you trying to say you are more important to him than me?"

"No! We are each as important as the other, I'm sure, but in different ways!"

Brigitte became upset and tears started streaming down her face. "You're being a bitch, Diana. Nobody is more important to me than Max. *Nobody!* We've been together since conception."

"What are you talking about now?" Diana was becoming tired of her.

"As his twin sister, nobody knows him better than me, not even you, Diana!"

Diana looked at Brigitte, shocked. "Twin sister?"

"Yes, of course."

"But – but – I never knew."

"Was it never mentioned before?"

"No, it wasn't!" Diana felt alarmed by the revelation. Alarmed that she had never been told. And yet so many of the things about Max and Brigitte's relationship suddenly made sense. The closeness,

Brigitte's neediness, their little world together. But why did Max never tell her?

Diana stood up. "I have to go, Brigitte. I told Paul I'd assist him with a new foal." And she quickly left.

That night Diana lay fast asleep in her bed. Suddenly a piercing scream jolted her awake. She quickly put on the light and sat up, listening. A few seconds later there was another scream echoing through the house. Diana realised it was Brigitte again and realised she must be having one her painful episodes. She thought about how Max had reacted to his sister's screams. How for some reason he had just ignored them. She had thought him uncaring at the time.

She got out of bed and quickly went to the door. She double-checked that the door was locked and then returned to her bed and turned off the light, ignoring any more screams from Brigitte that night.

The excitement and carnival atmosphere that had overtaken the town after war was declared had died down. With most of the men now gone the town seemed much quieter, with an empty feeling, as Diana made her way through it on Halcyon. She stopped outside the post office and tied Halcyon to a lamppost as she went inside.

"Good afternoon, Herr Richter," she greeted the friendly postmaster.

"Ah, good day to you, Frau Von Hoffsten. It is good to see you." He smiled warmly.

"Any news from your boys?" She had spoken to him before about his three sons who had gone to the front.

"They've finished their training. Two have gone to the Western Front, and the youngest . . ." Richter's face clouded with worry, "has been sent to the Eastern front."

Diana smiled sympathetically at him. "I'm sure they'll return to you and your wife unharmed. I'm sure they will."

Richter smiled at her. "Thank you. And I see plenty of letters coming in from your good husband."

"Yes, Max is settling into his new role very well. In fact, I wanted to post this letter to him." She handed him an envelope. "And I also want to post these." She handed over four envelopes to him. They were letters to each one of her family in Ireland. She had addressed the ones to her father and brothers to Garonglen, knowing her mother would know where to post them to on the Western Front.

Richter looked up at her, confused. "But these are to Ireland in the United Kingdom."

"That's right, to my family."

"But I doubt the post will get through! Delivery of post to the front is a priority but the rest of the post in Germany is severely disrupted. And as for posting to a hostile country, I imagine it's impossible. The British have set up a naval blockade, stopping anything getting in or out of Germany. They've even cut the German telegraph wires to the United States."

"Well, I need to get word to my family in Ireland. Will you please at least try to send it?"

"I will try, but you might never hear back," warned Richter.

"Thank you, Herr Richter," nodded Diana.

Richter watched her as she mounted Halcyon outside. As she rode off he examined the envelopes and who they were addressed to: *Maud & Simon Cantwell . . . Captain Dashiel Cantwell . . . Captain Warren Cantwell.*

CHAPTER 32

Diana wished, hoped and prayed that Max would get leave from the front for Christmas. But Max revealed in his scented letters that such a thing was impossible. As an officer he couldn't abandon his post and go home while his men remained stationed. Diana understood.

As the snow had arrived in December, it had added to her isolation on the hunting estate with so little staff left there and no visitors. She remembered the previous winter there. The skiing, the parties, the crowds of visitors and friends of Max's. At the time she longed for a moment's peace alone with Max. Now she would give anything to have the house filled with laughter and fun again.

She wondered what Christmas would be like at Garonglen that year. She hoped her brothers would get leave and they could have a traditional Christmas there. She felt so cut off from home as she remembered the incredibly happy times she had there.

To her surprise an invitation was issued to her from Conrad to stay with them in Munich for the Christmas period. She wondered if Max had forced it or if even Count Conrad Von Hoffsten realised the heartlessness of leaving her alone as her husband fought for Kaiser and country over Christmas.

As she arrived at the *schloss* on Christmas Eve, she could hear a piano playing and Brigitte singing 'O Tannenbaum' at the top of her voice.

As the butler showed Diana into the parlour Brigitte broke away from her piano and rushed to her to embrace her.

"Oh, Diana, you're here. I was worried with the heavy snow you might have been stranded!"

"I managed to get here just fine," said Diana.

"Happy Christmas," said Alexandra, who was standing over by the piano, smoking a cigarette.

To Diana's surprise she saw that Alexandra was pregnant.

Hugo came over and greeted her with a kiss on the cheek. "Merry Christmas, Diana."

She smiled at him. "And to you, Hugo."

She sat down and the butler handed her a glass of sherry.

"No Conrad?" she asked.

"He's busy with work. He'll be down later," said Brigitte.

"As always," Diana said under her breath before turning to Alexandra. "I believe congratulations are in order. When are you due?"

"Another three months," said Alexandra as she puffed on her cigarette and drank her port.

"Good for you," said Diana.

"Yes, we're very happy. It's a great pity you didn't get pregnant before Max went to war – it would have given you something to do."

"We were in no rush," said Diana.

"No, I suppose you weren't as this child will be the ultimate heir, and not yours and Max's," she said, touching her stomach.

After Diana was shown to her room and she unpacked she joined the family for the rest of Christmas Eve which was subdued.

That evening in the parlour she watched the snow come down in the gardens and wondered what kind of Christmas Max would be having.

"I hope Max gets the Christmas package I sent him," said Brigitte. "I usually give Max silk ties, or satin dressing gowns for Christmas and birthdays. This year I sent him thick woollen socks and gloves."

"That's very thoughtful of you." Diana smiled appreciatively at her.

"Certainly more practical," said Alexandra. "I can't imagine Max having much use for a satin dressing gown in the trenches."

Brigitte stared into space. "It must be so cold there, with the snow and frost."

"And he's not used to uncomfortable surroundings, let's face it," said Conrad. "Between The Ritz in Paris, Claridge's in London and the Hotel de Paris in Monaco, that boy has never known a moment's discomfort."

"It will hit him so bad," agreed Alexandra. "So much worse for him than the others because, as you say, he's spoilt."

Diana found herself becoming angry. "Actually Max is a very strong and capable person. I've never known him not to take any situation in his stride."

Alexandra sneered. "What situation has he ever found himself in before? Coming second at the regatta at Cowes, or sitting beside boring company at a dinner table? That hardly compares to living in trenches and being shot at by enemy fire."

"W-w-w-what of your own family, Diana? Any word from them in Ireland?" asked Hugo.

"I'm afraid not. The post is too badly disrupted and it's impossible to send a telegram. I hope they're all right."

"Two brothers fighting for the British, isn't it?" said Alexandra.

"That's correct," nodded Diana.

The atmosphere in the room became very cold as Conrad's face froze.

"Tell me," said Conrad. "At night when you pray, who do you pray wins the war? Your husband or your family?"

Diana looked at him squarely. "I pray that this will be over soon and everyone will go home to their families. That Max will come home to us and my brothers home to Ireland, safe and sound where they all belong." She stood up. "And now if you'll excuse me I'll go to bed."

"Pious bitch!" spat Alexandra once Diana had left the room.

That night Alexandra sat at the dressing table in their bedroom, applying cold cream to her face as Hugo sat up in bed reading a book.

189

"I don't know why she has to join us for Christmas. It's obvious she doesn't want to be here as much as we don't want her here," said Alexandra.

"We owe it to Max to be h-h-h-hospitable to her," said Hugo.

"We owe Max nothing, and her even less," snapped Alexandra.

"I think we can at least try to be civil to her," urged Hugo.

"Why bother? In fact I think you are being *too* friendly to her," she said harshly. She turned and looked at him accusingly, her face a smooth mask of white cold cream.

He looked down at his book and continued to read. She got up and walked over to him, sat on the side of the bed, took the book and placed it on the side table. She took his hand and smiled.

"I just want you to realise how important you are," she said softly. "You have lived in Max's shadow for too long. Diana is nothing without Max." She took his hand and placed it on her stomach. "It is our child who will be the heir and you need to act to protect our child's future at all times. Do you understand?"

"Y-y-y-es."

"You need to start acting as the head of this family and be stronger, tougher. Make me and your future son *proud* of you."

After church on Christmas morning, Christmas dinner was served. As Diana watched the Von Hoffstens being served by the staff she realised how Max was so essential to this family. He was the life and soul of it. His larger-than-life personality and sense of fun filled all the gaps that were so obviously there when he wasn't present.

"Thank you," Diana said to a maid who put carved turkey onto her plate. She turned to Conrad. "Oh, Conrad, I meant to tell you. You know Paul who runs the stables on the estate –"

"Of course I do. He was born on the estate. I've known him since he was a boy."

"Yes, well, he's very concerned," said Diana. "Because most of the workers went to war, a lot of the harvest wasn't saved in the autumn. He's worried there might be a shortage of foodstuff for the livestock during the winter. Also there just aren't enough workers to run the estate. He's very worried about next year."

Conrad stared at Diana as if she were mad. "And what would you have me do?"

"Well, I –"

"In case you hadn't realised there's a war going on."

"Well, I know that, but –"

"Do you realise that the British, your country, has declared the whole North Sea a military zone?"

"Well, I realise that –"

"They are blockading us in. No ships are coming into our ports. We are getting no raw materials. The coal we produce at home is being used for the military effort and basic rations for people. Do you realise what that means?"

"Of course."

"Obviously you don't. It means that we can't keep the brewery running here in Munich. The brewery that has been running for two hundred years is now on a go-slow, as not only do we not have the workers to work there but neither have we the raw materials to keep it running. That is taking all my attention, and you come to me about these other issues!"

"It's the same for Austria," stated Alexandra. "The French have blockaded the Austrians in at the Mediterranean, allowing no supplies through from America, South America. All the usual places that supply us."

Diana spoke sternly. "I am only passing on everyone's concerns."

"The running of my estate has really nothing to do with you," said Conrad, "and I'd appreciate it if you stayed out of my business affairs in the future."

Diana looked at Conrad, astonished. And then her astonishment turned into outrage as she glanced around at everyone and the staff standing impassively around the table. She suddenly found herself shaking with anger.

"The running of that estate *is* my business!"

Everyone's face dropped in shock. Even the servants were shocked out of their impassive expressions.

"Whether you like it or not, I am Max's wife. He chose *me*."

191

Diana turned to Alexandra. "*Me*, Alexandra, not you! He chose me, who brought nothing to the table, over all your titles and your palace and your supposed breeding. Although if your manners are a product of your breeding then both are exceedingly poor."

"Diana," begged Brigitte. "Stop now before you regret it."

"Oh, I'll never regret this, Brigitte. Max chose me because he loved me. I never thought anybody could love somebody as much as he loves me. He even allowed you, Conrad, to bully him into a left-handed marriage, denying our children their natural heritage because he loves me so much. And that's something you all will never understand. And I feel sorry for you, because you will never have what Max and I have."

Conrad turned around to the servants. "Leave the room," he ordered.

"No – stay!" demanded Diana. "Now, I'm going to say this just once. Max is your heir and he will be master of the estate and the brewery and this *schloss* here. I am his wife and, although because of you I will never be countess, I will still be the mistress of this house and the Von Hoffsten family. And I will not be disrespected in future. The running of the estate *is* my business as it will be my husband's. And while he is away at the front, I will protect his interests. He is your heir, something you couldn't change even if you tried to destroy everything for us and our children." Diana stood up. "And Alexandra – that child you are carrying will have a lifetime's wait until he is the heir. Now thank you for the invite for Christmas, but I think it's time I was going."

Diana turned and marched out of the room. Upstairs she packed, the tears flowing down her face. She put on her coat and hat and marched downstairs to the hall where she instructed a footman to bring down her luggage.

"D-d-iana!" called a voice and she turned to see Hugo there. "Where are you going?"

"I'm getting the evening train back to the estate," she said.

"But you'll be on your own t-t-to-night. Max wouldn't want you to b-b-b-e alone Christmas night," said Hugo.

"I can't stay under the same roof as them any more."

Hugo nodded. "I'll organise the car to take you to the station."

"Thank you."

"I-I-I-I never wanted any of this, Diana," said Hugo. "It was all Father's decision, the morganatic marriage."

Diana sighed. "You should have stood up to him, like Max did."

"I'm not strong like Max."

"Well, I feel sorry for you then, Hugo," said Diana.

CHAPTER 33

Despite Diana's warning, Conrad showed no interest in the estate. Her outburst didn't shock him into visiting it to see what was going on. Paul and the other workers endeavoured to run things efficiently, but the sparse foodstuff meant the livestock were malnourished and some did not survive the harsh winter. Most of the horses had been drafted to the war effort. Diana had just managed to hold on to her beloved Halcyon.

Brigitte continued to make visits to her.

"I can't believe you spoke like that to Father on Christmas Day, in front of the staff!" Brigitte admonished her.

"He left me no choice. The man has been nothing but ignorant to me from the moment I met him. I simply won't stand for it any more."

"But nobody speaks to His Excellency like that!"

"And nobody speaks to me in the way he does. He wouldn't dream of speaking to Alexandra like that," said Diana.

Diana was relieved when the snow began to retreat in the spring. As Easter approached, she had heard nothing from her family since the outbreak of war and she felt increasingly isolated from them. Only Max's scented letters kept her spirits up.

The war was showing no sign of stopping and even though the newspapers were reporting glorious victories for the German troops, the report back of constant casualties at the front illustrated the high price being paid for victories.

She walked down the high street to post her letters and saw the post office was closed. She peered through the window to see if she could see Herr Richter.

"It won't be open today, Frau Von Hoffsten," said a woman as she passed her. "News came that one of his sons was killed."

"Oh, I see." Diana's face dropped in horror. "Thank you."

Despondent, she got into the car and drove back up through the hills to the house. She drove through the arch into the courtyard and got out of the car. Thinking of kind Mr Richter, she wiped away a tear.

As she made her way to the front door she saw a figure walking through the arch into the courtyard. It looked like a man in a soldier's uniform and she squinted to see who it was. As the figure approached in the sunshine, her eyes widened as she recognised him. And suddenly she was running across the courtyard. Running and jumping into the man's arms.

"You're back," she whispered into Max's ear as he held her tightly.

"Why didn't you tell me you were coming back?" she said as they lay in each other's arms in their bed.

"I wanted to surprise you. I wanted you to think every day that I might be coming back to you that day and just show up unexpectedly. If I warned you I was coming, then you wouldn't have that expectation in the future when I go back to the front."

"Or the disappointment each night when you don't come that day," she pointed out.

"But you still have the hope again next morning," he said, smiling.

She reached forward and kissed him. "I've missed you so much."

She studied his face. He was much paler than before he had gone. That natural bronzed glow he always seemed to have was no more. He was thinner too and his eyes didn't seem to have the sparkly glint they used to have.

"Is it unbearable there?" She was frightened to ask.

"No," he gave a dismissive laugh. "It's not that bad at all. It's not The Ritz, but we make do."

"There are so many men from the town who have been killed. Some of them were in your regiment. But you never mentioned them in your letters."

Max suddenly smiled and jumped out of bed. "Right, let's make the most of every minute. I want to eat all the fabulous food I've been missing. And chocolate. I want chocolate and lots of it. And I want to go sailing on the lake with you for the whole day. I want to forget this war is even happening!"

Diana smiled and got out of bed.

The kitchens, in a side wing of the house, were large, light and airy. Diana made a visit and was looking at the empty larders with Gerti standing beside her.

"The lambing has started so we can have lamb. We've enough potatoes for some dinners but not so much that we can have them served every day this week," said Gerti.

"I didn't realise the larder was so far down," said Diana.

"It's very hard to buy anything because of the blockade. It's not my fault!" said Gerti, getting upset.

"I'm not saying it is!" said Diana. She smiled at Gerti. "I just want Max's stay to be as comfortable as possible. Do we have any chocolate and coffee?"

"There is no chocolate anywhere. It has run out. None is getting through the blockade and none is being manufactured. I manage to get a small amount of coffee for you every week. But not enough for His Lordship as well."

Diana nodded. "I don't need any coffee so make sure you just save it in future for Max. I'm sorry, I didn't realise you were having problems sourcing items."

"It's very hard to organise any food delivery here. At least you have livestock here so there is meat. Most people aren't getting any meat supplies."

Diana drove down to the local town and walked into the local grocer's which belonged to a woman called Angela Schneider. She had been in the grocer's plenty of times before, but was shocked to see the shelves weren't full of the usual abundance of products.

"Good afternoon, Angela," smiled Diana.

"Hello," said Angela, a middle-aged frumpy woman. "I believe your husband is home."

"Yes," smiled Diana. "It's wonderful to have him back."

"You're lucky. The local teacher was killed last week."

"Oh, how terrible! I remember him. He was such a nice intelligent young man. So pleasant!"

"Machine-gunned by the British." There was an accusing tone in Angela's voice as she looked at Diana coldly.

Diana noticed but ignored it. "I'm trying to make Max's stay as comfortable as possible so I wanted to buy some items."

"The lady of the manor never comes to do her shopping. Gerti usually arranges all the purchases for the big house," Angela said.

"Yes, but I believe Gerti is having problems getting some items."

Angela gave a dismissive laugh. "She's having problems because we don't have things to sell. All I have is what is on the shelves."

Diana was surprised at Angela's tone. All the people in the area had always given her the utmost respect as was fitting. But Angela's tone lacked respect.

Diana nodded and went to look at the shelves. There were soaps and detergents, but a severe shortage of food. There were cans of corned beef but when she checked she discovered they were out of date.

"I get the potatoes in on Monday. Whoever is here first gets served. Gerti usually makes sure she is here in plenty of time to get enough for the estate."

Diana turned and smiled at Angela. "What I'm really looking for is chocolate and coffee. Sugar. Max has a craving for them. And he wants bread of course and butter. All simple things, or at least they were."

Angela laughed derisorily. "There isn't a hope or a chance of getting such items. Not even for a Von Hoffsten, I'm afraid."

Diana looked to make sure no one was coming in and then leaned forward and spoke quietly. "I've heard that one can get such items if one is willing to pay more. I heard my sister-in-law say it.

I'm willing to pay quite a lot more."

Angela glared at her. "I've no idea what you're talking about. What you're suggesting is illegal. The black market."

Diana leaned forward again. "Name your price."

Angela stared at her and then she came from behind the counter. She locked the door and pulled down the blind. She then went out the back and arrived back a few minutes later with chocolate, coffee, tea, sugar and some other luxuries like biscuits, cake and fruit.

"I can only give you a small amount. I have to look after my regulars."

"I'll be one of your regulars," promised Diana.

Angela nodded while looking at the diamond necklace around her neck.

"You'll have to give me notice in future, and it's not cheap," said Angela, putting the items into a bag. "That will be two thousand deutschmarks."

Diana flinched when she heard the amount she was being charged. She opened her purse and handed the money over.

As she drove back to the house with her small stash of goodies, she thought about life before the war. The extravagance of the parties Max threw. The food that was constantly on offer to the guests. The bottles of champagne, the crates of caviar, the ice cream and bons bons and steak. And now she was begging for scraps and being exploited by a grocer's wife.

But it was all worth it that night as she and Max had an intimate dinner. As she watched his delight at being surprised with the chocolate and coffee and other items, she realised the pleasure he got from spoiling and surprising her all the time. As she watched his pale face light up when he tasted the chocolate, she realised it was so much more pleasure to give to a loved one than to receive.

For those few days in their Alpine retreat it was like the war didn't exist. They went sailing during the day on the lake or horse-riding up through the hills and at night dined on the treasures Diana got from Angela. She knew Max was not being honest with her about life at the front. His voice made light of everything, saying conditions were good. His eyes and his face said otherwise.

Brigitte was due to come and stay soon and Diana dreaded the visit, knowing that Brigitte would imprison Max, away from her.

Max was steering the small motor boat around the lake as Diana sat facing him in the prow.

"Max, why did you never tell me that Brigitte was your twin?" she asked.

"Did I not?" Max looked surprised.

"No. I was surprised when she told me. I never knew you had a twin."

"I suppose it wasn't that important or else it wouldn't have slipped my mind."

Diana sat forward. "You wouldn't confide in her anything you wouldn't confide in me, would you?"

"I don't understand you?"

"It's just you're so close to her. I know you're not telling me everything about the war and what you're going through. I just hope you didn't feel you couldn't tell me things but could tell Brigitte."

Max smiled at her. "Sounds like you're jealous of Brigitte."

"Maybe I am. And I'm missing my own family so much."

"No word at all?"

"There's no communication getting between the two countries."

"I wish you'd stayed in Garonglen that time."

"But then I'd have no communication with you and that's the one thing I really couldn't bear."

He smiled at her and reached out and took her hand. "You'll always have me, Diana. I promised you before and I meant it – I'll always come back to you."

CHAPTER 34

Diana opened the front door for Brigitte. Ignoring her, Brigitte raced right past her, across the hall and into the drawing room where she threw herself into Max's arms. Diana walked in after her and didn't know if she felt touched or disturbed by the vision in front of her. Brigitte was nearly strangling Max she was hugging him so tightly.

"Is it you? Is it you?" Brigitte asked loudly, pulling back and looking at him.

"Certainly looks like him," said Diana as she rang for tea.

"You look pale," said Brigitte as she sat down with Max, holding both his hands in hers.

"Ah, that's because I haven't been to the Riviera for a while," he laughed.

"You!" Brigitte slapped his arm playfully.

Gerti came in with the tray of tea and placed it on the coffee table.

"That's the last of the tea," Gerti whispered to Diana as she left.

Diana nodded quickly and went to pour the tea.

"What news in Munich?" asked Max, smiling.

"Alexandra has had her baby. A boy. George," announced Brigitte.

Diana's hand shook on hearing this and she spilled the tea slightly.

"Careful, Diana! We can't lose a drop of tea it's so scarce," warned Brigitte.

"The shortages are bad in Munich as well?" asked Diana.

"I imagine they are a lot worse than here as the population is so much greater. Our servants have to queue now even to get into a shop."

"And the boy is fine and healthy?" asked Max.

"Perfect in every way. Would Alexandra have it any other way?" Brigitte said knowingly.

Max looked into his tea. "The first of the next generation . . . Let's hope he'll never have to fight in a war."

"There are a lot of casualties arriving back in Munich. The hospitals are filled to capacity. Did I tell you I've started working at the psychiatric hospital?"

"No." Max was surprised.

"So many of the soldiers are arriving back with their minds broken. They are shaking and some can hardly talk. The army doesn't know what to do with them so they are being placed in the madhouse."

"With your training I'm sure you'll be a great help to them," said Diana.

"I hope so. All the women of our class are trying to do what they can for the war effort. You know the Baroness Von Flashan?"

"Of course," said Max.

"She is running a charity shop. People donate blankets and old clothes that are sent to the front. Her daughter is driving a tram!"

"I don't believe it!" Max was shocked.

"We all have to do our bit." Brigitte looked suspiciously at Diana. "I can help you find a suitable position with the war effort, Diana."

Diana looked uncomfortable.

"Let me see, what would suit you?" Brigitte studied her. "Have you ever done any nursing?"

"No, I haven't."

"But you can sign up to train."

"Brigitte, I won't be doing anything for the war effort."

Brigitte was astounded. "But of course you must. We all must! The women have to fill the men's places."

"It's impossible that I contribute, Brigitte."

"But why? What's wrong with you?"

"I can't contribute to the German side against my brothers and family on the other. I just can't do it. I'm sorry."

Brigitte looked surprised and then looked at Max who was staring off into the distance.

Diana took up her tea and started to drink.

The Von Hoffstens were having a gathering for Max in the *schloss* in Munich before he was to return to the front. Diana dreaded the prospect of staying there overnight and having to deal with Conrad and Alexandra again. Alexandra was appalling previously – she could only imagine how unbearable she would be now she had Baby George.

Remembering her own outburst at Christmas, Diana decided to continue the momentum and be in control of the situation. She dressed up and put on her best jewellery and proudly walked into the *schloss* on Max's arm.

The Von Hoffstens' close friends were gathered in the parlour and they all greeted Max warmly. Diana went straight to Alexandra who was with Baby George.

"He's a beautiful baby, Alexandra. Congratulations!"

"He never cries," said Hugo who stood proudly beside Alexandra, looking at George.

"Nurse, he needs his sleep – take him to the nursery," said Alexandra.

As Diana looked around the room she noticed there were hardly any younger men. What a strange society was being created by this war, she thought. As she watched Max effortlessly work the room, smiling and laughing, it was like nothing had changed. But he was going back to the front on the morning train. She could hardly cope with the feeling of loss.

"Ah, there you are, Diana," a strong stern voice snapped her out of her thoughts and she turned to find the Baroness Von Flashan there with a group of people.

"Good afternoon, Baroness."

"I just wanted to make arrangements with you to come and help in the charity shop I'm running in aid of the war effort. Brigitte said she did mention it to you?"

Diana felt awkward. "Yes, she did."

"I was thinking if you could do three days a week? It would also do you good. Get you out and not dwelling on the war up in that mountain lodge all the time. Why don't you come along tomorrow after you see Max off at the train station and we can make a start?"

Diana felt herself go red. "I'm sorry, Baroness, but I explained to Brigitte already that I can't assist you."

"Why ever not?" The baroness was astonished. "Do you think you're too good to do some shop work? My daughter is driving a tram, you know!"

"I realise that. But my brothers are fighting as well, you realise."

"I have unfortunately been made aware of that situation. All of Munich has at this stage." The baroness's voice rose so loudly that a hush descended on the room as everyone listened in.

"Then you see it's impossible for me," said Diana.

"I see this is an opportunity for you to nail your colours to the mast and show you are behind your husband and your adopted country one hundred per cent."

Diana's eyes began to fill with tears as all the staring faces waited for the answer.

Max suddenly walked towards Diana and put his arm around her. "I'm sorry, Baroness, my wife is being too polite to say. But she will not be involved in any work as I have asked her not to be."

"You have asked her, Max?" the baroness said, confused.

"It is my wish that she stays at the hunting lodge."

"But why?" demanded the baroness. "She should do her bit like the rest of us."

"I do not have to explain my reasons to you or anyone else, Baroness. I'm an officer in the army of the German Empire and returning to my post tomorrow."

The baroness became embarrassed. "Of course you don't, Max. Your bravery at the front is unquestionable. Forgive me, Diana."

203

But her face was set in stone as she moved away and everyone started talking and chatting again.

"Thank you," said Diana that night in their room in the *schloss*. "You shouldn't have taken the blame for my decision."

"They wouldn't have taken it from you," he said, holding her in his arms. They were silent for a while and then he said, "Imagine if I didn't have to go back tomorrow! If we ran away together."

"Where could we run to?" she asked.

"Italy is neutral. We could disappear down there to a little village where nobody knew us until the war is over. Or go on from there to America. Anywhere that's not in the war."

"You know you can't. You'd be shot!"

"I know. But I can dream, can't I?"

"I don't think I can bear going to the train station tomorrow morning and saying goodbye again."

The next morning when Diana woke up she turned and reached for Max but found the bed was empty. On his pillow was a red rose. She picked it up and smelled it. It was his sign to her. He had already left for the station. He knew neither of them could stand to say goodbye.

CHAPTER 35

A few weeks later it was Diana's birthday. She was disappointed there was no card or letter from Max that morning, but realised even the internal post was becoming increasingly late.

As she sat in the dining room having breakfast there was a knock on the door and Paul came in with his young daughter.

"Excuse me, but my daughter has a message for you," he said.

Diana smiled at the child. "Hello there."

The girl was holding a bunch of wild daisies picked from the meadows and she held out the posy.

"What's this?" asked Diana confused.

"Happy birthday, love from Max," said the child.

Tears started streaming down Diana's face as she took the daisies and held them close.

"He organised for me to do this before he went back to the front. He wanted to surprise you on your birthday."

"So typical of Max," said Diana as she reached out and hugged the little girl.

Each day Diana hoped that Max would just show up like he had the last time on leave. She knew he wouldn't warn her or tell her when he was due home. She didn't know if it was good or cruel. Each day she had a wonderful expectation, each night a bitter disappointment.

The ongoing war was affecting the 'home front', as it was now called, with worse and worse consequences.

"They should introduce rationing like Britain," insisted Paul whose usual relaxed manner was becoming stressed. "There's no control over essential food and products."

"Paul, go to the larder in the house and take what you want home for your children," insisted Diana.

"But that will leave you short," he objected.

"I'll be fine. There isn't too much there, but take what you want," she insisted, thinking she would pay another visit to Angela the grocer and pay her increasingly extortionate prices for black-market goods.

Paul looked at Diana. He genuinely liked her. She was easygoing and polite, not like the aristocratic women he was used to. But, according to everyone, she wasn't a true-blood aristocrat. She was landed gentry from a far-off country called Ireland. But she had an interest and understanding of the land and Paul realised it was from the farm she was brought up on. This place called Garonglen that she would speak of so lovingly and become misty-eyed over. He was glad she had this understanding because of the conversation he needed to have with her.

"Frau Von Hoffsten, has His Excellency made any decisions about the running of the estate?"

"I'm afraid not, Paul. I did bring it to his attention but I think he has too much to worry about with the brewery and his business empire. I got the impression this was the last of his problems."

"Then, with your husband away, you're going to have to make some decisions as the person in charge."

"How do you mean?"

"We didn't save the harvest. It was a poor harvest anyway because we couldn't import fertilizer. The snow is coming and the livestock won't be fed for the winter. They will die."

"I didn't realise it was so bad." Diana was shocked.

"Go look at the barns. There's hardly any hay."

"Oh, Paul!" She sat down, rubbing her temples with stress. "What can we do?"

"You'll have to sell all the livestock. Otherwise they will starve."

Diana thought long and hard before looking up. "What choice do we have?"

"None. The livestock will be dead by spring otherwise. At least with the shortages for livestock, you'll get good prices at market."

Diana stood up and nodded.

It was a harsh winter and Diana was glad the livestock were gone as they would have never survived without supplies.

She would have to spend Christmas and New Year alone at the house. An invitation was extended to her to go to Munich but she declined.

She had never been a person who scared easily. But now there was hardly any staff left, no staff lived in any more and she was alone in the big house at night. Then, she'd walk through the house, making sure the doors were locked and then sit in the drawing room alone rereading Max's letters or reading a book.

That Christmas Eve, an excited Gerti came in before she left for home. Her husband had managed to get leave for Christmas.

"I'm leaving now. I've prepared the food for you for tomorrow," said Gerti.

"Thank you."

"Also, Matilda gave in her notice. She's off to Cologne where she got a job in a munitions factory."

"Oh dear. That's the last of the domestic servants gone. Is there any point in trying to get another one?"

"I'll ask in the town. But I doubt it. They've all gone to take the men's jobs in the city."

"Not to worry, we'll manage somehow. Happy Christmas, Gerti."

"Happy Christmas," smiled Gerti as she turned to rush home to her husband. Then she stopped and turned around. "Frau Von Hoffsten, please don't think I am impertinent, but if you want to join me and my family for Christmas dinner, you are welcome."

Gerti's kindness touched Diana greatly. "Thank you, Gerti. But I'll be fine here. Enjoy your time with your husband."

Gerti bowed and left quickly.

Diana got up, sauntered out to the hallway and bolted the door. Then she turned off the lights and went up to bed.

On the Western Front, Max walked down the trenches. It was peaceful that night at least, he thought. A welcome lull over Christmas perhaps. He and some other officers were gathering in the mess later to have a Christmas drink. He looked up at the sky full of stars and took out a photo of Diana from his wallet and kissed it.

CHAPTER 36

At Easter 1916 the German newspapers gleefully reported the uprising in Ireland. Surely this was the turning of the tide, they said, when part of the United Kingdom was rising up against the government.

"This is wonderful, is it not?" said Gerti happily to Diana as she saw her read the newspapers. "Your country Ireland will now join Germany in the fight against England, no?"

"It's not quite like that, Gerti. The struggle for Irish independence is separate from the war and has been going on a long time."

Gerti looked confused and shrugged as she left the room.

Diana folded over the newspaper and frowned with worry about her parents and Garonglen. The British government had ruthlessly put down the rising in Ireland and shot the ringleaders for treason. For the British government to treat Irish rebels so ruthlessly made Diana think how dire the situation must be there. And she knew that treating the Irish independence movement in such a brutal fashion would only incense anger towards the British in Ireland and towards landed-gentry families like hers.

As the year progressed, conditions on the home front became increasingly bad. An early frost decimated the potato crop nationally which multiplied the food shortages. To try and counteract this, there was a late planting of turnips and Germany entered its 'turnip winter'. The dreaded turnip, usually reserved for feeding livestock, became the staple diet of the German populations as the naval blockade continued to block imports.

As Diana looked around she saw sights she never thought she would see in her lifetime. She had been brought up hearing of the barbaric conditions of the potato famine in the 1840s in Ireland. But here, in what used to be the richest country in Europe, she witnessed the increasingly desperate and malnourished population being afflicted by diseases such as typhus.

Diana had come into Munich to try and do some shopping. But she despaired as she saw the queues stretching down the streets. She had arranged to meet Brigitte for lunch and they met in a restaurant. Brigitte arrived in her nurse's uniform from the sanatorium. They kissed cheeks and ordered a small beer each and a lunch of bratwurst sausage and potato salad. Diana looked around the restaurant and recognised a lot of the faces she had met previously as Munich's elite, the only ones able to afford what was being served in the restaurant. She took a sip of her glass of beer and winced. It had been watered down and tasted odd.

"Do you see these prices?" moaned Brigitte as she looked at the menu.

"At least we can afford what they charge, unlike most people," said Diana.

"I suppose so," sighed Brigitte.

"Here we are, ladies," smiled the waiter, putting down the meals. "You're just in time – the chef has closed the kitchen for the rest of the day – we've run out of food."

"Thank you," said Diana.

She was used to eating without salt as it was unattainable now and she began to eat.

"How's work going for you?" she asked Brigitte.

"The sanatorium is packed out. We had a new delivery of solders this morning from the front. We've nowhere for them to sleep tonight!"

Diana was curious and intrigued. "And how exactly do they arrive in? Are they gone stark raving mad or what?"

"Most of them have shell shock."

"What's that?"

"Their nerves have given out from the sound of constant bombardment. They are shaking like epileptics."

Diana nodded, thinking of Max and how he wouldn't ever cope if he came down with that. Not Max who was so full of life and enjoyed every minute of living.

"I'm sure you're doing great work," she said.

"I read the situation in Ireland isn't good either," said Brigitte.

"Yes, they have put the country under martial law temporarily to control the situation. Ireland, where nothing ever happens under martial law! What is happening to the world? I miss my mother. It's strange – we used to get on each other's nerves so much, and now I'd give anything to be with her for an hour." Then she noticed the faraway look in Brigitte's eyes. "I'm sorry – that's insensitive of me, with you having lost your mother. I'm sure it's still very painful."

"Not really. Not any more. I got over it quickly enough."

Diana was surprised to hear this, considering how close she was to her family, particularly Max.

"Max rarely mentions your mother either," said Diana.

Brigitte smiled. "Well, she had a long illness, so it's upsetting to remember . . . My goodness, this bratwurst sausage is wonderful!"

"So it should be at the prices they are charging," said Diana.

That evening, as Diana made her way back to the train station, to get the train home to the Alps, the streets were only half lit by the streetlamps to conserve energy.

She was thinking hard about what Brigitte had said about their mother having had a long illness. Max had clearly said that their mother had died from a fall. She couldn't understand it but she had noticed before that nobody ever mentioned the deceased countess. There were no photos or paintings of her anywhere. And she had also noticed the strange atmosphere when she was ever mentioned. The subject was quickly changed. She also remembered Conrad laughing nastily when she brought the subject of his dead wife up.

She was suddenly determined to find out how the countess had died.

Diana called into the town hall where all the records were kept.

"I'm fascinated with the Von Hoffsten estate and want to find out about the history of it. The people who lived here and in the town," she said to the local administrator.

"Well, the Von Hoffstens used to rule the entire county. Everyone who lived here were their subjects," the woman said. "That was before German unification when all the kingdoms and counties and principalities were united under the Kaiser."

Yes, and they came up with cruel laws like morganatic marriages, thought Diana.

"Fascinating. I don't mean to disturb your work. I can look through the records on my own," she said.

The woman smiled. "If you want anything let me know. I am very busy – another batch of young men's death certificates to do today. All killed at the front."

Diana got to work and began riffling through the death certificates, finally finding what she was looking for.

"*Countess Helena Von Hoffsten,*" Diana read out loud. "*Cause of death – drowning.*"

Diana waited anxiously for Brigitte's next visit. She tried to understand what was going on regarding the former countess. Why were the family not telling the truth about her death? Why had Max not told her the truth? She had decided she would confront Brigitte about it.

Brigitte arrived for a weekend.

"You're very kind to continue visiting me and checking on me," said Diana.

"Oh, it's no bother at all. Besides, I promised Max I would," explained Brigitte.

Diana began to feel unnerved. "He asked you to mind me?"

"Of course he did. Why wouldn't he?"

"I don't want to be a burden to you. Please don't feel obliged to

212

visit me – you have enough responsibility at the sanatorium," insisted Diana.

Brigitte just smiled that elusive smile that so unnerved her.

"Brigitte, I'd like to ask you about something. When we met in the beer garden you said your mother had died from a long illness . . ."

"So?"

"So, Max said the countess died as the result of a fall."

Brigitte shrugged and smiled. "Well, she had a long illness and then she died from a fall."

Diana shook her head. "But she didn't die of either. She drowned."

Brigitte laughed lightly. "What are you talking about?"

"I've seen your mother's death certificate and it says she drowned."

Brigitte inhaled loudly. "I see! You have been busy, haven't you?"

"I just don't understand why nobody speaks of her or tells the truth about her death."

Brigitte stood up and walked to the French windows. "That's where it happened, out there in the Tegernfrei Lake."

"Was it a boating accident?" asked Diana, her face creasing in concern.

Brigitte laughed loudly then turned and walked slowly towards her. "Oh, it was no accident, Diana."

"What are you saying?"

"She killed herself. Our darling mother threw herself into the lake and drowned herself."

Diana's hand shot over her mouth in horror.

A gleeful unpleasant look came over Brigitte's face. "Oh, yes, you wanted to hear the details, so I'll tell you. She was quite mad, our mother. Not all the time, but often enough, especially in the later years. We lived here with her. Father was in Munich most of the time. The madder she became, the more he stayed away. And the more he stayed away the madder she became. It was like something taking over her mind and she would lock herself in her room and just scream."

"Oh, Brigitte, I'm so sorry," said Diana, Brigitte's own screaming fits springing disturbingly to mind . . . and Max's odd reaction to them.

"What's there to feel sorry for? Madness is quite natural, you know. Bend the mind enough and it will break like any other part of the body."

"And how did you cope? You were all so young?"

"We got used to it, because we didn't know anything else. Max and me took care of her, and Hugo . . . well, Hugo did what Hugo always does – kept quiet and did as he was told."

Diana shook her head sadly. "So much makes sense now. It's like you've given me the jigsaw piece that was missing. My poor Max. You've all been so long trying to pretend that everything is normal."

"But we are normal, darling Diana, in our own special way," Brigitte smiled.

CHAPTER 37

As 1916 led into 1917, the Western Front remained locked in an impasse. At least the winter was over, thought Max as he left the officers' mess and made his way towards the trenches for the next ordered attack. The men's morale was decimated and he saw it as his job to continue to keep their spirits up. But it was nearly impossible as not only had so many of their comrades been killed or horrifically injured but the conditions of their loved ones at home was demoralising them. It was hard for them to remain focused when they knew their families were hungry and cold from lack of fuel.

He thought of Diana. Her letters were not filled with such horror stories, but remained positive and upbeat, talking of when their life would return to normal after this terrible war was finally ended. His heart broke, thinking of her alone at the estate. But at least the timber from the estate woods would keep her warm and there would be enough food for her with what was produced on the estate – that was what she wrote to him anyway.

There was the constant pounding of shells in the distance and as Max walked down the area of the trenches under his control, inspecting the troops, he had a tight knot in his stomach. Evening was beginning to descend and the decision had been taken that this would be a good time to make an offensive. The darkening sky would act as a shield to them as they made their way across no-man's land. As he looked at the men his heart went out to them. They looked tired, hungry, exhausted. How different from the

215

enthusiastic and defiant troops who arrived three years previously in victorious mood.

He got to the end of the line under his command and turned and addressed his platoon.

"When I give the signal, we'll go over!" he shouted. "Remember, this will pass! We will go home. We will see our wives and loved ones again. We're doing this so we'll be home soon and then life will go back to the way we remember."

He felt his words were hollow as he voiced them. But they needed to hear this. They needed hope. As he looked at them, he wondered how many would survive the evening. He wondered if he would survive it and see Diana again.

"Get into position! Right – when I blow the whistle!" Then he blew the whistle hard and shouted, "*Go!*"

The men clambered up out of the trench and started racing across the no-man's land in waves. Max climbed over and ran with the men. The machine guns started firing from the British side and Max could see the British soldiers emerging from their trenches. As he prepared himself for battle he gripped his gun and insured the bayonet was secured. He began to fire shots at the oncoming British soldiers. All around him his men dropped to the ground. By his side a soldier dropped, letting out a bloodcurdling scream. Max kept storming on. He could hear the bullets whizz past him. As they made progress he and his men spread out further. They had one aim: to get to the enemy trenches. But the oncoming British soldiers' one aim was to ensure this did not happen. He could see his surviving soldiers up ahead, meeting the enemy and going into close combat with them.

The sky was darkening further, making visibility worse. Suddenly there was a British officer in front of Max, his pistol raised. Max raised his bayonet and thrust it at the man, stabbing him.

As Max withdrew his bayonet he glanced at his enemy's face.

To his horror he saw it was Dashiel facing him.

Dashiel's face went into shock as he managed to utter, "Max!" His face crumpled in shock and pain and Max watched in horror as he fell to his knees.

"Dashiel," gasped Max as he watched him slump forward.

He rushed to grab him and held him.

"Dashiel, I'm sorry," he gasped as he saw blood gurgle from Dashiel's mouth. All around the fighting, the shells, the screams and shouts continued as Max nursed Dashiel.

By the time night had fallen the battle was over. The shooting and shells had stopped. Only the distant groans and screams of the injured could be heard. Max was still kneeling in the middle of no-man's land, clutching Dashiel tightly. As he looked into his open blue eyes he knew he was dead but he couldn't let him go. As he stared at him he realised how similar Dashiel's eyes were to Diana's.

"Remember, Dashiel, when we were in Ireland and I arranged through you to meet Diana again at the Roundtrees' party? Remember we met in Dublin and we planned the whole surprise. You told me Diana loved surprises and that for me to just show up at the party would be the best idea to get her attention. You were right. She was surprised and she loved it. And we'll have good times again, Dashiel. When this war is over. We'll all meet up again. You can come to Germany to the hunting estate for the ski party and me and Diana will come to Ireland and stay at Garonglen and we'll be one big happy family again."

Max smiled at Dashiel as he wiped away the blood from his face.

CHAPTER 38

Diana thought a lot about Brigitte's revelation about their mother. How Max had suffered and witnessed such an appalling tragedy in his life. She wished he had told her. He seemed to always want to protect her. When the war was over she needed to be more supportive of him and for him to feel able to confide in her. She was his wife and partner and he had to rely on her because that was how she saw her role.

His letters kept coming, the familiar scent of his cologne on the paper always making her feel he was there with her.

Gerti came in as she was reading his latest letter from the front. "Frau Von Hoffsten, there is a guest to see you."

"A guest?" Diana was confused.

"A friend of your husband's from Munich – Claudia Von Garhart."

Diana remembered Claudia. She was part of the wealthy set Max hung around with before the war.

She rose and went into the drawing room where she found a fur-swathed Claudia, a glamorous blonde.

"Hello again," smiled Claudia, shaking her hand. "It's been a long time."

"Yes, you were a house guest here before the war and we met you at some events in Munich."

"That's right. How is Max?"

"He seems fine. I haven't seen him for a long time. He must be due leave soon."

Claudia smiled. "I was just passing by and so I thought I'd drop in to see how you are keeping."

"That's kind of you. Please sit down. May I offer you some tea?"

"No, thank you. Unfortunately I can only stay a few minutes."

They both sat, Diana on a couch, Claudia in an armchair facing her.

"It must get lonely up here in the mountains," said Claudia.

"I'd be lonely anywhere when Max isn't with me."

"I'm sure," said Claudia.

Then she stood abruptly and walked to the door. She looked out into the hall and then closed over the double doors.

Diana looked at her, perplexed. "I'm sorry – was there a draught?"

Claudia's expression switched from pleasant to concerned as she came hurriedly and sat beside Diana on the couch.

She spoke in a hushed voice. "I'll speak quickly as I can't stay long. I don't know who might be watching."

"Sorry?" Diana shook her head, confused.

"I have a message from you from your cousins, Elliott and Thelma Ashenbry."

"A message?" Diana was confused but excited. "How are they?"

"They're fine. I was great friends with them before the war. You are to travel to Geneva next Saturday."

"Go to Switzerland? But why?"

Claudia passed her a piece of paper. "This is a café near the train station and you are to be there for two in the afternoon. Thelma will be waiting for you there."

"Thelma!" Diana was astonished. She glanced at the paper. It was a pencil-drawn street map.

"Be sure to take your British passport," urged Claudia. "That is vital."

"But –" began Diana.

Claudia abruptly stood up and went and opened the doors again.

"The place is as beautiful as ever," she said, sounding loud and happy. "My goodness, is that the time? I'd better be going. Lovely to see you again, Diana. Please send Max my love!"

Claudia shook Diana's hand firmly and nodded to her before she left.

Diana walked out of the train station in Geneva and began to walk down the street, carefully following the directions on the map that Claudia had given her. She walked down a side street and spotted the small café. She pushed the door open and walked in. Surveying the half-empty restaurant she spotted Thelma in the far corner, dressed in a fur stole. Diana quickly made her way down to her.

"Diana!" said Thelma, rising up and embracing her. "I was frightened you wouldn't be able to make it."

"I had no problem crossing the border into Switzerland," said Diana as they sat down.

"Well, they are neutral but you never know," said Thelma and she smiled warmly at her. "It is good to see you."

"And you," smiled Diana, reaching across the table and squeezing her hand. "But what are you doing here?"

Just then the waiter came and they ordered coffee. Then Thelma took out a silver cigarette box from her handbag and lit up a cigarette.

"Thelma! You're smoking!" Diana said, shocked.

Thelma gave a light laugh. "Darling, all the women in London are now smoking. It gets us through! Smoking is the least of it! The city is being run by women, from the trams to the factories. Who'd have believed it before?"

"It's the same in Germany," said Diana. "With all the men at war."

"Yes, it's extraordinary."

Diana couldn't wait any longer and leaned forward. "How are Mama and Papa and the boys? How's everything at Garonglen? Are they all right? I can't get any information to or from them."

"I'll tell you all in a while. First I want to tell you why I'm here." Thelma looked around and leaned forward. "I've come up from Biarritz. I have an aunt and uncle and cousins who have lived there for years. But they got trapped there with the war."

"I see," said Diana.

"They've been living in relative comfort but now America has entered the war they are no longer neutrals. They don't feel safe there any more. They want to get out in case France is overrun by the Germans."

"I see," said Diana, taking it all in and considering the impact America's entry would have on the war. The German sinking of the *Lusitania* off the coast of Ireland had changed everything, dragging America into the conflict.

"We've decided that we can't take the chance of leaving them there any more. So we chartered a boat from Bournemouth and sailed right down the coast of France to collect them," explained Thelma.

"It's probably wise to get them to England," agreed Diana.

"Diana, the reason I've made this trip to Geneva is to fetch you as well."

"Me?" Diana was incredulous.

"Yes, Diana. I want you to get on the train to Biarritz with me now and return to England with the rest of us."

"You're out of your mind! I can't do any such thing," said Diana.

Thelma leaned forward and whispered urgently, "Diana, I don't think you realise the danger you are in."

"What are you talking about?"

Thelma reached down and took several newspapers and magazines from a briefcase that Diana now saw was on the floor at her feet.

"I've marked the pages concerning you," said Thelma, sitting back and smoking while she observed Diana.

Diana opened the first newspaper, *The Daily Mail*, on the marked page and to her shock saw a photograph of herself under the headline '*The Treasonous Countess – Diana Von Hoffsten.*'

Diana looked up. "What is this?"

"Read the article," urged Thelma, pointing her cigarette at the newspaper.

Diana picked up the paper and read the article.

'As Britain continues to suffer the hardship of war, one British citizen lives a life of luxury in Germany. Countess Diana Von Hoffsten, a native of County Meath, Ireland, is the wife of German officer Max Von Hoffsten. A socialite before the war who wooed London society, she has been ensconced in the Von Hoffstens' fabulous hunting estate in Bavaria for the duration of the war where she dines on an endless supply of steak, pork, potatoes and claret wine. Her name was brought up in a debate in the House of Commons last week when the subject of collaboration with the enemy and how collaborators should be treated was being discussed. The Right Honourable Cedric Willoughby MP said that the Countess Von Hoffsten was a disgraceful woman who had turned her back on her country at its most desperate hour and deserved to be charged with treason.'

Diana's head was reeling. She began to quickly scour through the other papers.

"The rest all say pretty much the same," said Thelma. "Some phrase it a lot worse."

"I can't believe it! Where are they getting all this information from, all of which is incorrect? I'm not leading a life of luxury. We're living on meagre rations like everyone else since the British and French have blockaded all supplies coming into Germany and Austria."

"I don't think the press are too interested in facts at the moment. They are just trying to rouse the public into more and more anger so the fight continues. They've reported some terrible things that aren't true – far worse than this – like about Belgian babies being bayoneted."

"They even call me a countess! The first time ever I've been called it! Don't they know I'm in a left-handed marriage?"

Thelma bent forward. "Diana, they don't care what kind of a marriage you're in. All they know is they see you in Germany supporting the enemy."

"And what would they have me do? Leave my husband?"

"Well – yes! You must return with me to London immediately. At the end of the day you are British and you can't stay in enemy territory any longer."

"I am not leaving Max, Thelma," Diana said sternly.

"I'm not saying leave him. Just wait for him in London or at Garonglen till the war is over," said Thelma.

"I'd be deserting him!"

"Diana, you don't understand how strong public feeling is at home. The people have turned very anti-German and you will be destroyed once the war is over."

"You seem very confident that the Germans will lose," said Diana.

"Of course they will once the Americans are on board," said Thelma.

Diana sat thinking and then said, "No – no, even if the Germans do lose, that's even more reason not to leave Max. If I left Max now, imagine what it would do to him? Imagine how he would be treated by everyone. He's already suffered enough marrying me."

"And what about your own family, Diana?" said Thelma crossly. "Have you thought about how this affects your parents and brothers, not to mention us?"

"Us? By which you mean the Ashenbrys?" Diana said.

"Yes!"

"My distant cousins the Ashenbrys who always treated the Cantwells as insignificant until I married Max? And now because of the war your connection to me is a source of embarrassment to you?"

"That's not true, Diana. I'm trying to save everyone here," said Thelma.

"I understand, Thelma. But you *must* understand the terrible situation I'm in." Suddenly she was blinking away her tears. "I can't desert Max, I just can't! No matter what the consequences are. I feel ashamed that you and my family must suffer because of your connection to me. But would you leave Elliot, if the shoe was on the other foot?"

Thelma sighed and sat back. "I suppose not."

"I am truly grateful that you've come all this way to try and rescue me, I really am, but I fear you've had a wasted trip. I'd follow Max to the ends of the earth, so I must sit and wait for him."

Thelma nodded and then sat forward again. "There's something else – Warren has been injured."

Diana paled. "How badly?" she whispered.

"I'm not sure. There are so many soldiers injured it's hard to get information about any one. It's not life-threatening, but it is serious. They've managed to get him back to Ireland for recuperation."

Tears sprang to Diana's eyes. "My poor Warren! I wish I could be there for him."

"You can be! Come to Biarritz with me now and take the chartered boat back to England with the others."

Tears started streaming down Diana's face. "I can't, Thelma. I'm sorry but I can't. When I married Max I committed forever. I could never leave him and I don't want to."

Thelma nodded slowly and sighed as she lit up another cigarette. "I've tried my best."

They spent the afternoon in that café, talking about everything. Then they made their way back to the train station.

As they stood on the platform, about to go to their separate trains, Diana handed Thelma letters for all her family.

"Will you make sure they get them?" she said.

"If I have to hand-deliver them myself. Last chance to come with me?"

Diana smiled at her. "Have a safe trip back to England."

"Until we meet in happier times then."

Diana reached forward and hugged her and then turned and quickly made her way to her train back to Munich.

CHAPTER 39

It was late by the time Diana got home to the hunting lodge. She drove slowly and carefully – she was out of practice as she used the car so rarely now that petrol was so scarce, often walking down to the town or riding Halcyon.

She saw some lights downstairs were on and thought it unusual as Gerti should have been gone by now. She let herself in.

"Gerti?" she called but there was no answer.

She walked into the drawing room and got a fright when she saw a man's figure standing at the French windows, looking out. She was about to say something and then her heart began to race.

"Max?" she whispered.

The man slowly turned around and she saw it was indeed Max. She raced across the room and embraced him.

"Oh, Max!" she whispered. "You're home!"

She pulled back and looked at him and got a terrible shock. He was deathly pale and thin. He had aged. But it was his eyes that scared her most. They stared at her, showing no emotion. And he wasn't embracing her back but just stood there like a block of ice.

"Max?" she said as she reached forward and kissed him. "My darling, are you all right?"

She quickly inspected him for an injury but there was no sign of one.

"You're freezing, Max. Come over here to the heat." She led him over to an armchair beside the fire and got him to sit down. She threw some logs on top of the dying fire and used the bellows to encourage the feeble flame.

225

"Are you hungry, darling? Do you want to eat?"

He nodded.

"Stay right there and I'll get you something. Gerti has gone home but I'll see what she has left."

Diana got up and raced from the room. She dashed across the hall and down the series of corridors that led to the other side of the house and to the kitchens. She felt panicked by how Max looked and how he was responding to her. He seemed to be in a trance. She began to frantically look through the larders and the cupboards but they were mostly bare. In one of the larders she found half a bag of the dreaded turnips but closed over the door, not wanting to serve them. Finally she managed to find some cheese and some bread she had bought from Angela the grocer the previous week. The bread was gone hard and she put the kettle on the stove and held the bread over the steam from it to soften it.

She put it on a plate with the cheese and poured a glass of goat's milk. She rushed back to the drawing room and found Max in the same position but bent over, his face buried in his hands.

She knelt beside him and gently touched his hands. He looked up at her, his eyes filled with tears.

"Is it really you?" he whispered, reaching out and touching her hair.

"Of course!" She smiled at him and kissed his hand.

"Can you ever forgive me?" he whispered.

Diana sat in their room that night, staring at Max lying on his back in a deep sleep. He had seemed to be physically and emotionally exhausted and so she had led him upstairs and put him to bed. He had been too tired even to talk. Her thrill at seeing him had been quickly replaced by her concern at how bad he seemed. She just wanted to mind him and nurse him. She thought how, if she had given in to Thelma, she would be on her way home to Ireland and she thought of what that would have done to Max when he arrived home to see she had gone. She knew she could never have left with Thelma and as she watched Max breathe deeply she felt such tenderness and love for him. Seeing him like this made her love him more than when he was providing her with yachts and rooms full of flowers.

The next morning, when Diana got up, Max was still in such a deep slumber she wouldn't have been surprised if he had slept the full day. She would head down to the town and get some supplies from Angela.

As she drove down the hills to the town she made a mental list of what she would get – sugar, tea, coffee, cheese, chocolate, sausages, bacon. She wondered if Angela had any cognac. She parked the car and walked down the street. As she passed the town hall she saw the long queue of women there, with their food stamps to get their weekly supplies, which Diana knew had been cut down to subsistence levels. Looking at the long queue of malnourished women and their children in the forecourt of the town hall, her mind went back to the festival day in that summer of 1914, the day Franz Ferdinand and his wife were killed. She remembered the tables all the estate workers and townspeople sat at with plentiful food and drink brimming. She remembered the happy, kind people celebrating their good fortune that day. It was hard to believe this was the same town.

She arrived at Angela's grocer's and found the door locked. She knocked on the door loudly and a minute later Angela opened the door.

Diana stepped in.

"Are you not open today?" she asked.

Angela gestured to the shelves which were all empty. "Not until I get the delivery, if I get it."

Diana approached the counter as Angela stepped behind it.

"I need extra stuff today, Angela. My husband is back from the front."

"So I heard." Angela seemed unimpressed.

"So I'll take whatever you have. I was hoping for sugar, tea, all the usual essentials. Whatever meat you have – bacon, pork? And I'd like some luxuries, chocolate and cognac – do you have any?"

"I'm afraid I've nothing," said Angela coolly.

"What do you mean? You must have something?"

"Nothing. You'd better go down and join the queue with your food stamps like all the other women."

Diana looked at her squarely. "I don't believe you. You always have stock. If it's a case of money and having to charge more, that's not a problem. Name your price."

"I told you I have nothing. Now leave," Angela insisted.

Diana looked at her incredulously and knew she was lying. She thought about all the times she had been ripped off by her over time, and about Max lying broken back at the house.

"We'll see if you have nothing!" said Diana and she marched in behind the counter to get to the rooms out the back.

Angela ran after her and grabbed her wrist. "I do not want you in my shop any more. Take your custom elsewhere."

"So you do have stuff?" Diana accused. "I told you to name your price."

"Your money is no good here. It's bad for my business for you to be seen coming in here. Bad for the other people in the town."

"But why?" Diana was shocked.

"Because you're the enemy! You're British. You are the reason we are all starving and the country is ruined!"

Diana was taken aback. "But *I'm* not fighting you."

"Your family is, your friends are. We don't want you here. Go!"

"But this food is for my husband! An officer in the German army!"

"He should have thought about that before he married you!" spat Angela.

Diana turned and walked to the door, then turned and faced Angela.

"You know you are insulting Count Von Hoffsten and his family?"

"Who cares about Count Von Hoffsten and his family any more? Times have changed. The war has changed everything! Look what's happened in Russia. The aristocrats have been thrown out like dirty bath water. It will happen here next."

Diana turned and walked quickly from the shop.

As she walked down the street she was very disturbed by the grocer's behaviour. She looked into her purse and saw the food coupons that had arrived to the house. She rarely used the food coupons as she had always acquired what she needed on the black market. Instead she had always given her coupons to Gerti or Paul, knowing they would have so much more need for them with their families. She had heard of desperate queues at the ration shops which had also deterred her. But with a husband at home to feed it looked like she had no choice but to go and queue along with everyone else.

She walked along to the town hall. The other women stared at her as she walked past them. She stood out a mile dressed in her chic dress and fur coat. She had deliberately dressed up that day so as to look nice for Max. She reached the end of the queue and joined it, smiling at the shocked women in front of her.

The women began muttering amongst themselves while looking at her.

She spotted a young girl who was the daughter of one of the workers on the estate who had gone off to war. She smiled and approached her. "Hello, Nicole, how are you?"

The girl's mother pulled the girl away from Diana. "Don't speak to her!"

Diana quickly returned to her space in the queue and ignored the hostile looks she was given.

It seemed like hours before she got into the town hall and to the top of the queue.

The man from the food rations war office at the desk looked at her and said, "Food coupons."

Diana smiled at him and handed over the coupons. "My husband came back from the front yesterday so I was hoping for some meat and –"

"Coupons are for turnips, bread and cheese," said the man and one of the workers fetched Diana's rations and put them on the table in front of her.

Diana looked down in horror at the tiny amount of rations.

"Why should she get rations? She's not one of us!" called a voice behind her.

"She's British! She's the enemy! Don't give her food!" shouted another woman.

"She's the Countess Von Hoffsten – she has larders full of food up at the estate," shouted an old man.

"That's right. She's a typical farmer hoarding all the food and not supplying the country while the rest of us starve!" screamed a woman.

"And then she comes down here in furs and jewels and robs our measly rations!" shouted the old man again.

Diana looked at them. "That's simply not true. The estate has no crops, the kitchens are bare and the livestock nearly all gone."

"'Nearly' isn't fully!" shouted a man.

The men who were running the food distribution looked on uneasily as the crowd turned hostile.

"Quickly – sign for the food and go!" snapped the man in charge. "There have been riots in the cities and we don't have the man power here to deal with one."

Diana quickly took the pen and signed.

"It's not right that a British aristocrat sitting in her palace should take our food!" shouted an angry woman, marching towards Diana.

It looked like the woman was going to hit her but the man stepped out from behind the counter and held her back. Suddenly a scuffle broke out and people in the queue took the opportunity to rush the counter and grab the food rations. Before Diana knew it her own rations had been grabbed and she was left with nothing. As she looked on at the near-riot a woman came up to her and spat in her face.

Horrified, Diana ran from the town hall. She could hear the commotion and jeering behind her as she raced down the street. She got to her car and raced back up the hills to the house.

Diana was still shaking as she drove into the courtyard and rushed into the house. In the drawing room she sat shaking on the couch, thinking of the terrible scene.

There was a knock on the door and she looked up with tears in her eyes as Paul entered.

"Frau Von Hoffsten, I wanted to ask you –" He stopped abruptly as he saw the state she was in. He rushed forward, fearing the worst: bad news from the front. "What's the matter?"

"It was horrible – I've never have seen anything like it. They were like scavengers." Her voice broke as she spoke and she looked up at Paul. "I went to queue to get food like everyone else, and a riot broke out. I caused it by just being me!"

Paul nodded. "They are hungry, that's all. There are food riots all around the country."

"It was more than that, Paul. It's because I'm the enemy." She wiped away a tear.

"You can't blame them for feeling this way. They are starving, their lives are ruined, their men dead or wounded. In Britain they are putting German citizens in jail until the war is over, just innocent civilians going about their business, and the same thing is happening here – only your status as Frau Von Hoffsten protects you."

"But those people were so welcoming to me when I came here. I recognised so many of them. They were so kind and respectful." Diana looked up at him.

"But that was before the war." Paul said it as the most natural thing in the world.

"But what will I do now? The grocer won't sell anything to me on the black market any more and I can't get food rations like everyone else. How will I feed Max?" She felt anguished. "Before the war Max went to extremes to provide me with happiness, and now I can't even provide him with some food."

"I'll go down to the grocer for you and make your purchases for you," offered Paul.

Diana shook her head. "I can't ask you do that, Paul. It's illegal and you'll end up in prison."

"If it wasn't for the black market everyone would have starved by now. They can't put us all in prison."

Diana managed to smile at him. "You're very kind."

"I think you should go and check on your husband, Frau Von Hoffsten. He won't be here for very long before he goes back to the front. Make it memorable for him."

Diana crept into their bedroom. The sun was shining through the

French windows and Max was still sleeping on his back. She went over, sat down on the bed and watched him for what seemed ages. Suddenly he stirred and opened his eyes. He saw her sitting over him, illuminated by the sunlight.

"Is this real? Are you really here?" he asked gently.

She bent over and kissed him. "I'm here."

Max was gently led down the stairs by Diana that evening.

"Where is everybody? Where are all the servants?" he asked.

Diana realised how everything must seem different to him. The army of staff that had kept the estate ticking like clockwork was gone.

"The men are at war, Max, and the women left for the cities. We don't really need them any more, we manage just fine. It's only me here."

She led him down the hallway and into the dining room. Gerti had laid out a spread with what Paul had bought earlier. Angela the grocer had charged an exorbitant amount but Diana just felt relief that she could welcome Max home in comfort. He sat down at the head of the table and she sat beside him. He stared at the food in front of him.

He picked up his fork and began to eat.

He seemed so fragile, Diana thought, as she poured wine into their glasses.

"This is quite a feast," he smiled. "Not what we are used to in the trenches."

She smiled at him and began to eat.

"Brigitte and your family will all be desperate to see you," she said.

He nodded and then said, "Don't tell them I'm home just yet. I'd like some time alone with you."

"Of course. Take all the time you need. You need to relax. We can go walking and riding," she agreed, relieved at his answer. He didn't seem fit for having the Von Hoffsten circus arrive in on top of him. "Halcyon is doing well."

"Halcyon." He said the name as if he had totally forgotten about the horse.

232

"I haven't heard a thing from Ireland. Not a letter or anything. But I met Thelma, yesterday in Geneva. She asked to meet me and she told me they are all fine."

Max suddenly stopped eating and put down his fork.

"Max? What's wrong?"

He looked at her and his eyes were filled with tears.

"Max?" she reached out and held his hand.

"I'm sorry. I'm not hungry. I just want to sleep."

"Of course. I'll take you upstairs." She went to stand up.

"No. You stay here. I'll be fine," he said, rising to his feet.

She watched him walk out and rubbed her temples with her fingertips.

Diana was sleeping that night when suddenly she heard a cry. Sitting up she saw Max beside her, calling out in his sleep. He was covered in sweat and his arms were flailing.

"Dashiel! Dashiel!" he shouted.

Diana reached out for him. "Max!"

Max's eyes suddenly shot open.

"Where am I?" he said, sitting up.

"At home with me. You were having a nightmare."

He was panting as she took him in her arms. "You're safe, Max. You're home safe with me."

"I thought I was there in the battlefield . . ." He looked at her. "How can you ever forgive me?"

She smiled at him. "What are you talking about, Max? I've nothing to forgive you for."

He gripped her tightly, his eyes wide and frightened.

"Max, darling, you were shouting for Dashiel in your dream," she said.

He said nothing but gripped her even tighter.

CHAPTER 40

Over the next few days Diana nursed Max. She made sure he got plenty of rest and sleep. She brought him out for long walks through the hills and meadows. And they went out sailing on the lake. He seemed like a different person most of the time from the carefree Max she had married. She could only imagine the horrors he had witnessed. And yet sometimes when they were alone she would get him back. For a few moments the expression on his face would change and she had her old Max back.

She suggested they go riding and they went to the stables.

"You remember your old friend Halcyon?" she said as she put the saddle on the horse.

Max stared at Halcyon.

"Most of the horses had to go. They were taken by the government for essential services. But they weren't taking my Halcyon," she said, leaning forward and kissing the horse. She turned around and looked at Max. "Come over and say hello."

He gently came over and patted the horse.

"Sometimes I wish I'd never taken either of you from Garonglen," he whispered.

"But then I'd be unhappy, Max. I've only ever been truly happy since I met you. I was looking for something beforehand and I didn't even know what it was. Now I do, and it's you."

As much as she tried to get through to Max, most of the time it was as if there was an invisible wall between them. He would sit and stare at her in a trance while she talked to him, sometimes with tears rolling down his face.

As the end of his leave approached she realised she had to do something to stop him returning to the front. She believed another return to the front would break him.

Max was due to go to Munich to meet the Von Hoffstens and, unknown to him, she made an appointment to see Colonel Otto Dorfman, a senior officer in charge of the officers on leave in Munich.

She dropped Max off at the *schloss* and made her way to the military building where Dorfman was based. She was led into an elaborate office where the colonel, a man of about fifty, sat behind a desk. Diana thought him well fed and glowing with health and imagined he had never seen a day at the front.

"Good afternoon, Colonel Dorfman – thank you so much for seeing me at such short notice," she said, shaking his hand and sitting down opposite him.

"My pleasure to meet the wife of one of our most esteemed officers," said Dorfman.

He studied Diana and she felt his appraisal was appreciative. He also had a curious look on his face, no doubt intrigued as to what had brought her here, she thought.

"How can I help you, Frau Von Hoffsten?"

"I'm not sure if you are aware but my husband is home on leave at the moment?"

"I'm fully aware."

"Colonel Dorfman, I'm extremely concerned over his state of health."

"It hasn't been brought to my attention that Major Von Hoffsten suffered any injuries?"

"I'm not talking about physical health, but mental health."

"I see," said Dorfman, sitting up.

"Max is extremely fragile. I think he has reached breaking point and I'm here to implore you not to send him back to the front."

Dorfman stared at her in amazement. "Is your husband aware you are here?"

"No. I came of my own accord."

"I see . . . Frau Von Hoffsten, your husband has been an exemplary officer, a credit to his rank, family and country."

"I don't doubt that for a second, but –"

"He has fought tirelessly and selflessly and gained the respect and admiration of everyone – in spite of his natural disadvantage."

"What disadvantage?" asked Diana.

"Being married to you! Married to an enemy woman."

Diana looked at him, startled.

"Your application is turned down. Good day." Dorfman took up a pen and started writing notes.

Diana reached forward and slammed her hand on the table. "Didn't you hear me? I told you my husband is on the verge of a nervous breakdown!"

Dorfman looked up. "He would not thank you for using those words. Now I suggest you leave before you get yourself into any further trouble."

"What are you talking about – further trouble?" demanded Diana.

"Goodbye, Frau Von Hoffsten," Dorfman said harshly.

Diana got up and marched out.

It was the night before Max was to return to the front. They enjoyed a quiet meal and then retired to the drawing room. She sat beside him, holding his hand as he stared into the roaring fire in the fireplace.

"Max?"

"Huh?" He snapped out of his trance and looked at her.

"I don't want you to go back to the front tomorrow."

"We don't get what we want in this world."

"Max!" She squeezed his hand. "This isn't you! This isn't you speaking. You always got what you wanted in this world. Anything you wanted you made sure you got. You went to ridiculous lengths to get what you want. Look how you got me!"

"That – that was before the war."

"And this war won't go on forever and we have to think about surviving it and making sure we are here to enjoy our life after the war ends."

"But what if it never ends? What if the war goes on forever? Month after month, year after year, death after death."

"Of course it will end. It can't go on forever . . . I've been thinking . . . you must to go to your superiors and tell them you need time off because you're suffering mentally."

Max pulled his hand from hers and looked at her, appalled. "What are you talking about?"

"You're not yourself, Max. You need time to recover. It would be inhumane to send you back to the front in your present state. They didn't listen to me, but if *you* told them –"

"What do you mean – they didn't listen to you?"

"Darling, don't be angry with me, but I went to see Colonel Dorfman when you were visiting your father and Brigitte. I told him the stress you are under."

He glared at her with a mixture of disbelief and anger. "You went behind my back?"

"Yes, I felt I had no choice."

"How could you? How could you? How could you?" He sank his face into his hands.

"How could I not? You're everything to me, Max, and I'd do anything to save you."

"But you've disgraced me."

"Of course I didn't disgrace you –"

"*You did*!"

"I'm just saying you need rest, a long rest, and to see a doctor. I've spoken to Brigitte a lot about her work in the sanatorium and the place is packed with soldiers who have been admitted. I think you need to talk to someone, a medical doctor, before you go back, and get a professional opinion."

"The madhouse? You think I should talk to someone in the madhouse?"

"It's not a madhouse. It's a hospital."

Max's eyes became dark and angry. "There's nothing wrong with me. Do you understand me?"

"I'm not saying there is, darling. I just don't think you're fit to go back to the front."

Max stood up abruptly and said angrily, "You will not talk about this again, do you understand me! *Ever*!"

She was shocked. She had rarely seen him angry before, and he had never been angry with her.

"I know about your mother, Max. Brigitte told me. About how she died and how she suffered before she died."

Max glared at her in disbelief.

"I just wish you had told me about it yourself."

"She had no right to tell you. I made her promise never to tell you. We never speak about it."

"It wasn't her fault. I uncovered most of it myself." She got up and walked to him and put her arms around his neck. "But why didn't you tell me? Why didn't you trust me enough to tell me?"

"How could you love me if you knew?"

"My love for you has nothing to do with your mother, Max. I love you all the more. I didn't fall in love with this perfect man who doused me in flowers and named yachts after me. I fell in love with *you*. Doesn't the fact I entered a left-handed marriage with you prove just how much I loved you for *you*, and not for anything else you had or pretended to be? All I wanted was for you to be honest with me. Trust me to love you so much that you could tell me anything. No more secrets, no more lies." She smiled at him.

"If you knew what I'd done you could not love me any more," he said as tears streamed down his face.

"I would, Max, I promise you."

He stared into her eyes. Her loving trusting eyes.

"Tell me," she urged.

He drew a deep shuddering breath. "I-I-I-I . . . killed . . ." he began, his voice slow and low.

"Yes?" she nodded. She could only imagine the horrors he had been forced into doing during the war and she wanted to know. She had to help him.

"I killed . . ." he began again.

"I understand," she said, nodding sympathetically. "It's war, you were under orders, you had to do what you had to do."

"But you don't understand . . . I killed . . ."

Diana nodded and pulled him close. "I know, darling. But it's war – you can't blame yourself."

As she cradled and soothed him, his tears dried up and he stared at the wall behind her and mouthed, not audible enough for her to hear: *I killed Dashiel.*

The next morning as Diana woke she knew Max would be gone. She turned, expecting the usual rose left for her on his pillow. But it wasn't there.

She got out of bed and put on her dressing gown. She could hear a car coming in the distance and she walked to the French window and out on to the balcony. She could see Max walking down the road towards the motor car sent to fetch him back for duty.

"Max! Max!" she yelled after him.

But he kept on walking, not looking behind. The motor car reached him and he opened the back door and got in.

Diana watched as the motor car turned around and began to drive back down the hill. She kept watching until it disappeared from view.

CHAPTER 41

Diana stayed away from the town after Max left, only venturing in to get her post. There seemed to be such a hostile feeling towards her she wondered how, when the war was over, she and Max could go on living there. She imagined they might have to relocate to Munich. When the war was over. But what world would be left for them, Diana thought. Not the world they had before. Could they go to London and the South of France any more, enemy countries? She often thought about the vicious hostility in the British newspapers towards her. She hoped her family weren't suffering any prejudice because of her, especially Dashiel and Warren at the front.

She came back one afternoon after riding Halycon and walked into the drawing room to find Conrad, Alexandra and Hugo seated there.

"And to what do I owe this unexpected visit?" she asked.

"We're moving in permanently, at least for now," said Conrad.

"Moving in?" Diana was horrified.

"Yes, we needed to get out of Munich – it's become too unpleasant and dangerous to stay there," said Conrad.

Alexandra spoke as she lit her cigarette. "The city is just too depressing to be in for words. The queues for the shops and stores go all the way down the streets. Women standing, no longer talking about the husbands at war, but about their starving children."

"The bloody British blockade!" hissed Conrad.

"I-t-t's all over the country," said Hugo. "Riots in Hamburg and

240

Berlin. People desperate for food and coal."

"There's revolution in the air. They are saying the communists will take over like they did in Russia," said Conrad.

"And we know what *they* did to the aristocrats," sighed Alexandra.

"That couldn't happen here!" Diana was aghast.

"At least here we are nearer the Swiss border if we need to make a hasty run," said Hugo.

"Who'd ever have thought it would come to this," said Diana, sitting down.

"The aristocracy's days could be numbered here like in Russia. Maybe everywhere," sighed Conrad. "It's a changed world and we no longer have the power we did."

"Also at least here there is wood to burn – impossible to get coal in the city. And we have meat here with the livestock. You know it's impossible to get pork in Austria – every last pig has been slaughtered."

"Well, I'm afraid there isn't much on offer here either," warned Diana. She smiled at Alexandra sarcastically. "At least you're still managing to get your tobacco, Alexandra."

Letters from Max were so much less frequent that, when she collected one from the post office one morning, she was thrilled. When she got back to the study at the house and sat at the desk, she opened it, waiting to get the strong scent of his cologne as usual. But there was no scent. She held the paper close but it hadn't been scented. She remembered what he had said about always scenting the paper as a sign everything was fine with him. Alarmed, she read the letter. Her face creased with worry. The letter was largely incoherent, with Max changing topics mid-sentence. And he wrote mostly about Dashiel. About how wonderful and kind he was. And how Max knew how much Diana adored him and loved him. But what frightened Diana was that Max wrote about Dashiel in the past tense, as if he were dead.

Suddenly the door swung open and Diana looked up, startled, to see Conrad coming in.

"Can I help you, Conrad?" she asked.

"No! I think you might have done quite enough. I've just gone on a tour of the estate. There's hardly any livestock left! I've been informed you sold it all?"

"Yes, the proceeds went into the estate account. It's all accounted for."

"I think you're missing the point! Who gave you permission to sell my animals?"

"Conrad, I had no choice! I tried to discuss it with you and you said you had more important things on your mind."

"That didn't give you authority to sell the livestock on my behalf! I understand you've been managing the whole estate in my absence!"

"Well, somebody had to! The estate manager was killed in Flanders last year. There are no managers here. Myself and Paul have been managing as best we can."

"But –"

Paul walked meekly into the office and stood near the door, holding his cap in his hands.

Diana rose to her feet. "Conrad, I may not be a blue-blooded princess, but I was brought up on a stud farm. I understand livestock. The harvest had failed and the animals would not have survived the winter. I couldn't just sit back and let them starve to death. I make no apologies. And as I stated before, I am Max's wife, and am entitled to make decisions on his behalf."

Diana stormed out of the room.

"Confounded woman!" blazed Conrad as he sat behind the desk. "She thinks she knows everything! I left her here at the estate so she would be kept out of the way, and she ends up taking over! I always knew she was a money-grabbing power-obsessed bitch. She may have taken Max in, but not me!"

Paul coughed. "Pardon me, Your Excellency, I know nothing of these things. But what she says is right. We failed to rescue the harvest so the animals would not have survived the winter once the snows came. If you'll excuse me, I'll be getting back to the stables."

Paul nodded and left.

Diana was not happy sharing her home with the rest of the Von

Hoffstens but she had no choice. Luckily the house was big enough to avoid them most of the time. It was only at mealtimes that she found herself trapped in the same room as them. Despite everything, the Von Hoffstens still dressed up for dinner every night and were served by the servants Conrad had brought with him from his *schloss* in Munich.

Diana arrived into the dining room to find Conrad, Alexandra and Hugo already sitting down. Brigitte was there too for her weekend visit from working at the sanatorium.

"Good evening, everybody," greeted Diana as she took her seat at the table.

"Any letter from Max?" asked Brigitte, her eyes filled with hope.

"No, none today," answered Diana. "Hopefully tomorrow."

"Our forces are at present launching a huge assault," said Alexandra. "Hopefully we'll break through this time and finish the war once and for all."

"Especially now we have the troops freed from the Eastern front," said Conrad.

"Yes, Russia conceding defeat has given us our first victory. Next it will be Britain and France," said Alexandra.

Diana had learned not to comment on the war. As far as she was concerned she now doubted the Germans could go on for much longer. The country was falling apart and the Allies had a huge resource with the Americans now behind them. The servants started to serve the food. A full plate of roast meat covered in a thick sauce of creamed mushrooms was placed in front of her. She was so used to eking out food, she was amazed by the sumptuous dish.

"This certainly beats turnips," she smiled as she raised her fork and began to eat.

Their glasses were filled with red wine.

"The rest of the country may be starving, but we are Von Hoffstens and will eat accordingly," said Conrad as he began to eat.

With his money and contacts, Diana realised Conrad could source any food he wanted.

"How is Baby George?" asked Diana.

"He was fine when I last visited the nursery," said Alexandra.

"He's a beautiful baby," stated Conrad.

"How are things going at the brewery with you all away from Munich?" asked Diana.

"We've had to close it temporarily," said Hugo. "When people have no food, they don't want beer."

They chatted away amicably for the rest of the dinner.

As always Diana wished to make an excuse and leave immediately.

"That was delicious," she said and smiled at everyone. "I'm going to have an early night as I'm going to take Halcyon out on an early morning ride tomorrow."

Brigitte and Hugo looked uncomfortably at each other while Alexandra sat back and lit a cigarette.

"I shouldn't bother getting up early, if I were you," said Alexandra.

"Why not?" asked Diana.

Alexandra said nothing but looked smugly at Diana.

"Why should I not get up early?" Diana requested again, looking at everybody.

"In war, we all have to make sacrifices," said Brigitte, her face earnest.

"What are you talking about?" Diana was becoming irritated by the atmosphere.

"Let's face it, the horse's best days were behind it," said Alexandra.

"And because of the war, he never got the opportunity to perform at the major races," said Conrad. "He was never going to be a champion now as he missed his time."

"And – and – and – when children are starving, it's hard to justify keeping a horse so well fed," said Brigitte, becoming more agitated.

"The horse should have been drafted into military service years ago anyway. I believe you prevented it from happening," said Conrad. "The horse wasn't a working horse – it was only kept as amusement for you."

"Halcyon," Diana whispered as she looked down at her empty plate.

She slowly looked up, tears stinging her eyes.

"You *bastards*!" she screamed.

"It was only a horse," said Conrad.

"But he made a most delicious meal, you said it yourself," said Alexandra, smiling at Diana falsely.

Diana jumped up from her seat and raced from the room. She didn't stop till she got to the bathroom where she vomited violently.

Diana stormed into the stables where she found Paul polishing a saddle.

"Why did you let him do it?" she shouted. "You know how much I loved Halcyon – why did you allow him to be killed?"

Paul shrugged. "He's the count. It would be unthinkable for me to disobey his order."

"Why didn't you come and warn me? Tell me?" she demanded.

"His Excellency told me not to. It's part of the war – people are getting food wherever they can."

She broke down crying. "It's more than that. He wanted to persecute me. And he thought of this way. He's a vile vile man who I hate with all my heart!"

"You mustn't speak of the count in that way."

"You all might have to respect him, but I don't. When this war is over, Max and I are going to leave here and have nothing ever to do with his family again. We'll go and live in Ireland with my family, at Garonglen. That's where we were at our happiest. I miss my family. I miss Max."

Paul came over and put his arm around her and comforted her.

Diana did not go down to have dinner with the family any more. She either went to eat in the kitchens, to the staff's dismay, or had something delivered to her room.

It was two weeks later and there was a knock on her bedroom door.

"Come in," she said, expecting it to be her lunch.

Gerti walked in nervously, holding a piece of paper.

"Frau Von Hoffsten, this telegram has come for you," she said, holding it out.

Diana reached out and took it.

Gerti hastily left the room.

Diana opened the telegram. It was from the Imperial army. It read: '*Major Max Von Hoffsten took part in the last battle of Amiens. Major Von Hoffsten has not been accounted for since the battle. It is therefore with great regret that we report that Major Hoffsten is missing, presumed dead.*'

She had hope in the first few days. It was like a heavy black cloud descended on the house. Everything was so silent, apart from Brigitte's wailing that echoed down the corridors at night. Diana didn't cry. She thought it was because she had been told he was missing as opposed to being told outright that he had been killed. The hope she initially had outweighed the grief. There would be another telegram saying Max had been found. But it didn't come. And when the hope began to ebb, the despair set in. She found herself in a strange limbo of not really believing he was dead. Where was his body? Where was the funeral? Where was Max?

She came down to the drawing room where she found the family sitting in deathly silence, apart from Brigitte who was sobbing. Even Alexandra looked shaken, her usual cool exterior vanished for now. Had Alexandra really loved Max, Diana wondered? Was that why she was so vicious to her?

Conrad had been using all his contacts to try and find any more information.

"Have you found out anything?" Diana asked.

"Only that he led his unit over the trenches and into the battle. He was last seen by his men charging with a bayonet. And then in the confusion and heat of the battle he was lost."

"But how do you get lost?" demanded Diana. "His body must have been found."

Conrad spoke coldly. "After the battles, it's too dangerous to go out and get the bodies because the rescuers will be shot by enemy fire."

"So they are just left there?" Diana wiped away a tear.

"Oh, yes," said Brigitte through her tears. "I've heard all the stories from the men in the sanatorium. Sometimes the bodies, after a battle, are out there for days, still alive. They can hear their screams and pleas from their trenches but can't go out to rescue them as they will be fired upon by the enemy."

"Oh, stop, please!" begged Diana, realising she was crying for the first time since she heard the news.

"Or the shells, the bombs. If a shell hits a soldier he is obliterated, never seen again," said Conrad.

"A British bomb," said Alexandra.

"But how can we be sure he wasn't taken prisoner of war?" demanded Diana.

"We're sure. I've made extensive enquiries. His name would be listed," stated Conrad.

Diana nodded. As she looked at them all she felt more of an outsider than ever. She felt she was intruding on their grief. That they wished she would go so they could mourn openly with each other. She got up and returned to her room. She picked up the photograph of Max that was on the bedside table. The photo was from before the war. He looked happy and healthy. He looked like the Max she married, the vibrant full-of-life daredevil. It was impossible to realise the pale gaunt fragile man who had come home to her on leave was the same man.

She thought of the last time she saw him – from the balcony as he walked down the road to his car, to be taken back to the front to his death.

He didn't deserve this death, alone in a battle in some foreign field.

CHAPTER 42

Diana was lying in bed even though it was the afternoon. She spent most days in bed, trying to come to terms with what had happened. She didn't follow what was happening outside the house. She had no idea about how the war was going and no interest. What did that matter to her now it had taken Max from her?

There was a knock on the door.

"Frau Von Hoffsten?" It was Gerti.

"Leave me alone, Gerti. I don't want anything to eat."

"But, Frau Von Hoffsten, Colonel Otto Dorfman from the Imperial army is here to see you."

Diana quickly sat up and got out of bed.

"Tell him I'll be down in a few minutes," she said.

She quickly changed into a dress. She remembered Colonel Dorfman well. He was the man she visited in Munich when Max was on leave to appeal for him not to be sent back to the front. She knew how senior Dorfman was and for him to be visiting her must mean he had news about Max. He must have good news. She sat down at her dressing table and quickly brushed her hair. As she looked at herself she got a shock. She was so pale and drawn. She applied some make-up quickly and walked out of the room and downstairs to the drawing room. Dorfman was standing there, accompanied by two other men.

"Good afternoon, Colonel Dorfman," she said, shaking his hand.

"Frau Von Hoffsten," nodded Dorfman.

"Please take a seat. We don't have much rations, but can I order you tea?" she asked, sitting down.

Dorfman sat down. "No, this isn't a social call."

Diana sat forward expectantly, her eyes lit with excitement. "You've heard something of Max. Have you found him? Is he alive? He was taken prisoner, yes? It's what I always expected."

Dorfman looked at his officers before looking back at Diana. "No. We've heard nothing back about Major Von Hoffsten. You should put any hope of finding him alive out of your head. You can be assured he's quite dead."

His words were like a punch in her stomach and she slumped back in her chair.

She wasn't even listening as Dorfman continued.

"The reason why we are here is about a completely different matter. We understand you are a friend of Claudia Von Garhart?"

Diana said nothing as she stared off into the distance in a trance, thinking of Dorfman's confirmation that Max was dead.

"*Frau Von Hoffsten!*" snapped Dorfman loudly.

Diana was jolted out of her trance. She stared at Dorfman.

"Claudia Von Garhart? She is your friend?"

"Who?"

Dorfman sighed loudly and angrily. "Claudia Von Garhart!"

"Oh, yes, Claudia. She's a friend of my husband's – was a friend of my husband's – in Munich," she said in a distant abstracted way.

"She visited you here on July the 15th last?"

"I don't know what date she visited, but she did visit me," said Diana.

"What was the purpose of her visit?"

Diana looked at Dorfman's hostile face and became annoyed. "I don't think that's any of your business."

"I'm afraid it is. Claudia Von Garhart has been arrested on treason charges. She was passing information back and forth to her high society friends in Britain."

Diana shook her head. "I really hardly know the woman. This has nothing to do with me."

"I'm afraid it has. The Saturday after she visited, you travelled to Geneva where you met the wife of a high-ranking colonel in the British army," stated Dorfman.

"Yes, Thelma Ashenbry – she's my second cousin's wife. How do you know this?"

"Frau Von Hoffsten, you have been a person of interest since the war started."

She looked aghast. "You've been following me?"

He opened a case beside him which was filled with letters. She immediately recognised them as the letters she had been posting to Garonglen since the war started.

"What are you doing with my letters?" she demanded.

"All your letters sent home to Ireland were intercepted by our censorship office."

"How dare you!"

"The letters are flagrant attempts by you to give information to the enemy about German military activity."

"What are you talking about?" demanded Diana.

"You are passing on information to your family who are in the British army about your husband's military activity."

"I am not!"

"Yes, you are. We have the evidence here." Dorfman took up a letter and, opening it, read out: "*Poor Max has just written to me. Conditions are getting bad there. He is attempting to boost the morale of his officers. Next week his company advances to Amiens.*"

Diana was shocked. "But that's just me being conversational!"

"You might call it being conversational – we call it being a spy."

"It's absurd! You're being ridiculous!"

"Attempting to give all this information to the enemy. And a colleague of Claudia Von Garhart. What information did you pass to Thelma Ashenbry in Geneva?"

"Nothing! She asked me to leave with her for London and I said no. I couldn't abandon Max."

"So you considered deserting to London?"

"Of course not. My family were worried about me. So they wanted me to come home. I'm not sure if you're are aware but the

British press have accused me of being treasonous to the British!"

"Yes, what a clever disguise for you as you went about your business spying here. We've had masses of complaints about you. From the locals in the town and friends of your husband's family. Baroness Von Flashan in Munich said you refused to help with the war effort when requested by her."

"That was my choice, I believe."

"We believe you have had activity on the black market, buying foodstuff."

"Who hasn't?" demanded Diana.

"Yes, but if you can trade food illegally, then you can trade information as well."

Diana stood up angrily. "I have just lost my husband for your war. I will not sit here and be accused of the most stupid things I've ever heard."

"At the outbreak of war all British citizens in Germany were interned. The British government did the same for German citizens there. Because of your late husband's position, not only in the army but in society, you were excused this imprisonment. Now, however, with your husband dead and the dangerous activity you have been engaged in exposed, we have no alternative but to arrest you. You will be interned at the Holminzhin internment camp until the war is over."

"You cannot be serious!"

"Please go pack a small suitcase and be ready to accompany us in ten minutes," said Dorfman.

"You're crazy!"

Dorfman nodded to his officer.

The officer walked over, grabbed Diana's arm and said, "Come on!"

"Let go of me!" she shouted at him, shaking herself free.

Dorfman stood up and approached her. "Please don't embarrass the memory of your husband. It would embarrass him for you to be seen dragged kicking and screaming from here. Which we will do if necessary."

Diana stood stock still.

"You have no choice," said Dorfman. "I'll accompany you while you pack."

Diana hesitantly turned and walked out of the room, followed by Dorfman. She walked up the stairs and opened her bedroom door.

"You can wait here," she said.

"I'll come in," said Dorfman, pushing the door open and entering the bedroom.

Diana went into her dressing room, took down a suitcase and started to pack.

"Please hurry. And no party frocks – you won't need them where you are going," said Dorfman.

She hardly knew what she threw into the case. When it was almost full she went to the bathroom and collected some items there.

Back in the bedroom, she opened a drawer and carefully took out all Max's letters to her and photos of them together, and placed them carefully into the suitcase before fastening it and putting on her hat and coat.

"I'll carry that for you," said Dorfman, reaching out for her suitcase.

"No need," she said, pulling it away from him.

Downstairs she was escorted out into the courtyard and, as she got into the back of the motor car, she looked up at the house and saw Alexandra staring down at her.

Dorfman sat beside her and they travelled in silence out of the courtyard. The other two men got into another car and followed them. They drove down the hill to the town.

She silently looked out the window as they drove through the streets.

Suddenly there was a huge amount of commotion as people came running out of their houses and shops into the streets. As Diana looked out she saw women shouting and crying.

"What the hell is going on here?" demanded Dorfman and instructed the driver, "Pull over."

The motor car came to a stop.

Dorfman beckoned a woman over to him and demanded, "What is happening?"

"The Kaiser has abdicated! The new government has asked for peace. The war is over!" she declared before hurrying off.

Dorfman sat in shocked silence before saying, "We've lost the war."

Diana turned to look at him. "Am I still under arrest?"

"No – you can go," said Dorfman. "We'll drive you back to the house."

"I don't want a lift from you," said Diana as she took her suitcase and got out.

As the motor car drove on, Diana walked through the streets that were filled with chaos until she reached the outskirts of the town. Then she walked back up the hill till she reached home. As she reached the stairs, she collapsed on the floor.

CHAPTER 43

The doctor examined Diana. "I'm pleased to inform you, Frau Von Hoffsten, that you are pregnant."

Diana stared at him in shock. "But my husband has been killed."

"Well, he has given you something to remember him by," smiled the doctor. "I'll inform Count Von Hoffsten of your condition."

The war was over. What Diana couldn't get over was that Max had lost his life so near the end. After four years of fighting and surviving, to be killed so near the Armistice was unthinkably cruel. And now she was pregnant and what should have been the happiest time of her life was now the saddest.

She continued to stay out of the Von Hoffstens' way, dealing with her grief alone, mostly in her room or on the long walks she took every day. Grief had not brought them together.

Brigitte had been sent to Switzerland to a rest home by her father. Her all-consuming grief was what had prompted Conrad to send her away for rest and recuperation.

"At least we won't have to listen to her eternal wailing each night," Diana overheard Alexandra say.

Nobody had congratulated her on the pregnancy, nobody offered support or asked after her health.

One day, from an upstairs window, she saw Conrad and Hugo get into a motor car with several suitcases.

"Where are they going?" Diana asked Gerti.

"They are returning to Munich. The blockade is over and so they are to reopen the brewery within weeks."

"What about Alexandra? Is she not going with them?"

Gerti shrugged. "No, she is remaining here."

Diana wished Alexandra had returned with them and left her alone in the house with her grief.

Diana went down to the town one day and into the bank to withdraw some money from the estate account.

"I'm sorry, but that account has been closed – you can't withdraw," explained the bank manager.

"There must be a mistake," said Diana.

"No mistake, I can assure you."

"In that case I'll withdraw the money from my husband's account."

"I'm afraid all accounts, your late husband's and the estate's, have been closed to you for withdrawals," said the bank manager firmly.

She drove back to the house and marched through the lobby.

"Have you seen Alexandra?" Diana questioned Gerti.

"She's in the study, Frau Von Hoffsten."

Diana went marching down the corridor into the study where she found Alexandra seated at a writing bureau. She was dressed in a long satin dress, her customary cigarette between her fingers as she wrote a letter.

"Alexandra, when is Conrad returning from Munich?"

"He didn't mention any plans to return. I imagine he is there for good," said Alexandra.

"I see. It's urgent that I speak to him."

"He's very busy with reopening the brewery. I shouldn't bother him, Diana."

"Well, I'm afraid I have to! I was unable to withdraw any money from the bank today," said Diana.

"Ah, good, the bank received our instructions then," said Alexandra.

"*Your* instructions?" Diana's eyes widened.

Alexandra reached over for a letter and handed it to Diana. As Diana read it, Alexandra crossed her legs and smoked while studying her reaction.

"What is this?" demanded Diana.

"It's a letter for you from the Von Hoffsten lawyer in Munich. Steps have been taken to declare Max dead. It shouldn't be a long process, merely a formality."

"You didn't waste any time!" Diana said in disgust.

"If you read on, the letter outlines where you stand legally in light of the now-existing circumstances. As you are fully aware, because of your morganatic wedding you are not entitled to anything from Max's estate. With Max's death Hugo is being declared the new heir to his father's title and estate."

"I see." Diana was dumbfounded but not really surprised by their callousness.

"As Hugo is the new heir, we are planning to make this house our permanent residence. So what are your own plans, Diana?"

"My own plans? I've just lost my husband. I have no plans!" spat Diana.

"That's what we feared. But I'm afraid we can't really accommodate you here any more. The war is over and we must all make new plans."

"And where do you suggest I go?"

"That's really none of my concern or business. I imagine you should go back to your own people in Ireland," said Alexandra, nonchalantly waving her cigarette in the air.

"You're kicking me out?" Diana said incredulously.

"Diana, you knew what you were getting yourself into when you entered a left-handed marriage with Max." Alexandra sighed in a bored fashion.

"You can bloody sigh, you bitch!" shouted Diana.

"Diana, there's no place for you here. There never really was and you have no rights here. Now *go!*"

Diana was shaking with anger and humiliation. "You can't just throw me out of my home, my husband's house, with nothing! Not when I'm carrying his child."

"Yes, we can. You freely entered into the left-handed marriage," insisted Alexandra. "I had better make it very clear, lest there be any confusion, that you are entitled to absolutely nothing of Max's estate. That includes all your jewellery, furs, clothes –"

"They are mine!" insisted Diana.

"I'm afraid not. They were on loan to you during the time of your morganatic marriage. I thought you might take this stance, so I had the servants go into your room while you were in town and we have taken all your valuables and put them into safe keeping."

"*You did what?*" screamed Diana.

"Well, we can't have you stealing anything from us," said Alexandra. "There were some old-fashioned gowns and trinkets that you obviously brought from Ireland. They are still in your room for you to pack. I would prefer for you to leave now. But it is getting late, so you may stay the night and leave first thing in the morning. I really wish you would now excuse me as I'm trying to write letters." Alexandra put out her cigarette, turned and began writing again.

Diana stared at her for a long time. She never had been a violent person but there was a red mist descending over her. She forced herself to walk to the door. She was trembling but forced herself not to show it as she turned around.

"You must have loved Max very much, Alexandra, for you to act to me the way you do. It must have killed you to realise you meant absolutely nothing to him and that he loved me with all his heart and soul."

"Goodbye, Diana," said Alexandra, not looking up from her writing.

Shaking with hurt and anger, Diana managed to climb the stairs and go into her bedroom. She went to her dressing table and, quickly looking through her jewellery boxes, she saw all her necklaces, bracelets and earrings were gone. She raced into her dressing room and saw it was stripped of all her clothes and furs.

She opened her purse and saw there was very little money there. She despaired as she realised she barely had enough money to get her to Munich, let alone home to Ireland. Slowly she walked to her bed, sat down on it and cried.

CHAPTER 44

The next morning Diana walked down the stairs, carrying a suitcase. It was a small suitcase as she didn't want to be laden down with heavy luggage with no transport provided. Not that Alexandra had left her with much to take.

Walking into the drawing room she found Alexandra there reading the morning newspaper.

"You're off? I'd like to offer you one of the staff to give you a lift to the train station but they are all busy with their work. The walk will do you good no doubt."

Diana turned and walked from the room and out the front door. She walked out of the courtyard and down the hill, not looking back.

Reaching the town, she made her way to the train station and used what money she had to get a ticket to Munich. She waited on the platform for what seemed like hours before the train arrived and then she got on it.

She had spent the night crying and she wasn't going to cry any more. She had too much to do.

Having walked through the main gates into the grounds of Conrad's *schloss* in Munich, Diana steadied herself as she went to the front door and pulled the bell. A minute later the butler answered.

"Can I help you?" he asked.

"I want to see the count," said Diana, marching past him into the marbled hall.

The panicked butler ran after her.

"It's quite impossible. His Excellency isn't here," the butler gasped, flustered.

"I just went to the brewery and it's not open yet and so I know he's here. Please fetch him," said Diana.

"It's out of the question. You must leave at once, young lady!"

"Not till I see my father-in-law." Diana marched over to the bottom of the stairs and shouted up, "*Conrad!*"

The butler blocked her from going up the stairs and shouted for the footmen.

"I'm not going until I see him!" insisted Diana.

The footmen arrived and the butler said, "If you don't leave at once I'll have no choice but to call the police!"

"*Conrad! Conrad!*" Diana shouted up the stairs.

Diana could hear a door open upstairs and then Conrad appeared at the top of the stairs, looking down at her.

"Conrad, I have to speak to you!" she demanded.

Conrad stared at her and then turned and began to walk away.

"Conrad! I'm Max's wife! I'm carrying your grandchild!" she shouted after him.

The butler nodded to the footmen and they each grabbed one of her arms.

"Let go of me!" screamed Diana, shaking them off, and then she turned and marched out of the house.

As Diana walked through the streets of Munich she began to despair. She had no money. Where would she sleep that night? She began to panic and shake. She reached into her pocket and took out the lawyer's letter Alexandra had handed her. Checking the address, she made her way to the lawyer's office.

She seemed to wait an eternity in the reception room before being shown into the office of Conrad's lawyer. He was a kindly-looking man in his sixties called Hans.

"Thank you for meeting me," said Diana, shaking his hand and sitting down.

He smiled uncomfortably at her. He had met Diana at some of

Max's functions before the war and had always found her charming and polite.

"I've come to talk to you about this," she said, holding up the letter.

Hans nodded. "It's all quite legal, I can assure you. You cannot contest your morganatic marriage if that is what you are here for."

"Whether it's legal or not is not the point. I have been treated in the most monstrous fashion by the Von Hoffstens. They have literally thrown me out of my home with no money, no possessions. I'm homeless, penniless. I don't even have anywhere to sleep tonight. All my family are in Ireland and London."

"Don't you have any friends?"

"Because of my nationality I became quite isolated during the war."

"I understand, but there's nothing I can do about it. These are Count Von Hoffsten's wishes and he is acting within the law of the marriage you freely entered into."

"But when I married Max I never expected to be a young widow with no rights," said Diana.

"The war has made everyone's circumstances difficult."

"Everyone except Hugo and Alexandra who have taken everything!"

Hans shrugged. "I'm sorry, I really am, about your situation. But there is nothing I can do."

Diana sat up straight. "I'm pregnant, Hans."

This news startled the lawyer.

"I see," he said, sitting back.

"I don't know what I'm going to do," she said, unable to keep the despair out of her voice.

The lawyer sat in thought before speaking. "I understand on the morning after your wedding Max gave you an emerald necklace as his morning present?"

"Yes, the gift given to a left-handed bride as the only thing she will legally receive from the wedding. I handed it back to Max."

"I know. Max brought it back to the family vault. I believe the necklace is legally yours as your morganatic gift."

Diana's face lit up with gratitude.

"I'll have to speak to His Excellency about it," said Hans. "But I will be informing him that the necklace is yours legally and should be handed over to you."

"Thank you, Hans. Will it take long for you to speak to him? As I said, I have nowhere to stay tonight."

"Please wait here, and I'll meet with the count."

An hour passed and Diana sat nervously until Hans arrived back.

"I met with His Excellency. The emerald necklace that was given to you is a family heirloom which His Excellency said Max had no right to give you."

Diana felt like bursting out crying.

"However, I explained to the count that whether it was his right or not is of no interest to me. It was given to you as your wedding morning gift and that makes it legally yours."

"Thank you," she whispered.

"His Excellency is willing to compensate you for the necklace to the sum of twenty-five thousand marks."

"It's probably worth a lot more," said Diana.

"It probably is," agreed Hans. "But it is getting dark, Diana, and it would take you a while to find the right buyer for such an item."

Diana nodded. "I'll take the money, thank you."

Hans nodded. "I'll fetch it from our safe."

Diana felt nothing but relief as she left the lawyer's office. She knew she had been ripped off in the matter of the necklace as it was worth much more than what she was given. But it and the kindly lawyer had been her saviours. She found a small cheap-looking hotel near the central train station and booked in for the night.

As she locked the door of her hotel room behind her, her sense of reprieve at not having to sleep in the train station, hungry, superseded the feeling of injustice and degradation she felt at the hands of Max's family. She would get up early and start planning her journey back to Ireland, leaving on the first possible train. Her life here was over and she needed to return home to her family and loved ones. She could hardly wait to leave.

CHAPTER 45

Present Day

Sam spent the first night in Munich and then he hired a car and drove south towards the Alps and Tegernfrei. The scenery took his breath away.

He booked into a small hotel in the town centre. As he walked through the town the buildings looked as if they hadn't been changed in centuries. The hotel manager had explained to him that there were strict planning laws in force in the area, preserving the traditional architecture. Sam imagined the town looked exactly the same when Diana arrived there to get married over a century ago, except that now it was filled with flash cars and designer-clad people. He discovered the area was a retreat for Munich's wealthy residents who came for the lake and the mountains.

He went into a restaurant and took a table overlooking the lake. The friendly waitress came and took his order.

"Excuse me, could you tell me how I get to the Church of St Benedict," he asked.

"Yes – you follow the road outside here to the left and it will lead you up around the lake into the hills. You go past the Von Hoffsten estate and about four or five kilometres farther you'll see the church. You can't miss it."

"The Von Hoffsten estate? That's the brewery family?"

"That's their place up there," she said, pointing to the hills past the town and a large manor house perched there in the distance.

"Is the estate open to the public?" he asked.

She started to laugh. "No! Anything but! There's a lot of security there. Particularly now after the kidnap attempt."

"Is he out of hospital?" asked Sam.

"Yes, he's up there recuperating with his wife," she said.

"Do you ever see them? Do they come down to the town?"

She laughed again. "No, of course not!" She headed back to the kitchens.

Sam followed her directions and drove up to the estate. He was hoping to be able to see the Von Hoffsten house from the road but it was impossible. He slowed as he drove past the entrance. The large electric gates were shut tight and he could see two security men inside them.

He speeded up the hill and finally came to a beautiful church looking down on the lake and valley. He parked the car and went up to the house beside the church and rang the doorbell. A minute later a priest, who looked as if he were in his seventies, came out.

"Hello. Father Schmidt?"

"That's right. You must be the young man from Ireland who rang about the records?"

"That's right," Sam smiled.

Father Schmidt led him into the records room.

"I was intrigued to get your telephone call. You are Diana Cantwell's great-grandson?"

"That's right. I believe she married Max Von Hoffsten in this church in December 1912."

"She did indeed and I got the record out for you here," said the priest as they both sat down at a desk.

Sam took the record and studied it intently.

"I'm only finding out about all this now," he explained.

"I take it you never knew her?" asked the priest.

"No, gosh, she was long dead before I was born."

"I instantly knew the name when you rang. You see my grandmother used to work at the big house on the Von Hoffsten estate when Diana was living there."

"Really?" Sam was amazed.

"Yes, my grandmother Gerti was the housekeeper there. When I

263

was a child she used to talk about her time working there and spoke of Diana often."

"What did she say about her?" Sam was brimming with excitement.

"She was very beautiful, very kind to the staff, but strong. I think there were quite a few arguments between her and the Von Hoffstens. She could hold her own in an argument."

"Well, that's good to know," smiled Sam.

"Herself and Max, the young heir, well, it was a love match without a doubt. The fact they had a morganatic marriage proves that."

"A what?" Sam asked.

"A left-handed marriage. It's when the wife doesn't have the rights to the husband's title and property and also –"

"Their children have none of the rights either," Sam finished the sentence as realisation dawned. He remembered he had come across morganatic marriages in his research as a historian. He sighed. "It all makes sense now. You see, I was curious as to why she didn't become a countess and why my grandfather, her son, was also bypassed."

The priest nodded. "It was all very unfair really. The old count, Max's father, didn't approve of Diana. He wanted Max to marry an Austrian princess called Alexandra. When Max refused, a left-handed marriage was forced on him and Diana. Alexandra then married Hugo, Max's younger brother, and they are the present Count Eric's grandparents. The title and everything else passed to Hugo when Max was killed in the war."

"I see," said Sam sadly.

"They threw poor Diana out, even though she was pregnant with Max's child at the time."

"So cruel!" Sam shook his head in disgust.

"I believe she went home to her people in Ireland."

Sam sighed. "Yes . . . and here I am today."

Sam drove back down the hill, consumed with sadness. He felt so badly for Diana, losing her husband and then having to fend for herself. He wondered how she coped, leaving this life of privilege and prestige.

There was a lay-by and he pulled over and parked. Getting out, he took in the view of the lake and the mountains – the same view Diana lived with while she was there in her left-handed marriage.

There was a path leading to the lake and he followed it down. Once he got to the lakeshore he walked along it towards the Von Hoffsten estate. When he came to heavy fences and many signs warning people not to trespass, he realised he had reached it. The fencing extended along the supports of a wooden pier which reached far into the lake. He climbed on a nearby rock to see if he could catch a glimpse of the house but there was no sign of it.

Walking along the fence he suddenly spotted a hole in it. Going up to it, he realised he could slip through. He thought about it for a moment and then made a decision. This was his one opportunity to get to see the house his great-grandmother had lived in.

He went through the fence.

He walked carefully along the lakeshore within the estate until finally he saw the house perched up on the hill. He strained to see it, realising he couldn't go any nearer for fear of being caught. It looked like a beautiful old house and it was hard to believe his great-grandmother was lady of the manor there.

Just then he saw someone walking along the beach towards him and he quickly hid behind some trees. As the figure came closer he saw it was the countess. He had only ever seen her with her hair tied back but that day it was long and loose, swaying as she walked. She was wearing a long white woollen cardigan over a white trousers and top and seemed lost in thought as she walked along. She had her arms folded and was staring at the ground.

When she reached the wooden pier she walked onto it and stood staring out at the lake and the mountains beyond it.

As Sam looked at her, he couldn't help but think how solitary and sad she looked. And then she suddenly put her face in her hands and began to cry. He had this overwhelming desire to go and comfort her.

"*Achtung!*" said a voice behind him. Turning around he saw a security guard there, pointing a gun at him.

Sam sat in the police station in Munich, having been arrested.

The door opened and in walked the Von Hoffsten's lawyer, Sophie Essen.

"Right, I have spoken to the count and countess and they do not wish to press charges against Mr Cantwell," she told the police officer present, "considering his generosity to the family in the past."

"Am I free to go then?" he said, standing up.

The officer nodded.

"Thank you, officer," said Sophie and she escorted Sam out of the room.

"What on earth do you think you were playing at, entering the Von Hoffsten estate like that?" she demanded once they were outside the station.

"I didn't know it was private property."

"Did you not read all the signs saying not to trespass?"

"They were all written in German. I can't read German!"

She shook her head in despair. "You know, from the first moment I met you I knew you were going to be trouble. Call it instinct."

"The first time I met you I knew you were a bitch – call that instinct as well!" he spat back.

"I don't know why you're being like this. I just saved you from a prison cell. There was an attempt on the count's life not so long ago, and then you just wander into his home! What are you doing here anyway?"

"I wanted to find out about my great-grandmother who got married here to the present count's great-uncle. It's quite a close connection, when you think about it."

"It doesn't sound close at all!"

"Well, it was close enough for him to take my blood! You know, if my great-grandmother and great-grandfather hadn't had a left-handed marriage, that title would have been passed down to me. I'd be Count Von Hoffsten now and you'd be working for me!"

Sophie sighed and studied him. "I haven't a clue what you're talking about . . . Sam, go home to your wife and children. You seem to have a happy life there. Don't go messing around looking for answers in the past, opening cans of worms – it will only bring you unhappiness. Goodbye, Sam. Thanks for everything and I hope our paths don't need to cross again!"

She patted him on the shoulder and walked off.

Sam thought it wise not to mention to Julia that he had been arrested while on his trip to Germany because of trespassing on the Von Hoffsten estate while spying on the countess. He sat in the dining room drawing out a family tree, waiting for her and the kids to arrive back from her mother's.

"Sam?" she called on entering the house.

"In here!" he answered and suddenly the two children were rushing in and hugging him excitedly.

"Presents from Germany up in your rooms," he told them and they rushed up the stairs.

Julia walked in and he stood up and kissed her.

"How did it all go?" he asked.

"Oh, fine, the same as usual." She gave him a quick smile and put her handbag on the table. "How was your Munich trip?"

"Great, did lots of sightseeing. Perfume for you on your dressing table upstairs."

"Ah, thanks, Sam!" She bent forward and kissed him again. She looked at the large sheet of paper with names and lines drawn on it. "What's all this? Is it for a lecture?"

"No, it's a family tree. You see, I visited the church where my great-grandmother Diana and my great-grandfather Max got married. I met the priest there whose grandmother used to work for them. Isn't that amazing?"

Julia looked at him, confounded. "I knew there was more to a trip to Munich than sightseeing!"

"Now look at this," he said. "You see Diana and Max had a son Christian, my grandfather. He died young, as you know. But first he had my father who then had me. But! Diana and Max had what was called a morganatic marriage. This meant that, although she was his legal wife, she and their children weren't entitled to his title or property. So when Max died in the First World War the title and estates passed to his brother Hugo, who is the present count's grandfather, whose life I saved."

Julia smiled sarcastically. "Brilliant! Now that we've solved your connection to that lot can you put all this away and lay the table for dinner? Thanks!"

She turned and walked up the stairs.

He followed her up. "But don't you get it?"

"Get what?" she asked, walking down the corridor and into their bedroom.

"If it wasn't for that morganatic marriage I'd be Count Von Hoffsten! I'm in the direct eldest male line."

"Fascinating!" she said, opening the box of perfume he had bought for her and spraying it on her wrist and smelling it.

"And you'd be a countess," he said.

"Countess Julia has a funny ring to it," she mocked.

"You obviously have no interest in this at all!" he accused her angrily.

She turned and faced him. "I don't know what you want me to say. Yes, of course it's fascinating that you are in some way descended from these people. But, Sam, you actually had eight great-grandparents in total, and only one, this Max, was an aristocrat. I am certain that the rest of your great-grandparents' backgrounds were normal enough to have diluted any blue blood you had into insignificance."

"Well, thank you for that!"

"Well, it's true. As for me being a countess, if the title had not been interrupted by this morganatic marriage, that wouldn't have happened either. Do you know why? Because you would have been brought up in a series of elite schools, mixing with elite circles, and we would have never met in that nightclub in town ten years ago! Now, the kids are starving – I'm going to put the dinner on. I only managed to do a quick shop so it's burgers, beans and chips. Sorry if that offends your patrician tastes!"

She marched past him out of the room.

Sam now knew, having spoken to Father Schmidt, that Diana had returned to Ireland when Max had been killed in the war. So she must have given birth here to their son Christian, he reasoned. He couldn't imagine there were too many Von Hoffstens registered at birth in Ireland at the time. And when he went onto the government's births registrations website he found it straight away. There was a copy of the birth certificate on the screen, showing Christian had been born in May 1919. The father was registered as Max Von Hoffsten and he was registered as deceased. The mother Diana Von Hoffsten, maiden name Cantwell, was registered as living at Garonglen Estate, Blakestown, County Meath. Sam found it exciting to see his grandfather there on the official birth cert with Max registered as his father. The address of Garonglen was obviously the name of the old Cantwell estate where Diana returned after being kicked out by the Von Hoffstens.

He had an afternoon free of lectures the following day and he decided to give County Meath a visit.

PART 3

1919

CHAPTER 46

On her last morning in Munich Diana entered the economy carriage of the train at the main train station. She couldn't help remembering how she had arrived spectacularly in Munich for her wedding all those years ago on the Orient Express.

As she looked around at her tired, hungry and poor travelling companions, she realised she was leaving in much less auspicious circumstances than the ones she had arrived in. But she had no choice – the money she got for the necklace had to see her home to Garonglen which meant careful economising. There was no first-class travel or luxurious hotels as she made her way across Europe in a series of train journeys.

As she travelled north through Germany she saw a country reduced to its knees by the war. But it was only when she hit the Belgian and French borders that she saw the true horrific scale of the war. Towns and villages laid bare. Only shells of houses left. Towns destroyed in a wasteland of destruction.

Often the train tracks were destroyed between towns and she had to get a lift in a motor car, a horse and cart or walk to the next train station. As she travelled she passed many displaced people. German soldiers or ex-prisoners of war walking or travelling in the opposite direction to her on their long journey home. Her eyes frantically searched the sea of faces of the men passing her, looking for Max somewhere among them. But she knew she was torturing herself. She knew he was dead. These were the lucky ones who were going home to their loved ones. Then there were the refugees she passed, the French and Belgians slowly making their way back to try and rebuild their lives in their destroyed homes.

As she travelled onwards towards the French ports, she left the battlefields behind. She finally arrived in Cherbourg and booked her passage on a boat to Ireland.

For the first time in years she was excited as the boat sailed away from the French coast and headed towards Ireland. She would be home soon with her mother, father and brothers in Garonglen. Garonglen, so far from the horrors of the war zone she had just passed through. A place untouched by this war.

As she sat in the bar on the boat, sipping a drink, she asked the barman for a newspaper.

"Certainly, ma'am," said the barman and he returned a minute later with a copy of the *Irish Times*.

"Thank you," she smiled.

"Were you a nurse at the front?" asked the friendly barman.

"No, I've just been away for a while. Looking forward to returning home," she smiled back.

Then her eyes fell on the headline of the newspaper.

'*Republicans Take Key Positions in Cork as Anglo-Irish War Rages.*'

She read the first paragraph with increasing shock at the news of the outbreak of war in Ireland.

"Oh my goodness!" she exclaimed.

"I know," said the barman, shaking his head. "As if the world didn't have enough of war over there, now it's flared up at home as well."

CHAPTER 47

The boat docked in Dublin and as Diana made her way to the city centre her joy at returning home was replaced with disbelief. The genteel sophisticated city she remembered from the Edwardian era was now a heavily militarised zone. She had known that Irish Independence had always been rumbling away in the background before the Great War. But like everywhere else in Europe the Great War seemed to be a catalytic event and it had now flared into a full-scale war of independence in Ireland.

Anxious to get out of the city as quickly as possible she made her way to the bus depot and got the first bus to the village near Garonglen.

As the bus made its way from Dublin to the country roads of County Meath she felt safer and all her youthful memories came flooding back.

She got off at the village and hurried down the road to Garonglen. Reaching the gates, it was like she had never left as she hurried past the gate lodge and up the avenue to the house. She could hardly contain herself as she turned the corner where the house came into view.

She stopped and stood still. Where the elegant manor once stood was now a shell of a house. Garonglen had been burned down.

She walked disbelievingly through the ruins of what had been her home. Apart from the walls there was nothing left. Roofless, windowless, the fire had destroyed everything. What had happened here, she asked herself in anguish. She stood in what had been the drawing room. A room that had harboured so many wonderful memories of family life, elegant parties, and where she had been courted by Max. Nothing remained now of that room but the four walls. Above was the sky, as the floor above and the roof had been destroyed in the fire.

She walked over to the front window and looked out at what once had been the excellently kept forecourt and gardens. By the look of the place the fire had been recent. As she looked out the window she saw smoke coming from the copse of trees down by the main gateway and realised it was coming from the gate lodge. She hurried from the house and down the avenue.

"Hello!" she shouted as she hammered on the door of the lodge. "It's me! Diana!"

A few moments later the bolt slid back, the door opened wide and there stood Maud.

"Mama!" cried Diana and rushed to her, embracing her and holding her tight.

"Mama! I'm home!"

She drew back and saw that Maud was deathly pale, her eyes lifeless. She seemed unable to hug Diana back.

Diana followed Maud into the small sitting room of the gate lodge. She got a start on entering the room. There were drawings and paintings of Dashiel everywhere. They all looked freshly painted. An easel stood in the centre of the room with a half-finished portrait of him on it.

"I'd given up hope of ever hearing from you again," said Maud. "We wrote to you every week but never heard anything back."

"I wrote to you too, but the censorship office in Germany wouldn't allow the post through." Diana had a pleading look on her face. "Where *is* everyone, Mama?"

"They're gone. All gone."

"What are you talking about?" demanded Diana, her eyes welling with tears.

Maud went over and touched Dashiel's face on the canvas she was painting.

"Dashiel was killed in battle in the last year of the war. He's buried in France. Your papa, my poor darling Simon, couldn't cope with it. He died of a broken heart not long after."

Diana slumped down on the couch, crying softly. Maud sat on an armchair opposite.

"Warren?" Diana was almost terrified to ask.

"He's alive. But he can't see."

"What do you mean?"

"He was blinded in a gas attack on the front. He's in a military home in Dublin, still recuperating."

It seemed hours before either of them said anything again. They just sat there in silence.

Diana shook her head and wiped away a tear. "And what happened here? To Garonglen?"

"The War of Independence erupted after Christmas and the rebels are burning down the 'Big Houses' all around the country. We were one of the ones targeted. They want our type, the landed gentry, out of the country and the best way to achieve that is to burn us out of our homes."

"The bastards!"

"Oh, they were incredibly polite for revolutionaries," said Maud. "They arrived one night and knocked on the door and told me that it was with regret they had to burn down my house as part of the struggle for independence. I explained to them that my house had no objection to them getting their independence and so not to take out their anger on Garonglen. I think they felt quite sorry for me, and even helped me take some possessions before they torched the place."

"They should be ashamed of themselves, burning the house down on a woman on her own!"

"Oh, don't be angry with them, darling. As I said, they were incredibly polite. They even gave me a lift down to the gate lodge here and made sure I was safely ensconced for the night before they set off on their mission to burn their next target. I believe in Russia the revolutionaries are just murdering the gentry on sight. We got off quite lightly here, I believe."

Diana shook her head in disbelief at her mother's benevolence.

She was reeling from the shock of Dashiel and Simon's deaths. And yet she felt quite numb.

As she looked at the fragile state her mother was in, she was scared to burden her with Max's death. The whole family had loved him like a family member. But she must tell her.

"Mama, I'm got some other terrible news. Max was killed in the war as well."

Maud showed no emotion as she got up and stroked Dashiel's face on the portrait.

"Good," said Maud. "I'm glad."

"Mama! What are you saying?"

"Well, he was the enemy, wasn't he?"

"Mama!" Diana cried.

Maud picked up her brush and continued to paint Dashiel's portrait.

"You know, before they torched Garonglen I didn't have time to rescue any photos of Dashiel. I have no photos of him. I have to paint from memory. I have to keep painting him so that I never forget his beautiful face."

Diana looked at her mother as she painted, surrounded by all the other portraits she had done of Dashiel.

Maud suddenly turned and studied Diana.

"You're pregnant."

"Yes."

Maud shook her head in despair and continued painting.

Diana and Maud were walking through the farm.

"And what of the land?" said Diana.

"We won't have it for much longer," sighed Maud. "We were always in debt as you know and so the land is for sale to clear the debts. That's what the locals want, to get our land, and now they may buy it at auction. If Warren was well or Dashiel still alive I suppose we could fight to keep it. But what's the point now? Our family has lost its future."

"Is there no other course?"

"No. Diana, we're not welcome here any more. I don't know

why the British are even fighting to keep Ireland – it's a fait accompli as far as I'm concerned. There will be an independent Ireland soon and there will be no welcome for the likes of us here. The burning down of our homes is telling us that."

"And what are the other Protestant landed families doing? Our friends?"

"Many are fleeing to England as soon as they can."

"What about the Roundtrees? Has their house been attacked?"

"Not so far. They lost their son Tommy in the war. Like many others, Hannah and her parents are keeping their heads down and hoping the rebels don't come knocking on their door like they did to us."

Diana felt despair but more worryingly she felt her mother had resigned herself to her fate. For a woman who was always so ambitious socially and planning for the future, it broke Diana's heart to hear her speak like this.

"If families like ours hadn't lost our sons, we might have a future. But what is left? Only the old people and women."

"What do you intend to do?"

"What can I do? I have a small pension to live on. I'll stay living at the gate lodge quietly. I'll plant a vegetable garden to help with the finances, and paint."

"Mama, I can't bear all this!" Diana's voice cracked. "You can't just give up!"

"I gave up the day I was telegrammed that Dashiel had been killed."

"I'm sorry I wasn't here, Mama."

"It's where you should have been. We sent for you. Thelma Ashenbry travelled to Switzerland to get you." There was an accusing tone in Maud's voice.

"I couldn't leave Max, Mama."

"Max who was at the front fighting for the other side!" Maud blazed at Diana. "Do you have any idea the terrible position you put us in?"

"Mama, there was nothing I could do. I loved Max. I couldn't desert him."

"So you chose to desert us instead! Have you any idea of what the British press said about you?"

"Thelma showed me the newspapers, yes."

"And yet you still didn't leave?"

"You were asking the impossible."

"We sent her to Geneva to fetch you. It took so much organising!"

"I couldn't leave Max."

"And why are you back now, Diana? Why now?"

"To see you, of course."

"And are you returning to Germany?"

Diana turned away. "No, I'm not welcome there any more. Hugo is the new heir and I have no rights."

"Because of your left-handed marriage?"

"Yes."

"The one we begged you not to enter when it was being forced on you and Max."

"I married Max because I loved him. I didn't marry Max for his money, or his title or his estate."

"Which is good, because you don't have any of it now!" Maud turned and walked off to the gatehouse.

Diana wandered through the burnt-out shell of Garonglen, trying to remember the wonderful times they had there. But as she looked at the burned walls it seemed like a different place. She sank to her knees sobbing.

"Papa!" she cried, looking up at the sky.

CHAPTER 48

Warren was being looked after in a military convalescence hospital, the Royal Richmond in Dublin.

Although Diana dreaded seeing him with his injury, she couldn't wait to visit him.

She got a bus to the hospital. As she walked up the avenue she was shaken to see all the wounded men in the grounds. Seeing so many of them trying to cope with their injuries and wounds, being assisted by nurses, made her shudder.

"I'm here to see Warren Cantwell – I'm his sister," she said to a nurse in the lobby.

"He's in his room," she said. "Please follow me."

Diana was led to an upper floor where the smiling nurse opened a door and let her in. It was small basic room.

Warren was sitting in a chair beside an open window.

Diana walked in and closed the door behind her.

"Hello?" Warren called, moving his head in the direction of the door.

"Warren," she said softly.

His head moved urgently around but she could tell he was unable to see her.

"Diana?" he asked, his voice breaking in emotion.

"Yes, Warren, it's me," she said, going to him.

He held out his arms to her and she fell into them, holding him tightly.

She sat in a chair beside him, holding his hands, and gazed into his eyes which were lifeless and staring into space, unable to see.

"I'm one of the lucky ones," he said.

"Yes?" she answered, trying to keep the pain out of her voice.

"Because I was an officer I get my own room. If I wasn't I'd be in a ward."

"That is good, very good." She gripped his hands even more tightly at his words.

"Mama didn't come with you?" he asked.

"No."

"She visits regularly . . . I can tell she hates coming here though. She's not able to see me like this. She's barely coping since Dashiel died."

"Don't you worry about her, Warren – you just worry about yourself getting better," she urged.

"Diana – I – I won't see again – I won't get better," he said softly. She stared at him.

"And you're not to cry," he said, releasing one of his hands from her grip, reaching out to her face and wiping away the tears.

"Is – is – is there nothing they can do?"

"Not to make me see again, no. But the government has said that they don't think blindness should be an obstruction to us leading full lives again. And, as we all know, if the government says something then it must be right." He didn't hide the sarcasm in his voice. "They give me lots of training to adapt to – my 'new circumstances', as they call it. Did you get the bus here? Did you see many signs of the war on the streets in Dublin?"

"There's a lot of military around," said Diana.

"As if we didn't have enough war over there – they start one over here."

"I'm sure it can't last for long."

"So I believe. Ireland will get its independence and that will be that – is it necessary to have a war on the way? It seems necessary to have a war for everything these days. Once Ireland gets independence I don't know what will happen here."

"What do you mean?"

"With the military hospital. They can't have a British military

282

hospital in an independent Ireland, can they? They'll probably move me to a military hospital in England."

"Don't worry about anything, Warren. I'll make sure you are looked after and provided for," said Diana, making a promise she feared she would never be able to keep in her circumstances.

"Any word from Hannah Roundtree?"

"Not since I got back," said Diana.

"She visits me when she gets the chance. She's very busy running the farm now since their Tommy got killed. She's a great girl, Hannah."

"Yes, she is," agreed Diana.

"I should have married her when I got the chance. Mama discouraged it, said she wasn't good enough for me."

"Maybe there's still a chance?" asked Diana.

"Of course there isn't. What use would a blind man be to help her run their farm?"

Diana put her hand to her mouth.

"And Garonglen is no more – burned down?"

"That's right, Warren," she said, trying to keep the emotion out of her voice.

"In a way I'm glad I can't see it. Now it will always be as I remember it. When the war started I was so excited. I'd get to see some of the world away from our home. Now all I want to see is our home."

CHAPTER 49

There was a knock on the gate-lodge door one morning. Maud was still in bed and Diana cautiously went to the window to look out. She was somewhat frightened as the war was raging around the country. She thought the rebels wouldn't return to Garonglen as their business was finished there, but she couldn't be too sure. The papers carried news every morning of atrocities being committed by one side or the other.

"Hello?" she said, carefully opening the window.

"Diana! It's me, Hannah."

Diana flew to the door and swung it open. She embraced her old friend.

"I heard you were back," said Hannah. "I could hardly believe it. I came straight here to see if it was true."

"Hannah, it's so good to see you," laughed Diana.

"You haven't changed a bit," said Hannah.

"Oh, I have, Hannah, believe me, I have."

To Diana's delight Hannah suggested taking her away for the day to her own family home. As Hannah drove them through the local village, the countryside had a heavy presence of British soldiers patrolling.

They were stopped at a check point.

"Where are you travelling to?" asked the soldier.

"Just up the way to my family home, the castle. I'm Hannah Roundtree."

"Carry on, miss."

"Thank you!" said Hannah as she drove on. She glanced at Diana. "They can't be too careful. The rebels are travelling incognito everywhere."

"I can hardly recognise the place," said Diana. "This quiet peaceful area now a military zone."

"It's amazing how you get used to it," said Hannah as she took a sharp corner.

"I could never get used to it. My home is gone forever."

Hannah gave her a sympathetic smile. "Awful what happened to Garonglen."

"They didn't come to you, the rebels?"

"No, so far so good – we've been lucky. We're keeping our heads down and hoping for the best – that's what Papa says we must do."

Diana sat in the conservatory at the back of the Roundtrees' house, letting the memories flood back. She remembered the parties there before the war. And the party that Dashiel had arranged for Max to show up at to surprise her. Everything else had changed so much it was strange to find one place the same.

Hannah came in holding a silver tray with a teapot and sandwiches on it.

"I'm afraid I had to rustle this up myself. All the staff left when the hostilities started. They didn't want to be seen working for a gentry family." She put down the tray and poured the tea. "We've had to endure our own cooking ever since!"

"Hannah, you should be grateful for the very fact you have food. If you saw the starvation and deprivation I witnessed in Germany during the war!"

"Well, it wasn't a picnic here either, you know – the rationing. We couldn't get sugar for a month once."

"At least you had food to ration."

"It must have been appalling. You don't think of the other side suffering. They said some awful things about you in the press. We all thought you were living on caviar and champagne."

"Far from it," said Diana.

"Poor you!"

"Hannah, what are your long-term plans now? What is your family going to do?"

"Sit tight and wait for this war in Ireland to be over."

"You won't be moving to England?"

Hannah laughed. "Heavens, no, why should we?"

"It's just that Mama was saying a lot of our friends are leaving."

"As long as they don't burn us out, we'll stay," said Hannah assuredly.

"But who's going to run the farm now without your poor brother Tommy?"

"Well, I was thinking I'd make a stab at it myself. I mean I'd been running things with Papa after Tommy went to fight in France and, after he got killed, I just kept on running it. I won't be doing anything I haven't been doing before."

Diana stared at her in admiration.

"I daresay," said Hannah, "if Garonglen hadn't been burned down and you weren't losing your land you'd be doing the same thing yourself."

Diana shrugged. "Perhaps I would. I was left mostly running Max's estate when he went to war. But that's no longer an option for me now."

"So what are you going to do?"

"Well, I'll have to stay here until the baby is born. After that, I don't know. I don't have many choices. But I'll have to provide for my child and build some kind of life for myself. I just have no idea how or what."

As the weeks went by, Diana and Maud lived quietly in the gate lodge. Diana realised they were both grieving. Maud seemed so bitter that Diana found it hard to deal with.

Diana thought hard about what she should do now. Ireland had entered a turbulent period and gone was the peaceful country of her Edwardian youth. It was true a lot of their friends were migrating to Britain. After the cost of getting back to Ireland, Diana realised she had very little money left. But what could she do in London? She had never worked a day in her life. She had no experience or training. She would be arriving in London at nearly thirty as a penniless widowed mother of one, with a notorious reputation in the British press.

One evening she was in the sitting room in the gate lodge, dwelling on her lack of options, as she watched her mother paint yet another portrait of Dashiel.

Maud suddenly turned around. "Whatever happened to that horse you owned – Halcyon?"

The disturbing memory of what had become of Halcyon flashed through Diana's mind.

"He died," said Diana.

"Like everything else of value . . . Halcyon. He was aptly named, wasn't he? A champion during those halcyon days before the war."

In Munich Hugo and Alexandra were in the drawing room of the *schloss*. Hugo sat deep in thought while Alexandra twitched nervously. The door opened and a middle-aged man walked in.

"Doctor?" asked Alexandra.

"There was nothing I could do. The count died peacefully a short while ago."

"Thank you, Doctor," said Alexandra and the doctor retreated.

Hugo looked stunned as he stared ahead.

Alexandra stood up, took his hand and said: "Our time has come now."

CHAPTER 50

Diana gave birth to a boy in May. She delivered him in the gate lodge, with the local doctor at hand. As she held the baby she felt a strange mix of delight, sadness and fear. Delight to have her child, sadness that Max wasn't there to see him, and fear for her baby's future . . . and what kind of a future she could provide for him.

"What are you going to call him?" asked Maud.

"Christian," answered Diana. "Max told me once if we had a son he would like that name for him."

"Christian Von Hoffsten. Sounds most aristocratic. To think that child should have been born a count, an heir to all that fortune. Instead what has he got?"

"He's got me, and I'll make sure he'll never want for anything, no matter what I have to do to get it."

"Brave words, Diana," said Maud dismissively.

Diana had hoped the birth of her first grandchild would somehow give hope back to Maud, that it would relight something in her. But Maud seemed as disinterested in Christian as she was now in everything else.

"I think he looks like Dashiel," said Diana.

"He looks nothing like Dashiel," said Maud firmly. "He looks exactly like his father – God help him."

The reality of motherhood came as a terrible shock to Diana. She hadn't been brought up in a world where mothers ever did any actual hands-on work with their children. She and her brothers had been brought up by a much-loved nanny – their food cooked by the cook – their clothes washed by the washerwoman – while Maud oversaw the upbringing, as always delivering advice and orders, but never actually getting her hands dirty. Even in a house like Garonglen, where money was always in short supply, the gentry had their set rules and regulations and a lady never did manual work. Now in the gate lodge, Diana found she was completely on her own. Except of course for Maud who still delivered advice and orders, but still did not get her hands dirty with any practical help with Christian. Diana found herself exhausted, cleaning the nappies, washing the clothes, feeding him, washing him, getting up at night to soothe him while he cried. It was something she had never been expected to do or expected herself to do. But now on her own and trying to conserve what money she had, she was forced into the role.

Although, every night as she finally managed to get Christian off to sleep and lay down beside him, she didn't mind at all. She would do anything for him. He was the only good thing left in her life. The one thing she had of Max. As she looked lovingly at Christian, she realised her mother was right about at least one thing: he was the image of Max.

Diana came out of the local post office, pushing the perambulator with Christian in it, after checking her account. She was extremely worried. She did not have much money left. She needed to make plans for the future. She couldn't wait any longer.

As she wheeled the perambulator down the street she suddenly came face to face with Caitríona, their old cook at Garonglen. Caitríona looked surprised to see her.

"Caitríona!" smiled Diana warmly. "How good to see you! How have you been?"

Caitríona looked coldly at her. "Oh, you're back, are you?"

"Yes. I'm staying with Mama."

"Are you indeed?" Caitríona's expression turned to smugness. "At the gate lodge?"

"That's right."

"You're no better than the rest of us now, and it's good enough for you!" spat Caitríona.

"Caitríona!" Diana was shocked.

"You and your lot have been lording it around here for long enough. It's about time you were cut down to size! That mother of yours with her airs and graces, bossing everyone around!"

"Good day, Caitríona," said Diana curtly as she pushed the perambulator past her and continued down the street.

"You're not welcome here any more! Go!" Caitríona shouted down the street after her.

When she got back to the gate lodge she found Maud planting vegetables out the back. It was such a strange and depressing sight. Her mother's hands had been made only to hold a glass of champagne or an artist's brush.

There was nothing for them at Garonglen any more.

"I've made a decision," said Diana. "I'm going to move to London."

Maud stood up from her work and looked at her daughter.

"And what do you propose to do there?"

"I don't know," said Diana. "But whatever it is, it's more than I'll be doing here."

Maud shrugged. "You must do what you see fit. Any words of advice from me would be ignored anyway. Besides, my days of giving advice are over. For all my advice and all my planning, look how we ended up."

"Will you come with us – to London?"

Maud started to laugh. "No, I will not. What would I do in London at this stage of my life?"

"Isn't it better than staying here planting carrots?"

"No, I imagine it isn't. I'm not going to London to live like a pauper. I might be living like a pauper here, but at least the Ashenbrys can't see me doing so."

"I think the Ashenbrys are very kind people. They might help us."

"You deluded creature! The Ashenbrys were only interested in

290

us when we might have been someone. I think you'll find that, now we are definitely nobodys, there will be no welcome on the mat. I certainly won't be going anywhere near them. Everyone has their pride."

"Mine's on the floor – where's yours?" snapped Diana. "So you won't come with me?"

"Definitely not!"

"And what will you do?"

"Stay here and plant carrots, as you said!"

"In that case we'll go alone. If I don't go soon I won't have enough money to get us to London and we'll be trapped here forever."

"Then I wish you and your little aristocrat all the luck in the world, and I think you'll need it."

CHAPTER 51

It was far easier to leave Garonglen than Diana had imagined. Saying goodbye to her mother was far easier than she had imagined. She realised they were both so exhausted from grief that there was no emotion to give. But it wasn't easy making the journey to London with a small child. Christian seemed to cry all the way on the boat and the train, almost driving Diana to distraction.

Even less easy was arriving in London and realising the busy metropolis wasn't very interested in her. When she had come to London before with Max, there had been chauffeured motor cars waiting to take them to the best hotels. Now all she could do was push the perambulator with Christian in it along the busy streets with everyone else.

For the first night they booked into a small cheap hotel. She was so tempted to just go to Thelma and Elliott and ask for help. But she wasn't sure what the reaction would be. After she had rejected Thelma's offer in Geneva they might be very angry with her. And then there was the notoriety of the press accusing her of being a collaborator with the Germans. Everything was so raw from the war and anti-German sentiment so high that it would be unfair to expect Thelma and Elliott to take her in. It could cause a backlash against them, if people knew she was staying with them.

She got a taxi out of central London to Notting Hill. She had heard there were lots of lodgings there that were cheap. And as she pushed the pram along the street she saw notices in windows advertising lodgings. She knocked on the door of one that looked clean but inexpensive, and twenty minutes later she had put the deposit down to rent a tiny one-roomed flat.

As she sat down on the bed, looking at the shabby furniture and the lace net curtain against the grubby window, she felt like collapsing with fear and fright. When she thought of the luxurious surroundings she was used to all her life! To have ended up here! She prepared food for Christian and managed to get him to sleep. She was so tired from him and the travel that she lay out on the threadbare carpet staring at the ceiling, feeling despair. She seemed to lie like that for hours.

She forced herself to stand up and opened up her suitcase. She looked through her dresses and there didn't seem to be anything there fine enough to meet the Ashenbrys in. She selected the nicest one and began to groom herself to look her very best.

Diana walked down the street of white stucco buildings in Belgravia, with Christian in his pram, until she reached the Ashenbrys'. She walked up the steps and rang the door bell. A moment later the butler answered.

"Could you tell Lady Ashenbry that Diana Von Hoffsten is here to see her," said Diana.

The butler winced at her German surname but allowed her into the hall. Diana stood nervously. She wondered if Thelma and Elliott would even receive her. Thelma had been angry with her in Geneva for not leaving with her, though she had seemed to have come to terms with it by the time they parted. But now she might have had second thoughts . . .

She was putting them in a terrible position, she realised. Asking them to be associated with her, with her reputation. She decided to leave and walked towards the front door.

"Diana!" cried Thelma, racing down the stairs and embracing her.

They sat in the drawing room having tea and sandwiches while Christian lay in his pram asleep beside her.

"Max never knew you were pregnant?" asked Thelma.

Diana shook her head sadly. "I'm afraid not."

"We were devastated when we heard he had been killed," said Thelma.

"Even if he was a German?" Diana asked cynically.

"Diana! You know how much we loved Max!" Thelma looked hurt.

"I know. I'm sorry."

"And how is your mother? Maud?"

"She seems to have given up on life. She's lost everything: Dashiel, her husband, Garonglen. She doesn't really even have Warren."

"She still has you and Christian!"

"I'm afraid that is not nearly enough."

"And what of you, Diana? What are your plans now?"

"I don't know! I've rented a flat for now. It's very nice, near Holland Park."

"But, Diana, you must come and stay here with us."

"I'm not going to do that, Thelma. It would be putting you and Elliott in a terrible position. The wife of a German officer under your roof. I know the depth of anger there is. It's frightening."

"Everyone's looking for someone to blame and hate. The losers of the war always pay the price . . . And the flat is nice?"

"Yes, it's lovely," Diana lied as she thought of her horrible one-roomed lodgings. "I suppose I need to get a job, although I have no idea what I can do. I believe women are doing all kinds of jobs now. Perhaps I could become a bus conductress?" She grinned to disguise the fact she was actually contemplating such a move.

Thelma laughed loudly. "Oh, Diana, you are a scream! Anyway, I don't think there's even any of those kinds of jobs going. The men are back from the war, fighting to get those jobs, and the women who took them during the war won't hand them back. There's a lot of unemployment."

Diana sighed loudly.

"Having Christian means things are so much less flexible for you. If you didn't have him I could have asked around for you to be a lady's companion to an older woman. But they won't take you with a child."

Diana forced herself to smile broadly to disguise the dire straits she was in.

"Oh, something will come along," she said lightly.

Thelma leaned forward. "I would advise you to drop your surname. A German surname will only hold you back. Go back to being Diana Cantwell."

"That would be such an insult to Max's memory!" Diana was horrified.

"Look, even the royal family changed their name from Battenberg because it was German. It's something you will just have to do."

"I see," said Diana, accepting reality. "I won't even have my surname now from my left-handed marriage."

"Well, maybe you should take heart from said royal family. I heard something recently – believe it or not, they're descended from a morganatic branch of the Grand Duchy of Hesse! And look how far they've managed to come!"

Diana had to laugh at that.

"We're having a soirée on Friday night," said Thelma. "You will come, won't you?"

"I can't – I haven't managed to employ a nanny yet," said Diana, thinking how ridiculous the prospect of her employing a nanny was, given her circumstances, yet her pride was forcing her to put on a front.

"No need to worry. We've plenty of staff here to mind him," said Thelma.

As Diana looked at Thelma she couldn't help but feel envious of her, and lament the life that had been lost to her.

"Are you still in contact with the Von Hoffstens?" asked Thelma.

"No. We never really got on," said Diana.

"I see. You didn't hear then?"

"Hear what?" asked Diana.

"Max's father Conrad died earlier this year."

"No, I hadn't," she said, shocked. "Although he was old, he seemed indestructible."

"Hugo and Alexandra are the new count and countess now," said Thelma.

"Just what they always wanted," sighed Diana as she saw her son's legacy stolen away.

CHAPTER 52

It had been so long since Diana had been to a social occasion that she felt awkward as she tried to mingle with the crowd at the Ashenbrys' party that Friday.

She was cornered by a man called Rupert and tried to appear interested in his conversation which mainly revolved around croquet. It was only after thirty minutes she realised he was actually chatting her up!

"Say, how about dinner next week? Shall we say Café Royal Thursday at eight?" he suggested.

Diana felt herself going bright red. "Oh, no, sorry. I can't possibly!"

"Oh!" Rupert looked surprised and disappointed.

Suddenly a striking woman with blonde hair was beside them. She spoke in a foreign accent. "Rupert, Mandy is looking for you."

"Oh! Is she?" Rupert said, looking round the room.

"She said it was quite urgent," said the woman.

"Oh! I'd better go find her then," said Rupert who looked disappointed to be leaving Diana's side.

The woman smiled at Diana. "I thought you looked as if you needed rescuing."

"I did! Thank you!" said Diana, relieved.

"I'm Olga, the Countess Varoski," the woman introduced herself.

"Pleased to meet you, I'm Diana . . . Cantwell." Diana felt it strange using her maiden name again. "You're Russian?"

"Yes, and I believe you're a cousin of the Ashenbrys from Ireland?"

"That's right, a distant cousin. You're a friend of theirs?"

"I know them socially. I'm seeing John Jake." She nodded at a man deep in conversation with Elliott. "He's a close friend of theirs." She paused. "But you should have accepted his invitation to dinner."

"I'm sorry?"

"Rupert's invitation. It would have got you a square meal in a fabulous restaurant."

"I've no interest in being in his company," explained Diana.

"What does that matter?" laughed Olga.

Diana spent the next couple of hours talking to Olga and found her fascinating. Her family had been fabulously rich in Russia, but had lost everything after the revolution.

"I was lucky to escape with my life. You and I are just two of the many impoverished aristocrats trying to find our feet in this new world," said Olga.

"You look as if you've found your feet very well," said Diana, looking pointedly at Olga's jewellery.

Olga studied Diana for a while. "I have to go back to Jake now but meet me for lunch during the week," she said then.

Diana felt it was more of a command than a request.

Diana pushed the pram into the Russian tea rooms where she had arranged to meet Olga.

Olga was already there and smilingly waved over to her.

They greeted each other and Olga made a fuss over Christian as Diana sat down.

Diana picked up the menu and grimaced as she saw the prices.

"It's all right, lunch is on me," said Olga.

"No! I couldn't possibly –"

"Diana, forget about your misplaced pride," Olga said gently. "You're no longer married to a millionaire aristocrat. Take a helping hand when it's offered."

Diana nodded and they each ordered a salad from the waiter and a glass of white wine.

"You seem to know a lot about me," said Diana.

"Well, you were quite the talk of the place at the Ashenbrys' last Friday," said Olga.

"Was I?" Diana was surprised.

Olga took a drink. "Diana, when I arrived in London, I was like you. No money, no job, no prospects. But, as I said, I was lucky I got out of Russia alive."

Diana was intrigued. "So how did you manage to survive here?"

"I got a job first as a seamstress. The pay was terrible and the work hours horrendous. Back in Russia my family had an army of staff to cater to our every whim. I only knew how to sew as a hobby and here I was sewing fourteen hours a day just to survive."

"How terrible!"

"But what I had was my background and my beauty. Being a countess, I managed to get invited to social occasions and I developed contacts. I met wealthy and powerful people. And you know a wealthy and powerful man likes to be seen out with a beautiful countess."

"It's all so odd. In my day, you did the Season, chose a husband and that was the end of it!"

"Well, that world is gone and you need to change with it. You're a beautiful cultured girl, Diana, with an exotic past. If you work things to your advantage this new world can offer you a lot of opportunities. Men will want to be in your company and you'll never be short of money."

"Are you talking about marriage? I never want to get married again," said Diana determinedly.

Olga laughed. "Who said anything about marriage? That will limit your options, dear. No, I'm talking about you being in control, not married to one man who you are enslaved to for the rest of your life. If you do it correctly, you can have everything you want, and you will be in control."

CHAPTER 53

Present Day

Sam had looked up the location of Garonglen on maps. Although he couldn't find an actual house called Garonglen, only a location of that name. He followed the route he had marked and drove along the country roads until he came to a large old gateway and pulled over. Getting out of the car, he saw the gateway was nearly overgrown with ivy and the gates themselves rusted with a padlock tying them together.

Ignoring the fact that last time he went exploring in grounds he didn't own he got arrested, he hopped over a wall to the other side. There, a little way from the entrance, was a small building that was once the gate lodge. Now, however, the windows were all missing and peering inside he saw it was being used as a hayshed by a farmer. He continued up the driveway which was overgrown. It was almost unimaginable to think a century ago this was a hive of activity of a thriving landed-gentry family. As he continued to walk up he kept expecting an old manor house to come into view, but none did. When he reached the top of the long avenue there was only a field, no sign of a house.

"Can I help you?" came a voice from behind him and he turned to see a man in his forties tending to cattle.

Sam walked over to him. "Hi, I'm sorry for coming on to your land. I'm just looking for the house Garonglen that belonged to the Cantwell family."

The farmer walked towards him, smiling. "Sure there's no house here."

"Was there ever a house here?"

"There was. The old landlord's house used to be standing just over there." He pointed to the area at the top of the avenue which was now just a field of grass being grazed by cows.

"What happened to it?" Sam was horrified to see it had vanished as if it had never existed.

"That would have been in my grandfather's time. This land has been in my family since then. The old landlord family's name was Cantwell all right, but sure there's no trace of them any more. The house was destroyed by fire and whatever stonework was left after that was later taken to build walls around the farm."

"Isn't that tragic!" said Sam, trying to imagine his ancestors' house in the field.

"Tragic for them maybe!" laughed the farmer.

Sam turned and smiled at him. "Thanks, sorry for disturbing you."

"No problem," smiled the farmer as he headed back to his cattle.

Sam turned and walked slowly back down the avenue.

In the local village Sam asked around in the shops and the pubs if anyone had any information about the Cantwell family, but nobody seemed to have even heard of them. Sam reckoned the only reason the farmer knew was because he now owned the land and the name would have been on the deeds.

"Why don't you go up to the Gordons and ask them?" suggested the woman who ran the coffee shop. "They are an old Protestant family who have been around here since Noah's Ark. They might have some information. They have a farm out the Dublin Road."

Sam followed the woman's directions until he came to a building that was part manor house, part old castle. Sam drove up to the house and wondered if Garonglen had looked something like this before it was destroyed.

He parked his car and spotted a woman trimming flowers in the garden. She was looking at him curiously.

"Hello there – are you lost?" called the woman.

Sam walked towards her.

"I'm sorry to bother you, but is this the Gordons' house?"

"Yes, I'm Molly Gordon," said the woman.

"I'm looking for some information. My great-grandmother was a Cantwell who used to live in the house that was at Garonglen. I'm trying to trace what happened to her. A woman in the village suggested I talk to your family."

Molly Gordon had heard of the Cantwells because her mother Gloria had mentioned them many times. Gloria was now in her eighties and lived there at the castle with the family. And now Sam was anxiously waiting in the drawing room for Molly to come back, to see if Gloria was up to meeting him.

Molly came smiling from the back. "She'd love to meet you, if you want to follow me, Sam."

"Great!" said Sam as he followed her through a maze of corridors and into a large conservatory where a very elderly woman sat looking out at the gardens.

"Now, Mother, this is the young man I was telling you about. He's Diana Cantwell's great-grandson."

The old woman looked thrilled to see him.

"Come sit beside me and let me look at you!" she said.

Sam went and sat at the table where she was, while Molly sat on the other side.

"Well, I never thought I'd ever meet a Cantwell!" said Gloria.

"Did you know her – Diana?" Sam was smiling eagerly back at her.

"No, she was gone from here before I was born, but my mother Hannah was a great friend of hers. Hannah Roundtree. This was her family's ancestral home. The Roundtrees had been here for centuries and were good friends of the Cantwells."

"How wonderful!" smiled Sam.

"My mother Hannah used to sing Diana's praises – they were the best of friends growing up. She missed her terribly when she was gone."

"When she went to live in Germany," said Sam.

"Yes. Diana was the belle of the county but everyone got a shock when she met and married this millionaire aristocrat. She met him through horses – she was a great horsewoman." Gloria's face became sad. "But he got killed in the Great War, like so many others. Whatever happened with his family I don't know, but Diana arrived back to Garonglen penniless after he died. But by then the War of Independence was raging and their house, Garonglen, had been targeted and burned down by the rebels."

"Awful times," said Molly, shaking her head.

Gloria looked at her daughter and spoke sternly. "We were lucky the rebels didn't arrive up here and burn the house down around us as well. It may have been just pot luck they didn't choose to burn this place down, but it was said it was Diana's mother that made them targets. She was full of airs and graces and related to Lord Ashenbry over in England. She wouldn't have been popular with the locals. She would have been better to keep her head down like my mother's family, the Roundtrees, did."

"And what happened to the Cantwells after the house was torched?" asked Sam.

"The problem was there wasn't much of a family left. Diana's brothers had been wiped out by the war, poor darlings, one dead, one blind. Mr Cantwell, Diana's father, dead too. That only left Diana and her mother. Once the baby was born, they headed to England. An awful lot of our class did that. Just got out of the country during those terrible times."

"That baby was my grandfather," informed Sam.

"Imagine! They never came back. Nobody around here ever saw them again. You're the first member of that family to have stepped back here since. I think Diana and her mother relied on their connections with the Ashenbry family when they went to London. I remember my mother had old magazines, *Tatler* and *The Lady*, kept from when Diana was featured in them. I think she became quite a socialite in London."

"You wouldn't have any of those magazines now?" asked Sam excitedly.

"I don't think so," smiled Gloria. "I'm the only old thing they keep around here! Now, young man, what do you do yourself?"

"I'm a historian. I lecture at Trinity," he said.

"And now you're researching your own family history."

"Exactly," he smiled.

"It was wiped out," Sam explained to Julia over a glass of wine that evening. "The whole house destroyed, nothing left."

"One way for the locals to drive out the landlords so they could then claim and buy the land, I guess," said Julia.

"They were such turbulent times, between the Great War and the wars that followed here in Ireland," said Sam.

"Well, at least Diana and her son survived, otherwise you wouldn't be here today. I think, Sam, you've taken this now as far as you can. Don't you agree? You've traced what happened to Max and Diana. It answers the questions you had."

"But I haven't really. I don't know what happened to Diana after she left for London."

"Didn't the old dear say she became a socialite in London? Sounds like she knew how to survive, that woman."

The following week Sam was sitting at his desk at the university, contemplating his trip to County Meath. He couldn't get over the tragedy that had unfolded there. For Diana to have lost her husband in the war and then to return to Ireland to find her own family and home to have been all but wiped out. It must have been such a struggle for her to re-establish herself and make a life for herself and her son.

Figuring he had better do some work, he looked at the stack of post on his desk and began to open it. Opening one large envelope marked for his attention and addressed to the History Department at Trinity, he was surprised to see several tattered old magazines inside.

He saw the note inside was from Molly Gordon.

Hello Sam,

It was lovely to meet you last week and my mother got great

pleasure from discussing your family with you. After you left she sent us searching through the attic where her own mother Hannah's stuff is kept. We found these magazines featuring Diana, and my mother wanted you to have them. I hope you find them of interest.
   Molly Gordon

Sam carefully took the magazines and began to examine them. There were copies of *Vogue*, *Tatler* and *The Lady* from the early 1920s. Molly had thoughtfully marked pages with stickers.

Opening the first marked page of *Tatler* from the year 1922, Sam was faced with a photograph of Diana. It was taken at a ball and she was dressed glamorously and standing beside a man in a tuxedo. Sam read the caption underneath: '*Miss Diana Cantwell and the Honourable George Felladale at this year's Ashenbrys' Ball, on June 12th.*'

He studied the photograph of his great-grandmother, her natural beauty obvious to see. He quickly went to the next magazine and saw Diana at a garden party posing with a different man. Looking at the next magazine she was with yet another man at a cocktail party.

At home that night he showed the magazines to Julia.

"Isn't it amazing? The way she managed to reinvent herself and get on with her life?" he said.

"She certainly seems to have known a lot of men. She doesn't look as if she was mourning Max too much!"

He gave her a disapproving look. "This was the 1920s – people had to get on with their lives. They were trying to forget the past, forget what had happened and who they had lost."

"She looks as if she managed to forget just fine! She looks like a right goer!"

"Julia!" he spat, his face disgusted. "This is my great-grandmother you're being disrespectful to."

"I'm just saying!" She tried not to giggle.

Sam tried to quell his annoyance. He returned to gazing at the photos. "She was just stunning, wasn't she? It's no wonder Max married her against his family's wishes." He looked adoringly at her photo.

"Well, that's what love does to people. I married you against my family's wishes."

"What are you talking about?" he snapped.

"They warned me you weren't grounded enough. I'm beginning to think they were right!"

He started gathering the magazines up. "I was thinking I shouldn't have shown them to you. I was right!"

She reached out and took his hand. "I'm sorry!" She looked suitably chastened. "Let's show them to the children in the morning. Eva will be thrilled to see her great-grandmother all dressed up like a princess."

"It's a countess she should have been, if they hadn't tricked her into that marriage. She should have been the Countess Von Hoffsten in those photos, not Diana Cantwell."

"Well, nobody said life was fair," she said, taking up a magazine and flicking through it.

"Careful, Julia! That's ninety years old!"

Julia threw her eyes to heaven and flung the magazine back down on the table.

PART 4

1924

CHAPTER 54

Diana leaned forward as she applied her red lipstick. She patted her lips with a napkin and rose from her dressing table. She walked across her large bedroom, elegantly furnished in Art Deco style, and picked up her gold purse from her bed.

It was eight in the evening as she left her room and walked across the large cream-tiled hallway of her flat into the nursery.

Christian was in his cot while her nanny Mrs Huddins played with him.

"I'm just off now, Mrs Huddins – will you be all right for the night?" asked Diana as she picked up her son.

"Everything's fine, Miss Cantwell, you go and enjoy yourself for the night," smiled the kind-looking woman, who was in her late fifties.

Diana held the smiling happy child close while she kissed him.

"And as for you!" she cooed at him. "You behave yourself for Mrs Huddins and I'll see you in the morning." She gave him a big kiss before handing him over to the nanny.

Diana walked down the long hallway towards the drawing room. She had been renting the flat in Regent's Park for two years and she loved it. It was a three-bed-roomed third-floor flat in an old neo-Georgian classical building. The rooms were spacious and high-ceilinged, and the front of the flat overlooked a crescent. At the top of the hall she turned right into the large drawing room, again furnished in elegant Art Deco furniture.

Her mother Maud was sitting on the couch, reading a magazine.

"Did you visit Warren today?" questioned Diana.

"Yes, he was asking after you," said Maud.

"I'll go see him on Wednesday."

Diana had arranged for Warren to be transferred from Dublin to a private nursing home outside London.

"My taxi will be here any minute," said Diana as she walked past her mother to the mirror.

Maud looked up from her magazine. Her face was masked with a look of disapproval as she studied Diana who was dressed in a glitzy cocktail dress, her hair and make-up done to perfection.

"Which boyfriend are you out with tonight?" asked Maud.

"I'm meeting Carl along with Thelma and Elliott and a few others," said Diana.

Maud looked even more disapproving. "He's old enough to be your father."

"He's not actually. He's only ten years older than me. The war and excessive drinking has aged him prematurely." She continued to fix her hair in the mirror.

"What a carry-on!" said Maud under her breath.

"I should have thought you would have been delighted that I was a friend of someone like Carl whose father is a lord. You would have practically thrown me at him if I had ever done the Season all those years ago."

"That's before you were widowed with a young child, he was divorced with a drink problem, he was one of several boyfriends you have and no doubt you are one of several girlfriends he has! Hardly the stuff of young love!" Maud flung down the magazine on the coffee table in front of her.

Diana turned around from the mirror and smiled. "Well, Mama, if you ever get tired of disapproving of my lifestyle, there's a gate lodge in County Meath you can return to at any time!"

Diana walked past her to the door.

"But your taxi hasn't arrived yet," Maud pointed out.

"I know, but I want to be gone before your motley crew arrive to do your séance in the dining room," Diana said, indicating the dining room across the hall that had already been set up for Maud's séance that night.

"We're making excellent progress with the spirit world, as it happens. I think we might actually get through to Dashiel tonight," said Maud.

Diana raised her eyes to heaven. "The only spirits you'll be making contact with are my decanters of whiskey which will no doubt be consumed by your spiritual friends during the course of their séance!" She smiled at her mother and walked on towards the front door of the flat.

"You know, before the war only prostitutes wore that much make-up!" Maud called after her.

Diana paused for a second before quickly opening the door and stepping outside the flat into the bright spacious corridor.

The taxi left Diana off outside a new drinking club that had opened up near Piccadilly. Diana tipped the driver generously and then walked up the steps into the club.

"Good evening, Miss Cantwell!" greeted the doorman with a smile as he held the door open for her.

"It is a nice evening, isn't it, Miss Cantwell?" smiled the manager as he came out to the reception to greet her.

"Are my friends here?" she asked.

"Already seated at your normal table, Miss Cantwell," smiled the manager as he held open the door into the restaurant for her.

As Diana walked across the restaurant she attracted looks from the other diners.

"Who is that?" a man asked his female companion as she walked past their table.

"That is Diana Cantwell."

"Who?"

"She's the one that married a German count and spent the war years in Germany. Remember, she was the one that everyone accused of treason."

"Oh, that's her!"

"The husband died in the war and his family, the Von Hoffstens, kicked her out penniless and her family in Ireland lost everything in the War of Independence. Not that you would think it the way she swans around London as if she owns it. She's seeing Fraser Havington now."

"I heard she was seeing Sir Roger Hadley," said the woman opposite her.

"I heard she was seeing both of them and an American millionaire," said another.

Diana arrived at her table. "Hello, everyone. Sorry I'm so late!" She went around and kissed everyone at the table.

"We were about to give up on you," said Thelma as she kissed her cheek.

"Never give up on me, Thelma – you should know that by now!"

Diana reached a man who was seated in the middle of the group.

"Hello, Carl," she said and bent down to kiss his lips briefly before taking a seat beside him.

"How is Christian?" asked Elliott.

"Perfectly fine. Looks more like Max every day," she said and there was a moment of sadness on her face. "As for my mother!" She took the glass of champagne Carl had poured for her. "She's having another séance tonight."

"Ohhhh," said Thelma, getting all excited. "Has she had any luck getting through?"

"Of course she hasn't. These mediums are such frauds it makes me want to laugh or cry. Only she can't see it!"

"You never know. My cousin managed to get through to her husband on the other side last week, she told me," said Carl.

Diana sighed in a bored fashion. "This new obsession everyone has with the spirit world is ridiculous. I, as much as anyone, know how many people we lost during the war. And of course it's impossible to understand and comprehend how all those loved ones were lost so quickly and brutally. But once you are gone you are gone! No matter how many séances and mediums and what-not you engage in, it is not going to bring the person back."

Elliott looked sad. "But if it helps people to deal with all the loss?"

Thelma quickly moved to head off a dispute between Diana and

Elliott and said brightly, "There's a new club opened in Soho. We can go after dinner. A jazz band plays there that is supposed to be the best in London!"

Turning over in the bed, Diana saw Carl still fast asleep beside her. She got out of the bed and got dressed.

Carl stirred awake, opened his eyes and looked at his watch. "It's only nine in the morning, Diana. Come back to bed."

"I can't, I've a lot to do today," she said, smiling at him.

He got out of bed and put on his dressing gown.

"I've got something for you," he said as he went over to a cabinet and opened it.

"What is it?" she said as she finished dressing.

He came over to her and handed her a small box. Smiling, she sat down on the bed and opened it. There was a beautiful sapphire brooch inside.

"Do you like it?" he asked, sitting down beside her.

"I love it!" she said, before turning to him and kissing him.

Diana and Carl, still in his dressing gown, went downstairs and walked into the drawing room.

She sat down on one of the couches as he tugged the bell pull.

"So what's so pressing that you have to disappear off so early? Why can't you spend the day with me?" he asked.

"I told you – I have things to do," she said, opening her make-up bag and beginning to put on her make-up.

"Like what?"

"Like seeing Christian for starters!" she said.

Carl went over to the drinks cabinet and poured himself a vodka.

She watched, concerned. "It's a bit early for that, isn't it?"

"No, it's never too early," he said, turning and sitting opposite her.

The maid came in with a tray of coffee and placed it on the coffee table.

"Ah, Jane, you've saved my life with that coffee!" smiled Diana as Jane poured a cup and handed it to her.

Diana took a drink of the coffee and closed her eyes, sighing. "To think I spent a whole year in Germany during the war with hardly a cup of coffee! Thank you, Jane!"

Smiling, Jane left the room.

Carl waited till she had left before sitting forward. "I was wondering if you had given any more thought to my proposition last week?"

"Carl, I told you then – I can't marry you. I'm sorry."

Carl looked upset. "But why?"

"Because I don't love you and you don't love me!"

"But I do! I'm crazy for you!"

"You're not – you only think you are because you're searching for something since the war!"

"That's not true!"

"It is, Carl. And whatever you are searching for, it isn't me! You'd quickly discover if we were married that you're not that crazy for me at all and you'd be searching for something else to fill the void." Diana put down the coffee and began to do her make-up again.

"I could offer you a lot, Diana."

"Everything except happiness, I'm afraid. And you're not happy either, Carl. You haven't been since the war and you're – grasping – on to something you think will make you happy. Me!"

"But you do make me happy."

"I wouldn't if you lived with me all the time . . . Have you seen a psychiatrist about your drinking?"

"No!" said Carl sulkily.

"Well, I think you should."

"Why are you such a believer in therapy?"

"I don't know. My sister-in-law Brigitte was a great advocate, not that it did her any good."

Diana put her make-up bag away and studied Carl, then she went over and sat beside him. "I think it might be a good idea if we don't see each other for a while, Carl."

"*What*?"

"I just don't think it's fair on you because you think you've developed feelings for me. It would be unfair to keep on seeing you under the circumstances."

"Are you seeing Fraser Havington? Tell me you're not!"

"If you don't want to know the answer then don't ask the question!"

Seeing he was getting upset, she put her arms around him. "Oh, Carl, my not seeing you again has nothing to do with Fraser or anyone else. I'm not the girl for you. I don't want to get married ever again. I loved Max so much and he loved me so much and it only brought terrible pain. I don't want to ever go through that again. As for you – go see a doctor, Carl. We're all handling our own ghosts since the war, but I think yours are going to consume you. Will you see a doctor?"

Carl nodded.

"Promise?"

"I promise," he sighed.

Diana walked down Bond Street later that morning and turned into a small jeweller's. A man in his forties was serving a customer but when he saw Diana he beckoned to his assistant to take over the sale and went to Diana.

"Good morning, Diana, you're looking happy with yourself today," he smiled.

"That's probably because I am, Mr Carter."

"Have you anything to show me?"

"I might very well have," she teased.

"In that case shall I show you into my office?"

"I think you should, Mr Carter."

Diana followed him behind the counter and into an office at the back.

She sat down at the desk as he sat down behind it and she handed him the box Carl had given her that morning.

Carter opened the box and began to study the brooch.

"A very nice piece. It looks as if it's been commissioned?" He looked up at her quizzically.

"I believe it has."

"Hmmm," he said studying the brooch carefully. "I'll take it off your hands for forty pounds."

"Not a chance. Fifty."

He studied her and then the brooch again. "I'll give you forty-five pounds."

Diana went to stand up, looking irritated. "I'm not going to sit here haggling."

"All right! Fifty!" conceded Carter.

He went to the safe behind his desk and, opening it, counted out the money.

"You drive a hard bargain," he said, handing the money to her.

"I just know the value of jewellery and I'm in a position not to be ripped off. I once didn't understand the value of jewellery and was not in a position to argue. I was defrauded of an emerald necklace which would have made you faint if you had seen it." She stood up and smiled, putting the money into her purse. "That won't be happening again."

"Hello, darlings," said Thelma as she came into the drawing room where Diana was playing with Christian.

Christian ran to greet her and she bent down and kissed him.

"You're right, he's looking more like Max every day," she said.

Diana smiled, delighted at her comment. "He's just about to go to the park with Mrs Huddins to play," she said.

Mrs Huddins came bustling in. "Good afternoon, Lady Ashenbry," she said.

"I'm afraid I must take this little man away from you."

Christian ran to take her hand.

"See you later, darling," said Diana. "Be a good boy for Mrs Huddins."

Diana and Thelma waved goodbye as the nanny and child left the flat.

"I'm here on a mission of mercy," said Thelma as she took off her coat and sat down on the couch.

"Carl sent you?" asked Diana as she poured two gin and tonics.

"I'm afraid so," smiled Thelma. "I believe you've dumped him?"

Diana handed Thelma a drink and sat on the armchair opposite her.

"I haven't dumped him, Thelma, because I was never really in a serious relationship with him in the first place!"

"That's not what it looked like to everyone," said Thelma.

"I warned him not to get too close and let his emotions run away with him. I told him from the start that nothing was going to come of it."

"Which makes it all right then?" Thelma raised a cynical eyebrow.

"I bet you he'll find somebody new by the end of the week. Let's face it, London is awash with enough women desperate for husbands."

"However, you're not one of them?"

"No, I'm not! I've tried marriage once and never intend to try it again."

Thelma studied Diana who was dressed in a grey satin flared trouser suit and was lighting a cigarette.

"You can judge me all you want, Thelma. I'm used to it at this stage. The truth is I like my life just as it is. I go where I want when I want. I see who I want. When I came to London, the anti-German feeling was so strong I had to change my name back to Cantwell. People believed all that rubbish about me being a traitor and living a life of luxury in Germany while you all suffered the war. The truth was I was going through hell there. They were about to intern me when the Armistice was declared."

"I know all that," said Thelma. "No need to tell me."

"I lost my husband on one side and my brother on the other, and the simple truth is I just have to get on with things now," Diana said, her voice cracking. "We all do. The war is over and I'm actually finally enjoying my life. I provide for my son. I pay for my other brother's accommodation and medical bills. And I look after my mother while I put up with her constant disapproval! I have an electric refrigerator in my kitchen full of food that I would have to have begged, borrowed or stolen for in Germany during the war!"

"I know –"

"The world is changed and I've changed with it. Carl doesn't love me. He's broken from the war and clinging on to me like a lifeboat. But we're all broken from the war and now we all have to stand on our own two feet."

Thelma shrugged. "If you put it like that . . ."

"It's fine for you, Thelma – Lady Ashenbry, married to Elliott and all the protection that gives you. I got no protection from my marriage to Max. The Von Hoffstens kicked me out without a red cent because of my left-handed marriage. My son should be the rightful heir to the Von Hoffsten fortune and the future Count Von Hoffsten, and I should be a countess."

"Fate has been cruel to you and Christian."

"I really wish now that Carl will see our relationship for what it was and find happiness."

Thelma sighed and nodded. "I'll report back to him that he needs to get on with his life."

"Thank you." Diana smiled appreciatively at her as she stubbed out her cigarette.

They sat in silence for a while.

"Are you going to Grace's party this weekend," asked Thelma.

"I can't, I'm afraid. I promised Fraser I'd go to his country house. He's having a ball."

Thelma smiled. "That will be nice."

Thelma stayed the afternoon chatting and then Diana saw her to the door.

Diana closed the front door and leaned against it. Then she walked slowly down the wide corridor to her bedroom. Entering her room, she went and picked up the large photograph of Max that was in a silver frame on her bedside locker and held it close to her heart.

CHAPTER 55

Diana hadn't been to Fraser Havington's country house before and, as the car that had been sent to collect her from the nearby train station swept up the avenue, she saw that the house was a four-storey neo-classical pile set in the beautiful Yorkshire countryside.

The car pulled up in front of it and as she stepped out she saw Fraser coming down the steps surrounded by several large dogs.

"Welcome, my dear," said Fraser, kissing her. "Good journey?"

"Very pleasant. I immersed myself in F Scott Fitzgerald on the way up," she said, linking his arm and climbing the steps.

"Do I need to be jealous of this Fitzgerald man?" he asked, looking alarmed.

She took the book out of her handbag and showed it to him, arching an eyebrow.

"Oh!" said Fraser, laughing at his own misunderstanding.

Diana liked Fraser. His family were merchant bankers. They weren't aristocrats but their banking saved them from the money problems besieging most of her aristocratic friends.

That Friday evening there was a small dinner party for Fraser's family and close friends, but it was the following night, the Saturday, that was the highlight of the weekend as Fraser was hosting a ball.

Diana was happy to get the opportunity to be out of the city for a couple of days. The countryside reminded her of Ireland and she was looking forward to going riding the following day. It was also a good opportunity to make connections with a new circle and get to know Fraser better. Fraser was in his forties, handsome, with an often detached manner. Already divorced, she was certain he would not develop any Carl-like love obsession for her.

The guests for the ball arrived early on the Saturday evening and as Diana looked out at the forecourt she saw it was now filled with swanky cars, with tuxedoed gentlemen and chic ladies swanning around. She made her way downstairs and across the crowded hallway into the ballroom. A jazz band was playing loudly and French windows were open, looking onto a fountain in the manicured gardens of the back of the house. Diana quickly spotted people she knew and joined them.

By midnight the party was still in full swing as the crowd became rousingly drunk. As a young woman started dancing crazily on a table, Diana could only compare these antics to the parties she had attended back before the war. She would have been shocked if she had seen these antics back then. But then she would probably be shocked if she saw her own antics now as well.

She hadn't seen Fraser for a while and she wandered out the French windows to take some air.

She stepped over tuxedoed bodies in the gardens that looked to be dead, but she was quite sure were only drunk. She kept going as far as the large fountain, only to see a young woman emerge fully dressed from the water.

"I went for swim," said the dripping wet girl as she climbed out.

"I hope you don't catch cold," Diana said.

"I'll have to have some whiskey to warm me up!" said the girl as she raced back inside to the party.

Smiling to herself, Diana leaned against the fountain, took out a cigarette and lit it.

As she was looking at the party from afar, a man stepped out from the shadows.

"Do you have a spare one?" he asked in a strong American accent.

Diana got a start. "Oh, yes, of course. Be my guest." She held out her cigarette case and offered one.

He took it and lit it with his own lighter. "Thanks. Jimmy

Barclay." He smilingly stretched out his hand.

She shook his hand. "Diana –"

"I know who you are, Miss Cantwell. I've heard all about you," he said.

"Only good things, I hope?"

"Certainly interesting things. A countess, reputed to have been a collaborator during the war, who is now only ever seen in the company of very rich men."

"And are you a very rich man, Mr Barclay?" she asked, his comments not having fazed her in the least.

"Unfortunately not. I'm a broke writer."

"Well, since I am, in that case. not presently in the company of a very rich man, I think you can take it for granted that the other tags you gave me are untrue as well."

"What a pity. You'd sounded very interesting." His handsome face was mocking her.

"Sorry to disappoint you." She looked at him. "I don't think I've met many writers."

"You are wise to avoid us. We're a horrible breed. We'd sell our young for a story."

"And where can I find one of your books?"

"Nowhere – none have been published. I'm presently making my living by selling short stories until I write my classic."

"Well, we all have to start somewhere, Mr Barclay," said Diana.

"Indeed we do," agreed Jimmy.

Fraser just then emerged from the French windows. "Diana? Diana – are you here?"

"Your rich man is calling," said Jimmy.

Diana dropped her cigarette on the ground and stamped it out. Then without saying another word she flashed a smile at Jimmy and headed back to Fraser and the party.

CHAPTER 56

Diana sat in the drawing room in the flat, looking through a magazine showcasing the latest fashion from Paris. It was two weeks after she had returned from Fraser's party in Yorkshire. As she was flicking through the pages, looking at the different fashion styles featured, her eye was suddenly caught by a short story by Jimmy Barclay.

She immediately remembered the young man by the fountain who had asked for a cigarette. Curious, she began to read the story. To her surprise the story was set around an extravagant party held in a Yorkshire manor where a male guest meets a girl at a fountain. Intrigued, she read on as the pair became entwined in a secret affair.

Diana arrived for Elliott's birthday party at the Ashenbrys'.

"Am I late?" she asked the butler as she handed over her coat. She could hear much laughter and merriment coming from the drawing room.

"Not overly, Miss Cantwell."

"Diana, there you are!" said Thelma, coming down the stairs and seeing her. They approached each other and kissed each other's cheek.

"Anyone interesting here?" asked Diana as Thelma put her arm around her and led her into the party.

"The usual faces. A couple of new ones. I've found the most brilliant young writer. He's one of ours, American. Jimmy Barclay."

They came face to face with Jimmy who was in the centre of the room.

"Ah, Jimmy, I was just speaking about you."

"Only good things, I hope," he said, smiling knowingly at Diana.

"Of course," said Thelma. "I was just saying you were American and a writer – isn't that a positive recommendation of you?"

"Many might disagree," smirked Jimmy.

"Jimmy, this is Diana," began Thelma.

"We've met," said Diana.

"Oh, really?" said Thelma.

"At a fountain," said Jimmy.

"I guess there are worse places you could meet!" said Thelma, confused at the way Diana and Jimmy were eyeing each other intently. "Excuse me – I'd better go and get them to bring out Elliott's cake." She hurried off.

"You're certainly getting around, Mr Barclay," said Diana.

"Aren't I? Not bad for a farm boy from the middle of nowhere who's only been in London six months."

"Not so surprising. London is always looking for a new plaything to be amused by," said Diana.

"And I thought it was my great literary talent that was wooing everyone," said Jimmy, taking two glasses of champagne from the tray of a passing footman and handing her one.

"I actually read one of your short stories today," she informed him.

"Really?"

"I wouldn't call you a *great* literary talent, not just yet in any case," she said.

"You're a cruel reviewer!" His voice was mocking.

"But your story did make me laugh."

"But it wasn't supposed to be funny!"

"Oh dear!"

"Which story was it?"

"It was about a man who met a girl at a fountain at a party in Yorkshire," she said, looking knowingly at him.

"Was it?" he said, pretending to look surprised.

"You weren't joking when you said writers would sell their young for the idea of a story, were you?"

"Indeed I wasn't."

"In your story the pair ended up in a clandestine affair."

"Lucky guy!" Jimmy moved a bit closer to her. "If only life imitated art, don't you think?"

She held his gaze. "Aren't all young American writers supposed to be in Paris while they wait to be discovered?"

"Alas, I don't have the passage fare to take me there."

"Oh dear. You need to find a rich widow in that case – there are plenty of them about after the war."

He smiled at her, reached out and took her hand. "I think I've just found her."

Diana was taken aback and felt herself become embarrassed and yet excited.

She pulled her hand back and smiled. "Well, I'm afraid you're wasting your time if that's your game with me. I can assure you I am a widow, but not a rich one."

"Oh dear, we'll just have to be impoverished together then," he said.

"You're very sure of yourself," she said, laughing.

"I have to go now," he suddenly said.

"Oh!" She felt disappointed. "So soon? The party is only starting?"

"No, I'm not leaving the party – I'm leaving you. I'm accompanying that lady over there tonight." He pointed over to a woman dripping in jewels, glaring at them from the other side of the room. "So it really would be very ungallant of me to leave her alone any longer."

Diana noted the woman's hostile stare. "Yes, I think you might be right. I wouldn't want her throwing any of those rocks she's wearing at me. They might knock me unconscious."

"So we can continue this conversation on Friday."

"Friday?"

"I'm taking you out to lunch."

"Are you indeed?" She was amazed.

"What's your address?"

"15 Chester Terrace, Regent's Park. Flat 14."

Mrs Huddins opened the door.

"Jimmy Barclay to see Miss Cantwell," smiled Jimmy.

"I'm in here!" Diana called from the drawing room.

Jimmy smiled at Mrs Huddins and walked in. He found Diana fixing her hair in the mirror over the fireplace and a small boy playing with a train set on the ground.

"Hello there, and who are you?" asked Jimmy, kneeling down on the floor beside the child.

"Jimmy, this is Christian. Christian, say hello to Jimmy," said Diana.

"Hello!" said Christian.

"What an amazing train set," said Jimmy as he began to play with the train.

"I got it for Christmas," said Christian.

"Did you? Well, you must have been a very good boy all year to get a present as good as this! I'm absolutely jealous!" said Jimmy.

Christian looked at Jimmy, his eyes getting bigger with amazement at this big brash American.

Diana looked on fondly as they began to play with the train.

Diana looked at her watch. Jimmy had been playing with Christian for nearly an hour. She stood up.

"Jimmy, we'd better go or the restaurant won't hold the reservation!" she said.

"Oh, they said there's no time limit on it," he said as he continued to play.

"Well, that sounds unlike any other restaurant I've ever been to," she said.

Jimmy stood up. "Okay. Well, we'd better be off, little man. I'll see you later."

"Bye!" smiled Christian.

"Bye, darling." Diana bent down and kissed him before she walked out with Jimmy.

"I thought you said you weren't rich?" said Jimmy, inspecting the Art Deco furniture as they walked out.

"I'm not. It's all for show, believe me." She smiled at him before calling out, "Mrs Huddins! We're off out for the rest of the day."

Mrs Huddins came into the room. "Very well, madam."

Jimmy drove through the streets of Chelsea.

"You haven't told me which restaurant we're going to," she said.

"It's a surprise," he said as he drove away from the King's Road and down towards the river. To her surprise he drove across Chelsea Bridge.

"Where *are* we going?" she demanded as she saw they were leaving anywhere fashionable behind.

He took a turn into Battersea Park and pulled up beside the river.

"What are we doing here?" she asked, looking around bewildered.

He hopped out and, opening the back, took out a large basket.

"A picnic?" she asked disbelievingly.

"Beautiful day, why not? Better than being cooped up in some restaurant – and as I said no fuss about what time we arrive or leave."

"I haven't been on a picnic for years," she said, following him to the river. "We used to have them back in Ireland before the war. The whole family used to go and have one by the river at Garonglen."

"Garonglen?" he asked as they made their way through the high grass, looking down at the swaying Thames.

"It was our old house in Ireland," she answered.

"Who lives there now?"

"Nobody," she said. "It was burnt down during the War of Independence."

"I'm sorry."

"Why? You didn't burn it down."

She watched as he flattened the grass, spread out a blanket, knelt down and began to lay out the food from the basket.

326

"Who needs the Ritz, eh?" he asked, smiling, as he began to spread a soft cheese on crusty bread. "We should have brought Christian."

She looked at him, surprised, as she took a glass of red wine from him.

"We couldn't have brought Christian."

"Why not?"

"I don't bring my son out when I meet a friend, a male friend."

"Why not?"

"Well – well, usually we are in a high-class restaurant and so I couldn't bring a child there."

"Exactly. Today is different. He would have loved being here."

She shrugged. "Perhaps."

"So – are you going to marry Fraser Havington?"

"Of course not." She looked at him, surprised.

"Why not?"

"Well, I don't think he has any intention of getting married in the first place. And then neither do I."

"Not to anybody? Ever again?" His eyes widened in disbelief.

"No. I don't want to try it again. Max, my husband, was the love of my life. I'll never get that again. The things he used to do for me, you would not believe. He dedicated his whole life to making me happy."

"So why do you see Fraser and the others then? If there's no future in it?"

"For many reasons. You probably wouldn't approve of some of the reasons. I probably don't approve of them myself. They are my ticket to the life I want to have, the places I want to be."

"But you can't live like that forever."

"I'm not interested in forever. I don't think about forever. I think about now. If the war taught me anything it is to live in the present and only think about today. Anyway, what about you? What about that bejewelled woman you were with at the Ashenbry party?"

"Ah, her! She was one of those rich widows you advised me to marry."

"Well, you should have invited her here today instead of me, then."

"Are you kidding me? Did you see the size of her? She'd eat all the food and leave none for me!" he said, taking a bite from the bread and cheese as she started to laugh.

Diana was putting on Christian's coat in the drawing room.

"Where are you off to today?" asked Maud.

"We're off for a drive in the country with Jimmy."

"Who is Jimmy?"

"Jimmy Barclay – he's my new friend."

"Is he indeed? You don't usually take Christian out on your dates."

"Jimmy's different," Diana said, smiling to herself.

Maud studied her daughter with concern.

"And this Jimmy's family? Who are they?"

"Oh, you wouldn't have heard of them. They're from the mid-west," said Diana.

"The mid-west of where?"

"Of America, of course!" laughed Diana.

"America. You mean he's an American?"

"That's right."

"And what does he do?" quizzed Maud.

"He's a writer."

"An American writer! Oh, Diana!" groaned Maud.

"What?"

"Do not get in any way serious about this American. You've already had one marriage that left you penniless – please do not choose another!"

"Oh Mama!"

"What does he write?" asked Maud.

"Short stories."

"Well, let's hope that's exactly what your relationship with this man will be – a short story!"

The doorbell rang.

"I'll get it," said Diana, running out into the hall. She reappeared a few seconds later with Jimmy.

"Hello there, little guy! Are you all ready for our trip to the country?" he said, sweeping a delighted Christian up in his arms. He looked over at Maud and smiled. "Hi there!"

"Hi – indeed!" said Maud.

"Jimmy, this is my mother, Maud Cantwell," said Diana.

"My daughter has just been telling me all about you, Mr Barclay. I believe you're a writer from the mid-western section of America?"

"That about sums me up!" smiled Jimmy.

"A rather short resumé, in that case!"

"We'd better go!" said Diana, taking Jimmy's arm. "Goodbye, Mama."

"See ya later, Maud!" sang Jimmy as he carried Christian out of the room, linking arms with Diana.

Maud stared after them, shaking her head in despair.

CHAPTER 57

Jimmy unlocked the door of his flat and let Diana in.

She smiled as she looked around. "Oh, it's big! Bigger than I expected."

"That is because it's in an area not known for its high rents," said Jimmy.

She looked around. The furniture was a little shabby.

"It's not quite the ritzy environment you're used to," said Jimmy, opening a bottle of wine and pouring two glasses.

"You'd be surprised. I lived in a place much worse than this when I first moved to London after the war."

"Really?" He was shocked. "How did you get to where you are now?"

She took the glass of wine from him. "Let's just say I have kind friends."

She went over to the typewriter on the table and began to tap the keys.

"And this is where you exercise your creativity?" she asked.

"Most of the time."

"Perhaps this flat will be famous one day as the place Jimmy Barclay lived in," she laughed.

"And perhaps not!" He pulled a face.

"I've always wanted to see where a writer lives and now I have," she said, sitting down on the couch.

He came and sat beside her, smiling.

"Jimmy, I think this should be the last time we meet," she said.

"Why?" His expression fell.

"I just don't think we'll be very good for each other."

"Don't you enjoy the time we spend together?" he asked.

"That's the problem. I do. Too much. I'm surprised how much I actually enjoy your company. I didn't think I ever would enjoy another man's company so much after Max."

"Then what's the problem?" he asked, reaching for her hand.

She reached forward and laid a hand on his cheek. "It's so clear that you weren't in the war. I think that's what attracted me so much to you. There you were in America, so far from the war. You haven't been touched by it. And I love that about you. It's what the rest of us try so hard to pretend to have, but we never succeed. We pretend to each other or pretend to ourselves. We fill our time so much with stupid things, nightclubs and parties, because if we stop – well – we start remembering the horror of it all."

He took her hand from his face and held it. "Then let me help you to forget."

She smiled at him. "Do you think you really could?"

He reached forward and kissed her.

Maud was reading a magazine at the table in the dining room while having breakfast with Diana.

"You're in the gossip column again," she said as she handed over the magazine. Diana looked at the large smiling photograph of herself and scanned through the article about her, detailing different venues she had been at during the week and whose company she had been in.

"I really don't understand the interest these papers have in people like you!" said Maud. "Who on earth is interested in what so-called society girls are getting up to? It's all very vulgar, if you ask me. They call you a flapper!"

"Well, I've been called much worse over the years," said Diana, putting down the magazine. "I'd better rush – I'll be late for lunch."

"Are you meeting your American friend, Mr Barclay?" Maud's face was disapproving.

"No, I'm meeting Thelma for lunch. But I am meeting Jimmy later, for your information."

"Again! I imagine he won't be around for long. He looks as flighty as you do!"

"Thank you, Mama!" Diana got up and left the room.

She chose a coat from her wardrobe and then went into the nursery to say goodbye to Christian and Mrs Huddins.

"Will you be home for dinner?" enquired Mrs Huddins.

"Yes, I'll be home for dinner, but I'm out later to the theatre," smiled Diana.

She walked down the hallway.

"Goodbye, Mother!" she called as she opened the flat front door.

She stood stock still.

There, outside the flat door on the floor was a single red rose.

She stared down at the rose for a while and then reached down and picked it up. Then she burst out crying and came back into the flat.

"Whatever is the matter with you?" said Maud, coming out of the dining room.

"This!" said Diana holding up the rose. "Somebody left a rose outside the door."

"So?" Maud looked perplexed.

Diana wiped away her tears quickly. "It's nothing. It's just that Max hated saying goodbye when he went back to the front and so he'd slip off before I awoke and leave me a rose."

"I see. Peculiar custom."

"It just brought back the memories," said Diana.

"And who left it there now?"

"I don't know," said Diana as her voice became harsh. "But I've a pretty good idea!"

Diana entered Fortnum and Mason and made her way to the table where Thelma was. She bent down and kissed her.

"Are you all right?" asked Thelma who could tell she had been crying.

"Not really. I'm going to have to speak to Carl and tell him not to bother me again."

332

"Why? What's he done?"

"He left a rose outside my flat door."

"Did he?"

"Well, I'm sure it was him – who else would do such a thing?"

"Fraser?"

"Fraser Havington is hardly known for romantic gestures, is he? It must be Carl. But leaving a rose for me isn't going to win me back – if anything it will drive me further away."

"He probably thought it romantic," sighed Thelma. "I'll have a strong word with him for you."

"Thanks, Thelma."

"Did it upset you that much?" Thelma was surprised that it had caused Diana to cry.

"It wasn't Carl leaving the rose for me that upset me. It was that it reminded me too much of Max. Max always left a rose for me when he was going back to the front."

"Oh, I see." Thelma smiled sympathetically at her.

"It just brought back all my memories of Max."

"I see. Any word from Fraser?"

"Yes, he rang a couple of times."

Thelma studied Diana. "I hear that you've been seeing a lot of Jimmy Barclay."

"Yes, I have," Diana smiled.

"I'm quite surprised."

"Why?"

"Well, he's not your usual type. He's quite broke, you know."

"I know," Diana laughed.

"So what's the story between the two of you?"

"He makes me laugh, Thelma. He actually makes me laugh. I'd forgotten how to," smiled Diana. "And he's interested in me. Actually really interested. Not just interested in being seen with me. He asks me questions and I can talk to him. And he's so good to Christian. He's the first man I've met who hasn't considered my son an inconvenience. We spent last weekend together in the country. Christian came too."

Thelma smiled at her. "Then I'm happy for you."

CHAPTER 58

The Zanzibar Club was one of the numerous nightclubs and bars that were opening all around the city centre as London embraced the roaring twenties.

Jimmy and Diana entered the club, his arm around her waist, and spotted the Ashenbrys. They were at a round table positioned near the stage where a group of dancers were moving energetically around to loud music.

"Hello, everyone!" said Diana. There was a chorus of hellos. "Does everyone know Jimmy?"

"Hi, all!" smiled Jimmy.

Diana sat next to Thelma with Jimmy beside her.

Diana applauded as the posse of outrageous dancers left the stage and a singer called Joe Clifford came on and began to serenade the audience with a medley of songs.

"I spoke to Carl about the rose incidentally," said Thelma.

"Did you tell him I was very cross?"

"Yes."

"He was probably drunk at the time and can't remember!" said Diana.

"Perhaps. Anyway, I've made him promise me he won't bother you again."

"Thanks, Thelma."

Thelma looked at Jimmy who was busy charming the people at the other side of him.

"I take it you and Fraser Havington are over then?" Thelma asked.

"Oh, we never even got started," said Diana.

"Well, would you mind telling him? He's wondering why you haven't returned his calls."

Diana looked guilty. "I'll call him next week."

"This week!" insisted Thelma.

"All right!"

"Diana, I hope you know what you're doing with Jimmy," cautioned Thelma.

"Don't worry, Thelma. For the first time I really do know what I'm doing. I've never felt like this about anybody, except Max of course."

"I absolutely love this place," said Diana as she listened to Joe Clifford sing yet another of a series of songs requested by customers.

Jimmy smiled at her and refilled her glass of wine.

The song finished, Joe spoke to the audience.

"Ladies and gentlemen, I hope you are enjoying the evening," he said. "The next song is a request for Diana Cantwell."

"Oh!" said Diana, surprised but delighted. "Which one of you did that?"

"It wasn't any of us," said Elliott. "And we can prove it! We haven't left the table."

"She's here!" called Jimmy, pointing to Diana. "This is her!"

A light shone down on Diana and she self-consciously smiled.

"And it's a beautiful song for a beautiful lady," smiled Joe Clifford.

He walked to the front of the stage, looked down at Diana and, as the band struck up, began to sing.

"If you were the only girl in the world . . ."

Diana's face froze in alarm. And then suddenly tears began to fall down her face, every word of the song frightening her more.

As Joe Clifford finished the audience clapped.

"Diana? Are you all right?" asked Jimmy, putting his arm around her.

Diana suddenly stood up and marched around the stage and through the door that led to the backstage area. Concerned, Jimmy, Thelma and Elliott hurried after her.

"Diana, what is wrong with you?" demanded Jimmy.

The chorus girls were making their way onstage as Joe Clifford walked off.

"Who asked you to sing that song?" demanded Diana, standing in front of the singer.

"I'm sorry?" asked Joe Clifford.

"The song 'If You Were the Only Girl in the World' – who requested it to be sung for me?"

"I don't know, madam. The requests are taken by the stage manager," said Clifford, pointing in the direction of a man who was running around organising the acts backstage.

Diana rushed over to the man.

"Who put in the request for 'If You Were the Only Girl in the World' to be sung for Diana Cantwell?"

The stage manager looked startled. "I don't know!"

"Think!" demanded Diana.

"The requests are written on slips of paper and collected by the waiters and left on the desk over there. I gather the slips and hand them to the singers. I don't know which waiter took the request or left it there."

"Where's the slip of paper with that request on it?" demanded Diana.

"Still on the desk, I imagine."

Diana rushed over to the desk and frantically began to look through the slips of paper. "It has to be here!" she gasped.

"But what's the point in finding it?" asked Jimmy.

"To see whose handwriting is on it, of course," said Diana.

"Diana, will you calm down? What on earth has got into you?" asked Thelma.

"That song was Max's song for me. He used to have it played for me. Once he booked the whole restaurant of The Ritz in Paris for us and he came in singing that song."

"So what's your point?" asked Thelma.

"Only Max would know what that song meant for me."

"Diana, anyone here tonight could have placed that song request for you. It's just a coincidence," urged Jimmy.

"But who *did* place it then and where has the bloody request slip gone?" demanded Diana.

Thelma stepped forward and held her shoulders tightly. "Diana, you have plenty of admirers in the city. Any of the customers here tonight might have seen you and put in a request. I think we should go home. You are being irrational."

Diana sighed. "All right. I'm sorry for ruining everyone's night."

"You're tired and that song just brought back memories of Max and made you emotional. But that's all there is to it. It was just requested by an admirer of yours. Why don't you come back and stay with us tonight?"

"No. I'll go home. Order me a taxi, please."

As Jimmy walked Diana back into the main club, Elliott and Thelma looked at each other, worried.

Thelma called over to see Diana the following afternoon. Diana was just about to leave, to take Christian for a walk in the park.

"I'm sorry about last night," she said. "What must everyone think of me rushing around backstage like that like a madwoman?"

"It's understandable. The song just brought back memories. As for the request, you obviously have a secret admirer." Thelma smiled at Christian. "Right, little man, let's go for that walk then."

"Well, I can do without that kind of admiration in future," said Diana as she led Christian down the hallway after Thelma. "Goodness knows what Jimmy thought of my outburst! He'll think I'm a raving lunatic and never contact me again."

"I doubt that very much if the looks he was giving you last night are anything to go by!" said Thelma over her shoulder as she reached the front door.

She pulled it open and halted in her tracks. A red rose had been placed outside on the floor. She looked back, concerned, at Diana.

Diana stepped forward and carefully picked up the rose.

"Another rose!" she said. "It wasn't here when you arrived?"

"Definitely not," confirmed Thelma.

Diana rushed to the balcony of the landing and looked down to the hallway three floors below.

"Anybody there?" asked Thelma.

"No," said Diana, turning around. "The front door of the building is left unlocked during the day so anybody can just come in."

"Do you think it's Carl again?" asked Thelma.

"I don't know," said Diana, her face a mask of worry.

Suddenly she went racing down the landing and started to knock on a door. It was answered a moment later by her neighbour.

"Hello, Mrs Falcon. Did you see anybody come into the building over the past while who doesn't live here? Somebody carrying this rose?"

Thelma looked on, concerned, as Diana continued to knock on all her neighbours' doors in the building, interrogating them about the rose.

Diana knocked loudly on Carl's front door and a minute later his housekeeper Jane answered.

"Oh, hello, Jane. Is His Lordship home?"

"He's in the drawing room," said Jane, allowing her in.

"Thanks, Jane. I'll show myself in," Diana said, walking down the hall and into the drawing room where she found Carl pouring himself a drink.

"Diana!" he said, delighted to see her.

"Carl, how are you?"

"Much better for seeing you!"

Diana sighed. "Carl, I need to ask you to do something for me?"

"Anything."

"Please leave me alone. I'm not in love with you and I need you now to concentrate on yourself and getting on with your own life."

He looked crestfallen and confused. "I don't understand."

"The rose, Carl. The rose you left outside my flat door today."

"I didn't leave any rose there today!"

"And what about the one before? And the song in the club?"

He stared at her bleary-eyed.

He looked half drunk and she wondered if he could even remember what he had done that day.

CHAPTER 59

A few days later Diana was over at the Ashenbrys'. They were about to go to the theatre and were having a drink beforehand.

"Where's Jimmy?" asked Elliott, having got used to Jimmy being a permanent fixture on the scene when they were with Diana.

"He's meeting us at the theatre," said Diana.

"I believe you visited Carl?" said Elliott.

"Yes, I decided to confront him myself. He denies it's him," said Diana.

"I wonder if it's another ex-boyfriend?" said Thelma.

Diana shook her head. "I don't know . . . I've spoken to all the neighbours in my building. I'm trying to see about having the front door of the building locked during the day for security reasons. I'm not getting much support though. People don't feel the need to lock doors when they live an area like Regent's Park."

"Do you know my parents' apartment block on Fifth Avenue has a twenty-four hour concierge?" said Thelma. "There would be no mystery roses if London used concierges as well." She stood up, ready to leave.

"Sounds like a good system to me!" smiled Diana.

They made their way out to the hall where the butler got their coats and they began putting them on.

The telephone on a side table rang and the butler had to leave off helping Elliott put on his coat to go and answer it.

"Hello? 149 Connaught Square." He listened and then laid the receiver down on the table. "Miss Cantwell, phone call for you."

He hurried back to assist with the coats.

Diana moved quickly to the telephone. "It's probably Mama or Mrs Huddins. I hope everything is all right with Christian."

Thelma began chatting to the butler as he handed her her gloves.

Diana picked up the telephone receiver. "Hello?"

There was no answer, only silence, and Diana again said, "Hello?"

Suddenly there was a crackling on the phone line and what sounded like a gramophone record began to play 'If You Were the Only Girl in the World'.

Diana froze.

"Diana? Is everything all right?" asked Thelma, seeing Diana's horrified expression. She quickly approached her. "What's wrong?"

Diana swayed and then fainted onto the ground.

"Just go home and get some rest," suggested the doctor after examining Diana.

"Thank you, doctor," said Diana.

She was in the Ashenbrys' drawing room.

They had contacted Jimmy at the theatre and he now sat beside Diana, comforting her.

Elliott came back into the room. "Well, I've spoken to the butler and he can't give any more information. All he said was that a man's voice asked for you. He was flustered at the time with trying to help us with our coats."

"Did he say the man had an accent?" demanded Diana.

"He can't recall. We were all in the lobby making a lot of noise."

Diana turned to Thelma and grasped her hand. "You heard it, Thelma, didn't you? You heard 'If You Were the Only Girl in the World' playing down the telephone?"

Thelma looked stressed. "I heard something, yes. I heard a song play. I can't say which song it was. I was too busy looking at your terrified expression!"

"Who is tormenting me?" demanded Diana, walking up and down. "What is going on?"

"Well, whoever it is knew you were here," said Elliott.

"So somebody is following me?" Diana began to shiver uncontrollably.

Thelma looked at Elliott, concerned, then addressed Diana. "Diana, are you sure nobody spoke?"

"Quite sure!"

"Are you sure it wasn't your mother and there was just a gramophone playing in the background?"

"Of course I'm sure! It wasn't background music – the telephone was right up against the gramophone!"

"It's just with the roses and everything . . . you might have only heard what you hoped to hear," ventured Elliott.

Diana looked at the concerned expressions on the Ashenbrys' and Jimmy's faces.

"You think I'm being paranoid, don't you?" she demanded.

"Nobody's saying that, Diana," said Jimmy quickly.

"No, of course not," said Thelma. "I saw the rose myself outside your flat and heard some kind of music on the phone out there . . . I just think you might be building it up into something it's not."

"And what about the request at the Zanzibar Club?" demanded Diana.

"I don't understand what you're implying is going on?" said Thelma. "What are you implying, Diana? That this has something to do with Max?"

"Of course not," said Diana. "I just want to know who is behind these things and why they are doing it."

Elliott moved towards her. "As the doctor said, you need a good night's sleep. Why don't you stay here tonight?"

"No. I want my own bed."

"I'll give you a lift home then," he said.

"No need, I'll take her home in a taxi," said Jimmy.

"I ruined enough of your night, Elliott," said Diana. "I seem determined to ruin everyone's nights at the moment."

"Not at all," said Elliott. "In that case, if you will accompany her, Jimmy, I'll get my chauffeur to drive you there."

Elliott went out to arrange for the motor car and Thelma went over and put a comforting arm around Diana.

"I'm not going mad, Thelma."

"Of course you're not. Nobody is suggesting that for a moment." Thelma looked at Jimmy. "You'll make sure she gets into her flat safely?"

"Of course I will," said Jimmy.

In the motor car Diana stared out the window at the rain.

Jimmy reached forward and took her hand. "Are you all right?"

"No, I'm far from all right, Jimmy. I need to know what's going on. I could see by Thelma and Elliott's faces that they didn't believe me. But I did hear that bloody song being played down the telephone!"

Jimmy put his arm around her and soothed her. "Of course you did."

She started to cry and looked away, trying to hide her tears from the chauffeur.

Thelma and Elliott sat having a pot of tea in their drawing room.

"I'm worried about her, Elliott," said Thelma. "I mean, is she suggesting that all this has something to do with Max? Part of me thinks she wants it to be. She's never really let him go, you know. Not in her heart."

CHAPTER 60

Present Day

It was Saturday afternoon and Julia was preparing the children to take them to the park.

She walked into the dining room where Sam was sitting with several thick tomes open in front of him and busily flicking through the internet.

"Are you sure you don't want to come to the park with us?" she asked.

"No, thanks. I've too much to do."

"I thought you said you had to correct essays," she said, taking up one of the books and looking at it.

"Eh, yes – later," he answered distractedly.

"What's this?" she asked and then read out the book title. "*German Matrimonial Rights, Customs, Laws and By-laws* – some light reading for the afternoon?"

"It's just some research I'm doing."

"For what?"

"Julia! I'm trying to concentrate!" he objected, glancing up at her from the computer screen.

"All right then, we'll leave you to it." She turned and walked out of the room, calling for the children.

Sam sat outside Thomas's office at the law chambers. Beside him was a file of papers and several books.

"Shouldn't be long now," said the secretary, smiling over at him.

He nodded back.

Five minutes later Thomas put his head around the door.

"Hi there! Come on in," he said.

Sam gathered his papers and books and, going into the office, took a seat. He put the books and papers on the desk.

Thomas glanced down at them. "I'm taking it this is not a social call?"

"No. I need your opinion on something."

Thomas sat back in his chair and put his fingers together. "Fire away."

"Well, you know all this that's been going on about the Von Hoffstens?"

"Hmmm."

"Remember I was telling you that my great-grandmother entered a morganatic marriage which caused the title and property to bypass my grandfather?"

"Yes, interesting tradition – no legal comparative in the UK or Ireland," observed Thomas.

"Well, I've been researching whether it really had legal status in Germany after the war," said Sam.

"In what manner?"

"In 1919, after the war, a republic was declared in Germany."

"Yes, the decadent days of the Weimer Republic."

"Exactly. Prior to the republic the nobility, like the Von Hoffstens, had special rights and privileges and laws unique to themselves, including the left-handed marriage law. But when the republic was declared all these rights and privileges of the aristocracy were abolished. They became just regular people like everyone else. A series of laws dismantled their special rights, like for example a law on March 28th 1919 specifically got rid of an aristocrat's right to tell his heir who to leave his estate to. This meant morganatic marriages had no legal standing any more. My grandfather was born after that date, meaning he shouldn't have been by-passed."

"Go on."

"This means that the old Count Conrad could not dictate that Max's and Diana's son be bypassed in favour of Hugo any more. Max was his heir and by the system of primogeniture then in practice in Germany, the eldest son would inherit – which would have been my grandfather, and should have been my grandfather."

"If that was the case then why didn't Max and Diana enforce it?" asked Thomas.

"Because Max was dead, and Diana had been kicked out of her home in Germany and was back in Ireland, obviously unaware of what these changes meant for her and her son."

"That was a pity for her, wasn't it?" said Thomas.

"Well, they did her! They did her and her son out of what by then was legally theirs."

"They sound like a cruel lot. So, Sam, what's that got to do with me? Why are you here?"

"Well, that's what I understand from my reading but I want you to investigate if what I'm saying is, in fact, legally correct."

"For what purpose? Just so you can be even more bitter about how your family was treated?"

Sam sat up straight. "No . . . I want to mount a case against the present Von Hoffstens to the effect that they are pretenders to the title and that the property they inherited back in 1919 when the old count died was not theirs to inherit, but rightfully belonged to my grandfather, Max and Diana's son."

Thomas stared at Sam in disbelief and then he lay back in his chair and began to hoot with laughter.

"I don't see what's so funny," said Sam, his face a mixture of irritation and anger.

"Let me get this straight – you want to take a case to claim you are the count and everything that belongs to them belongs to you?"

"Exactly."

"Have you lost your marbles, man?"

"No."

"Have you told Julia?"

"No."

"Figures. She wouldn't let you make a fool of yourself by even suggesting it."

"I don't care what anyone thinks. I don't care what anyone says. I owe this to my great-grandfather Max and great-grandmother

Diana who suffered so much." Sam stood up. "I'm leaving you the paperwork and the books with the pages marked. I would appreciate it if you gave it your serious attention. If you don't get back to me about it, I'll find someone else who will listen."

Sam turned and walked out of the room.

Julia was relieved that Sam hadn't mentioned the Von Hoffstens or this Diana Cantwell for a number of days. She had begun to regret advising him to go to his distant relative's assistance in Munich. The whole experience appeared to have taken him over and begun to dominate his life.

It was a Friday night and they were both in the sitting room, curled up watching television. They had a full weekend of activity ahead with friends and Julia was looking forward to things getting back to normal.

The doorbell rang.

"Who on earth is that at this time of the night?" she asked, seeing it was after ten.

She went out to the hallway and answered the door. To her surprise Thomas was standing there, looking excited and flustered, carrying a few files.

"Is Sam home?" he asked, walking past her into the house.

"Hello, Thomas, is everything all right?" she asked, but he had made his way into the sitting room. She closed the front door and followed him in.

"Thomas!" said Sam, sitting up surprised.

"Hi, Sam," said Thomas, sitting down on an armchair and beginning to spread the files he carried across the coffee table.

"Is everything all right? Colette isn't ill or anything?" asked Julia.

"No, everything's fine. Right – I've been doing a lot of investigating since you visited my office last week, Sam."

Julia looked at Sam, surprised. "What were you doing visiting his office?"

"And I think we've got a case, and a strong one," said Thomas excitedly.

"A case for what?" asked Julia, shaking her head in confusion.

"Go on!" urged Sam, ignoring his wife.

"As you said, this left-handed marriage Diana and Max entered into had no standing in law once the German monarchy was abolished and the republic was declared in 1919. In fact, a law was passed in 1919 in Germany that all citizens were equal before the law in August of that year, so the offspring of a morganatic marriage could not then be declared ineligible to be the heir. From your notes I see Max was killed in the war in 1918. The old Count Conrad died at the beginning of 1919. So when your grandfather was born in May of that year he was born the rightful count and heir to the Von Hoffsten estate. But his uncle, Hugo, had seized the title and estate by then, which he had no right to."

Julia looked at Sam, shocked. "You've been investigating this legally?"

Sam glanced at her. "Yes."

"Without telling me?"

"I wanted to know if we had any legal standing before worrying you," explained Sam.

"But what for? What's the purpose of all this?" asked Julia.

"Sam wants to launch a lawsuit to reclaim the Von Hoffsten title and property," said Thomas.

"*What*?" screeched Julia.

"*Shhh*, Julia! We can talk about it later – let's hear what Thomas has to say first. Go on, Thomas!"

"To sum up," said Thomas, "I think the best way to handle this is by asserting that your grandfather's title and property were taken from him unlawfully, on the grounds that he was born the count, as morganatic marriage was no longer recognised by the time he was born, and all property rights belonged to him at the time. And that his uncle, Hugo, illegally claimed the title and estates."

"I've never heard anything so ridiculous! You can't go back into history and claim something like that! It's like – nearly a century!" said Julia incredulously.

"That is where you're very wrong, Julia," said Thomas. "There are presently hundreds if not thousands of such cases going on, on the continent."

"But how?" demanded Julia.

"There are many actions being taken – mainly by aristocrats, but also by regular people, to reclaim property that was taken from them by the Nazis and Communist regimes," Thomas said triumphantly.

"Of course," said Sam, remembering having read articles about it.

"Throughout Germany, the Czech Republic, Hungary, Poland, much property was seized by the then Nazi and Communist regimes and those families are now pursuing the return of that property through the courts."

"And how successful are they?" said Julia, becoming more alarmed as the situation Thomas was explaining was now making sense.

"They are complicated cases, and can take years to prove, but some are successful. A Hapsburg was handed back a castle that belonged to his family in Romania, an Argentinean managed to successfully reclaim a castle and lands that belonged to his family in the Czech Republic. Most importantly to our case, there are many such actions being taken in Germany by aristocrats reclaiming property taken in the 1930s, 40s and 50s by the different regimes. It sets a precedent for us that I think we can exploit."

Julia was becoming stressed. "Thomas, you are approving of Sam's crazy idea!"

"I do approve! There's a clear case the title and property were seized illegally by Hugo Von Hoffsten, when his nephew was the rightful heir. I'm not saying that the Von Hoffsten empire is going to be handed to Sam, but I do think the Von Hoffstens must compensate Sam for his loss of inheritance."

"And the title?" asked Sam.

"Titles were officially abolished in Germany after the war but the heirs of aristocratic families continued using them by incorporating the titles into their birth certs and by so doing continuing to address themselves by their historic titles. The Von Hoffstens did this. We would be insisting the present count, not being the direct heir, had no right to incorporate that title into his birth certificate and that he should relinquish the right to use that title or compensate you fully to continue its use."

"Oh, Thomas, you're just speaking like a lawyer – the first whiff of money and you're off, even with this cracked idea," said Julia.

"I've investigated this fully and explained my stand on it," said Thomas.

Julia stood up. "Sorry, Thomas, but could I ask you to leave? Myself and Sam have a lot to discuss."

"Of course. Call me if you need to know anything. I'll leave these files for you to read."

"No, don't!" said Julia.

"Yes, do!" insisted Sam.

Thomas smiled awkwardly and left the files where they were. "I'll see myself out."

Julia waited until she heard the front door close before she turned on Sam.

"What the fuck has got into you?" she demanded loudly.

Sam sat back with his hands behind his head, looking a mixture of excited and scared, and said, "I can't believe it!"

"*You* can't believe it! How do you think *I* feel?"

Sam jumped up and grabbed her hands. "Julia! Do you know what this could mean to our lives?"

She snatched her hands back. "Sam, you are not seriously considering pursuing this?"

"Of course I am – why wouldn't I? You heard Thomas. We have a case."

"And you would actually go through a court case to get – I don't know – what exactly are you looking to get?"

"I'm looking to get what is rightfully ours, and what would have been ours if we hadn't been swindled by that Hugo Von Hoffsten all those years ago," said Sam.

Julia shook her head. "You're not thinking straight, Sam. You heard Thomas – these are complicated legal battles that can go on for years. Do you really want to go through that, and put our family through that for years? And what about the costs involved?"

"We've got a lot of equity in the house and our savings and this is our priority."

"*Sam!*"

"If it means getting what is rightfully ours! Besides, I'm sure Thomas would be willing to delay his costs until we win and are compensated. You see how confident he is!"

"But you're trying to rewrite history," she said.

"No, I'm trying to *correct* history," he maintained.

"But all our friends and family will think we're demented," she said.

"Let them – Thomas doesn't."

"Thomas is a lawyer salivating at the thought of getting his hands on the Von Hoffsten empire. And they are an empire, Sam, from how you describe them. How could we possibly take them on?"

"Well, that's exactly how people like that function, Julia. They think they can do whatever they want to whoever they want. That's how they walked on poor Diana all those years back and made her life hell. And I've experienced them, Julia. When I was in Munich. They never came near me – I wasn't even allowed to speak to them. They think they are so superior. I can only imagine how they destroyed Diana all those years ago."

"So you are on some kind of vendetta?"

"Not exactly."

"Or is this your own pride? There you are, Sam Cantwell, with all your students hanging on your every word, and your qualifications, and then you meet this family, the Von Hoffstens, and they make you feel worthless, unimportant. Is this your way of making yourself important to them? To make the countess notice you perhaps?"

"Don't be ridiculous," he said angrily. "They've got away with everything, and it's time I stood up to them – not just for myself but for Diana and Max and their descendants right down to me. All the people they stole from. They've lived a life of outrageous luxury while my family have struggled through the years. That needs to be corrected."

"And just say, Sam, that after years of wrangling and fighting you get what you want? You get the title and get huge compensation from the Von Hoffstens. What then?"

"What do you mean?"

"Our lives would never be the same again. How could we fit in with our circle here with you a multi-millionaire count?"

"That's their problem."

"Do you honestly think a count and countess could fit into suburban Dublin? Do you honestly think that all that money could bring us happiness? Has it brought the present count, who got shot in a kidnap attempt, and the present countess, who seems unable to even say hello to anybody, happiness?"

"I think it's you who's being selfish," he said.

"*Me?*"

"Yes, you! You're not thinking of us or the children at all. When they are struggling to get a job and get a mortgage in years to come, do you think they will thank you for not ensuring that their rightful inheritance was secured when there was an opportunity to get it?"

"That's not fair, Sam!"

"Of course it's fair. I'm doing this as much for them as Diana and Max. They don't deserve to scrimp and save all their lives while their distant cousins enjoy our money."

"Don't bring the kids into it," she insisted.

"Of course I have to bring them into it. It's about their future too. I'm willing to fight for what is rightfully theirs and you aren't and that's the bottom line."

"I want them to be well-rounded happy people, not living behind secluded walls," said Julia.

"And that's what they will be – well-rounded happy people – with us as parents and their rightful inheritance in place," said Sam.

PART 4

1924

CHAPTER 61

Diana sat at the kitchen table in the flat drinking coffee, almost in a trance.

"Diana!" Maud called.

"Yes?" Diana answered.

"Just come to the drawing room, Diana. I've somebody I'd like you to meet."

Diana raised her eyes to heaven as she finished her coffee and left the kitchen. Maud was seated in the drawing room beside a rotund bohemian-looking woman who looked like she was in her fifties.

"Diana . . . this is Madame Souska."

"I'm so happy to meet you – your mother has been telling me all about you," said Madame Souska in a thick foreign accent.

"She's Polish," Maud explained. "Take a seat, Diana."

Diana sat down opposite them.

"Madame Souska is a clairvoyant," announced Maud. "She's the lady I've been telling you about who has been running the séances here for me for the past few months. She's brilliant!"

"Your mother has been telling me everything that has been happening to you," said Madame Souska. "The roses, the song being requested, the telephone call. It absolutely sounds to me like somebody trying to contact you from the other side."

"Oh, for goodness sake!" said Diana.

"It makes total sense, Diana," said Maud. "We've been holding séances here trying to get through to Dashiel, and we've ended up getting Max instead!"

"After all, this is your home, Diana, so when we reached to the other side, it was your husband who came through," said Madame Souska.

"So you're trying to tell me it's my dead husband Max who's leaving the roses and playing songs to me down telephones?"

"Yes! The spirits move so strangely and often I've heard they can intercept telephone lines to do their work," said Madame Souska excitedly.

"I'm afraid that's just nonsense!" said Diana.

"She's a non-believer," said Maud with a disappointed look at the medium.

"You don't have to be a believer if someone on the other side needs to contact you," said Madame Souska.

"How else do you explain it, Diana?" said Maud. "The song, the roses – you said only Max would know these things."

"Thelma and Elliott say they're just coincidences and it's a secret admirer," said Diana.

"What do they know?" Maud dismissed the notion. "Besides, if Max is looking on from the other side, the antics of your lifestyle have probably shocked him into coming back to you! I imagine he's trying to tell you he disapproves of your lifestyle, particularly your new-found beau, Mr Barclay."

Madame Souska closed her eyes. "I'm feeling a great love between you and your husband. A love that survived the grave . . . and he now wants to make contact with you."

"My poor Max didn't even get a grave. His body was never found."

"Oh, not to have a grave!" declared Madame Souska. "It's no wonder his soul can't rest."

"I suggest a séance!" said Maud.

"Tonight!" said Madame Souska.

"No!" snapped Diana. "I don't want a séance and think I would prefer if you didn't have any more séances in my home! I don't really believe in ghosts, but I also don't like the idea of you trying to disturb people who are dead. Who knows what mischief you're causing?"

"It's all done in a very controlled way," said Madame Souska.

"And if, as you say, we have disturbed Max's spirit then we ought to have a séance now to finish the job," said Maud.

"Otherwise he could become a malevolent spirit – if he feels nobody is listening," said Madame Souska.

"Will you stop this!" demanded Diana, rising quickly. "I don't want to hear any more about ghosts and spirits. I'm going shopping. I would really like it if you were gone by the time I get home."

With that she rushed out of the room.

Thelma was the patroness for a charity that raised money for the deprived children of the East End. She held parties and balls to raise funds. The charity often arranged days into the country for the children or parties in parks to give them a break from the monotony of their daily lives. Diana often assisted on these days. When she saw their malnourished faces it reminded her of the starvation back in Germany during the war.

One Saturday the charity had arranged a party in a park. The children had competed in sports during the morning and now were being served lunch. There were tables laden with treats and food.

Thelma and Diana walked through the tables of delighted children.

"Poor loves," sighed Thelma. "You know these days that we organise are the only time most of them will ever have ice cream or sweets. For most of them it is a battle to get fed every day, their families are so poor."

"Let's hope this new Socialist party will change all that," said Diana.

Thelma grimaced. "Don't let Elliott hear you say that. He maintains Labour is going to tax the aristocracy out of existence."

"That would be so British! The Russians shot their aristocracy, the Irish burned them out and the British aristocracy are subjected to a slow death by taxation!"

Diana bent down at a table to resolve a dispute between some children about the sharing out of sweets.

"No more roses?" Thelma asked as they walked on. She was almost afraid to ask.

"No. Mama is convinced it's all being done by Max's ghost. That my lifestyle has shocked him back from the dead to try to point out the error of my ways!"

"One solution, I guess!"

Just then a man came up to them. "Lady Ashenbry, would you be able to come up to the stand to present the prizes to the children who won in sports this morning?"

"Of course."

Thelma and Diana followed the man up to a row of chairs on the stand which were already nearly filled by the other dignitaries involved in the charity.

"Ah, Lady Ashenbry, there you are! What a wonderful day for the children," said the vicar who ran the charity.

"Yes, Reverend, great work by everyone," said Thelma.

"Miss Cantwell, please take a seat with the others," said the vicar, gesturing to the row of chairs.

Diana sat and looked out at the tables of joyful children. There were many parents there as well, assisting on the day.

"Children, children!" called the vicar, waving his hands in the air to quieten them down. "Now we are going to present prizes! Lady Ashenbry will present them!"

There was a cheer from the children and parents.

"Winner of the 100-yard sprint is young Tommy Byrne. Tommy, where are you?" called the vicar.

Diana watched as a series of children were presented with prizes of toys.

When all the prizes were presented, Thelma readied herself to say a few words of congratulation.

"Ladies, gentlemen, children," she began but stopped when a young girl of about eight years old walked up the steps, hands behind her back, and onto the stand.

She was smiling as she reached Thelma and the vicar.

The vicar looked very flustered. "Who are you, little girl? Did we forget to give you your prize? What is your name?"

The little girl ignored him, walked past him and Thelma, and up to Diana. She stood in front of her, smiling.

"Hello there!" said Diana, leaning forward and smiling at her. "What's your name?"

The little girl brought her hand out from behind her back and presented Diana with a bunch of wild daisies.

Diana stared at the daisies. She had a flashback to the festival for the estate workers in Germany, on the day Franz Ferdinand was assassinated, and the little girl who had presented her with a bunch of daisies then. And then on the morning of her birthday, how Max had arranged for Paul's daughter to present her with daisies when he was away at the front.

Trembling, Diana knelt down beside the little girl and, trying to hide the stress in her face, smiled at her. "Who told you to give those to me?" she asked.

The little girl said nothing but continued to hold the flowers out to Diana.

Diana leaned forward to her and asked again, "Who sent you with them?"

"Diana! She's trying to give you flowers!" said Thelma, concerned at Diana's reaction.

Diana's voice cracked as her face became upset. "Please tell me! Who told you to give me the flowers?"

The vicar and the other dignitaries looked on, concerned.

"Miss Cantwell, are you quite all right?" asked the vicar, moving towards her.

Diana reached out and took the little girl's free hand as tears slipped down her face. "Please tell me!"

The girl remained silent but seeing Diana's tears was obviously making her agitated.

An older boy ran up from one of the tables.

"Let her alone! She can't speak! She's dumb!" the boy declared.

After the incident, Diana hurried to the car park, followed by Thelma. Thelma's chauffeur opened the back door of the car and Thelma and Diana sat in.

"Diana!" said Thelma as they drove off. "What on earth was all that about?"

Diana was staring out the car window as it began to rain.

"When we lived in Germany, before the war there was a festival for the estate. On that day a little girl came up and presented me with daisies just like those."

"So?"

"And then when the war started and Max was at the front, on my birthday he had organised for a little girl to give me daisies as well."

"What are you implying, Diana?"

"Don't you see? It's too much of a coincidence. Whoever is behind the roses and the playing of the song got that little girl to give me flowers! I just know it!"

"Oh, Diana!" Thelma looked exasperated. She reached for a cigarette and lit it.

"And why me?" asked Diana. "Why didn't she give you the flowers or one of the other women?"

"Who knows?" said Thelma.

"Only Max would know about that day in Germany, the day of the festival." Diana had a far-off look in her eyes. "It was the day Franz Ferdinand was shot and the war began. It was a beautiful summer's day. Everyone from the estate and the town was there. Max and I and his family were seated at the top table and the little girl came up and presented me with the daisies. It was the last day we were truly happy before the war changed everything."

"So then perhaps your mother is right," said Thelma sceptically. "Perhaps Max's ghost is coming back, giving you signs. But how a ghost communicated with a little girl is beyond me."

"But maybe Max isn't dead," Diana declared.

Thelma stared at her in disbelief. "Diana . . ." she began.

"What if Max isn't dead?" repeated Diana. "It was never confirmed. His body was never found. Nobody reported back from the battlefield saying they saw him being killed. He was reported missing, presumed dead. But not confirmed."

"But if Max didn't die then, where's he been all this time?" Thelma was incredulous.

360

"Well, I don't know!"

Thelma leaned towards her. "Diana, I think you really need to see a doctor. We have an excellent doctor and I can arrange an appointment for you in the morning."

"I don't need to see a doctor!"

"Well, I think you do!" said Thelma. "You were clearly upset by being given those flowers today. The vicar was very concerned about you."

"Well, I'm sorry if I upset the day."

"Diana, Elliot and I are seriously worried about you. You've gone through a terrible time, what with losing Max and the way the Von Hoffstens treated you. And then finding out Dashiel was dead and everything else that happened with your family and Garonglen."

"I'm very tired," Diana conceded.

"And maybe you threw yourself into building a life for yourself after the war and maybe it's all just catching up with you now."

Diana sighed. "Okay, make the appointment."

CHAPTER 62

Jimmy drove Diana to the doctor. He parked the car and walked her into the reception.

"Do you want me to come in with you?" he asked.

"No, Jimmy, I think he'd prefer to see me on my own," said Diana.

"I'll be waiting just outside," he reassured her as he gave her a hug and a kiss.

She nodded and headed in for her appointment.

Doctor James Canning specialised in stress-related disorders. He listened attentively as Diana described everything that had been going on.

"Miss Cantwell, you're an intelligent young woman and I don't think I need to tell you that you have no direct evidence that your husband is still alive," he said.

"But the fact that his body was never found also means that there is no direct evidence that he was killed either!"

"He has been declared dead though, Miss Cantwell." The doctor's face became sympathetic as he leaned forward to her. "I treat many soldiers from the war who are going through a kind of living hell. I treat them for the trauma they are suffering. And I think you are going through your own trauma from what you tell me you have endured during and after the war. Because Max's body was never found, I don't think you ever truly believed he was gone. This was a man who led you to believe he could do anything! Win any race, buy any yacht, provide you with anything you wanted. It's hard to accept that such a hero came to the same fate as millions of others. Just another casualty on the battlefield. But for your own sanity, Miss Cantwell, you must now accept that he is dead and move on with your life."

"But I never doubted he was dead until all this stuff began to occur!"

"You're piecing together coincidences and clinging to hope. If you continue to look for hope where there is none, it's your sanity that I fear for."

"But the roses?"

"An ex-boyfriend of yours."

"The request of the song in the club?"

"A secret admirer."

"The daisies at the park?"

"A sweet little girl giving you a gift."

"The song played down the phone at the Ashenbrys'?"

"Did you really hear that song? Or was it just in your mind?"

"Well, the butler took the call and the Ashenbrys were there!"

"By the time you got to the telephone there was a crossed line, hence the music. As you know the telephone lines are full of crossed lines. I went to answer my own telephone yesterday and there was a crossed line of the most terrible argument I'd ever heard between a married couple. These things happen. I believe only in reality. If you want to have different answers then follow your mother's advice and have a séance – not that that will give you any correct answers."

Maud was waiting anxiously at home for Diana. She heard the door unlock and Diana came in, accompanied by Jimmy.

"Well?"

"All in my mind apparently," said Diana, sitting down on the couch.

"What does he know?" said Maud.

"That's what I said," said Jimmy.

"But, I suppose what he said makes sense. There is no cold hard evidence. And I love Max so much perhaps I am just reading things into these coincidences."

"Madame Souska says –"

"Stop it, Mama! I'm not interested in what she has to say. All in my mind, that's what the doctor said." Diana sat in thought. "He's right, of course. Do you know, I'd better be careful or they'll be putting me away in the nuthouse. Elliott and Thelma already think I'm half doolally. I've been letting all this take me over. I'd better just put it out of my mind and move on with my life."

"That's fighting talk!" praised Jimmy.

She stood up, smiling. "I think I'll throw a party."

"Not another one!" sighed Maud.

"Just to show everyone that the old Diana Cantwell is back with no more hysterics about flowers and songs."

"Can I invite Madame Souska?" asked Maud.

"No!"

CHAPTER 63

"You look marvellous, Diana," complimented Thelma as she and Elliott were shown into the drawing room of the flat which was already half full of people, the night of the party.

"I feel a lot better. Thanks to that doctor you sent me to."

"I'm so glad you're feeling better." Thelma was relieved.

"We're all still fragile after the war, Diana, no matter how we hide behind everything," said Elliott. "It doesn't take much to send us back to the dark place."

"I'm just very lucky I have such good friends and family," Diana said, kissing them both before glancing over at Jimmy who was chatting away to a group of people. "And Jimmy, he's been so supportive of me during all this . . . Drink?"

"Yes, please. A Manhattan," said Thelma.

Diana began to mix the drinks. "And some music. Jimmy, put on the gramophone, will you?"

"Certainly," said Jimmy, going over to the gramophone. "What song will I put on?"

"Anything but 'If You Were the Only Girl in the World'!" Diana said.

Thelma and Elliott looked at her and they all started to laugh.

It was eleven at night and the party was in full swing as the Charleston played on the gramophone and couples danced.

"It's a whole new world!" said Maud as she sat on the couch looking at the spectacle of the party in front of her.

"They are the bright young things," said Elliott.

"Well, they don't look that bright and some of them don't look that young either!" said Maud. "*Things* is the only part of that description that suits them! When I think of the dances we used to have before the war at Garonglen! Oh, beautiful genteel evenings where the men were all gentlemen and the women were all ladies, and dressed accordingly." Maud gave a girl sashaying past, dressed in a tasselled short cocktail dress, a disproving look and looked in despair at a young man who seemed to be wearing make-up.

"I believe it's even more shocking in Berlin," said Elliott.

"Well, it would be, wouldn't it?" said Maud. "How do you think Diana is this evening?"

"Much better!" He looked at her in the centre of the room, laughing with a group of people as she told a story.

"I do worry about her, Elliott. She's gone through so much and never thinks of the future, just the present. She can't continue living this life forever. I had thought that these reminders of Max might have been a warning to her to slow down. To stop this lifestyle. But she seems to have bounced back fully!"

Elliott looked at Maud, concerned.

"And as for this Jimmy character! What do you make of him?" she asked.

"He seems . . . charming," said Elliott.

"*Too* charming, in my estimation!" Maud stood up. "Anyway, I'd better be going. I'm retiring to my room."

Diana heard the phone ringing out in the hall and went out to answer it. She closed over the door from the music and picked up the receiver.

"Hello?"

"Diana?"

"Yes?"

"*You know I'll always come back to you,*" whispered the man's voice.

"Max!" Diana cried out but the line went dead.

The party was hastily cancelled and everyone sent home. Diana sat in an armchair with a tumbler of neat whiskey in her hand. She was still shaking as Thelma tried to comfort her.

"You can't be sure it was him," said Thelma. "The music was blaring, the guests were loud. You said it was a whisper."

"But it was what he said. He said: '*I'll always come back to you.*' I told you it's what Max always said to me before he went back to the front. It was his promise to me. He used to finish his letters always with that." She suddenly put down her whiskey and, jumping up, ran out of the room.

She returned a minute later holding some of Max's letters.

"See!" She showed them where he had written it.

Jimmy came in and knelt down beside her, holding her hand.

"Madame Souska says the telephone can be a medium for spirits," said Maud. "That they can infiltrate the lines."

"What nonsense, Maud!" snapped Thelma.

"You seem to think this is all real, Maud?" questioned Elliott, studying her.

"There are some things that we can't understand, Madame Souska says."

"Well, putting aside the possibility that Diana is being haunted by Max's ghost for a moment," Thelma spoke with authority, "let's just say for argument's sake that Max did survive the war and he is alive. Then what the blazes is he playing at? Why is he playing these pranks? Why on earth is he hiding?"

Diana began pacing and down.

"Mama, do you remember when Max's father came to dinner at Garonglen?"

"How could I forget? Ignoramus!"

"Do you remember in the ensuing row that Max said there was a large degree of insanity running through their family?"

"Vaguely! But having witnessed that family, I am in agreement with that prognosis!"

"Well, he was right. As I told you before, Max's mother suffered from insanity and killed herself due to it."

"Very tragic family," said Maud, shaking her head.

"And Brigitte. I'm sure she was veering to madness half the

time," said Diana.

"A most unusual girl to be fair," agreed Maud.

"Well, maybe it's not me gone mad, but Max?"

"Because it runs in his family?" asked Elliott.

"Yes! And maybe the war drove him to madness. The last time he came back on leave he wasn't the Max I knew and loved."

"What was he like?"

"He was a shell of a man. Very broken. Whatever had happened him in the war had broken him. He hardly spoke and I had to lead him everywhere. His eyes had this emptiness. He was like as if he was in a trance all the time. I pleaded with his superiors not to send him back to the front, that he wasn't well enough. But of course they ignored me."

"So what do you think could have happened to him when he went back to the front?"

"What if he had a complete breakdown and got lost somewhere in the battlefield? Maybe he wandered off somewhere and was admitted into a hospital in France. Maybe he has been recuperating all this time."

"But why is he here in London? Why didn't he go back to Germany to his family?" asked Thelma.

"He traced me here and followed me here. I was the most important thing to him."

"But why doesn't he step forward then and claim you back? Reunite with you?" Thelma was flabbergasted.

Jimmy looked hurt at this. "Excuse me, Thelma, but Diana has moved on with her life. He can't just come back and reclaim her like luggage he forgot to collect!"

Diana ignored Jimmy's outburst. "But, that's my point, Thelma," she said. "Maybe he's still not the old Max. Maybe he has gone insane."

"Perhaps seeing you going out with a series of other men has deterred him from coming forth as well!" said Maud. "If he has gone insane, and he did love you so much, he's probably insane with jealousy if he has been looking on at your life. He thinks you don't love *him* any more!" She gave Jimmy a vicious stare.

"Well, I think I should stay here the night," said Jimmy. "To make sure you're all right."

"There's absolutely no need, thank you, Jimmy!" objected Maud.

Diana squeezed Jimmy's hand and smiled. "I'll be fine."

CHAPTER 64

Diana was in a daze over the next couple of weeks. She turned down invitations and stayed home mostly.

"I'm just heading over to a friend," said Maud as she came into Diana's bedroom and found her lying on the bed.

"All right."

"Can I get you anything while I'm out?"

"No." Diana sat up and swung her legs on to the floor. "I'm going out as well. I'm meeting Claire Charter for lunch."

"Oh, that's good. Better than hiding yourself away all the time."

"I don't feel like going, but I don't want to let her down."

"Good girl!" Maud came over and kissed her daughter before leaving.

Diana got a taxi to Knightsbridge where she met Claire.

"I've been hearing all about these strange goings-on with you. What's really happening? They said Carl was bothering you, but seemingly it's something to do with your poor dead husband?"

"I don't really want to talk about it," sighed Diana. "The last thing I need is for all this to become public knowledge."

"Well, you can't stop people from gossiping."

"Don't I know," sighed Diana.

It was five by the time Diana got back to the flat. She let herself in.

"Mrs Huddins!" she called, taking off her coat. There was no answer and she realised that the nanny hadn't returned from taking

Christian to the park yet. She checked through the mail that was left on a side table in the hallway and, seeing nothing of interest, she left the letters in a drawer of the table.

Then she went to her bedroom and walked in.

She stood staring. Her whole bedroom was filled with flowers. There were vases everywhere. She walked slowly through the room, staring at the flowers. Then she turned and quickly went out into the hallway, looking up and down.

"Mama! Are you home?" she called loudly but there was no answer. She began to slowly walk down the corridor and then she ran to the front door and let herself out. She ran down the landing to her neighbour's door and started knocking loudly.

"Help me! Please, open the door!" she screamed.

The police were called and Diana sat beside Jimmy in the drawing room of the flat as a Sergeant Hollingford questioned her.

A concerned Mrs Huddins stood nervously beside her while Maud, Thelma and Elliott were seated opposite.

"And you just arrived back and found your bedroom full of flowers?" asked the sergeant.

"Yes!"

"And you have no idea how they got there?"

"No! Of course I don't. I'd hardly cause all this commotion and call the police if I knew, would I?" snapped Diana.

"She has a point!" said Jimmy.

"But how did the intruder get in?" asked the sergeant.

"I think through the back door," said Mrs Huddins. "I leave it unlocked on Thursday afternoons for the grocery delivery when I take Master Christian to the park."

"The back door leads to?" asked the sergeant.

"Down a flight of steps that are used by the building's servants and for deliveries," said Maud.

"And nothing has been stolen?" checked the sergeant.

"No," confirmed Diana.

"We usually investigate a break-in when there's burglary, not when the intruder leaves a shop full of flowers," said the sergeant, mystified. "Have you any idea why anyone would break in and leave flowers? An admirer, I take it? Has anyone been pressing his attentions on you unduly?"

Diana shook her head. She was shivering as she rocked back and forth and Jimmy put his arms around her.

"Max," said Diana. "Once when we were in Berlin staying in a hotel, he did the same thing. We arrived back to find the whole bedroom filled with flowers. The exact type of flowers that are in my room now!"

"Who is Max?" questioned the sergeant.

"My dead husband," said Diana to the sergeant's astonishment.

"I think you had better sit down, Sergeant," said Thelma. "We had better tell you the whole story."

The sergeant was leaving.

"I'll make a full report on the matter. But there has been no crime committed really. Nothing was taken."

"But what about this persecution Diana is suffering?" said Thelma. "What are you going to do about this?"

The sergeant looked baffled. "As I understand it, you are making a complaint about somebody who is dead? Your deceased husband Max Von Hoffsten?"

"I know how bizarre it sounds," said Diana.

"And even if by some strange event he is alive, all he has done is give you flowers and play a song to you?"

"But the whole thing is sinister, Sergeant, and threatening," said Thelma.

"If anything else happens let me know immediately. In the meantime I will inform the police in the area to keep an eye on this flat. Keep all doors locked at all times – no more leaving doors open for deliveries."

"Yes, Sergeant," nodded Mrs Huddins.

"Whoever did this is obviously watching the place – they knew that when the deliveries were coming in they could get access," said Thelma.

"We will keep a watch for any strange activity in the area," said the sergeant.

"Thank you, Sergeant," said Diana.

Mrs Huddins showed him out of the room.

Diana looked at Thelma. "Now, is it all in my mind?"

The sergeant suddenly reappeared. "Just a thought, but have you checked with his family in Germany? Have they received any contact?"

"That's a good point," said Jimmy.

"Oh, I don't want to contact those people ever again!" said Diana.

"I think it's necessary," said the sergeant.

It pained Diana to put pen to paper to the Von Hoffstens. The memory of them filled her with revulsion. She decided that Hugo was the best person to write to. Alexandra loathed her and Brigitte was too fragile.

Flat 14
15 Chester Terrace
Regent's Park
London

Dear Hugo,

It is as much a surprise to me as I'm sure it is to you that I'm writing to you. I never expected to be in contact with the Von Hoffstens again. But it's important that you are made aware of what has been happening here in London. I have been receiving indications and messages that lead me to believe that Max was not killed in the war but somehow survived. I really need to know if you or any of the family have received any news of Max and whether he is still alive. I'm naturally out of my mind with worry about him. If you have not received any information, I appreciate that this news will come as a shock to you. But if Max is alive, I feel he is reaching out to us and I know our mutual love for him will allow us to put aside our past and work together in whatever way we can to help our darling Max. I look forward to hearing from you at your earliest convenience.

Yours sincerely,
Diana Cantwell Von Hoffsten

Diana waited and waited for a reply from Hugo but none came. She realised how bizarre her letter must have appeared. And she was fully aware that the Von Hoffstens' hatred of her made it unlikely they would ever want to hear from her again or to encourage any sort of communication. But she had hoped the idea of Max being still alive might stir them into a response. She'd obviously been wrong.

CHAPTER 65

Mrs Huddins left the morning post on the coffee table in front of Diana as she sat in the drawing room.

"Thank you, Mrs Huddins," she said and poured herself a cup of tea.

Then, as she took a sip of tea, she suddenly got a strong smell. She paused as the scent brought memories flooding back. Max's scent, his cologne. Panicking, she got up and quickly looked around for the source of the scent. And then she realised the smell was coming from the batch of letters left on the coffee table. She grabbed the letters and flicked through them. She stopped on seeing the plain white envelope addressed to *Diana Von Hoffsten*. Nearly all her mail was addressed to Diana Cantwell. But this wasn't what stopped her in her tracks, nor even the strong scent wafting from that envelope, Max's cologne. But the handwriting. It was Max's handwriting. She quickly tore open the envelope and inside on a white sheet of paper was written: *As if I could deny you anything.*

Diana sat in the Ashenbrys' drawing room while Thelma poured them tea and Elliott paced up and down.

"The whole thing is outrageous," said Elliott. "Sending such a letter – for what? Why doesn't Max just show himself to you?" He inspected again the letter Diana had been sent.

"Careful, Elliott, you speak almost as if you believe Max is still alive," cautioned Diana.

Thelma looked embarrassed. "I'm sorry we ever doubted you, Diana."

"Then you believe it's Max doing all this?" questioned Diana.

"I don't know," said Thelma. "But somebody is doing it and I'm apologising to you for us doubting that something sinister is going on."

Diana took up her teacup and saucer and started to sip her tea. She suddenly shivered.

"Are you all right?" asked Thelma.

Diana managed to smile. "Not really."

"And nothing back from his family in Germany?" asked Elliott.

"Not a jot, no surprises there."

"Well, I'm going to write to them myself," he said. "I'm going to tell them exactly what's been going on here and that it's become a police matter. And that we are going to going contact the German embassy to tell them we suspect that a German citizen all this time believed dead is still alive."

"Oh, Elliott, I don't want you to have to get involved!" objected Diana.

"We are involved, Diana. You are family to us and, in the absence of your father and husband, I have a responsibility to you. And we were very close to Max. If he is in some kind of danger or needs some kind of psychiatric help, then we want to help him too."

She got up and went and kissed him on the cheek. "Thank you, Elliott."

Jimmy had gone to Cambridge to attend a literary festival. He had begged Diana to go with him, but she had declined. She wasn't in the mood to go anywhere with everything that had been going on.

"Any messages?" asked Diana as she and Christian entered the flat after a walk in the park.

"Yes, Lord Ashenbry's secretary rang," said Mrs Huddins, taking Christian's coat off. "He said Lord and Lady Ashenbry are going for dinner in The Ritz and you are to join them there at seven."

"Oh, I don't feel like going. I'll telephone Thelma back."

"She said Lord and Lady Ashenbry are out for the day and going straight to The Ritz and it was important for you to go as they had some information," said Mrs Huddins.

Maud appeared from the drawing room. "They're probably just trying to get you out and about again. It's not healthy for you to stay in all the time."

"I thought you used to object to me going out all the time," said Diana.

"I object to you going out with men all the time. Elliott and Thelma are different," said Maud.

"All right. I'd better get ready. I haven't much time," said Diana with a sigh.

Diana made her way up the steps and into the foyer of The Ritz. She walked to the restaurant where the manager was waiting for her.

"Good evening, madam. Miss Cantwell?" he checked.

"That's right," she said. She was used to people recognising her at the social venues around London.

As Diana looked around the restaurant at the other diners but couldn't see Thelma and Elliot.

"Am I early?" she asked.

"No, madam. If you could follow me." She followed the manager through the restaurant to a central table and pulled out a chair.

Confused, she sat down.

"Did I get the time right? Seven?"

"Seven is the correct tine, madam."

"Where are Lord and Lady Ashenbry?" asked Diana.

"I'm sorry – who?" The manger smiled, confused.

"I'm meeting Lord and Lady Ashenbry here at seven."

Music suddenly started up and Diana froze as she heard the strains of 'If You Were the Only Girl in the World'.

Tears in her eyes, she turned to the manager and demanded, "What is going on here? Where are Thelma and Elliott? Why are you playing that song?"

The manager looked shocked. "Madam, your table was booked for the night by your host and we were ordered to play that song on your arrival."

"*By whom*?" Diana screamed, causing the other diners to look.

"By Mr Max Von Hoffsten of course!"

Half an hour later Sergeant Hollingford arrived at the restaurant and began to question the manager and staff.

A few minutes later, Thelma came rushing in.

"Diana! What's this all about?"

"Mrs Huddins received a call from your butler telling me to meet you and Elliott here at seven."

"My butler did no such thing! We were supposed to be at the Hollanders' tonight," objected Elliot.

"And then I arrive – and am shown to my table that has been booked by Max and that damned song is played again!" Diana was distraught.

"And you say it was Max Von Hoffsten who booked the table?" asked the sergeant.

"Yes!" said the manager.

"And did you meet him? Was he here?" asked the sergeant.

"No. The booking was taken over the phone by one of my staff."

"So you never met him?" checked the sergeant.

"My staff speak to hundreds of people a day on the telephone so they can't remember the details but it was written into the book that the dining guest would be Miss Diana Cantwell and she should be immediately shown to her table and that song played for her."

"He did the same thing ten years ago when he booked the entire restaurant in The Ritz in Paris, including playing that song," said Diana.

"Did he give any other details?" asked the sergeant.

"Just the gentleman's address. It was written in our book," said the manager, hurrying to the front of the restaurant and getting the book.

They followed him over.

"Here it is – Mr Max Von Hoffsten, 23 Hartley Place, Chelsea."

Twenty minutes later the sergeant was driving them down Hartley Place. "Here it is . . . Number 20, Number 21, Number . . ." The sergeant stopped the car.

Number 22 Hartley Place was the last house on the row. There was no Number 23 Hartley Place.

Jimmy came bounding up the stairs to Diana's apartment that night after rushing back from Cambridge and knocked loudly on the door. Mrs Huddins opened the door and he rushed past her and into the drawing room where he found Diana with Thelma, Elliott and Maud.

He put his arms around her. "Are you all right?"

She smiled at him. "I'm fine. Just recovering from the shock of it all."

Jimmy looked up at Elliot and Thelma.

"Any more news?"

"No more than what I told you on the telephone," said Elliott.

"Right, that's it. I'm staying here tonight and I don't care what you say," said Jimmy.

"I don't think that's wise!" objected Maud.

"I don't care! It's Diana I'm concerned about," said Jimmy.

"I'm sure you are," said Maud under her breath.

"I can sleep in the spare room," said Jimmy.

"Thank you, Jimmy, but Mama is right. That's not wise," said Diana.

"Why not? If this is Max, then he needs to know that you've moved on. That he's come back too late. That you don't love him any more," insisted Jimmy.

Diana looked at Jimmy's earnest face and then turned to the others.

"Could you give us a minute alone, please?" she asked.

Thelma and Elliott stood up but Maud made no attempt to go.

"Come along, Maud," said Elliott, taking Maud's arm and escorting her out of the drawing room.

379

As Maud shut the door after her she didn't close it fully and kept it slightly ajar.

"Maud!" objected Thelma, seeing her listening at the door.

"*Shhhh!*" snapped Maud.

Diana reached for her cigarettes and lit one.

"Jimmy – I think it might be an idea if we don't see each other for a while," she said.

"What are you talking about?" said Jimmy, his face masked with confusion.

She turned and looked at him and bit her lower lip. "Just with everything that's going on, I think it's wise you don't come here again."

Jimmy stared at her. "You're dumping me?"

Diana stood up and began to pace up and down. "Don't put it like that, Jimmy."

"Well, how should I put it then?"

"If Max is alive, imagine what he thinks seeing me in your company all the time."

"He'll think the truth – that we are seeing each other!"

"But if he's alive, I've no right to see anybody. I'm his wife."

"This is ridiculous. You're finishing with me because of your dead husband?"

"I don't know if he is dead, and if he is alive he's certainly not going to approach me with you here all the time."

He got up, walked over to her and stared her in the face.

"You want him to be alive."

"Of course I want him to be alive. He's my husband, the father of my son . . . I warned you at the beginning he was the love of my life."

"But – I've fallen for you," he said, reaching out and touching her face.

She stared into his eyes. "And I had fallen for you."

"Had?" His voice turned stern.

She turned away from him and folded her arms. "I can't see you – I can't see anybody until all this is cleared up. Until I know what's happening."

380

"I feel I was just being used by you, an entertainment in the absence of your husband," said Jimmy.

She took his hand and kissed it. "I'm sorry, Jimmy . . ."

Jimmy snatched away his hand and spoke angrily. "When you're willing to start living a normal life again, instead of worshipping the ghost of Max, call me."

He turned and stormed from the room. As he swung the door open Maud, Thelma and Elliott jumped back. He glared at them and then marched out of the flat.

Diana was opening the post at the breakfast table.

"Nothing from your dead husband today?" asked Maud sarcastically.

"You were quite happy to believe it was Max when you thought it was his ghost. Now there's hard evidence he's alive you're not so keen on the idea."

"Well, I still think it is a ghost," said Maud.

"How do you explain the letter then?"

"Madame Souska says spirits can take control of other people and get them to do their bidding. He took possession of a living person and that's who's doing all this."

"*Shhhh!*" said Diana as she saw a letter addressed to her from Germany. She tore it open and saw it was from Hugo.

"Who's that from?"

"Hugo. He's invited me to meet with them in Munich to discuss what's been going on."

Maud was horrified. "You're not going, are you? Not after the way those people treated you? I never thought they would respond."

"I have no choice."

CHAPTER 66

Present Day

There was a coolness between Sam and Julia following the revelation he intended to reclaim his family title and property, and Julia was angry with Thomas for encouraging the situation. And yet she knew that Thomas was a shrewd and exact barrister and would not waste his time on something he did not think plausible.

As she sat at the table one evening, having dinner with Sam and the children, she looked across at him and for a moment felt she didn't know him. She had met, fell in love and married a kind steady history lecturer, the son of two teachers. A man who was on the exact same wavelength as her, her family and their large group of loving friends.

They were happy. She had thought they were happy. She had thought they had their life arranged exactly as they wanted it. They had worked hard to have their life the way it was. And then suddenly there was this discovery of who and where he'd come from. And he seemed less like the man she married. It intimidated and confused her that he was descended from this count and Diana, this trailblazer who still glowed from magazines many decades later, exuding her glamour and beauty. The truth was she was terrified that this was turning Sam's head. Making him dissatisfied with his life, dissatisfied with her. And if he entered a lawsuit against these Von Hoffstens and lost, she knew their life could never be the same again. And if they won, what would their lives be like then? She had always pitied people who won the lottery.

How could they ever expect to be happy when they weren't used to so much money? And the tales she'd heard of Sam's brief encounter with the Von Hoffstens were not appealing – being kidnap-attempt targets, being shot, living behind lawyers and fortresses. Julia for one was very happy that Diana Cantwell had accepted a left-handed marriage all those years ago. She shuddered to think what Sam's life would be like now if she hadn't.

Sam was chatting to the children, studiously avoiding eye contact with Julia across the table. He was very disappointed with her reaction, not only to discovering who he was but also the attempt to reclaim who he was.

She just didn't seem to understand what this meant for him. He had always felt a part of him was missing. A feeling he didn't belong. Never knowing his grandfather might have contributed to that. And his grandmother had never been interested in talking much about her dead husband's past. Sam often wondered if she even knew much. They met young, married young, and in the full bloom of love he was snatched away from her. They didn't have the time to mature and to ask all those questions that come later. His own parents were too busy with day-to-day living to worry about the past. Perhaps this was what had drawn Sam to history. He loved exploring the past and what had happened to all those magical characters in times gone by. To now discover that his own great-grandparents Diana and Max weren't just ordinary people but had this magical past was unbelievable to him.

He had continued to unearth more information about Max before he died. He seemed like a larger-than-life hero. Racing yachts, racing cars, flying aeroplanes, falling in love with a woman his family hated. What a character! What a life, cut down so brutally by that war. His own life could hardly compare when he thought about his daily routine of standing in that lecture hall and preaching to barely interested students. He did feel robbed when he looked at the Von Hoffstens' lives when he was in Germany. And he never wanted his own children to have that feeling. He didn't want them to have a mundane ordinary life. He wanted them to live as exciting lives as Max and Diana had.

Julia came downstairs after an afternoon nap. She could see the door at the end of the hallway was open and she could hear talking outside. She walked to the door and looked out. Sam was at the garden table in the sunshine with Eva and Brian. He had papers spread out between them.

"And you see this photo?" he was saying to them. "I found this on the internet. It's a photo of your great-great-grandfather Max Von Hoffsten and it was taken at Cowes, after he had won a yacht race."

"He looks like a prince," said Eva excitedly.

"Well, he kind of was a prince – he was going to be a count, but he died young."

"How did he die?" asked Brian.

"He died in a big war many years ago. Many people were killed in that war and it changed many things. People's lives changed."

"There won't be any war like that again, will there?" asked Eva.

"No, I hope there won't be anyway," smiled Sam.

Julia came out to the garden and sat down at the table.

"Now, kids, time to go off and play," said Sam, beginning to put away the photos and articles.

Julia reached forward and picked up the photo of Max at Cowes.

"You look a little like him," she said.

"Do I?" He was surprised.

"Yes, all you need is the sailor's suit!" She started to laugh.

He reached over, took the photo from her and put it in a file.

"Okay," she said. "I'm behind you on this lawsuit if you really need to do it. But if it gets too much for me or the kids, you have to promise me you'll stop at once?"

He reached over, took her hand and smiled. "I promise."

The next few weeks seemed to pass in a blur as Sam and Thomas worked around the clock. Sam used his knowledge of history and Thomas his knowledge of law to prepare the case to show that the morganatic wedding of Diana and Max was no longer considered morganatic after the war when the republic was declared in

Germany and their son Christian was born.

Before she knew it, Julia was sitting inside Thomas's office beside Sam on the day they were filing the law suit.

"This will hit them for six when they receive it," said Thomas. "I'm sending the papers to their Munich lawyer, Sophie Essen."

"The charmer who watched me like a hawk when I was in Munich!" said Sam.

"Thomas, what if we win?" Julia felt herself panicking as she looked at the paperwork about to be filed. "We have no idea of how to run a brewery in Munich and manage all those people who work there – we have no experience of business. Not to mention all those properties."

"I don't think it will come to that, Julia," said Thomas. "They will fight tooth and nail that the building of the Von Hoffsten brewery globally was done by the present count and his father, so it's unlikely that would be handed to you. What we are fighting for is compensation for the fact they took the brewery in the first place. And also historic property belonging to the family including the estate in the Alps and the *schloss* in Munich, or compensation to the value thereof."

Julia started shivering slightly. "I'm even a Socialist! I don't believe in the aristocracy or people having that much money!"

Sam smiled and reached over for her hand. "We can set up a charitable foundation when we win."

"The present-day count and countess already have a huge charitable foundation," Thomas told her.

"Are we not depriving them of funds by doing all this?" asked Julia.

"Julia! Now is not the time for doubts. Let's just file the lawsuit and get on with it," said Thomas.

"Okay," she nodded, but she was worried.

PART 5

1924

CHAPTER 67

Elliott insisted on travelling to Munich with Diana.

"I have the biggest favour to ask you," she said before they left. "Would you accompany me to meet them?"

"I wouldn't possibly let you meet them on your own," said Elliott. "Not after the way they treated you in the past. They have to see you're not on your own this time. You have the Ashenbrys behind you now."

They travelled to France and got a direct train to Munich where they booked into a hotel.

It felt strange for Diana to be back. All those memories came flooding back. The treasured memories of Max. And the dreadful memories of the war and being at the mercy of the Von Hoffstens.

Their appointment to meet Hugo and Alexandra was the next day and they arrived up at the *schloss* by taxi at the appointed time.

"Are you all right?" asked Elliott as they approached the front door, noticing she was pale and nervous-looking.

"I am because you're here. I don't think I'd be brave enough to go in on my own."

He took her hand and squeezed it. "We're here to find out the truth. To find out what they know about Max."

The butler answered the door and showed them in.

"They will probably leave us waiting for hours before they deign to meet us," whispered Diana.

As she looked around the familiar space she imagined how different their lives would have been if it hadn't been for the war.

She, Max and Christian would now be living in that house, he having inherited the title and estates after Conrad died.

To her surprise she saw they were being shown straight away to the main drawing room and not one of the reception rooms.

The butler knocked on the door and opened it. Inside, sitting on large armchairs by the fireplace were Hugo and Alexandra.

"Your Excellencies, Lord Ashenbry and Mrs Von Hoffsten," announced the butler before showing them in.

As Diana entered all the past upset and hatred came flooding back to her. Hugo had matured and looked far more distinguished than when she had seen him last. Alexandra looked more or less the same, her make-up and hair in the same style, wearing her trademark long satin dress with her signature cigarette in one hand.

As Diana looked at the new count and countess living in splendour, she couldn't help but feel resentful that they had stolen the future that should have been hers and Max's. If it wasn't for the war and the left-handed marriage.

"Hello, Diana – good afternoon, Lord Ashenbry," smiled Alexandra.

Hugo rose from his seat and came to Diana.

"You're looking well, Diana," he said, reaching forward and kissing her cheek.

It was a cold awkward kiss, Diana felt.

"So do you, Hugo," said Diana. "This is my cousin, Lord Ashenbry."

"Hello." Elliot shook his hand and smiled over at Alexandra. "We met a few times before the war at Max's parties and events."

"I remember you well . . . please take a seat," said Alexandra, gesturing to the couch near them.

Diana and Elliott sat down.

"I read your letter with great interest, Lord Ashenbry," said Hugo.

"Did you not get the letter I sent to you before that?" asked Diana.

"I did. But it was hard to take what you were saying seriously. But then when I read the details that Lord Ashenbry sent I thought it best we should meet."

Diana was annoyed. "I shouldn't be surprised that you just ignored me when I wrote to you. This family has never been civil to me."

"So!" smiled Alexandra. "If what you say is true, it is most disconcerting. You believe Max is still alive?"

"I don't know what I believe any more. I'm trying to find answers. Have you heard anything from him?"

"Not a thing," said Hugo.

"I don't know whether to be relieved or disappointed," said Diana.

"A bit of both, I imagine," said Alexandra. "And you have got the police involved, I understand."

"Of course," said Elliott. "Diana's flat has been broken into and some of the stuff happening is sinister. We feel she is under threat."

"Under threat from Max? But he adored you," said Hugo.

"The old Max did," said Diana. "But we don't know what his present state is, after the war and whatever has happened to him between then and now."

"You speak as if you accept it is Max doing all these things," said Alexandra.

"There's stuff that only he would know. Intimate stuff between him and me."

"The things you describe in your letter, Lord Ashenbry?" said Alexandra.

"That's right," said Elliott. "What we can't understand is why he's doing it, if it is him."

Alexandra smirked and shrugged. "Why did Max ever do anything? He lived life as if it was one big game. He enjoyed doing things and watching people's reactions. It amused him."

"So do you think it's possible that he survived the war and has re-emerged all these years later?" asked Diana, sitting forward.

"Who knows?" said Hugo. "Can we see the letter you were sent?"

Diana reached into her handbag, took out the scented envelope and handed it to Hugo.

Both he and Alexandra studied it acutely before handing it back.

"It's his handwriting," said Diana.

"It looks like it," said Hugo.

"You're the first people who aren't sceptical," said Diana.

"Perhaps that is because we knew Max better than them," said Alexandra. "The question is, if he has come back – what has he come back for?"

"For you, Diana, obviously," said Hugo.

"Of course we are only saying this in the event it is Max. But in all reality – how could it be?" said Alexandra.

"Has Brigitte heard anything? They were so close – if he was going to contact anyone other than me it would be her," said Diana.

"If she has heard anything she certainly hasn't said," said Hugo.

"I'd like to meet her. Is she here?" asked Diana.

"No, she has been in London this past year," said Alexandra.

"London! What is she doing there?" Diana was astonished.

"Working in a hospital."

"I need to meet her – what hospital is she in?" asked Diana.

"The St John's Hospital for the Criminally Insane," said Hugo.

"I see," said Diana.

"We don't have that much to do with her any more. She took Max's death very badly," said Hugo.

They sat in silence for a while.

"How is George?" asked Diana.

"He's very well. Young as he is, he's already taking an interest in the brewery. I've no doubt but that he will make a fine captain of industry one day," said Hugo proudly.

"Your nephew is doing very well too," Diana said, realising they weren't going to ask after Christian.

They nodded, disinterested.

"What of the estate in the Alps? How is that?" asked Diana.

"We go there at weekends or for the holidays," said Alexandra.

"The Count and Countess Von Hoffsten and your wonderful lives," said Diana, unable to keep the bitterness out.

"Diana!" warned Elliott.

Diana stood up. "I think we'd better go. I feel we've made a wasted journey. We only came all this way as you ignored my letter in the first place and you invited us out here. "

"Not at all," said Alexandra. "We found your visit most informative. You will keep us informed of any further developments, if there are any further developments?"

"Yes, we will," said Elliott. "Thank you for your time."

Diana was already marching to the door, followed quickly by Elliott.

"Goodbye, Diana!" Alexandra called after her.

Diana walked quickly from the house and to their waiting car.

"You can take us straight back to the hotel," Elliott informed the driver as they sat in.

Diana sighed loudly as they drove away.

"Are you disappointed?" asked Elliott.

"I thought they might be able to shed some light on everything that has been going on. They seem as much in the dark as us. Why is Brigitte in London? They were so close, her and Max. Perhaps he's with her. Perhaps that's the reason she is in London – because he's there."

"You think she's a part of this?" asked Elliott.

"They did everything together. He used to confide in her all the time. She even arranged our wedding and helped him arrange all those surprises for me."

CHAPTER 68

On the night of their return to London Diana shared a taxi with Elliott. She stared out the window as the rain hit against the glass.

The taxi pulled into the crescent in front of Diana's building.

"Thank you for everything, Elliott," she said. She kissed him goodbye and got out of the taxi cab, but Elliott followed her out.

The driver took her suitcase out of the boot.

"I'll carry that up for you," said Elliott, taking the suitcase from the driver.

"No, Elliott, Thelma will be waiting for you."

"Diana, you look exhausted and fit to drop. Give me the case," he said forcibly. He took the case and followed her to the front door of the building which she opened with her key. They went into the lobby and she pressed the button calling for the elevator. They could see the elevator come down through the shaft. They got in and she pressed for the third floor.

"You know, growing up in Garonglen, we always heard about our wealthy and titled cousins the Ashenbrys. In a way I was always jealous of you even though we'd never met. I'm just so glad that you and Thelma are such an important part of my life now." She smiled at him as the elevator hit the third floor and he pushed back the door. She walked across the landing and, taking her key, opened the front door.

Inside, the flat appeared to be in darkness.

"They must have all gone to bed," said Diana as she entered along with Elliott and went to turn on the light.

Then she stopped short of touching the switch as she heard somebody speak.

The voice was coming from the dining room.

"Max, are you there? Can you hear us? We want to make contact with you."

Diana crept over to the dining-room door which was slightly ajar and peered in.

The room was lit by candles and gathered around the table were Maud, Madame Souska and three others, two men and a woman.

It was Madame Souska who was speaking. "Max, if you are there, give us a sign . . . please give us a sign."

Diana reached into the room and turned on the main light switch.

"*Ahhhh!*" screamed Maud in shock.

Diana marched into the room. "What is going on here?"

"Diana! You nearly scared me to death!" said Maud between gasps.

"I told you I didn't want any more séances here," said Diana, going around blowing out the candles.

"We weren't expecting you back so soon," said Maud.

"Obviously! And what do you think you're doing trying to contact Max? Whatever about contacting Dashiel, how dare you have a séance for Max!"

"We had to, dear," said Madame Souska. "We have to find out if it is his spirit doing all these things to you. If it is, we need to give him rest."

"You're not going to give him much rest calling him down to a flat in Regent's Park!" said Diana.

A tall man stepped forward, smiling. "I'm Madam Souska's husband, Marcus." He put out his hand for her to shake which she ignored. "Would you care to join our séance to contact Max?"

"I certainly would not!" snapped Diana.

"But, Diana, if he did make contact then he could tell us what's going on," said Maud. "And if it's not him then he could tell us who exactly is behind this campaign!"

"It's a fascinating case – I've written an article about it for our society's magazine," said Madame Souska.

Diana stood stock still as she looked at the table. Laid out there were all of Max's letters to her. The ones he had written to her from the front.

"My letters! Max's letters! What are they doing here?"

"We needed something personal of his to help contact him," said Maud.

"Letters are so intimate we thought they would be the best thing," said Marcus.

"How dare you!" Diana was enraged. "How dare you go into my room and rummage through my personal belongings and take my letters!"

"It was for your benefit!" said Maud.

"My beautiful letters, the only thing I have of Max and you just lay them out for all these strangers to view!" Diana was aghast.

"Maybe we should go?" said Madame Souska to Maud.

"Yes, go!" said Diana. "Just all of you get out of my home!"

Madame Souska, Marcus and the others grabbed their belonging and left.

"You were very rude!" said Maud, standing up from the table and marching out to the drawing room.

"Mama! Why did you take my letters?" demanded Diana, following her.

"I told you, to try and make contact with Max. I've used them before to try and contact him, if the truth be known."

"Have you read them?"

"Of course not!"

"Liar!" Diana was horrified.

"Diana!"

"I'll never forgive you!"

"Forgive me for what exactly?"

"For even touching my letters!"

Elliott walked into the drawing room, holding some of the letters.

"He was sentimental, wasn't he?" he said. "In this letter here he starts by saying he was sorry he couldn't say goodbye to you,

Diana, but he hoped you enjoyed the red rose he left on your bed as he always did . . ." He smelled the paper. "And even after all this time it still smells of his cologne."

"So?" said Maud.

"I bet Max reminisced about the details of your life together, Diana. Tell me, Maud, is the time he booked The Ritz in Paris in the letters? And the times he sang the song 'If You Were the Only Girl in the World'? Are all those details in the letters?"

"How should I know?" Maud demanded.

"I'm remembering the time at the party here when you said you hoped the roses and the song being played would have made Diana snap out of the life she lives."

"Are you saying *I'm* behind all that's been going on?"

"You had the information from these letters you had access to and you had the motive – to shock Diana into changing her ways. And with your séances and mediums you could pretend that it was all a voice from the spirit word. Max speaking beyond the grave."

"And could I make the telephone calls, the man's voice, and coordinate everything else?"

"I'm sure Madame Souska and your friends from the spirit society would have assisted you."

"I'm not staying here listening to any more of this," Maud snapped and strode out of the room.

"Mama!" Diana called after her. "Oh, Elliott, what have you done?"

Diana ran down the hallway after her mother and tried to get into the bedroom but the door was locked.

"Mama! Come out and speak to me!" she begged.

There was no response.

"Mama!" Diana knocked again and again. "Mama!"

At last the door opened and there stood Maud in her hat and coat, carrying a suitcase.

She walked past Diana and towards the front door.

"Mama, where are you going?" demanded Diana, quickly following her.

"I'm going to stay with Madame Souska for now," said Maud

and she paused at the drawing-room door. "Good night, Lord Ashenbry. For a man who never bothered to even send us a Christmas card before Diana met Max, it's amazing the profound interest you have in us since then!"

"I really didn't know you back then!" Elliott retaliated as Maud opened the front door, exited and slammed it after her.

Diana walked into the drawing room where Elliott was sitting deciphering the letters.

"I'm sorry for looking through Max's letters, Diana, but I think we've got our culprit," he said. "It's all in there. I'm sure it's all there – the roses, The Ritz, the song. The handwriting could be easily copied."

Diana sat down beside him. "Oh Elliott, Mama isn't behind all this!"

"How can you be sure, Diana?"

"She can be cruel but she can't be *that* cruel."

"I wouldn't be so sure! You know how she disapproves of your lifestyle and is terribly worried about you. She would do anything to change that – she sees it as saving you from yourself."

Diana picked up a letter and began to read through it.

"She would have all the inside knowledge to have the flowers put in your room," said Elliott.

"Well, it doesn't make sense to me," said Diana, shaking her head firmly.

"Perhaps you don't want to believe what I'm saying. Perhaps you want to hold on to the belief that Max is alive."

"Of course I do! Of course I want to believe Max is alive."

"But if it's not true, then it's not true." He passed her back the letters. "Read the letters for yourself and see if it's all there. I'd better get back to Thelma."

He leant forward and kissed her cheek before leaving.

CHAPTER 69

Diana walked through the grounds of the large hospital and up the steps to the main entrance.

Inside, she walked over to the reception.

"Hello, could you tell me if Brigitte Von Hoffsten is working today?"

The woman behind the reception went to look up the schedules.

"She's due in at one o'clock," she said.

"Thank you, I'll wait," said Diana and she went and sat on a bench against the wall. She watched the different staff walk in and out over the next hour, anxiously looking out for Brigitte. She felt increasingly nervous about seeing her. How would Brigitte react on seeing her? What's more, how would she react when she saw Brigitte?

Finally she saw the unmistakable figure walk through the front doors and towards the wide staircase at the bottom of the foyer.

Diana got up and walked towards her.

"Hello, Brigitte," she said.

There were extensive grounds around the hospital. There were various patients in the grounds, either sitting or being escorted around by members of staff. Diana and Brigitte walked slowly through the lawns.

"What made you come to London?" Diana asked.

"The psychiatrist I assist was transferred here from Vienna, and I accompanied him. We are researching the effects of the war on the mental health of the soldiers. How did you find out I was here?"

"I saw Hugo and Alexandra and they told me," said Diana.

They walked on for a while before Brigitte began to speak.

"After Max was killed I had to be sent away to a rest home in Switzerland for long while. I was in despair. I couldn't see any future for myself without Max. My family kindly put me in the sanatorium in Switzerland. The trouble was, after a while I realised they also gave instructions that I wasn't to be let out."

"How did you manage to escape?" Diana was disgusted but not shocked by the Von Hoffstens' behaviour to Brigitte.

"I managed to get one of my psychiatrist friends in Vienna to insist I was sane and they had to release me. I went back to Vienna and threw myself into my work. It helped me survive."

"Did you know I was in London?" asked Diana.

"Oh, yes, I follow your adventures in the gossip columns with interest." Brigitte had a look of disgust on her face.

"You could have made contact with me."

"I didn't want to," Brigitte said.

"Not even to see your nephew? Max's child?"

"I have no interest in seeing your child. Max was everything to me, his child could never be a substitute."

"He's the image of Max."

"In that case it would be definitely too painful to see him. It would only be too painful a reminder of what I lost with Max. Why have you come to see me, Diana? We were never close."

Diana stopped walking and faced Brigitte.

"I wanted to ask you . . ." She searched for the right words. "Has anything strange been happening with you recently?"

"There's always something strange happening with me. What are you talking about?"

"I know how absurd this sounds . . . but I'm not sure if Max was killed in the war."

Brigitte looked at her, baffled.

"I've been receiving messages," Diana said.

"What kind of messages?"

"From Max. It started off with red roses being left at my door, something Max always did before he went to the front. I dismissed it at the beginning. But then our special song was requested for me in a club, and played for me down the telephone when I answered it. I know how ridiculous all this sounds –"

"Yes, it does!" Brigitte began to walk away quickly, back to the hospital.

Diana hurried after her. "And I refused to believe it in the beginning. But then he rang me one day and told me he would always come back to me. Then a restaurant was booked by him for me. But he wasn't there."

Brigitte stopped walking and faced her. "Why are you saying all this?"

"Because it's true. And then I received this." Diana handed her the letter.

Brigitte took the letter, studied the handwriting, and opening it read the line inside.

"Do you recognise the cologne? It's his cologne – he used to put it on all the letters he sent back to me in the war. And it's his handwriting, isn't it?"

"It certainly looks like his handwriting. But handwriting can be easily copied." Brigitte handed back the letter. "I think you are a victim of a practical joke."

"But who would do such a thing?"

"Probably one of those idiots you run around with. The bright young things. Aren't you all notorious for playing practical jokes on each other? If you're not on treasure hunts, you're doing cocaine, because –" Brigitte adopted an upper-class English accent, "everything is such a lawf!"

"Now you're being ridiculous! Why would any of my friends do such a thing?"

"Ask them! They are renowned for doing stupid things."

"But these are intimate details between me and Max. How would they know what cologne he used, or what flowers he gave me or what song he made mine?"

"I have patients waiting. I have to get back to work."

"Brigitte! Do you not understand what I'm telling you? Max

could be alive!"

"He's not alive, Diana. Why not show himself if he is?"

"I don't know. But Max never did anything straightforward since the time I met him. He was always doing things behind my back, plotting and planning. It was like he always playing with me, teasing me. Testing how I would react. So really this behaviour now doesn't surprise me in the least."

"He just wanted to make you happy, Diana. He loved surprising you. I know because I often helped him with his surprises. I helped him come up with the surprises and plan them. We were two of a kind – he was the love of my life."

"I know how close you were."

"And I tell you this. If he could see you now he would be heartbroken. The way you've led your life over the past few years. Whoring around London and disgracing his memory. How quickly you forgot him. You were never worthy of him."

Diana became angry. "Brigitte, have you any idea how desperate I was after the war? I was heartbroken, pregnant and alone. Your family kicked me out, literally on the street. And where were you? In some rest home in Switzerland getting the best of treatment. Did you ever think of me? Did you ever wonder how I survived or if your nephew did? Max would be disgusted with *you* if he was alive now. If he *is* alive now. For the way you abandoned me and his son. You treated us like dirt!"

"I wish he had never met you." There was hatred in Brigitte's eyes. "If he hadn't met you then he might have followed Father's wishes and married Alexandra. And she would have made sure he didn't go to war like she did with Hugo and I would still have him now. You as good as killed him! If he is alive now he probably hates you and I hate you too!"

Brigitte turned and stormed back to the hospital.

Brigitte's words hit Diana hard. They were delivered with such venom. That night alone in her bedroom she took out Max's letters and read each one from start to finish. They were written with such passion, his love for her so obvious. And then towards the end of the war, they became more disoriented, as the war was obviously affecting his mental health more and more.

The following day Diana put on her coat and gloves and set off to visit her mother at Madam Souska's to try and mend what had occurred between them.

As she walked down the street she looked out for a taxi. A red bus passed her by and pulled over to the bus stop. As she went to cross the road she saw Jimmy sitting at the bus window looking out at her. She stood still and they stared at each other. He smiled at her and gave a little wave. She smiled back and waved at him as the bus began to take off.

CHAPTER 70

"Where's Grandmama?" asked Christian as Diana was doing a jigsaw puzzle with him in the drawing room.

"Grandmama is taking a little holiday," she said.

She had tried a few times to contact her mother but Maud was refusing to see her.

"Why didn't we go with her?"

"I think Grandmama needs a little time to herself at the moment. She's staying with her friends."

"Will she be home soon?"

"I hope so," said Diana, finishing the jigsaw puzzle.

The telephone rang in the flat and Diana let Mrs Huddins go to answer it.

She came into the drawing room a few seconds later.

"Miss Cantwell, Countess Von Hoffsten is on the telephone for you," she said.

"Alexandra?" Diana was astonished. She got up quickly and went out to the hallway to the telephone.

"Hello?"

"Diana, it's Alexandra."

"This is a surprise."

"We're in London, staying at Claridge's."

"Oh!"

"We were hoping to see you if it was convenient?"

"What about?"

"I'd prefer not to talk on the telephone."

"I'm busy for the rest of the day. Tomorrow would be fine."

"Excellent. Shall we say three in the afternoon? We'll come to you. Your address is still 15 Chester Terrace?"

"Yes, Flat 14."

"We'll see you then," said Alexandra and the telephone went dead.

Alexandra and Hugo arrived exactly on time at three.

Diana heard the doorbell ring and Mrs Huddins showing them into the drawing room. She took a look at herself in the mirror, steadied herself and left her room.

Walking into the drawing room she saw they were seated beside each other on a couch.

"You look tired, Diana," said Alexandra with no greeting.

"So everyone keeps saying," said Diana as she sat down, dispensing with greetings in turn. "How long have you been in London?"

"Just over a week," said Hugo.

"Have you heard anything from Max?"

"No, not a thing," said Alexandra.

"In that case, how I can help you?"

Alexandra reached into her handbag and, taking out her cigarette case, took a cigarette and lit it.

"Well, we were very taken aback at your visit, so decided to come to London to check on everything that has been happening," she said.

"I see," said Diana.

"We've been to the police and met with that nice Sergeant Hollingford who has been investigating the case," said Alexandra.

"We gave him a statement," said Hugo.

"And what did you say in your statement?" asked Diana.

"I said that without any doubt my brother was killed in the war," he said.

"But you had no right to say that!" snapped Diana. "You had no right at all! All the evidence is pointing to Max surviving the war and being here in London!"

405

Alexandra took a drag from the cigarette and smiled sympathetically. "We also informed Sergeant Hollingford about the severe case of paranoia you suffered from in Germany during the war."

"What are you talking about?" Diana's eyes widened in horror.

"We told him that you had a history of paranoia. Believing everyone was against you. Becoming a recluse in the hunting estate."

"Everyone *was* against me! I was British living in the enemy country. My post was being intercepted and the special police nearly arrested me!"

"As we said – paranoia," said Hugo.

"We've been doing a lot of enquiring over the past few days and we think all this is having a terrible effect on your mental state. We obviously have a responsibility to you as Max's wife –"

"You never expressed such responsibility before," spat Diana.

"And an obvious responsibility to my nephew, Christian," said Hugo.

"The child you have never even seen or expressed an interest in seeing!"

"We've arranged for you to go and stay at a rest home in Switzerland," said Alexandra.

"*What*?" Diana shouted.

"You'll get the very best of care there. The doctors are world-renowned," said Hugo.

"I don't believe I'm hearing this!"

"We only have your interests and Christian's interests at heart," said Alexandra.

"Is this the same rest home that Brigitte was in? The one that she wasn't allowed to leave and would be still in today if her friends in the medical profession hadn't rescued her?"

"While you are recuperating Christian can stay with us. His closest family," said Hugo.

"As if I would entrust the two of you with the care of my son!" spat Diana.

Hugo and Alexandra looked at each other.

"If you don't agree to what we are suggesting, we'll have to go to court and take Christian away from you legally," said Alexandra.

"On what grounds?" demanded Diana.

"You're an unfit mother," said Hugo. "Your antics in London have been shameful. And now you are suffering from a delusion that your dead husband is still alive."

"We've spoken to your neighbours who complain you bang at their doors, screaming," said Alexandra. "We've spoken to your friends who say you are just not yourself."

"Even your mother can't put up with your behaviour any more and has left."

Diana stared at them. "My God, am I such a threat to you?"

"You're no threat at all!" said Alexandra.

"Now you have everything, the titles, the brewery, the property – are you so terrified of losing it to me that you would do all this?"

"How are you a threat to us?" asked Hugo.

"As long as Christian is Max's son he is a threat to you. Are you afraid he might one day take it all away from you?"

"As we said, it's your interests we have at heart," said Alexandra.

"It's *your* interests you have at heart, as always!"

"Make it easy on yourself, Diana," said Hugo. "If you don't agree to what we are saying we will start the legal process immediately."

Diana sat back, thinking. "Elliott accused my mother of reading Max's letters and finding out all the details. But there was somebody else who had access as well. You two were in the estate. You could have entered my room when I was out all day, walking or riding, and read Max's letters. Are you behind all this? Did you want everyone to think I was going mad?"

Alexandra laughed derisorily. "What purpose could we possibly have to do all that?"

"To maintain control."

"Nonsense!"

"Is it, Alexandra? By getting me out of the way and becoming guardians of Christian you would be making sure you have control over him – you would be ensuring that there would never be a threat to you or your own son's future from him."

Diana stood up, walked to the window and stood there, staring out.

"I want you to leave, please," she said.

"Diana, this is what we are talking about – your paranoia!" said Alexandra.

Diana didn't turn around. "I said get out!"

Sighing, Alexandra put out her cigarette. "Unfortunately, all we have seen today here is reinforcing our opinion that we must act."

Alexandra and Hugo stood up and turned to leave.

Diana stared out of the window. Down in the crescent she could see a man looking up at her. She leaned closer to the glass and studied the man. Then she gasped.

"*It's Max!*" she suddenly screamed. "*Max!*"

"What are you talking about?" demanded Alexandra as she and Hugo quickly rushed over to the window.

"Max . . ." Diana whispered. "You're here! You're alive!"

Alexandra and Hugo scrutinised the man down below.

"Is it Max?" asked Hugo incredulously. "It looks very like him."

"Quickly, run down and see!" Alexandra ordered and Hugo raced out of the flat.

The man in the crescent turned and began to walk away.

Diana began to bang on the glass with her knuckles. "*Max! Don't go! Don't leave me again!*"

The man reached a taxi cab at the end of the crescent just as Hugo burst out of the front door of the building. He turned and waved at Diana before getting into the cab and being driven away.

"*Max! Don't leave me again!*" Diana screamed.

CHAPTER 71

Mrs Huddins opened the front door.

"Where is she?" asked Thelma as she and Elliott rushed into the flat.

"In the drawing room," sighed Mrs Huddins.

"You poor darling!" cried Thelma, rushing in, sitting beside Diana and putting her arms around her.

"It was him!" said Diana. "It was Max. Standing outside in the crescent. And then he waved to me as he got into the taxi."

Elliott looked at Hugo and Alexandra.

"Did you see him?"

"We saw somebody," said Alexandra.

"Was it Max?" demanded Thelma.

"*Yes!*" shouted Diana.

"It looked like him," said Hugo.

"But it was down in the street, not beside us," said Alexandra.

"He's alive!" Diana grabbed Thelma's hand. "I know it for a fact. I've seen him. He's come back. He's come back to me."

"Well, he hasn't come back to you or else he'd be sitting here beside you," said Alexandra. "Whatever is going on in his mind."

"Why is he torturing me?" demanded Diana.

"He doesn't think you love him any more," said a voice at the drawing-room door.

Everyone looked over to see the speaker was Mrs Huddins, standing with her coat and hat on and carrying two suitcases.

"I beg your pardon?" said Thelma.

"It's obvious. Any husband who came back and saw his wife carrying on like Miss Cantwell does, with her men and her parties – well, it's just not decent. And he's punishing her, that's my opinion."

"Mrs Huddins! I don't think anyone is particularly interested in your opinion!" Thelma was outraged at the housekeeper's behaviour.

"That's as it may be, but I'm just letting you know that I'm off!" said Mrs Huddins.

"Off where?" Diana demanded.

"Anywhere but here! I hand in my notice. I can't stand it here any more. I could just about put up with the loose morals, the parties, the drinking, women wearing trousers, men wearing make-up! But what with the séances, and the arguments, and husbands back from the dead, and break-ins and flowers being left! It's not the right environment for a woman of my moral character, I can tell you that. Good afternoon, Miss Cantwell. I hope your husband can put up with the drama, because I can assure you it's enough to wake anyone from the dead!" With that Mrs Huddins turned and walked off with her head in the air.

"Well, I never!" said Elliott. "What is the world coming to when servants speak like that? I blame the Socialists!"

Alexandra waved a cigarette in the air, anxious to get attention back from Mrs Huddins' outburst. "Diana, what are you going to do now?" she asked.

"All I can do is wait until he makes his next move," said Diana. "Alexandra and Hugo, I'd like you to leave now."

Alexandra looked at Hugo and reluctantly stood up.

"We are staying at Claridge's," said Hugo.

"Diana, you must come and stay with us tonight," said Thelma.

"No, I'm not leaving. What if Max comes back?"

"That's why I'm saying you must come to our house. Your mother's not here and now, with Mrs Huddins gone, I don't like you being here on your own."

"I can't leave, he might telephone," said Diana.

"In that case we'll take Christian to stay with us," said Elliott.

"You're too traumatised to look after a child on your own tonight."

"No, we'll be fine," objected Diana.

"We insist. You need a good night's sleep, you look exhausted. Christian will be fine with us."

Alexandra and Hugo walked to the door.

"You will contact us as soon as you hear anything?" asked Alexandra.

Diana stared at them. "Why would I tell you anything after the cruelty you showed me earlier?"

Elliott, fearing an argument, turned to Alexandra and Hugo. "I think you'd better leave. I'll show you to the door."

"We'll show ourselves out," said Alexandra as she and Hugo left.

Diana started to smile as she turned to Thelma. "All that grief and he's not dead, Thelma. I've seen him with my own eyes."

Diana was a having a dream. She was in Garonglen again and Max was there and her whole family were there, happy and laughing. Then she and Max were at the hunting estate in Germany, walking through the meadows, arms around each other's waists. Then there were bombs falling and bullets firing and Max was pulled away from her. Pulled away into the distance, into the battlefield where he disappeared.

She woke up with a start and sat up in the dark. She calmed herself as she realised she had been having a nightmare. She rubbed her face and bent over to switch on her bedside light but it didn't come on. Sighing, she got out of bed and walked over to the main light-switch to turn it on. But when she tried it she realised there was no light there either. She opened the door and walked out into the corridor. No light there either. Either the lights had fused in the flat or there was a power failure in the area. She walked to the drawing room to get a candle.

Going into the darkened room, she went to the sideboard where candles were kept.

As she went to open the drawer she heard a noise in the dark.

She quickly turned around and saw a figure in the darkness.

"Mrs Huddins?" she asked.

The figure began to move slowly towards her and, consumed with fear, she made a dash across to the door. She let out a scream as the figure moved more quickly than her and knocked her to the ground. She started to scream but the man was on top of her and a leather-gloved hand came over her mouth.

He was far larger than her and her feeble blows had no effect on him. She kicked and fought but to no avail. One of his hands still over her mouth, he reached over for a table lamp on the sideboard and pulled it to the ground. Grabbing the cord of the lamp he looped it around her neck. Then, taking his hand from her mouth, he began to tighten the cord around her neck with both hands. All she could do was gasp as the cord tightened around her vocal cords. It was impossible for her to fight him or push him away. She reached out above her head towards the curtains. With all her strength she grasped the heavy curtain and tore it from its railings, causing the light from the streetlamp outside to fill the room.

The sudden light startled her attacker and he pulled back, covering his face. It gave Diana an opportunity and she reached for the lamp and hit it against his head, knocking him off balance. She pushed him from her, scrambled to her feet and began to run to the door. He reached out and grabbed her ankle, but she kicked him in the face with her other foot. She stumbled out of the room and to the front door, where she frantically unbolted it. Then she raced onto the landing.

She tried to scream, but all she could do was gasp as she ran to her nearest neighbour's door and started hammering on it.

"*Help!*" she managed to scream. "*Help me!*" she continued to scream as she made her way down the landing banging on the doors.

CHAPTER 72

Present Day

Sam's mobile rang as he was walking across campus to a lecture hall.

"Sam, it's me," said Thomas. "They've got back to us already."

"Who exactly?"

"The Von Hoffstens' lawyer Sophie Essen."

Sam steadied himself, expecting a furious response from her.

"They want to meet us."

"What?"

"They have suggested we meet with them to discuss the situation. Do you know what this means, Sam? They are taking us seriously. They believe we have a case."

Sam stopped walking. "Really?"

"Absolutely. The fact they want to talk means that they're worried, and I would say very worried."

Thomas got in contact with Sophie Essen who suggested that Sam, Julia and Thomas travel to Munich.

"What she is suggesting is mediation and has recommended that an independent qualified person be present," said Thomas one night as they discussed the recent development at Sam's house.

"But this mediator might be one of their lackeys taking their side," observed Sam.

"No, both parties have to agree on the person. I've lots of contacts in the legal world in Germany to suggest a suitable person."

"So, we don't have to go through with the case now?" asked Julia.

"Well, who can say?" said Thomas. "It depends on what comes out of the meeting. If they are going to be unreasonable or try to bully us in any way, then we'll walk and continue with the case. But I reckon they don't want that. I reckon they want a quick easy solution and will probably agree to our terms. They face losing an awful lot here, and the fact they want to talk shows they realise that."

"And who will be at this meeting?" asked Sam.

"Sophie Essen of course, and her clients Eric and Nova Von Hoffsten," said Thomas.

"The count and countess themselves?" Sam was surprised.

"They have to be. This is one thing they can't delegate to one of their lackeys."

Julia looked at Sam. "And to think I thought you had gone mad with all this!"

"I thought I was going mad myself at times," said Sam. "But the truth wins through and Diana and Max are going to get justice after all this time."

Brian and Eva were being left with Julia's sister while their parents were away on their trip to Munich.

Thomas and Sophie Essen had finally agreed on a mediator to officiate the meeting. His name was Dominick Meyer, a retired judge who had a reputation for being fair but strong.

"He's the best man who was recommended to me," said Thomas as they sat in the plane en route to Munich. "He will give everyone a fair hearing and won't be in any way intimidated or awestruck by the Von Hoffstens."

"Good, because I can tell you, they are fairly intimidating when you meet them," said Sam.

"Well, you haven't let them intimidate you so far, so don't let them start now," advised Thomas.

The plane landed in Munich Airport and they got a taxi to the hotel.

"I've always wanted to come to Munich, but I would never have guessed it would be to contest for a title and family fortune," said Julia.

The meeting was scheduled for the next day at noon and that evening Thomas and Sam stayed in the hotel going through the minute details of their claim.

Julia went out to investigate the city, leaving them to it. As she walked around the city centre she wondered what it must have been like for Diana arriving there a century before to marry into this family. It must have seemed like a million miles away and a different planet to what she was used to at home. It was strange that her arriving a century before was the cause of them being there now. The cycle had repeated itself.

PART 6

1924

CHAPTER 73

Sergeant Hollingford walked into the hospital room. Diana was sitting up in bed, Thelma and Elliott seated on either side of her.

"Sergeant, have you found anything at the flat?" asked Thelma.

"The intruder got in through a window at the back of the flat. He came up the fire escape till he got to the kitchen window and forced the window open. He then turned off the electricity at the main electricity board in the kitchen. You didn't hear anything, Miss Cantwell?"

"I did wake – maybe I heard something."

"And you didn't see his face?" asked Sergeant Hollingford again.

"No, I told you before. The flat was in darkness. I saw nothing."

"It has all the hallmarks of a burglary that was disturbed," said Sergeant Hollingford.

Thelma became angry. "Of course it wasn't a burglary. It was Max!"

"You have no evidence of that," said the sergeant.

"What more evidence do you need? He's been following her for months. And yesterday he was seen by both Diana and the Count and Countess Von Hoffsten outside the block of flats. He's been staking it out." Thelma's voice rose to near hysterics. "He wants to kill Diana. That's what all this has been about!"

"It wasn't Max who attacked me," Diana said quietly, causing everyone to stare at her.

"How can you say that?" demanded Elliot. "Thelma is right. We

419

now know he was never killed in the war and he's back seeking some kind of vengeance on you. That's what this has been about – he's been tormenting you, making your life hell and now he wants to kill you."

"Max would never hurt me," said Diana. "Never! He loves me too much!"

"Exactly!" said Thelma. "He loves you *too* much. It's an obsession, a sick kind of love."

"You said yourself, Diana, he wasn't the same man the last time you saw him," said Elliot. "You said he was broken. He's obviously been driven to insanity by the war."

"Maybe he was always insane, like his mother," said Thelma.

"It runs in his family – you said he admitted that himself," said Elliot. "Diana, Max was trying to murder you last night."

"It *wasn't* Max!" Diana's voice rasped. She buried her face in her hands. "I *know* it wasn't Max who tried to kill me last night." She started to sob.

"After you escaped from him and raised the alarm he fled back the way he came in, out the kitchen window and down the fire escape," said Hollingford. "I'll file my report. If you can think of anything else let me know immediately. With everything that's been going on, I don't think it's advisable for you to go back to your flat right now."

"Especially with your mother away and Mrs Huddins left," said Thelma.

"She's coming to stay with us," said Elliott. "The doctor said he wants to keep her in for observation tonight but we'll collect her in the morning and take her to our house in Connaught Square."

Sergeant Hollingford nodded and left.

Diana wiped away her tears. "I need to rest."

"Of course," said Thelma, standing up. "We'll collect you in the morning."

Thelma and Elliott bent over and kissed her cheek.

CHAPTER 74

Diana rested over the next few days at Elliott and Thelma's. She hardly left the house as she recovered from the attack but stayed in mostly, minding Christian.

"I honestly think that Sergeant Hollingford is quite useless – perhaps you should request a new officer on the case?" suggested Thelma.

"He's doing the best he can," said Diana.

"If that's the best I wouldn't like to see his worst!"

Maud had moved back into the flat but the Ashenbrys insisted Diana continue to stay with them.

"I suggested to Maud she stay here too, but she declined," said Elliott.

"My mother is made of sterner stuff than to let an intruder scare her off," said Diana. "Besides, I'm sure she has Madame Souska and half her spiritual society staying with her, merrily having séances through the night without me disturbing them."

"It's just – if Max does break into the flat again –" began Elliott.

Diana lost her temper. "*For the last time it wasn't Max! He wouldn't hurt a hair of my head!*"

Elliott and Thelma were taken back by her outburst.

"Right," said Thelma. "Well, we are off for the day to a charity event for the children. Won't you come with us, Diana?"

"No, thanks. I really wouldn't be in the mood."

"Very well." Thelma and Elliott turned to go.

"Thelma – Elliott!" she called and they turned around to her. "I'm sorry for shouting. I owe so much to you for everything you've done. I love you both very much."

Thelma smiled. "You just relax for the day – take it easy."

Diana had a late breakfast brought into her in the dining room. She took up a newspaper and read it. She found an article on herself inside.

Still No Lead in Regent's Park Break-In.

Police still have not made any further progress after the break-in at a flat in Chester Terrace , Regent's Park, last Tuesday. The home of socialite Diana Cantwell was entered into by an unknown assailant at three in the morning. Miss Cantwell, who was home alone, was attacked during the attempted burglary and the police are treating the incident as extremely serious. Miss Cantwell . . .

Diana threw the newspaper down as the article continued into reporting idle gossip about her and listing the men whose company she had been seen in around London.

The butler came in. "Pardon me, Miss Cantwell, but there has been a letter put through the letterbox for you. It's a hand delivery, no stamp."

Diana stood up, grabbed the envelope from the butler and saw the unmistakable handwriting on the front with the word *'Diana'*.

She tore the envelope open and on the letter inside was one sentence: *Be outside St Paul's Cathedral at three this afternoon – Max*

Diana stared at the letter.

"Is everything all right, Miss Cantwell?" asked the butler.

Diana looked at the clock on the wall and saw it was nearly one.

"Yes, of course. Could you get my coat?" she requested.

"Certainly," said the butler as he headed out.

Diana left the letter on the coffee table and went to the mirror over the fireplace to check her appearance. Then she hurried out to the hallway after the butler who helped her on with her coat.

"Will you be back for dinner, Miss Cantwell?" he asked as she hurried to the door.

"I don't know, I'm not sure," she said as she swung the door open and hurried down the steps outside. In her haste she didn't close the door after her. The butler went over to the door and watched her walk quickly down the street until she disappeared from view.

It was eight that evening by the time Thelma and Elliott got back to Connaught Square and the butler let them in.

"You know, it makes it all worthwhile, all the fundraising, when you see the joy on their little faces," Thelma said to Elliott as she handed over her coat.

"And with the huge unemployment we're going to have to fundraise all the more in the future."

They walked into the drawing room.

"Is Miss Cantwell upstairs, Gordon?" Elliott asked the butler.

"No, she went out before lunch, my lord," said the butler.

"Out where?" asked Elliott.

"She didn't say. A letter arrived for her and –"

Thelma picked up the letter Diana had left on the coffee table. "Elliott!" she said, alarmed. "Look at this!"

Elliott took the letter and read it. "Oh my . . ." He turned to the butler. "She left after receiving this letter?"

"Yes, my lord, it was put through the letterbox for her."

"Gordon, get Sergeant Hollingford on the telephone for me at once," instructed Elliott.

The butler quickly left the room.

"Elliott! She's gone to meet him!" said Thelma, terrified.

"What was she thinking? Putting herself in such danger? If it was he who tried to kill her –"

"Or if it was somebody else who's behind all this, she's run into their trap! Oh, I shouldn't have left her today!"

"Darling, she would have gone anyway."

"But I could have gone with her!"

"She wouldn't have told you or shown the letter as she would have known you wouldn't let her go on her own. This is her one chance of meeting him. Nothing was going to stop her going."

"Sergeant Hollingford on the telephone, my lord," said the butler at the door of the room.

"Coming," said Elliott as he headed to the hallway.

Thelma sat down slowly on the couch, clutching the letter.

CHAPTER 75

One Month Later

The train had left Munich and was now making its way to its destination up farther in the foothills of the Alps. It pulled into the small station at Tegernfrei.

"Last stop!" shouted the conductor and the passengers began to disembark.

The woman stepped out of the carriage and looked up and down the platform. Dressed in a smart cream suit with a large brown collar, she was wearing a hat with a netted veil that was down over her face. She didn't want anyone in the town to recognise her. She made her way across the platform, through the station and out onto the street. There was a Mercedes waiting, with a chauffeur standing beside it. She made her way over.

"You're from the Von Hoffsten estate?"

"Yes," said the chauffeur, quickly moving to the motor car's back door and opening it for her. She sat in.

Looking out the window as they drove, she thought the town hadn't change at all, except for the people. There were men there now, young men going about their business alongside the women and children. And the people didn't look hungry any more. The motor car continued on its journey up the hills and into the Von Hoffsten estate. The fields were being worked by plenty of farm hands and as they approached the house it looked painted and well kept, like it had been before the war.

The motor car drove under the arch and stopped in the forecourt. The chauffeur opened the back door and she got out.

She made her way to the front door and pulled the bell.

Almost immediately a maid opened the door.

"Frau Von Hoffsten?" said the maid.

"Yes."

"The count and countess are waiting for you."

"You're new here."

"Yes," smiled the maid. "I started last year. If you would like to follow me?"

"You don't need to show me the way – I was the lady of the manor here for many years," said Diana as she walked on and into the drawing room.

Inside, Hugo and Alexandra were sitting waiting for her.

"Diana," greeted Alexandra. "Welcome back."

Diana nodded to them. "I was never welcome here in the first place, so I doubt I'm welcome back."

"Oh, Diana!" smiled Alexandra, lighting a cigarette.

Diana walked over to the French windows and looked out at the view past the balcony patio. "It's as beautiful as ever."

"Yes. We like to spend the summers here now."

Diana sat down on a couch opposite them.

Diana smiled at Hugo. "And how are you, Hugo?"

"G-g-g-good," he said nervously.

"Oh, your stammer has returned! What a pity."

"So," said Alexandra. "You said you needed to speak to us urgently. That you had news of Max."

"Yes." Diana smiled at them. "I can confirm that he is alive. I have met with him."

Alexandra remained expressionless while Hugo twitched.

Alexandra held out her cigarette and looked at the door behind Diana. "Where is he then? Hiding in the hall?"

"He is in London. I came alone."

"Why?"

"Because if he put foot into Germany he would be arrested on sight."

Alexandra looked confused. "Why – what terrible crime has he committed?"

"Desertion," said Diana. "Max wasn't killed in the war. He

426

deserted. He was in a terrible state of mind the last time he went back to the front, we all know that. In that last battle he went over the trenches and as he was fighting, in the heat and confusion of battle, he just hid. Then when night fell he walked. But he didn't go back to the German trenches. He made his way to a nearby forest and hid there. He kept going through the forest and found his way to the Dutch border. He waited until night and crossed into neutral Holland. From there he got on a boat to neutral Spain. And that's where he's been ever since. Hiding in Spain."

"So why is he suddenly coming out of hiding now?" asked Alexandra.

"He had read about me in a society magazine that had been left by a British tourist in Madrid and came and found me. And discovered he had a son, Christian. When he came to London, he was going to come straight to me. But then he saw me out with a boyfriend. He was frightened that I would not love him any more. He was terrified how I would react to the fact that he had deserted and hid in Spain all these years. That he had led me to believe he had been killed. He was frightened to just show up at my door. Frightened I could never forgive him. So he sent me the flowers and everything to let me know he was still alive. And then when he did send for me and if I went to him he would know I still loved him. But if I didn't go he would realise I didn't love him any more, and he would disappear, never to be seen again."

"A-a-a-and you obviously do," said Hugo.

"I adore him, I always have. I thought I had lost everything when my Max – when we thought Max was dead. I've been handed back my life."

"You love him even though he tried to murder you?" asked Alexandra.

"I think all three of us here know that it wasn't Max who broke in and tried to kill me that night," said Diana.

Hugo tensed.

Diana leaned forward to him and whispered, "I saw you, Hugo. I saw your face when I pulled down the curtains and the street lamp shone through."

Alexandra stood up abruptly. "It's a lie! Outrageous!"

"We know it's the truth. When you saw Max that day out of the window in my flat you knew he was back. And you knew if he came back, the risk was he would claim back the Von Hoffsten title and estate . . . and leave you with nothing. You thought he was back for me, so if I was dead, then he would go away again back into hiding for whatever reasons he had to hide."

"If you believed you saw Hugo that night as your attacker then why didn't you go to the police?" demanded Alexandra as she began to walk up and down.

"Because when I saw Hugo's face I knew the two of you would have left the country immediately for Germany. And if I said it was Hugo, you Alexandra would have provided him with an alibi saying he was with you all that night. And with everyone doubting my sanity at the time, who would they believe – me or Count and Countess Von Hoffsten?"

Hugo began to tremble.

Diana leaned forward towards him. "Why did you pause once I pulled down the curtain and I saw your face? Was it that you could kill me in the dark, but you couldn't look me in the eye and kill me?"

Alexandra stubbed out her cigarette.

"You can't prove anything, Diana. I will vouch that Hugo was with me in bed all that night. And you have no case to take to the police at this stage."

Diana sat back and crossed her legs. "I'm not going to the police."

Alexandra's face brimmed with frustration and anger. "So why are you here? What do you want? Why don't you go and live happily ever after with your Max and leave us alone?"

"But that's exactly what I want to do."

Alexandra waved her hand in the air. "Then go! Depart! Leave!"

"It's not that simple. We have no money, no property, no bonds. We are broke."

"You looked as if you were doing all right in London!" said Alexandra.

"My flat is rented. I live from month to month."

"W-w-w-what has this to do with us?" asked Hugo.

"Everything!" said Diana. "Hugo, as we all know Max as the eldest son is the rightful Count Von Hoffsten and all this, the estate, the *schloss*, the brewery, the money belongs to him. You only became count because it was believed Max was dead. Now he is alive, he is Count Von Hoffsten, not you, and you are sitting in his house, on his estate. Because of our left-handed marriage, after Max is dead the title and estates will not pass to our child but to you, Hugo, if you're still alive, and ultimately to your son. But Max is still a young man and I'm delighted to say in perfect health, so that will not be for another fifty or sixty years."

Alexandra sat down. "You said yourself Max can't come back to Germany. He will be arrested, not to mention disgraced when it is learned that he deserted."

"And he doesn't want to come back here. If he was arrested he wouldn't be shot for desertion as the war is over, but he would face a lengthy prison sentence and the disgrace would be almost unbearable for him."

"Well then!" declared Alexandra, sitting back and crossing her legs triumphantly.

"But he's willing to do it. He's willing to go to jail and face the public humiliation in order for him to reclaim his title and fortune. He says it's better to face five years in prison and for me and Christian and him to have our proper position and entitlements for the next fifty years."

Hugo looked at Alexandra nervously.

"Of course," said Diana. "There's a way around this that will make all of us happy."

"Which is?" demanded Alexandra.

"Share the fortune. Max says if you give him one million dollars he will not return to Germany. We will go and live quietly out of the way and you'll never hear from us again. You can continue being the count and countess and continue owing the property and brewery and everything else. He wants American dollars as the German currency is becoming worthless outside of Germany with the rampant inflation."

"One million dollars!" Alexandra laughed loudly. "You're crazy! We're not giving you anything!"

"Then you will lose everything. Max will come back and claim everything."

"And go to prison and be disgraced and hated for desertion?"

"Yes! If he put up with four years of the trenches, which was more than you ever did, Hugo, he can put up with anything. And I will take great pleasure in kicking you out of this house with nothing, the way you did to me, Alexandra."

"Damn you!" spat Alexandra.

"And you will be left with nothing. I believe your family estate in Austria was lost, Alexandra. And the Austrian government stripped you of your title along with all the other aristocracy. When Max comes back you won't be a countess any more either. Neither of you have ever suffered poverty. I can assure you, you will not like it. And Max won't give you the crumbs off his table after what you did to me."

"Not a chance! We are not giving you a mark!" insisted Alexandra.

Diana stood up. "We gave you the opportunity."

She walked to the door.

"W-w-wait!" said Hugo.

Diana turned around and looked at him.

"A million dollars is a large part of the Von Hoffsten fortune."

"It's leaving you with the bulk still," said Diana.

"Please sit," said Hugo.

Diana returned to her seat.

"It will take a while to organise it. Inflation is rampant in Germany. To raise American dollars we will have to sell a lot of art and property," said Hugo.

"*Hugo! We are not negotiating with her!*" screamed Alexandra.

"*Shut your fucking mouth!*" Hugo screamed back at her.

Alexandra sat back quickly.

"How is the money to be transferred?" asked Hugo to Diana in his normal calm voice.

"Through a lawyer called Launderbeger in Geneva," answered Diana.

"And what insurance do we have that you won't come back and look for more money in the future?" asked Hugo.

"On the receipt of the money the solicitor will give you a document signed by Max renouncing his rights as Count Von Hoffsten and all other rights, including property rights, that are aligned to it. He will officially abdicate."

"You've thought of everything!" spat Alexandra.

"Max thought of everything," said Diana.

"I will begin to arrange the raising of the money straight away," said Hugo.

"Our solicitor will be in contact with you. Then our business is concluded," said Diana as she stood up.

She nodded to both of them and walked out the door.

Walking across the lobby she didn't look left or right as all the memories of her time there came flooding back. She left the house and went to the motor car where the chauffeur was waiting for her. She climbed in and they drove out of the courtyard, under the arch and down the drive to the road that led them down the hill back to the town. It was only when she got to the train station and safely on the train back to Munich that she began to breathe normally again.

PART 7

CHAPTER 76

Present Day

Sam and Julia woke early in their hotel room in Munich the morning they were due to meet with the Von Hoffstens for mediation. They met Thomas in the hotel lobby and made their way by taxi to the Von Hoffstens' lawyers' offices, based in a modern office block in the city's business district.

Julia observed that Thomas, in the front passenger seat, had gone into lawyer mode, all hints of the jovial character he was outside work evaporated. Sam, beside her, looked nervous as he stared out the window. She reached over and took his hand and gave it a squeeze. He turned and smiled at her as the taxi pulled up outside the building.

"Here we go!" said Thomas as they entered.

Thomas announced them to reception and they were directed to an elevator which brought them to an upper floor. They were shown into a waiting room and they sat in silence for a further thirty minutes before a severe-looking man entered.

"If you could follow me, please," he said.

They got up and walked down a corridor to a double door which he opened. He gestured for them to enter. Thomas entered first, followed by Sam and Julia.

The boardroom was large with floor-to-ceiling windows on one side, offering a view of the city.

At the top of the table sat a man in his sixties. He was serious-looking but Julia judged him to have a kind face.

The man stood up. "Hello, please come in. I'm Dominick Meyer who will be mediating today."

Thomas led them to the top of the table.

On one side of the table sat Sophie Essen, looking cool and unfazed. Beside her sat a man of around sixty with grey hair. He was tall and athletic-looking.

Beside him was the unmistakable Nova, the Countess Von Hoffsten.

"I'm Thomas Powers, and these are my clients Sam and Julia Cantwell."

"We meet again," said Sophie, standing up and shaking Sam's hand, giving him a glacial glare.

"Indeed," said Sam.

"And these are my clients," introduced Sophie. "Eric and Nova, the Count and Countess Von Hoffsten."

As Sam offered his hand Eric reached out and shook it. For Sam it was a surreal moment. Hands reaching across the generations.

Julia judged Eric with his unsmiling face to be a no-nonsense man. But it was the Countess Nova that captured her attention. Having heard Sam's description of her, and built her into almost a superhuman in her mind, it was good to see that she was after all just a woman, if a very beautiful woman.

"Shall we get on with the matter in hand?" said Dominick as the shaking of hands finished and the two parties took their seats facing each other across the table.

"Due to a required medical intervention, Mr Cantwell has discovered that he is a relative of Count Eric Von Hoffsten. It is his belief that due to the manipulation of Eric's grandfather, Hugo Von Hoffsten, the inheritance that was rightly belonging to his grandfather, Christian, was unlawfully taken . . ."

As Dominick continued giving the background of the case Sam studied Eric across the table. He had put so much work into the case and researching his family, it felt surreal to be there in the same room as him. He tried not to stare at Nova beside Eric, but she still possessed that elusive quality he remembered her having. She sat there almost as if she were removed from everything, her eyes vacantly looking past them to the wall behind them. Her face was impassive and she looked as if she wasn't even listening to the proceedings, or hadn't any interest in them.

"I believe," continued Dominick, looking at Sophie, "that to begin with there is no doubt or objection that Sam Cantwell is who he says he is. That he is the great-grandson of Diana Cantwell and Max Von Hoffsten?"

"We have no objection to that claim. We accept that," said Sophie.

"That is good. At least we are not dealing with a case like that of Anna Anderson, the woman who claimed to be Russian Princess Anastasia for years through the courts. Of course DNA now can prove everything in a matter of hours, but that is not necessary."

"No," confirmed Sophie.

"It is then the circumstances of the morganatic marriage that –" continued Dominick.

"May I interrupt?" said Sophie. "To save us all much time I think I should make it clear that Mr Cantwell is not aware of all the facts."

"In what way?" asked Dominick.

"Mr Cantwell is under the illusion that his great-grandfather Max was killed in the First World War. This is in actual fact an untruth."

"I beg your pardon?" said Thomas.

"*What?*" said Sam.

"Max was not killed in the war. He deserted. He fled to Spain for the duration of the war and spent some time there in the years after the war to nobody's knowledge, not even his wife Diana's."

"That's a lie!" snapped Sam.

"Mr Cantwell!" objected Dominick. "Continue please, Ms Essen."

"In 1924 he then made contact with Diana who was living in London. He didn't make direct contact at first in order not to frighten the woman or perhaps to test her love as by then she was engaged in many relationships with many men."

"What are you talking about?" demanded Sam.

"Diana reported the incidents to the police, fearing firstly her life might be in danger from her husband as he might have suffered some mental breakdown. I have in fact a copy of the police file from the time here." Sophie passed the file to Dominick. "The file clearly shows Max was very much alive and – the modern term for it would be 'stalking' his wife in an attempt to woo her back. Diana and Max did finally reunite. Diana then made the journey to Germany to visit Eric's grandfather and grandmother, Count Hugo and Princess Alexandra. In that meeting she disclosed that Max had no intention of returning to Germany due to the fact he faced imprisonment and disgrace due to his military desertion. In return for one million dollars, a sizeable part of the Von Hoffsten estate at the time, it was agreed that Max would remain abroad and not return to Germany to claim his rightful title and property. In exchange Max signed a document on the 24th of October 1924, through the Swiss law firm Launderbeger, abdicating his title, renouncing all claims to the Von Hoffsten title and estate for both himself and his heirs."

Sophie picked up a document and handed it to Dominick.

Sam's heart had started pounding as the details emerged. He reached over, taking the document from Dominick. "Show me that."

"That is a copy. The original is held in a safe and it is quite authentic. Its execution can be verified by the Launderbeger law firm in Geneva as also can be the payment of the one million dollars which was done through the same law firm in 1924 to the account of Diana Cantwell."

Dominick reached over, took back the document and began to read it as everyone sat in silence.

Thomas glanced at Sam who sat almost in shock.

"This certainly throws a new light on the whole subject," said Dominick eventually. "It would appear that your claim to the title and estate is not valid, Mr Cantwell. Your great-grandfather signed away all rights."

Sam stared at Eric who didn't look smug but maintained the serious thoughtful expression he had from the beginning. Nova still looked impassive.

"We request time to analyse this new information," said Thomas.

"I suggest that this claim by your clients is dropped immediately," said Sophie. "And that the count and countess are allowed to return to their lives, without any further annoyance from the Cantwells."

Dominick looked at Sam. "It would appear you do not have a claim any more. I think you should be grateful that the count suggested this mediation before you began costly court proceedings."

Sam sat in shock. He felt that somebody had punched him in the stomach. Julia looked at his face and felt his pain. She reached out and took his hand. It was the only move that elicited an emotion in Nova as she looked inquisitively at Sam and Julia.

"Can we request a recess for me to discuss this development with my clients?" asked Thomas.

"By all means," nodded Dominick.

Thomas, Sam and Julia were shown into the waiting room.

"I'm so sorry," said Julia as she hugged Sam.

"You can't argue with that document," said Thomas. "It's valid, Sam. The Swiss law firm will verify that it was signed in 1924 and verify all the other details."

"What do we do now?" asked Julia.

"I think we had better get in there and grovel," said Thomas. "Before they start coming after you for costs or some other trumped-up claims."

"They won't, will they?" asked Julia, concerned.

"I doubt it but they will want you to sign disclaimers and acknowledge you have no rights over the title and estates," said Thomas. "Otherwise they could come after you for wasting their time."

Sam had tears in his eyes as he sat down and put his face in his hands.

Julia knelt beside him. "Oh, Sam, let's just get home to the children and put all this behind us. Let's just get out of here, please!"

Sam quickly controlled himself. "Yeah, let's just get this done as quickly as possible." He stood up.

Thomas turned to Julia. "There's no need for you to come back inside, Julia. You can wait here."

Julia nodded. She reached forward and kissed Sam before the two men left the room and closed the door. It was only when they were gone that she began to crumble. And what made her crumble was the look on Sam's face which was filled with disappointment and rejection.

Julia was sitting in the waiting room and looked at her watch. She had been there nearly an hour and she wondered what was going on in the boardroom.

The door opened and she looked up expectantly but was taken aback to see Nova come in and close the door after her. Nova looked startled to see Julia sitting there and she walked slowly past her to the wall of windows and stood with her back to her, looking out at the city.

"You should have spoken to him that day," said Julia.

Nova turned around to look at her.

"In the hospital corridor when Sam went up to you and spoke to you. You shouldn't have ignored him and walked past him. I know Sam and none of this would have happened if you had just been civil to him. If you and your husband had shown some gratitude and hadn't treated him in such a dismissive fashion. You angered him and then when he discovered how Diana was treated all those years ago, he wanted some kind of justice."

"I didn't know who he was when he came up to me that day – I didn't realise he was the distant cousin helping us," said Nova.

"Would it have mattered? You shouldn't just ignore people. Who do you think you are? You should treat people with respect."

"You know nothing about my life, our lives," said Nova.

"And I don't want to know. All I know is that you are arrogant and selfish people and I wish you had never contacted us and that we had never heard of you. We were happy before we heard the name Von Hoffsten."

"And you can be happy again. You can return to your life tomorrow," said Nova.

"That's easy for you to say. Sam is going to be very hurt from all this, especially after hearing all that about Max deserting and everything."

"What then do you want me to say?" Nova walked towards her. "You are just today's problem. Tomorrow there will be another problem to deal with, and the day after that, and that. When you are people like us there are always people coming after us, wanting from us. We are constantly fighting people away. The kidnap attempt and the shooting was just the worst scenario. We have no peace."

"Then change your life. Remove yourselves from all this crap in your lives," said Julia.

"We've tried our best. We hardly ever go out of the estate any more. I worry about my children's safety all the time, and yet I have to let them try to lead normal lives. Do you have children?"

"A boy and a girl."

"Exactly what we have. But your children can lead normal lives, mine can't."

Julia studied her. "You know, before today I was intimidated by the sound of you. I dreaded meeting you. I thought I'd feel inadequate. Now I just feel sorry for you."

"Don't feel sorry for me, Mrs Cantwell. I have all the money in the world to make me happy," said Nova, speaking bitterly.

The door opened and Sophie Essen came in and was surprised to see the two women together. "Countess, your car is waiting. We have concluded our business and need to go."

Nova nodded and began to walk past Julia. She looked as if she was going to walk by but then she stopped.

"Good day, Mrs Cantwell – I hope you have a safe journey home," she said.

"Thank you," said Julia.

"Countess, we really have to go!" demanded Sophie.

Nova nodded and walked on.

That evening Sam and Julia walked through Munich with their arms around each other.

"Will Thomas join us for dinner tonight?" asked Julia.

"No, he's nursing his sorrows back at the hotel bar. Poor Thomas, he was sure he was on the verge of the biggest case of his career."

"He'll get over it. But will you?"

"Of course I will. I'm just trying to revaluate my thoughts on my great-grandparents. I had built Max and Diana up into these amazing people who could do anything. But now I know they were just as human as everyone else. Max wasn't a fearless winner. He deserted. I don't blame him for deserting. It must have been terrifying, the war. But he had to live with the shame and fear of being discovered for the rest of his life. And Diana along with him."

"Did you find out anything further about them?" asked Julia.

"The Von Hoffstens never heard from them again after paying them the money. They believe they went to live in Spain. But they couldn't shed any more light on what happened to Max and Diana after that."

"I'm sorry, Sam," she said.

"Why are you sorry? All you've done is support me even though I knew you didn't want any of this."

"I'm just sorry how things turned out for you."

He smiled at her as they passed a restaurant. "What do you think of this place?"

"Looks great. Let's go in."

They walked into the busy restaurant.

"There's a long waiting time. There won't be a table for thirty minutes," warned the manager.

"But we're Von Hoffstens!" said Sam, laughing.

"Sorry?" said the manager, confused.

"Ignore him," laughed Julia. "We'll wait at the bar, like everyone else."

CHAPTER 77

It was a sunny day in northern France and the farmer decided to take advantage of the weather and plough his fields. He sat in his tractor, ploughing the land. He had been doing extensive work on the farm recently. His farm had too many hedges in it and small fields. Over the past months he'd had the hedges removed, turning the small fields into one large one. It was so much easier for him to plough and work the land now. As he drove the tractor along something caught his eye up ahead of him. He slowed the tractor down and turned the engine off. He walked towards what was glinting in the sun. Reaching it, he bent down and began to dust away the earth around the shiny object. Getting more curious, he began to dig the area away with his hands. Pulling away the soil, he saw the shiny metal was part of a helmet. He paused and studied it. It looked like a German helmet. He had found a couple of interesting artefacts over the years. Once he had found a revolver. All echoes from a war fought there a hundred years ago. As he continued to dig he suddenly fell back, shocked at what he was unearthing.

The farmer immediately contacted the police. They came with a forensic team and quickly established that the skeleton had been there for many years and, from the uniform on the body, it was a German soldier from the First World War. They excavated the body and it was transported to the forensics laboratory in Paris for a full examination.

Dr Pierre Montalan was examining the body which was laid out on a slab in his lab in Paris. He was the head of the forensic anthropology department at Paris Descartes University. He'd been intrigued when the Department of Justice had contacted him, saying the body of a soldier believed to be from the First World War had been uncovered in northern France. The body had been brought to him and now he and his assistant Natalie began their work to uncover as much of the facts and details of the find as possible.

"It's well preserved considering the amount of time he's been buried," commented Pierre, inspecting the now tattered uniform on the body. "The cause of death was probably a gunshot as can be seen by this bullet hole through the uniform's chest."

"Would he have died quickly?" asked Natalie.

"From where he was shot, I don't imagine instantly," said Pierre. "Poor boy."

"The area where his body was found was the site of a major battle in the closing months of the war. He was obviously killed in a German advance," said Pierre.

"How come his body wasn't found at the time?" asked Natalie.

"He would have been killed in no-man's land and it would have been unsafe to go and get the body. The body was left there and all the shells exploding would have shifted the soil and the body was covered," said Pierre.

"And that's where he's been for the last century, just waiting to be found," said Natalie.

"Tragic for his family. He would have been reported missing presumed dead, but they would never really have known what happened to him," sighed Pierre who began to delicately remove what was left of the jacket. "He is wearing an officer's uniform." He began to search inside the pockets and pulled out a leather wallet. "Ah, hopefully this will give us a clue as to who this gentleman was. Ah, yes . . . this wallet has his name engraved on it. Max Von Hoffsten."

"Von?" said Natalie. "He was an aristocrat?"

"He must have been," said Pierre as he continued to look through the wallet. He took out a photograph and looked at it.

"She's beautiful," said Natalie. "There's an inscription on the back!"

Pierre read out the inscription which was in English. *"To my darling husband – love forever – Diana."*

"Diana," Natalie repeated. "How she must have missed him!"

Pierre took out another photograph and they studied it. It was a picture of Max and Diana on their wedding day.

Natalie suddenly reached into her pocket, took out a tissue and started wiping her eyes.

"What's wrong with you?" asked Pierre, looking slightly amused.

"They just look so in love and it was all taken from them. Robbed in a moment. Did she ever recover? It's hard to think that man in the photo came to this end and is here today."

"Do you want to take a break?" he asked.

"No, let's continue," she said.

Pierre looked down and addressed Max's body. "We won't be too long, my friend, and then we'll see about getting you back to your family."

CHAPTER 78

Back in Dublin, Sam and Julia returned to the life they had been living before the Von Hoffstens had intruded on it. Sam began to concentrate on his work again, Julia on her PhD. They quickly fell back into their routines. Dinner parties, rotating between friends' houses on Fridays, barbeques, christenings, birthdays. Life returned to normal to Julia's great relief.

And yet the whole experience still lingered in Sam's mind. What happened to Diana and Max eventually? Where did they go to? He remembered Sophie Essen saying in Munich that they believed Diana and Max had gone to Spain.

One evening at home while correcting essays he couldn't help but push them aside and start researching on the computer. He tried to see if he could find anything on Diana in the Spanish genealogy sites. He imagined a name like Diana Cantwell would be extremely rare in Spain at the time, Von Hoffsten even more so. He was stunned as he suddenly came across the death certificate for Diana Cantwell Von Hoffsten.

"*Julia*!" he roared at the top of his voice.

A few seconds later Julia came rushing in.

"Look at this, I found Diana's death certificate!"

"Oh," said Julia, slightly concerned as she had hoped Sam had left all that behind. She sat down beside him, hoping he was just tying up loose ends.

"Look at this, Julia – it's her. Born Garonglen, Ireland, April 19th 1890, and she died June 16th 1950. She outlived my grandfather. I always presumed she had died before him. Look, it has her residence at Villa Bonaventura, Avienda de los Ceros, Alicante, and her resting place as Con Vista Al Mar also in Alicante."

"Have you found anything for Max?"

"Let me check . . . No, nothing at all," said Sam.

Sam swung around to his computer and typed Diana's address in Spain – Villa Bonaventura, Avienda de los Ceros, Alicante – into the Google search page.

A few seconds later a website came up for a hotel and Sam went on to the website.

"This address on Diana's death certificate is a boutique hotel. It looks beautiful, up in the hills overlooking the sea."

"Perhaps she lived permanently in the hotel. She certainly got enough money out of the Von Hoffstens to do so," said Julia.

CHAPTER 79

Sophie Essen drove into the courtyard of the house at the Von Hoffsten estate in the Alps. Getting out of her BMW, she walked up to the front door where a servant let her in.

"They are in the drawing room," said the maid.

Sophie was shown across the hallway and into the drawing room. There, Nova and Eric were waiting for her.

"Well?" asked Eric as he gestured to her to sit down opposite them.

"I can confirm that the DNA test on the body found in northern France matches and he was a Von Hoffsten. I think we can safely say, considering the wallet, photos and letter found on the body, that it was Max Von Hoffsten, your great-uncle."

"I can hardly believe it," said Eric, shocked. "My family always believed that he had deserted and not been killed. That's what his wife Diana told my grandparents."

"Your grandparents Hugo and Alexandra were obviously the victims of an elaborate hoax constructed by Diana Cantwell to get the money out of them," said Sophie.

"What a clever woman!" said Nova. "To have fooled them like that!"

"A dishonest woman," said Eric. "All these years we have believed that Max was the black sheep of the family. A coward who fled the war. We never told anybody outside the family because of the shame involved. Until we met the Cantwells from Ireland and told them in order to dismiss their court action."

"I think Diana was only claiming what she believed was hers," said Nova. "She was kicked out without anything, with a young son. Your family treated her appallingly."

"The question is, what do we do now?" asked Eric.

"Diana obviously had Max's signature forged on the abdication document," said Sophie.

"Does this open up their whole case again, Sam and Julia's claim?" asked Nova.

"I had Sam Cantwell sign a document when we met them at my offices in Munich the day of the mediation that he would no longer make any claim for the Von Hoffsten title and estate," said Sophie.

"And he signed willingly?" asked Eric.

"I told him we would slap a multi-million-euro lawsuit against him for wrongful assertion and for wasting our time if he didn't," said Sophie.

"I knew there was a reason we pay you so much," smiled Eric.

"After signing that document he can't come and back and claim again. Besides, Diana was paid one million dollars in 1924, regardless of whether Max was alive or dead, and I think any judge will say that was adequate compensation for that branch of the family," said Sophie confidently.

"And what about the body, Max's body? What's to be done with him?" asked Nova.

"I suggest we say nothing to the Cantwells," said Sophie. "I think we have had enough messing about with them. Just have the body buried and that's the end of it."

"But they could find out. It will be in the news that the body of a soldier has been found," said Eric.

"I think we have a duty to tell Sam Cantwell," said Nova. "He is Max's great-grandson and it should be his decision where the body should be buried."

"I strongly advise not getting in contact with those people again, Eric," said Sophie.

"But, I think –" began Nova.

"Countess! This is for your own good. Follow my advice and say nothing," said Sophie sternly.

"But –"

"No contact with them," reasserted Sophie.

Nova sat back silenced as Sophie and Eric began to discuss other business.

Then she suddenly sat forward and spoke loudly. "Actually, *no*, Sophie!"

Sophie and Eric looked at Nova, startled.

"To say nothing to Sam and Julia Cantwell is the wrong thing to do. If they have no claim any more then why hide this from them?"

"Because why should we bother ourselves?" demanded Sophie.

"Because it's the right thing to do." Nova turned to her husband. "Eric, they are no threat to us any more. I spoke to the wife that day and she had no interest in any of the case. If we don't tell the truth now and it comes out later they will be so angry and upset that they might pursue the case again."

"I told you they have no claim any more," stated Sophie sternly.

"Then why hide this from them?" said Nova. "Diana and Max's marriage was so short and the aftermath so unkind. Why not finally give them peace now? Give Max's body to his great-grandson Sam."

Julia was out in the garden when the phone rang. Irritated to be disturbed from her work, she got up and went inside.

"Hello?" she asked.

"Is that Julia?" said the foreign accent.

"Yes, who is this?"

"It's Nova Von Hoffsten, Julia. I'm sorry to disturb you but I've some startling news that we felt you would like to know."

Sam found Julia waiting for him when he got home.

"Everything all right?" he asked, seeing her worried expression.

"I think you had better sit down," said Julia.

Sam and Julia sat out in the garden as she told him of the phone call she'd received that afternoon from Nova Von Hoffsten.

"So, according to Nova," said Julia, "the body that was accidently uncovered by a farmer in France is your great-grandfather Max."

Sam stared at her, trying to take it all in. "But I don't understand. How was Max buried in a field all this time?"

"The forensic anthropologist who carried out the examination on the body said he was killed in battle and somehow the ground was moved with all the explosions and he was buried there all this time," said Julia. "Seemingly it's more common than you think. Nova said they were emailing us on the anthropologist's report."

"But what about the million dollars paid to Diana back in 1924 and the fact that Max had deserted and signed that abdication document?"

"Nova said that Diana must have concocted an elaborate hoax to get the money from Hugo and Alexandra," said Julia.

"So I find out my great-grandfather Max was actually not a coward and deserter but my great-grandmother Diana was a fraudster?"

"And a very good one at that from all accounts. I don't blame her in the least. It's shocking she was forced into a left-handed marriage that left her and her son unprovided for. If she did defraud the Von Hoffstens, she was only getting what was rightfully hers and her son's. In fact I quite admire her."

"That's obviously why she spent the rest of her life in Spain. She couldn't come back in case the truth was ever discovered," said Sam. "She could lose herself in Spain. What I can't understand is why Countess Nova rang you. Why did they contact us at all? It undermines their position with the law suit."

"Nova was quite open and honest. She said it was already in the newspapers about the discovery of Max and we would probably find out about it eventually. She did point out she hoped it wouldn't inspire you to reignite your court case and pointed out you had signed a document saying you wouldn't pursue them again."

"How pragmatic of her! No, I've no intention of pursuing that again. Besides, Diana was paid off in 1924, regardless of how she swindled the money. And that's where our tree of the family relinquished any rights to the Von Hoffsten estate, morally and I imagine in law."

"I think there was more to it than that, though – I mean, why

451

Nova personally phoned. I think she felt bad about how they treated you when you went to Eric's assistance."

"What makes you say that?"

"We were alone in the waiting room that day in Munich and I gave her a piece of my mind," said Julia.

"Did you?" Sam was shocked and started to laugh. "I'd say that was the first time anyone had spoken to her like that."

"I think Nova and Eric Von Hoffsten feel quite bad about their behaviour. In a way I don't blame them for how they were. You know, they are so removed from reality they hardly have any idea what's going on. She didn't even know who you were when you went up to her in the hospital. She actually said today that both herself and Eric are, what word did she use – profoundly – grateful to you for helping to save Eric's life."

"Really?" Sam's eyes widened in surprise.

"And Nova wanted you, as Max's great-grandson, to decide what you want to happen to Max now. She said they were quite happy to take care of it and have Max buried at the Von Hoffsten family plot, but it was your decision."

"I think there's only one place Max can be buried, Julia," he said.

"I thought you'd say that, so I've already investigated flights to Spain," she said, smiling at him.

Sam and Julia took a flight to Alicante and a taxi to the Villa Bonaventura which was the address given on Diana's death certificate as her residence. Sam had checked and it was close by the cemetery where she was buried. They decided they might as well stay there while they conducted their business.

"I imagine this place looked very different from when Diana lived here," said Sam as the taxi passed apartment blocks.

However, when the taxi got to the hills the rate of new buildings lessened. It travelled up the twisty wooded road high up into the hills before pulling off the road and into the forecourt of the Villa Bonaventura Hotel.

As Sam paid the driver, Julia looked up at the old Spanish manor house that was meticulously kept. Pulling their suitcases behind them, they walked in through the glass-and-iron front doors and into the cool reception.

The hotel was furnished in Art Deco style. And at the end of the lobby Julia could see open French windows that led into beautiful gardens with a swimming pool and a view down the hills to the sea.

"Hello," smiled the receptionist.

"Ah hello," said Julia. "We've reserved a room – Sam and Julia Cantwell."

"Yes, I have you here. I hope you had a nice journey?" The receptionist began to tap on her computer.

"Yes, lovely, thank you."

"If I could see your passports, please?"

"Of course. Sam, the passports!" called Julia,

There was no response and she turned around. Sam was walking slowly towards a fireplace over which hung a portrait.

It was a portrait of Diana.

"Sam?" said Julia, coming over to him and staring up at the painting.

"It's her," said Sam, remembering all the photos he had seen of her in the magazines sent to him.

"Is everything all right?" asked the receptionist.

"Yes, sorry . . . it's just this painting. Who is it?" asked Sam.

"Ah, we call her *La Bella Dama*. She's a woman who lived in this house for many years. She was a friend of my father's family."

"Where's your father now?" asked Sam.

"He's upstairs doing the accounts. He's seventy-eight but he still insists on doing them!" laughed the woman.

"Could we meet him?" asked Sam. "It's just that this woman in the painting is my great-grandmother."

Sam and Julia were shown to their room and then the receptionist rang up to say her father was out in the back gardens and would love to see them.

Sam and Julia walked down the staircase and out past the lobby into the back gardens which were beautifully manicured with the old swimming pool as the centrepiece. At a table by the pool sat a very strong, healthy-looking man in his seventies.

"Mr Cantwell?" called the man, waving to them.

"That's right. I'm Sam and this is my wife Julia," said Sam, going over to him and shaking his hand.

"Welcome to my hotel. I'm Alano Sandoval. Please sit down."

Sam and Julia sat down.

"You are related to Diana Cantwell?" he checked.

"Yes, she was my great-grandmother. But I never knew her. We tracked her down to here from her death certificate. Did you know her?"

"Yes, I knew her when I was a child. She lived here at this house. This house was in my family for many years but by the 1920s they had fallen on hard times. She arrived one day, fell in love with the place and rented it from my father. My father was delighted as, without the money she paid us in rent, I don't know what would have happened to us. We moved to a smaller house down the hill."

"So she didn't live here when it was a hotel?"

"No, she lived here for many years and it was her home. It was only after she died that we converted it to a small hotel and that's what it's been ever since."

"And you actually knew her?"

"Of course. Me and my brothers and sisters used to visit here all the time – she was very kind."

"I met somebody in Germany whose grandmother knew her. Then in Ireland I met a neighbour of her family whose mother knew her. And here finally I've met somebody who actually knew her," smiled Sam.

"She was known around here as *La Bella Dama* – the beautiful woman. We still call her portrait in the lobby that," said Alano. "Not that she drew attention to herself. She and her boyfriend and son lived here quietly."

"Her boyfriend?" asked Julia, surprised.

"An American called Jimmy Barclay. He was very devoted to her. At first when they arrived they had serious money. But I believe they lost a huge amount in the Wall Street crash. She sent her son –"

"That was my grandfather Christian," said Sam.

"– to boarding school in Ireland. She wanted him to be educated there, and especially after the Spanish civil war started she wanted him in the safety of Ireland."

"So that's how my grandfather came back to Ireland," said Sam, seeing all the pieces of the jigsaw coming together.

"She spoiled him incredibly," said Alano. "There was nothing he wanted for. When he came back on holidays from university he would be driving around in a sports car dressed in the best American clothes. But one day he told her he was marrying a girl in Dublin. Diana was furious as in her opinion this girl wasn't good enough for her son."

"It's like history repeating itself with her own marriage," said Julia.

"He ignored her and married the girl. He died then in a car crash in a sports car Diana had bought him and she was utterly heartbroken. She became mostly reclusive after that, just living here with her Jimmy. Our family were the only people she would see."

Julia reached out for Sam's hand and held it.

"After she died, Jimmy Barclay organised the funeral for her and then closed up the house here and handed us back the keys."

"Where did he go, this Jimmy?" asked Sam.

Alano shrugged. "Who knows? Maybe back to America. We never heard of him again."

Sam nodded and looked down at the floor.

"We're come here for a reason," Julia said to Alano. "Diana's husband Max has been found. He was a soldier in the First World War and he's been missing all this time. We've come to rebury him here with Diana."

"I see," said Alano.

"We just thought it would be the proper and fitting resting place for him, beside his wife," explained Julia. "We've made all the arrangements. His body arrives tomorrow from France and burial is on Wednesday."

The Con Vista al Mar cemetery was further up the hill from the hotel. It was an old disused cemetery that looked down the hill to the sea.

Sam and Julia met the priest they had been arranging the burial with, to finalise the details. Diana's grave was at the very edge of the cemetery. Sam instructed the gravediggers that Max was to be buried to Diana's left-hand side.

"She might have been a left-handed bride in life, but now she'll be close to his right hand as she should always have been," said Sam to Julia.

As they were returning to Dublin the day after the burial, Sam had made sure the engraving was done before the burial. The words '*Max Von Hoffsten, Beloved Husband*' were added to the stone beneath Diana's name.

Max's body arrived into the local airport and was transported out to the cemetery the morning of the funeral. Only Sam and Julia were there as the priest prayed while Max was lowered into the grave beside his wife. As the priest continued with the prayers, Sam felt in a trance looking out at the sea, thinking of the journey that had brought him there. Thinking of the journey that had brought Max and Diana there that day.

"I saw you got a taxi here. Can I offer you a lift back down the hill to your hotel?" offered the priest.

"No, thank you. It's a nice day for a walk," smiled Sam, shaking his hand.

"As you wish," smiled the priest.

"Thank you very much for everything," said Julia as she shook his hand.

He headed off to his car and drove away.

They stood at the end of the grave and Sam reached out and took Julia's hand.

"They are together at last," said Julia.

Sam nodded, turned to her and said, "Let's go home."

They walked out of the overgrown cemetery and closed the rusty gate behind them. Then they walked back down the road in the sunshine.

CHAPTER 80

Epilogue 1926

The afternoon sun blazed down on the Villa Bonaventura which was set in the densely wooded hills of Alicante in Spain overlooking the Mediterranean. Diana sat beside the swimming pool as Christian played in the pool. He came out of the pool and hugged her.

"Will I take him in for a while out of the sun?" asked the Spanish nanny.

"Yes, thank you, Consuela, it is getting very hot." She kissed the little boy then Consuela took his hand and Diana watched as the two of them walked happily up the steps and into the coolness of the house.

Diana walked around the pool and looked at the azure sea stretching out in the distance. It was an idyllic place. The old colonial-style manor house renovated in Art Deco style was three miles from the nearest house. It was a beautiful secluded location, the back gardens and pool area carved out from the thick trees around the house.

Diana walked over to the table and chairs beside the pool and began to write her letter to Thelma and Elliott.

Dear Thelma and Elliott,

I was thrilled to get your last letter and to hear everything is fine in London. Thank you so much for minding Mama. I do hope to get over for a quick visit this year. At the moment we are just enjoying life too much in the sun. Max and Christian are now firm friends. All the shyness Christian showed his father at the beginning

457

is now gone. After everything we went through, we are now just enjoying this time being a family.

Diana paused and sat back in her chair to admire the view of the sea. She turned then to continue writing but there was a figure standing by the pool. She couldn't make out the figure as the sun shone from behind it. She squinted and held up her hand.

"Hello, Diana," said an unmistakable voice as the figure stepped forward.

It was Brigitte.

"Brigitte!" Diana gasped. "What are you doing here?"

"I've come to see my brother of course."

Diana stood up. "But how did you find us?"

"It wasn't easy. But I figured if Max could track you down after the war, then so could I."

"Did you ring the doorbell? I didn't hear anything." Diana was flabbergasted.

"I came around the side of the house. Where is Max?"

At that moment Jimmy Barclay came bounding out of the French window from inside the house, holding a cocktail shaker.

"Say, darling, do you think it's too early to start the cocktails?" he asked.

He stopped in his tracks as he saw Brigitte.

"Brigitte, this is –" began Diana.

"I know who he is. I saw a photo of him in papers before. Tell me, Diana, does Max not mind having your ex-boyfriend as a house guest?"

Jimmy walked down the steps towards Diana and put the cocktail shaker on the table beside her.

Brigitte walked towards them. "I always knew Max was dead. I never believed for a second he had survived the war. It wasn't just that I would have felt it in my heart if he was alive – but there was no way that Max would have been alive and not contacted me. He wouldn't have hidden in Spain without letting me know. And he certainly wouldn't have come to you, Diana, before he came to me, no matter how much he loved you. I was his twin, his confidante, he told me everything. That he would send you roses and book restaurants for you without involving me was impossible . . . it would never have happened."

"Brigitte –" began Diana.

"So which of you came up with the idea, the plot? The idea to make Hugo and Alexandra believe he was still alive so that you could extract the money from them?"

Diana's eyes filled with tears. "It wasn't planned, I can assure you. We had no part in the beginning of it. I was distressed and confused as to what was going on when all the strange things began to happen. The roses, the song being played at the club, the telephone calls, the letter, the restaurant. That wasn't us."

"Who was it then?" demanded Brigitte.

"It was Maud," said Jimmy.

"Yes, my mother . . . She hated my lifestyle in London and when I fell in love with Jimmy she was terrified I'd make a pauper's marriage with him. So she and her medium friend Madam Souska and her husband did all that to make me believe that it was Max's ghost trying to warn me away from Jimmy."

"And it worked. Diana did finish with me," said Jimmy. "We stopped seeing each other."

"Then when Elliot and I arrived back from Germany after seeing Hugo and Alexandra we found Maud and her friends having a séance with Max's letters on the table. Elliott suspected it was Maud who was the culprit, getting the details from reading Max's letters to me. That day I met you in the hospital in London, when you insisted Max was dead, I knew he had to be if you knew nothing of him being alive. That night at the flat I read all Max's letters and as Elliott suspected I realised my mother got all the information from them."

Jimmy put his arm around Diana. "Maud worked in tandem with Madam Souska who was planning on becoming a famous medium through the case. She even wrote an article about it in a spiritual magazine."

"So what happened then? Why didn't it end there?" asked Brigitte.

"The day after meeting you at the hospital, I was walking along the street on my way to confront my mother when I spotted Jimmy on a bus. When he saw me he jumped off and I told him what had happened – that it had all been my mother."

"It was then we decided to turn the situation to our advantage," said Jimmy. "We decided that, instead of exposing Maud and Madam Souska, we would continue with the charade and try and convince the Von Hoffstens that Max was still alive in order for them to pay Diana off to get rid of him and stop him from returning to reclaim his inheritance."

"You are despicable!" spat Brigitte.

Diana's tears became angry. "Myself and Elliot had just returned from visiting Hugo and Alexandra in Munich. When I saw the opulence they lived in and how Christian and I had been left with nothing, I became so angry. You left me with nothing! Your family kicked me out, pregnant with Max's child, without any concern for our safety or future. If we hadn't been forced into that left-handed marriage, they could never have done that. I was only taking what was rightfully mine and my son's."

"I suppose you couldn't have kept on living the life you were living in London forever. What age are you now, Diana – thirty-six? How many more gifts of jewels would be coming your way from boyfriends to fund your lifestyle?"

"Well, that's the truth of it! I had to make sure our future, mine and my son's, Max's son's, would be secure. I was only taking what was rightfully ours."

"But it wasn't rightfully yours. You and Christian had no right to any of it once Max was dead."

"Legally true perhaps, but not morally," said Jimmy.

Brigitte looked at Jimmy. "Oh, Diana, did your mother teach you nothing? I thought a girl with your background was taught to fall in love for money. You seem to have the unfortunate habit of falling in love with men who do not give you security. First Max left you penniless with the left-handed marriage and now you fall for this penniless gigolo."

"I did love Max, Brigitte, more than you'll ever know. I married him knowing I'd have no rights to his fortune, didn't I? And then, yes, I did fall in love with Jimmy. I didn't think I'd ever fall in love again after Max, but I did. I deserve happiness after everything I've been through."

"And the Ashenbrys, they knew nothing?"

"Of course they didn't. Only me and Jimmy knew."

"But you needed them all on board for your scheme to work. To convince Hugo and Alexandra that Max was alive, they had to vouch for what you said was happening." Brigitte looked at Jimmy again. "The roses, the songs, the restaurant – that was all Maud and her cronies?"

"Yes," Jimmy nodded.

"After you visited me at the hospital, Diana, I got a visit from Sergeant Hollingford as part of his investigation. Alexandra and Hugo had already made a statement to him and he thought he had better get one from me as well. He told me that you, with Hugo and Alexandra, saw Max outside your flat window waving up to you. Who was that impersonating my brother?"

"It was an actor we hired," said Jimmy. "We searched for somebody who looked like Max. We told him it was a practical joke we were playing on a friend, a bright young thing."

"We knew Hugo and Alexandra had to see him to believe, in order to hand over so much money," said Diana.

"What are you going to do now?" asked Jimmy.

Brigitte shrugged. "Nothing. What can I do even if I wanted to? You're holed up here in Spain. The financial transaction you made in Geneva is probably impossible to trace. Besides, what do I care if Hugo and Alexandra are a million dollars poorer?"

Diana visibly relaxed on hearing this.

"I could always tell the Ashenbrys what you did . . . but what would that achieve? Max is still dead, and nothing is going to bring him back."

"Thank you, Brigitte," said Diana, breathing a sigh of relief.

"Don't thank me. I'll say nothing for Max's sake, not for yours. He loved you so much, Diana. And that's what killed him in the end."

"What are you talking about?" asked Diana.

"He always told me everything. Absolutely everything . . . That last time he was home on leave when he was so bad, so broken, a shell of a man. Do you know why he was like that?"

"Four years of the war of course," said Diana.

Brigitte shook her head slowly. "No. He could face the war and the trenches. Max could deal with that. When he was home on leave he told me that the last time he went over the trenches and he was charging forward, suddenly your brother Dashiel was there. Right in front of him, charging in the other direction."

Diana stared at her in disbelief.

"Max told me that he didn't realise it was Dashiel until after he bayoneted him . . . Max killed Dashiel."

"What – what?" Diana felt her legs go weak.

"Dashiel dropped to the ground and Max stayed with him for hours, nursing him as he died. It broke Max. He couldn't cope with what he had done. And when he came home on leave and saw you, the guilt overcame him. He told me he would never be able to look at you again. Because every time he looked at you he saw Dashiel. He told me before he went back to the front that he couldn't live with it, that he wanted to die. He didn't go back to the front wanting to survive, he went back to die."

"No . . ." whispered Diana.

"I'll leave you to get on with your lives now. Goodbye, Diana."

Brigitte turned and walked away through the trees at the side of the house.

Diana stared after her. She touched her mouth with her fingers and turned to Jimmy.

"I – she –" Diana began but the words wouldn't come out.

"Diana –" said Jimmy, moving towards her and putting his arms around her.

"It – it can't be true," she managed to say. "Oh, Jimmy!"

She grabbed on to his shirt with her hands as she started to whimper.

Jimmy tried to hold on to her as her legs gave out from under her and she fell to her knees, weeping. He went down with her, holding her.

"It's going to be all right," soothed Jimmy as the two of them knelt there, clinging to each other.

"Max, oh, Max!" she started to cry out over and over again as her sobbing evolved into a heart-wrenching wail that carried down the forested hill and out to sea.

THE END

If you enjoyed reading
The Left-Handed Marriage
Here's an exclusive sneak preview of
The Secrets of Armstrong House prologue.

PROLOGUE

Present Day

The man came rushing out of the front door of Armstrong House into the winter's night. He was dressed in a black tailored Edwardian suit and his cloak blew in the wind as he quickly made his way down the steps in front of the house and across the forecourt to his awaiting phaeton two-seater carriage. Jumping in, he whipped the horse and took off at high speed.

The carriage raced out of the forecourt and down the long winding driveway that led through parklands. The bare branches of the trees swayed in the wind and stretched out against the clear moonlit sky as he drove past. He continued his journey down the driveway which hugged the lakeshore until the large stone gateway came into view. As he approached it he pulled on the reins and the horse slowed to a walk to go through the gateway.

Suddenly from the shadows of the night a man stepped out in front of the horse, blocking the carriage's journey. The horse drew to a halt. Dressed in shabby clothes and a peaked cap, the man on the road produced a shotgun and aimed it squarely at the carriage driver whose face twisted in panic.

The man in the peaked cap pulled the trigger. The driver screamed in agony and fell back onto the leather seating of the carriage. At the sound of the gunshot the horse plunged forward through the gate and bolted down the road.

"*Cut! Cut! Cut!*" shouted the director in frustration.

Kate Collins quickly made her way to him.

"It's no use, Kate!" he snapped, annoyed. "This can't be the way the shooting happened!"

"It is, Brian! I've checked and checked it with the inquiry and the newspaper articles at the time," Kate defended herself. "Lord Charles Armstrong was just coming out of the main gates of the estate, exactly here, when he was ambushed and shot."

The film's firearms expert joined them. "It's as I said – the horse would have bolted with fright when Charles was shot and there was no driver to control it."

"So then, Charles couldn't have been found here as you insist, Kate!" said Brian. "The gun we're using is a blank-firing gun which has the same explosive sound and flash as if it was shooting for real. So the horse is reacting as it would to a regular gunshot. The horse would have been terrified by the gunshot and raced down the road to somewhere else, as we've just seen."

"No! All the reports say Charles was found here at the gateway, shot in his carriage," Kate insisted. "Even his mother Lady Margaret testified at the inquiry that she was the first to arrive at the scene and found him at this exact spot."

Brian shook his head in despair. "Well, we've retaken this scene three times and each time the horse has bolted, and we've used two different horses!" This was the second night of trying to film the scene, as Kate had insisted the horse be changed.

Kate's husband Nico Collins stepped forward. "Brian's right, Kate. I've grown up with horses all my life and they don't just hang around stationary after something like this."

Kate sighed in frustration. "Well, this *is* how it happened. Maybe Charles' horse was tame and timid?"

Both Brian and Nico looked at her sceptically.

"Okay, I think we'll call it a day, or a night!" said Brian and the film crew all heaved a sigh of relief. "It's late and everyone's tired and cold and wants to go home. We'll film around this scene for now."

"Thank goodness for that!" said Nico who had feared they would have to re-shoot the scene when all he wanted to do was get out of this freezing cold and back to the warmth of their home, Armstrong House.

"Are you sure?" questioned Kate, ever the perfectionist. It had taken a long time to get right the exact circumstances of a crime that had taken place over a century beforehand and Kate didn't mind in the least if everyone had to work through the night to get this crucial part of her docudrama correct.

"Yes, Kate!" insisted Brian.

The film crew was quickly dismantling the equipment and taking away the props.

"What we'll have to do is use a replica prop gun which won't make a noise, as the firearms expert advised," said Brian, "and we can dub the gunshot sound to it digitally later. Then we won't frighten the horse."

"Come on, Brian!" Kate protested. "I've been on enough movie sets to know those replica guns just don't have the same effect. I know no director who likes to use them and they're only used as a last resort."

"This is a last resort!"

"But the scene has to be as authentic as possible!" objected Kate.

The actor who was playing Charles was trotting the horse and carriage back up the road after regaining control of the animal. He pulled up at the gateway.

As Kate was talking in depth with Brian about the next stage of filming, Nico walked around the carriage. He had to admit it all looked very authentic to him. The carriage, the long winding driveway behind it and the lights of Armstrong House in the distance. He imagined what he had just witnessed being acted looked very like the real crime back in 1903, the night this shooting actually took place. Nico got an eerie feeling. For the film crew it was just another day's filming. Even though his wife Kate cared passionately about the history of Armstrong House, she was still an actress by profession and had the professional training to be able to look at the filming in purely objective terms. But for Nico it was different. At the end of the day they had just filmed the shooting of his great-grandfather, Lord Charles Armstrong. And he would have to be made of stone not to have somehow been affected by seeing his ancestor being shot down in cold blood, albeit for a docudrama.

It took an hour for all the props and film equipment to be taken away. Then Kate came over to him as he waited patiently for her in their Range Rover.

"Well, I'm at a loss as to why the original horse didn't bolt away after Charles was shot back in 1903!" she said in exasperation as he started the engine.

Nico just shrugged.

They drove back up the driveway to Armstrong House and pulled up in the forecourt.

She saw his unhappy expression. "Don't you find it all fascinating?" she asked as they stepped out of the car.

"Well, it's fascinating all right . . . but just remind me why we're making this programme again?" He looked at her cynically as they walked up the steps to the front door.

"For the money, honey," she said. "This house is costing a lot to upkeep, and we need the money."

Both of them knew that was not strictly true. Ever since he had known Kate she had been fascinated with the history of Armstrong House and Nico's family who had lived there for generations. They had been married only a couple of months when she had come up with the idea of a documentary about life at the Irish 'Big House' during its golden age of the late Victorian and early Edwardian period. She had discussed the idea with film-producer friends of hers and managed to get the project agreed to. Kate had always known it would be harder to convince her husband to agree to it than the film producers. Nico disliked the idea of their home and his family history being held up to public scrutiny. However, with acting roles thin on the ground for her lately and his architect's practice struggling, she had used the financial rewards offered by the film as the lever to get him to give the go-ahead.

"So are you going to use a prop gun as Brian suggests?" Nico asked as they walked into the drawing room.

"No, not yet anyway. I want to know what the police report has to say first."

"Police report?" Nico asked, surprised.

"Yes, when the horse bolted last night I decided to send away for the police report on the crime to see if that could shed any more light on it."

Wearily, Nico sat down on the couch. "And how long is that going to take?" he asked, frowning.

"I'm assured it won't take long at all. I've a friend in the police press office who said he would help locate it for me in the police archives. A couple of days at most. I haven't told Brian yet because he'd be furious, seeing it as causing a further delay."

Kate noticed Nico's frown become more pronounced.

"What's the matter?" she asked, pouring two glasses of wine.

"I just didn't realise when we started all this we'd be concentrating so much on the shooting of Charles. I thought it was going to be about the social life at the house."

"Of course we have to include the crime – that's the hook for the whole film! Audiences love to hear about a glorious crime!" She handed him a glass and sat down beside him, leaning her head on his shoulder.

"It's easy for you to be so clinical about it – it's not your great-grandfather being shown in such a bad light."

"No, my great-grandfather was probably one of the peasant farmers who cheered when he was shot!" she laughed. Although Kate had mostly been brought up in New York, her family originally came from the area.

"It's not funny, Kate. I feel I'm betraying my heritage with all this. I mean, I'm not saying Charles was a saint –"

"Far from it!"

"But I'm just saying we shouldn't be concentrating on all his bad points."

"Oh come on, Nico! Everyone would love an aristocratic cad in their family's past. You should be proud!"

"Well, it's too late to back out now, I suppose," he said.

"Yes, it is! And I've put too much work and time into this for you even to say such a thing, Nico. I need your support on this!" She looked hurt.

He had to admit she had been working round the clock on it. He knew his wife and when she decided to do something she gave it everything. She had dug up a copy of the inquiry into Charles' shooting and meticulously studied it so she could get the filming of it perfect. She had pored over all the newspaper reports of not only the crime but the terrible land war he had engaged in with his tenant farmers.

He smiled at her. "I'm sorry. Of course I support you, and if I'm proud of anyone it's you, for working so tirelessly on what you believe in."

"Thanks, Nico." She smiled at him. "Let's go to bed – we've an early start with more filming tomorrow."

Kate walked through the ballroom at Armstrong House, speaking as the camera filmed her.

"The ballroom here at Armstrong House witnessed many extravagant receptions. The Armstrongs were known as being generous and hospitable hosts and as one of the great 'gentry' families in Ireland residing in what was known as a 'Big House' would have considerable wealth to fund their lifestyle. The source of their wealth was the several thousand acres in the vicinity rented to tenant farmers whose own lifestyle was in stark contrast to the one led here at the house.

"It was the relationship between these tenant farmers and Lord Charles that erupted into a land war that ultimately led to the attack on Charles. At the inquiry, there were numerous accounts of the increasing animosity and aggression displayed on both sides. Chief witness at that inquiry was Charles' mother, Lady Margaret Armstrong. Lady Margaret at the time lived at Hunter's Farm, a dowager house down the road from the main entrance to Armstrong House. Lady Margaret testified that on the night of December 8th 1903 she heard a gunshot. Concerned, she went to her front door and said she saw what she described as a peasant man race past her house from the scene of the crime, holding a shotgun.

"Suspicion then fell on a tenant farmer called Joe McGrath. McGrath had recently been evicted from the estate. With a history of violence and known to the police, McGrath had threatened to kill Charles in retaliation for his ruthless eviction. Lady Margaret later identified the man she saw running with the gun as McGrath, from a police photograph. Police made extensive searches for McGrath, but he had fled from Ireland to America before he could be apprehended and interviewed, where it is presumed he disappeared into one of the teeming ghettos of New York or Boston, never to be found."

"*Cut!*" said the director. "Great, Kate!"

Kate was glad when the filming was done for the day. Her friend in the police press office had come up trumps and located the file on Charles' shooting. Kate had been handed the file by her researcher that morning and she was looking forward to spending the evening reading through it, to try to get to the bottom of the mystery of why Charles' horse hadn't bolted, as everyone was suggesting must have happened.

She waved off Brian and the rest of the film crew for the day, then walked through the hall and down the stairs to the kitchen where Nico had made them dinner.

They sat up at the island in the kitchen, eating spaghetti carbonara, as they discussed the day's filming.

"Well, I haven't managed to do a jot of work all day with all those strangers in the house filming," complained Nico as they finished eating. "So I'll try to catch up now while I have some peace!"

"I'll leave you to your architect's board then," she said as she stacked the dishwasher.

"And I'll leave you to your police report!"

Nico went into the library and Kate went into the drawing room where she poured herself a glass of wine and put on some music. She took the police folder from the sideboard and settled back on the couch to read through it. She started to decipher all the handwritten reports and then stopped when she found a black-and-white photograph. She picked up the photo. Along the top was written: *Morning of 9th of December 1903 – Crime scene, shooting of Lord Charles Armstrong*.

Wonderful! She had found an actual visual of the crime scene! Now they could compare it to how they had filmed the event. She studied the photo and her face creased in bewilderment.